A
THUNDER
ON
NEPTUNE

Books by Gordon Eklund

The Eclipse of Dawn
Beyond the Resurrection
All Times Possible
The Grayspace Beast
If the Stars Are Gods (with Gregory Benford)
Find the Changeling (with Gregory Benford)

A
THUNDER
ON
NEPTUNE

GORDON EKLUND

WILLIAM MORROW AND COMPANY, INC. / *New York*

For
Jeremy Eklund

At the water's edge, where the smothering ferns lifted
Their arms, "Father!" I cried, "Return! You know
The way . . ."
Among the turtles and the lilies he turned to me
The white ignorant hollow of his face.

—STANLEY KUNITZ
"Father and Son"

A
THUNDER
ON
NEPTUNE

PART
ONE

BROTHERS

ONE

The fat little detective resembled a gnome, with his bald, wrinkled dome of a skull and his flesh the color of cotton candy. Acting as nervous as a cat in a kennel of dogs, he gulped ersatz coffee, lit, puffed, and extinguished one untobacco cigarette after another, and informed Danny Hawkins that he'd located Danny's missing brother George here in Clarkegrad, the largest city—actually the only real city—in the southern hemisphere of Mars.

"Are you sure it's really him?" asked Danny, who had been thinking about this moment the last six M-days—since the shuttle from Phobos had first set him down here—without much real expectation of its ever taking place. For some reason he had nearly convinced himself that George must be dead. Maybe just because it would be so much easier that way.

"Take a look for yourself." The detective laid a photograph on the tabletop, a blurry snapshot of a slender, handsome, elegantly dressed (even for Mars) young man strolling along a neon-lit street. "This him?" the detective said. "This your brother."

Danny studied the photograph. There was a definite resemblance, yes, but he couldn't be sure. "It's been four years—Earth standard years—since George left home, Mr. Lucero. But he's just two years older than me. He'd only be fourteen now."

"I figured that out myself."

"Well, George—this person"—Danny touched the photograph with the tip of a finger—"he looks more like eighteen or nineteen."

"That's the way he's trying to look." The detective, Matheson Lucero, lit another cigarette, puffed, exhaled a cloud of gray-brown smoke that wreathed his head like a dirty halo, dropped the cigarette on the sandy red concrete floor and ground it out under a clear glass boot heel. "Look at the face, Danny. Ignore the moustache—it's fake—and concentrate on what's underneath. Look close and it's the face of a kid."

Danny tried to look close. He shook his head. "I'm sorry, sir. I just don't know."

"Well, I do. It's him. I got a set of his prints last night and checked them this morning against the warrant from Earth. It's the same guy. George Hawkins."

Danny continued to gaze at the photograph. So it was him. George. Try as he might, Danny couldn't feel a thing—no jolt of recognition, no welling up of brotherly affection. Well, it had been four stanyears. And when you were only eight—Danny's age when George left home—a month might seem like a year. And they'd never really been close. Too different—even back then. And now . . . ? Well, it was the face of a stranger.

"What's the matter?" Lucero said. "You still don't believe me?"

"I believe you, sir." Danny looked up from the photograph. "We were pretty positive all along George was on Mars if he wasn't dead. He grammed my mother once from here, but that was two years ago and—"

"I know. I've seen a copy of the gram. It wasn't much help. George was always a careful guy."

"Yes, but . . . but you said his name wasn't in the data banks, and so I—"

"His name never will be." Lucero kept glancing past Danny's shoulder to the café door, which stood partially open to the always mild, artificially maintained air of the domed city. It was fairly late—a few minutes short of Martian midnight—and the room was only sparsely occupied. Fewer than a dozen people, even counting themselves, older people mostly—old for Clarkegrad, that is—in their thirties and forties. For the young—here in the city's notorious Glitznik district—there were too many other, more exciting ways to spend an evening than sipping ersatz coffee in a dingy café. "Your brother's used a fistful of names since he first showed up on Mars, but his real name was never one of them."

"Because of the warrant from Earth?"

"He wouldn't have to worry about that here."

"Then what? Has George been mixed up in something crooked?"

"Something?" Lucero laughed. Besides his glass-heeled boots, he was wearing a suit jacket of luminous green plastic, matching knee-length trousers, and a huge pink-and-yellow polka-dot bow tie. Anyone walking around dressed like that in the ruined rubble of Seattle—the only other city Danny had ever visited—would probably have been arrested as a lunatic. But this wasn't Seattle. In fact, as Danny had to remind himself frequently, it wasn't Earth. On Mars, in Clarkegrad—especially here in the Glitznik district—people seemed to dress as they pleased. Matheson Lucero looked no more out of place—no odder—than another tree in a forest.

"What's so funny?" Danny asked.

"Because you might better have said everything crooked. Right now in my office I've got a dossier I put together on George thicker than both my thumbs stuck together. A week ago it wouldn't have existed. A week ago I would've had ten dossiers with ten different names on them."

"Can you tell me what he's done?"

"Name it, son, he's done it."

"Murder?"

Lucero's moon face registered his shock. "Hold on. This isn't the old Earth. We don't put up with degenerate activity on Mars. If your brother's killed anybody, it's always been a fair fight, and as far as I know, he's never killed anybody."

"Then what has he done?"

"Scamming mostly. Miners and dusthogs come to town looking for a good time, and your brother fleeces them this way and that. He tried picking pockets for a while but got caught and had his fingers broken. Last summer he was wholesaling yo-yos out at the Kropnik diggings but tried to unload a weak batch and had to make a run for it."

"Yo-yos? You mean like—" Danny made an up-and-down motion with his arm.

Lucero grinned. "Close. It's a drug. Takes you way up, then way down, then back up again. Like a roller-coaster ride, actually, and it's all over in twenty minutes, so you can find the top of your head, put it on again, and get back to work."

"But is any of that so unusual?" Danny waved a hand at the door. "For around here, I mean."

"Not really, but the problem is, your brother is unaffiliated. You make a lot more money that way, but it's awfully dangerous. George is lucky to be alive. No, I take that back. It's not luck. The kid's smart—goddamn smart."

"I thought you said people didn't murder each other on Mars."

"I said it'd be a fair fight. And it would. The affiliates would send a trigger after him—one on one. The trigger dies, they send another. Sooner or later they get George, but it's always a fair fight, every time. Lately your brother's specialized. He's become a card player."

"But there must be twenty casinos around here."

"Only fourteen. One for each affiliate. That's the way it works."

"But there's still nothing wrong with playing cards."

"The way George plays there is."

"He cheats?"

"The affiliates would say so. But, look, maybe I shouldn't have said anything. The deal was made, I find your brother and let you talk to him. That's as far as it went, right?"

"Will I get to talk to him?" Danny asked.

"Sure. Why not?"

"I thought you might have to put him under arrest."

"What for?"

"The drugs, the people you say he stole from, the—"

"What's any of that got to do with you or me?" Lucero looked genuinely confused.

"But the law—"

"There aren't any laws on Mars, son. Not that anybody's ever written down. We seem to get along fine without them."

"Then I don't understand. What do you do? I mean, you're the police and—"

"No, I'm not."

"You're a detective."

"That's different. I'm for hire. Somebody wants to find out something, they hire me, I find it out, then charge them a fee. That's as far as it goes."

"Then there's nobody who can do anything about George?"

"There's plenty of them. All the people he's burned. Including the affiliates. But they didn't hire me. Not this time. If they had, it'd be a different bowl of soup."

"Would you arrest George, then?"

Lucero shook his head. "That's what I've been trying to explain, son. I can't arrest anybody. There aren't any jails on Mars, for one thing."

"Then what would you do? Would you kill him?"

"Me? Heck, no. I'm no trigger."

"But I thought you said—"

"Not that I didn't. Look, son"—his tone was patient—"the only people I ever killed in my life were people who were trying to kill me. That's the way it is—the way it ought to be. If we Martians were the sort of degenerates you seem to think, then we'd have plenty of police, because we'd need them."

"I guess I just don't understand," Danny said. Mars—it wasn't just a different planet; it was like a totally different universe. Everything on Earth turned upside down, topsy-turvy.

"It's not easy to understand," Lucero said. "When people first come here from Earth—people like you, who are used to laws and police and governments—they never do understand. But they learn. They figure things out. If they don't, then they don't stick around. They go home. Now your brother, he—"

Lucero stopped, abruptly tense, and slowly rose to his feet, sliding a hand inside his jacket as he did. Danny glanced back over his shoulder and saw that a man had entered the café, a man of about forty stanyears, almost totally bald, a heavy black beard concealing the bottom of his face. The man walked up to the counter and spoke to the robot waiter. The machine poured him a cup of coffee from its nose spout. The man took the cup and went back outside.

Lucero let out his breath and sat down again. He folded his hands on the tabletop.

"Do you know that man?" Danny asked.

"I thought I did. A case of mistaken identity. But like I was saying, every person on Mars is free to do whatever he wants till he runs into the guy next to him, in which case it's up to the two of them to work things out. Your name's Hawkins, by the way. I've been wondering. Are you any relation to Michael Hawkins?"

It was something most people got around to asking Danny in time. "He was my father."

Lucero nodded somberly. "I figured it was something like that—when you said Sam Goble gave you my name. Old Sam and Mike were almost like father and son themselves. But I never knew Mike had kids of his own."

"George and me."

"He never said a word to me about kids."

"You knew him?"

"Off and on." Lucero stiffened again. Danny glanced back and saw that someone else had come through the door, a girl this time. The dress she wore was more like a few strings of thread held together by metallic clasps. Danny couldn't help staring. The girl couldn't have been much older than he was.

Relaxing again, Lucero said, "Mike spent a lot of time on Mars, you know. Before Sam Goble came that last time and took him away to Uranus or wherever . . ."

"Neptune," Danny said.

"And then I heard that he'd died."

"You were actually his friend?"

Lucero lit another untobacco cigarette and appeared to consider. "As much as Mike had friends, I guess I was one. Not that he wasn't a friendly man. It was more like he had his own world—his own private place—and nobody was ever allowed in there except maybe, like I said, Sam Goble. Now that I think about it, maybe it wasn't so weird he never talked about you. Mike wasn't the sort to talk much about personal stuff."

"What did he talk about?"

"Actually, he didn't talk that much at all. Only when he had something to say."

"Then he was a quiet person?"

"Well, I wouldn't necessarily—" Lucero broke off, glancing sharply at Danny. Perhaps the desperation hidden in his tone had leaked through. "Didn't you know him?"

"Not . . . not really well. He and my mother didn't live together after I was born. Dad didn't like Earth. He said the gravity made him feel old. He was used to Mars and the satellites and space."

"The gravity must be tough on you too. With your legs the way they are."

"I'm used to it," Danny said curtly.

"It's better for you here, though, isn't it? Better than Earth?"

"Well, a little. Without my leg braces—they work through electrical impulses that stimulate the remaining muscle tissue—I couldn't walk a step."

"What was it? An accident of some kind?"

"Polio. When I was a little kid."

"I thought they had that under control."

"They do now. Especially where I live—in the old United States. Some of the plagues are still pretty bad in other places—Africa and Asia especially. I was just unlucky."

"That's a tough break, all right."

"It was worse before I got the braces. That was Dad. He showed up one day when I was six with two men from Luna who fitted me with the braces. The next morning when I got up, he was already gone. I never saw him again."

"That sounds like Mike. You shouldn't take it personally, though. Mike has a sort of wanderlust. All real spacers do. There was one time, I remember, when he was trying to convince the affiliates to put up the capital to finance a ship to travel to the stars. He had it all mapped out, which ones were the most likely to have habitable planets and so on. The Combine had turned him down on Luna, and he couldn't think of anywhere else to turn. The craziest scheme you ever heard of."

"It could be done, though," Danny said. "A real starship. The technology exists. But it would take years to get anywhere."

"A couple of hundred, Mike told them. But you'll be dead, they said. Not our grandchildren he told them. Like I said, crazy. Why do it?"

"To find out what's there," Danny answered automatically.

"What if it's something we don't want to find?"

Danny shook his head. "People—the human race—you can't just remain stationary in one spot forever. You have to move forward or else you'll shrivel up and die."

"Now you sound just like Mike."

Danny felt a flush of pride and averted his eyes. He was about to thank Lucero for the comparison when—all at once—he realized that the chair across from him was empty. Matheson Lucero had vanished.

Danny started to turn his head and look around when the gunshot sounded from behind. Later—calculating mentally—he estimated that the bullet must have passed within ten centimeters of his left ear. The chair Lucero had occupied burst into plastic splinters. Something struck Danny on the cheek. He felt a stinging pain, reached up and touched blood on his face.

Only then did Lucero reappear from under the table. He was holding a gun in his right hand. To Danny, this close, the gun looked as big as a cannon. Lucero fired one shot. A voice cried out in agony.

Lucero was on his feet, standing over Danny, holding out a handkerchief. "Kid, are you okay?"

"Something hit me. A splinter. From your chair, I think."

"Christ, I'm sorry. Here, take this. It'll stanch the bleeding. If I'd known the fool was going to come charging in like that . . ."

Still somewhat dazed, Danny turned and saw a man seated on the floor close to the café door, holding his stomach with both hands. There was blood flowing through his fingers like paste. The man looked about thirty stanyears old, with long flowing blond hair. As Danny watched, the man's hair fell off the top of his skull and landed in his lap. Underneath the wig he was almost totally bald. And about ten years older in appearance.

"Who—Who is he?" Danny managed.

"Someone we had to take care of before we see your brother, a man named Vladimar Arabatov, George's partner."

"But why was he trying to shoot you?"

"To keep me away from George. Vladimar found out I was looking for your brother, figured it had to mean trouble, and decided to stop me. Vladimar has reasons of his own—financial reasons—for not wanting George's life interfered with right now."

Danny felt dizzy, light-headed. It wasn't his own pain, or even the blood which had pretty much stopped. It was having to watch the other man's suffering. "Can't we do anything for him?"

"The robot'll get a doctor. They're programmed for this sort of thing. This café probably averages a shooting a week."

"He won't die?"

"Uh-uh. I aimed to miss anything vital. Like I told you, I don't like killing people."

"But George, he—"

"Your brother probably didn't even know this was happening." Lucero was reaching down, helping Danny to his feet. "Come on. We'd better get moving. I want to catch George before he hears about this."

"But where is he?" With Lucero's assistance—he was surprisingly strong in spite of his small stature—Danny managed to make it across the floor. His legs—even with the electronic braces—felt heavier than lead right now.

"Club Monte Carlo, the last I heard."

"Isn't that close by?"

"Right around the corner. It's why we've got to hurry."

TWO

A month earlier Danny was sitting up in bed reading a book in the back downstairs room of the big two-story drafty old white shingle house he and his mother shared on a lonely wooded island in Puget Sound. It was March and the weather was its normally damp and drizzly gray self, but Danny couldn't have been feeling any more content. The rain never really bothered him anyway, not the way it sometimes did his mother. He sort of liked it, in fact—the steady, comforting rhythm of raindrops striking the wet muddy ground outside his bedroom window—and even when the sun did come out—a rare occurrence this time of year—Danny seldom cared enough to go outside, unless his mother goaded him with complaints about his health, and even then all he'd usually do was wander out into the surrounding woods till he found a dry spot away from the trees and then plop down and go back to whatever book he was currently reading. It was an okay way of life, Danny believed, if a person was primarily a bookworm, and Danny admitted that was pretty much all he was right now, at this particular stage in his existence. Bookworm was the word his brother George had used to describe him back when George lived at home too. (If George had ever read a book in his life, Danny had never caught him doing it.)

In the privacy of his room Danny sat with his shoulders propped against the wooden headboard—where somebody (George, he supposed) had once carved Danny's name in the paint with a knife—a paperbound book held open in his lap, and his stockinged feet balanced in the air on two fat pillows. Not that his legs ever hurt him anymore—only occasionally, any- way—but for some reason he always felt less aware of them—of the numbing, draining weakness of the muscles—when they were slightly raised this way.

Danny had contracted poliomyelitis when he was four years old. It had been a season of epidemics on Earth—the last, it was hoped, of many such seasons—and Danny realized that he had actually been fortunate to escape with his life. A good many others—hundreds of thousands worldwide— had not. As for the major consequence of the polio, his withered legs, Danny had long since reconciled himself to that. In truth, he had a lot of difficulty remembering what it had been like before, back when he could run and jump and skip and hop like a supposedly normal person, and besides, since he wasn't interested in football or dancing—his mother had once been a ballerina, he knew—or anything else active, then what real difference did it make in his life that he was as he was? Very little, he preferred to believe. None at all in the really important aspects. Being crippled wasn't for Danny the genuine handicap it might have been for another person. For him it was just the way he happened to be. And, of course, it was also the way he always would be.

Because of that, even though he was only twelve years old, Danny had already made up his mind what he intended to do with the remainder of his life. Naturally it wasn't something where he would need to hop and run —or even walk, for that matter. Danny intended to become a scientist—a theoretical physicist, to be precise. He knew it wasn't a common choice in the present day and age—at least not on Earth it wasn't, where everyone was expected to work to help rebuild the wartorn planet, with much noisy encouragement from the handsome, youthful, always optimistic World President Armelino in Perth, and the bluesuits of the Reconstruction Corps who carried out his desires. There was nothing wrong with theoretical physics, he would be told, but it was insufficiently practical as a profession at the present moment. It was like wanting to become a gourmet chef or a musician or a poet. (Danny's mother was a poet.) It was a luxury.

Danny didn't necessarily dispute that. He had gone to Seattle several times with his mother and seen what utter devastation the war had caused. But he didn't care either—he honestly didn't—and if that meant he was being selfish, then, okay, he was selfish; but being also what he was—a hopeless cripple, a victim of the war, too, in his own way—ought at least to allow him the privilege of living his life the way he wanted to live it, and if there wasn't a place for him on Earth right now, then he would leave and go to a world where he would be made welcome. There were a lot of scientists on Luna, for instance—the Combine was headquartered there, for one thing—and a number of them were theoretical physicists. Danny had even exchanged grams with two such men in recent months, when he had written asking about books and papers his mother had been unable to obtain for him in Seattle. Their replies had been helpful and encouraging— Danny hadn't mentioned his age—and they had sent what they could.

And anyway, it wasn't as if—with his legs—he was going to be able to rush out and enlist in the bluesuits and decontaminate a hot zone or put up a dam or build a bridge. "You could always design the bridge," his mother had explained. "You could become an engineer." Danny had thought about that—but it just wasn't enough. It wasn't mere bridges that interested him. It was things far beyond that—beyond almost everything—the stars and the galaxies and the frayed and blurry edges of the universe. He had read over and over about such phenomena by now, and envisioned them—if only in his mind's eye—and because of that, everything else— everything on Earth, in fact—seemed dreary and mundane in comparison. And that included bridges—building them or designing them.

It had really begun for Danny when he was five, going on six, still recuperating from the polio and getting around only in a wheelchair, just before his father made his last brief visit and presented him with the electronic leg braces he now used. Danny was wheeling around in the yard behind the house one autumn day, with his mother in her upstairs study writing and George off in the woods with his dog Rowdy, when a sudden rain shower had driven him into the garage for shelter. They didn't own a car—nobody on the island did except for the postman and his wife, who also ran the ferry service to the mainland—and the garage was actually used as a storage shed for a lot of old and mostly useless junk, some of it dating back fifty years, which was as long ling as his mother's family—the Domincas—had lived here. On this particular day something caught Danny's eye on a low dark shelf half hidden in a far corner, something he had either never noticed before or which had failed to attract his interest if he had. It was the bent dog-eared corner of a book sticking up out of a wooden crate.

Curious, Danny wheeled over—dodging a broken baby carriage and a headless wooden horse—and took a look inside. The entire crate was stuffed with books, and not just this one crate either. There were a half-dozen others just like it, all jammed back in this one corner, all stuffed with books. Although he had been able to read since before he could remember—like walking and talking, reading was something Danny had always seemed to be able to do—it was only during the last few months alone in bed that he'd really turned into a full-fledged bookworm. (George was already calling him that every chance he got.) But Danny had gone through all of his mother's books that held any interest for him, most either weird poetry he had trouble following or else old novels that were often even tougher to follow since they were set on a thriving, bustling Earth that seemed more alien to him than any distant planet.

Whatever, Danny was definitely ready for something else, so he reached into the crate and picked up the book that had first caught his eye. There was a black-and-white photograph on the dust jacket showing a sad-eyed man with a bushy moustache and a comically wild shock of hair. The book was apparently the story of the life of the man pictured on the cover, an old scientist of some kind, Danny gathered. Since he could still hear the rain beating on the rooftop, he opened the book in his lap, intending to read until it was safe to go outside again.

Two hundred fourteen pages later, somebody touched his arm.

Danny blinked, twisted his head, and found his mother kneeling beside him with a quizzical expression on her face. Sara Dominca was a tiny woman, though muscular, not frail, and the top of her head was barely at the level of his even though he was sitting down. "Where have you been, Danny? I was getting concerned."

"Just in here."

"You've been gone nearly two hours."

"I was reading."

"It's rather dark in here for reading, Danny."

He turned his head as if just noticing the fact. "I guess so."

Sara looked at the book in his lap. "Einstein?"

"You know him?"

"I know of him, yes. But he"—she waved at the crates of books—"he knows a lot more."

"He?"

"Michael. Your father. These are all his books back here. I'm storing them until he wants them."

"Dad's a scientist, too, isn't he?"

"Well, not really a scientist. He doesn't hold a degree or anything."

"But he knows about physics, the things Einstein knew."

"Some of it. In space you have to know what you're doing."

"Einstein was a genius."

"So I've been told. But you'd better come in now. It's getting late."

Danny went with her, taking the Einstein biography along, and early the next morning was back in the garage looking through the crates for something else to read. In time Danny read every one of his father's books, some more than once. Most turned out to be scientific texts, ranging from the basic and fundamental to the advanced and highly technical. For Danny the toughest part (along with the math—he never seemed to know as much math as he needed) was figuring out in what order he ought to be reading. Science was like a ladder, he soon realized. It worked best when you went up it one rung at a time. Before Danny turned ten his elementary scientific education was reasonably complete, though there were definite gaps remaining in his knowledge, since his father had naturally leaned toward acquiring books that dealt with subjects he would most need to know for his life in space. As a result Danny knew much more chemistry than biology, more astrophysics than chemistry. When he finally finished with the last of the books in the crates, his mother agreed to help him obtain additional books from Seattle, where a new public library had just opened in the decontaminated zone. And then there were the two physicists on Luna as well.

But the book Danny was rereading this afternoon (for the fourth time) wasn't strictly about science, even though he had originally come across it among the books in the garage. It was a novel, actually, a work of pure fiction, and very old too—over a hundred years, from the date in the front. In spite of this the entire story took place not on Earth but on Mars, which Danny had at first thought peculiar since the book had been written a good fifty years before Cosmonaut Ovinnikov first set foot on Mars. The crazy thing was how totally believable the story turned out to be, at least as long as you were reading it. Danny was not expert on real-life Mars—he had never been there, of course, he had never even been to Oregon—but he did know enough to realize that almost nothing in the story was completely impossible even today, although very little of it had actually turned out to be the way things really were. Maybe that was why the story seemed so believable. It wasn't like a fairy tale or a dream. It always made clear, logical sense.

The book was so engrossing, in fact, that Danny didn't even glance up when his dog Rowdy started making a lot of racket in front of the house, where the dirt road leading from the ferry dock ran past, a probable sign that somebody was coming. Sure enough, a few moments later Danny heard the noisy rumbling of an automobile engine. That was unexpected— the mail had come two days ago and wasn't due again for another eight. Presumably it was a visitor, someone from the mainland with a car. The car stopped, a door slammed, Rowdy's bark of warning turned into a yip of welcome, and then Danny heard the muffled sound of a fist rapping at the front door.

"Now who?" said Sara Dominca in a slightly perturbed voice as she went past Danny's door on her way from the kitchen into the living room. In a moment Danny heard the front door open, the sound of voices—his mother excited and surprised—and then the door closed and the voices drifted off into the living room, where Danny could hear them only if he strained.

He went back to his book, figuring the visitor—a man, from the sound of his voice—must be another of Sara's old friends from the mainland. It surprised Danny how many people she seemed to know from years past, when as long as he'd known her—all his life, of course—she'd kept so totally to herself here on the island.

The voices in the living room formed a low background murmur as Danny zipped through the book. The one part he probably liked best in the whole story was one of the few things that not only wasn't true, but never could have been. There was life on this version of Mars—native life, real genuine Martians. Danny's favorite was a little creature named Willis, a Martian animal shaped like a furry basketball with legs. Danny had often thought about the overall question of alien, non-human life in the universe and had found a couple books in his father's collection describing early, unsuccessful attempts at locating it. His personal opinion was that such life almost certainly had to exist somewhere. It was a matter of probabilities, if nothing else. Not in the Solar System, of course, since that had by now been fully explored, but elsewhere. The universe was so huge and the portion explored by humans no more than a single grain of sand in a vast, nearly endless beach. Yet if intelligent life did exist elsewhere in the universe, what would it be like? Something warm and cuddly and friendly like Willis, or else . . . ?

Danny was half reading, half pondering the question of intelligent life in the universe when there was a gentle tap on his bedroom door. "Mom?" he called out, knowing it had to be her wanting him to come out and say hello to her friend, whoever he might be. Even though he was primarily an introvert—something he had picked up from one of his father's books, a psychology text—Danny didn't really mind meeting new people. The only thing he hated was when they thought they had to say something about his legs, how terribly sorry they felt about his handicap. Danny never liked it when people felt sorry for him, especially people he didn't already know. What business was it of theirs?

The bedroom door opened and his mother peered through the gap. To Danny's surprise her face looked drawn, her smile tense. "There's a man here, Danny, who wants to talk to you."

"To me?" he asked.

"He has something to ask you about."

"It's not school again?" That was something Danny definitely did not want to have to go through again. Four years ago two bluesuits had come to the house explaining that a new presidential edict required all children living outside the savage zones to attend school when schools were available. There was no school on the island—Danny and George were the only children living there—so they would both have to go and stay in Seattle in a dormitory. Sara said no. The children were learning more at home than they'd ever learn anywhere else. The bluesuits said they were sorry but that was the way President Armelino wanted it done and only he knew what was best for the future of the world. Sara asked for a week to get things ready, and the bluesuits said all right but not to try to run away, because there was no place to go. As soon as they left, Sara went, too, telling George to please try and take care of things till she came back. She didn't return for three days, and when she did, told Danny it was all right now. She had contacted an old friend in Perth and fixed it so that Danny would not have to go anywhere. Listening to her, it surprised him to discover that he almost felt sorry to have to be staying. Sure, he would have missed her and the house and his books and everything else, but still . . . the universe was so big and he had seen so little of it, even if he was just a kid. He never told Sara how he felt, though. Four days later the bluesuits returned and George went away with them. They never saw him again. It was a long time later when they received a brief gram from him saying he was living on Mars.

"No, it's not school," Sara said.

"Then what?"

"I think it would be better if he—the man—if he talked to you himself."

Danny nodded and laid his book aside. "Okay. Give me a minute."

"Do you want me to help?"

Danny frowned a warning. "You know I can manage, Mom."

She smiled apologetically. "Of course. I'm sorry."

Danny kept his leg braces on a shelf above the bed. While his mother waited patiently, he reached up, brought them down in his hands, and placed them beside him on the bed. He pushed his pant legs up as far as they would go and then rolled the braces on over the exposed skin. The braces resembled long wire-mesh stockings that attached snugly to his legs from the tops of his thighs to his ankles, like chain mail, except that neither weighed more than a few ounces. There were two tiny levers on each brace, directly behind where they fit over the kneecap. Danny thumbed the levers and felt an immediate surge of electricity rushing through his legs. The sensation was as if something were tickling his muscles way down under the skin. He slid his pant legs back down, sat up, twisted his body and let his feet drop to the floor. This was always the hardest part. Standing. He tensed his arms and let his biceps do the actual lifting. Once he was on his feet, walking was a comparative breeze.

"Is this man an old friend of yours?" Danny asked as he crossed the room to his mother. His gait was more a shuffle than a genuine walk, although there were moments when one foot or the other actually came entirely off the floor.

She caught his elbow in her hand. "I've know him a long time, yes, but that's not why he's here today."

"Why then?"

"I thought I explained, Danny. He wants to talk to you."

"Why me?"

"Because, I gather, he's decided you're somebody special."

"I don't understand. Special how?"

"You'll have to let him explain, Danny. I promised him he could."

His mother continued to clasp his elbow as they went through the door. Danny's bedroom had originally been part of the dining area, but Sara had put up a wall, partitioning it off from the rest of the room when he'd first gotten sick and been unable to reach the other bedrooms upstairs. That was still almost impossible for Danny, climbing stairs on his own. As they entered the L-shaped living room he removed his arm from her grasp. It seemed to make her feel better to think she was helping, but it wasn't as though he was going to fall on his face either.

THREE

The man waiting in the living room dressed in a loose-fitting bright green kimono and matching suede boots, was huge and red-bearded, with a face like a wrinkled prune. He occupied one entire end of the sofa, a coffee cup dwarfed in his big right hand. Danny was startled to discover he recognized the man from an old newspaper photograph he had found among his father's books in the garage.

"You're Dr. Samuel Goble," he blurted out.

"I'm Sam Goble, if that's what you mean," the man said smoothly, draining his coffee in a gulp and bounding to his feet. "And you're Danny Hawkins. It's high time you and I met, son."

"My father went on the Nemesis expedition with you. You were his commander."

"Mike and I went out there together, Danny. He was the best friend I ever had." Sam Goble crossed the room in what seemed like two dexterous, bounding leaps and grasped Danny's hand in his. Glancing at Sara, he beamed. "He looks like you, not Mike. Except for the nose. That little tilt at the end. Remember, Sara?"

"I remember," she said, a little stiffly.

"I understand your other boy more closely resembles his dad."

"George is two years older. He doesn't live here anymore, you remember."

"I do. His, ah, later desertion had nothing to do with me, by the way."

"I never thought it did."

"Youthful high spirits, I'm sure. The lust for adventure. It's certainly nothing to blame yourself for either."

"I don't."

He looked at her closely. "Are you sure?"

"Always the amateur psychologist, aren't you Sam?" she said, smiling faintly.

"Amateur?" He cocked a bushy eyebrow. "I've never charged a fee, if that's what you mean."

"I meant that the only person you ever studied with was a Buddhist monk."

He laughed, shaking his head. "But theirs is the only psychology that works worth a damn, Sara. In the long run—where it counts." Sam was gazing down at Danny. He was not only just big, but a tall man, too, a full two meters, Danny thought. "Want to sit?"

"No, that's okay," Danny said. Having to stand in one spot actually seemed harder for him than walking. His leg braces did nothing to ease the strain on his knee joints. "I'm fine, sir."

"Well, I'm not." Sam went back to the sofa and plopped down. "It's been a damn long day for me. Arrived at San Lucas from Luna before dawn. Hired a plane from there to get me to Seattle. Had to find a ferry to bring me and a car across to here. This is certainly an isolated pocket of the cosmos you've found for yourself, Sara."

"It's what we thought we wanted at the time, Sam, Mike and I."

Sam pursed his lips, started to say something, then turned his attention back to Danny. "You think you've got it tough? What about me?" He patted the roundness of his stomach. "How would you like having to haul three hundred pounds of fat-padded flesh everywhere you went?"

Danny grinned, went over, and sat beside Sam. For some reason he felt comfortable around the man, as if he'd known him for years rather than minutes. Maybe it was the way Sam resembled a youthful Santa Claus, back before his beard turned white. Not that Sam was young. Danny calculated he had to be at least fifty, maybe more. The expedition to the dark star Nemesis had taken place twenty years earlier.

"I hear you want to be a scientist, Danny," Sam said.

"Well, yes sir."

"No, wait. Call me Sam—or Doc. The last time I let anyone call me sir, I was a shavetail second lieutenant in the United States Air Force."

"I never knew that," Sara put in.

"I was twenty-two. An academy graduate. It was the quickest way at the time of getting into space. As soon as I got to Mars I resigned my commission. They didn't really like it but there was nothing they could do. The Russians were trying to melt oxygen out of the polar caps back then. I thought I'd give them a hand."

Danny automatically added at least another two decades to Sam's age, even if he didn't look it.

"So what about science, Danny?" Sam said. "Physics, Sara tells me, and astronomy. I know a thing or two about both fields, as a matter of fact."

"Sam knows a thing or two about every field," Sara said.

"I try to keep my mind active," Sam said, as if he'd failed to notice the sarcasm in her tone. "Reading and thinking, Danny. To me both are more important for true good health than anything else—except eating." He smiled. "So tell me a little of what you know."

"Well, I'm no expert, sir."

"Who is? The only real experts I've ever met are the ones who damn well know they're not."

"I've just read some books and—"

"Mike's books," Sara said.

"A good place to start," Sam said. "Your dad always told me when it came to science he was just another student. I don't know how much he ever learned, but he never quit trying either. Mike was a man of action, a doer, not a sitter or a thinker like me. Maybe that's why the two of us worked so well together. How many moons does the planet Neptune have?"

"I—" The sudden question caught Danny by surprise, but he didn't have to think to answer. "It has fifteen."

"Do you happen to know the name of the only one we've bothered to colonize?"

"That'd be Triton."

"Ever been there?"

Danny laughed. "I've never been to Oregon, sir."

"How would you like to? Not Oregon. Triton."

"Well, I . . ." Danny's voice faded as the full significance of Sam's words sank in. He glanced automatically at his mother, but her expression was blank and impassive. "Did you say . . . well, I mean to me? To Triton?"

"That's what I said." Sam put a hand in a pocket, removed a sheet of paper and handed it to Danny. Scribbled on the paper were a series of questions numbered one through twelve, all dealing with different aspects of astronomy and physics. Black holes. Elementary particles. Plasma. Quantum mechanics. Cosmology. Nothing really advanced.

"Do you want me to answer these, sir?" Danny asked.

"Can you?"

"Well . . . yes. Except for question eight. When you ask about different varieties of quarks, do you mean the different flavors or the different colors? There are six different flavors and each of them comes in three different colors, so I guess you could say that makes eighteen actual varieties, unless you also mean—"

"Never mind. I figured as much." Sam grabbed the paper back from Danny and tucked it away. "Now that you've passed my little test, let's discuss my actual proposal. I mentioned Triton. Our real goal is Neptune itself. The directors of the Combine on Luna have given me the job of putting together a project designed to place a human being on the surface of that world."

"But Neptune doesn't have a surface," Danny said, without thinking. "It's a gas giant."

"It was, yes."

"Sir?"

"Let me finish. This will not be our first attempt at sending people to Neptune."

"My dad was killed there five years ago."

"Yes. Of course you'd know. That was the first attempt—the first project. It was a flop."

"Were you involved in that, too, Dr. Goble?"

"I was chief project officer, yes. My reason for coming here today is to find out if you'd be interested in following in your dad's footsteps, in picking up the fallen staff that slipped from his—"

"Sam," Sara broke in. "I don't want you putting things that way. It's not fair to Danny."

He nodded slowly. "Yes, right. Danny, I apologize. There was a time when I was young when I earned my living as a traveling boot salesman on Mars, and it's left an indelible stamp on my personality. Let me try to put things objectively. It is imperative at present that the human species establish a physical presence on the planet Neptune. It is further—"

"But, sir," Danny broke in, overcome by bewilderment, "I'm only twelve years old."

"In this project everyone will be twelve years old. Some a little more, some a little less, but twelve is a good median age. I'm not going to go into the details now, but the fact is that there exists good reason for believing that a group of children can succeed in reaching Neptune—and surviving —where others—adults—have failed. I've managed to put together a short list of children who appear to be the best qualified in the Solar System for the job by reason of intelligence, real and potential scientific aptitude, sheer imagination, and raw courage. Your name is on that list, Danny."

Danny looked again at his mother, but there was no help for him there. "When will you need my answer?"

"Now."

"Today?"

"I can give you thirty minutes. I have to be at a Corps camp in Ohio by nightfall to pick up another recruit, a boy even younger than you."

Danny spread his hands, facing his mother. "What do you want me to do?"

Her voice was controlled. "Are you certain you want me to tell you, Danny?"

"Well . . . sure." But didn't he already know what she would say?

"Then"—Sara looked grim—"the honest truth is that even though I understand how you must feel about Sam's offer—he can be a persuasive man—I really think you must—"

Sam was up out of his seat and across the room in a flash of motion. He caught both Sara's hands in his and bent down, his bulk dwarfing her smallness, and gazed into her eyes. His voice was as soothing and gentle as a song. He said, "I can remember an occasion not so long past as it might sometimes seem when a certain young woman told me there was something she felt she could not rightfully do because of her obligations she believed she owed to another. The woman was a dancer—a magnificent dancer, I might add, though young—and there was a certain older man—a truly great dancer, the greatest of his time—who had taken her under his wing and been her mentor and who loved her as well. Then, suddenly, a strange character entered the woman's life seemingly from nowhere, with an amazing proposition totally different from anything she had known before, an offer to go with him on an expedition to what was to her the far side of the universe. He explained that her name had been selected by a master computer. He lied. He had seen her dance—just once—and decided then and there that she was what he needed for his mission."

"I never knew that, Sam," Sara said.

"But you guessed?"

"Later, yes."

"She was dismayed, this dancer," Sam went on, "but also excited. The strange man had tapped into a part of her soul she hadn't known was there. Yet she owed so much to the older dancer, her teacher. And he loved her. How could she walk out and leave him now? As I recall, I told her at the time that she must follow her own heart's desire, that only in listening to our hearts—and our souls—do our heads ever find out what it is we truly wish to do. I told her it wasn't possible to live one's life for the sake of another, because it was hard enough to learn to live it for one's own self."

"You told her to be selfish, Sam. And she was. It's something she's felt bad about ever since."

He shook his head. "She shouldn't."

"Dyvinski killed himself three days after our ship left Lunar orbit."

"I know. So?"

"So how can I feel anything except guilty?"

"By not lying to yourself."

"How am I lying to myself?"

"By pretending that you do feel guilty."

"Oh, Sam, you always make it sound so easy." Shaking her head, she removed her hands from his. "But this isn't the same. Danny is only a boy."

"The woman we were discussing was only a girl."

"She was seventeen. And grown-up."

"No, not then. Later, yes. But not then."

"And she was . . . healthy. Danny requires constant care."

"What you mean to say," Sam said, "is that if Danny leaves, you'll be left alone here, a lonely, aging, bitter woman."

Her eyes were angry. "That's not fair."

"But it's what you think."

Her voice tightened. "This is what you've had in mind all along, isn't it? When you helped get Danny out of going away to school, it had nothing to do with me. You just wanted him here where you could get your hands on him when you needed him."

"The possibility existed, yes," Sam said. "I wasn't completely sure, but it seemed likely even then that the key to Neptune lay in using children."

"Then I can't think of any reason why I should help you now."

"Nor can I," Sam said, looking grim. "But it's not really your decision alone. Twenty years ago you made a choice that you've managed one way or another to live with ever since. Why not let Danny have the same privilege?"

"Because, damn it, he's a boy. A poor sick boy."

Danny felt puzzled. From some of what Sara and Sam were saying it seemed as if they must have known each other very well at some point in the past, quite apart from whatever connection Danny's father had given them. But when? he wondered. And how?

Danny tried to help Sara explain: "I think what Mother means to say,

Dr. Goble, is that with my legs the way they are, I can't do the things you'll want me to do anyway."

"Forget that," Sam said, his eyes still fixed on Sara. "Your legs won't matter where we're going."

"But, sir, how can I explore Neptune when I can't even run across my own backyard?"

"I told you not to worry about it. And do me a favor. Stop feeling sorry for yourself. To tell you the truth, it turns my stomach."

"But I—I—" Danny stammered.

"Don't talk to him that way," Sara said.

"Why not? It's the truth. I always try to speak the truth."

"Not here you won't. This is my home. And it's not the truth. Danny doesn't feel sorry for himself."

"Of course he does. What other choice have you given him, stuck here all his life like a fish in a bowl? Don't you think that's been more selfish of you than anything else you might ever have done?"

"What else could I do?"

"I don't know. Nor do I care. That's the past. It's the future I'm concerned about now. Danny's future. If he's got one."

"Sam, I . . ." Sara looked away from him, staring into space.

"Was that true, what you said before? About Danny's legs. He'll really be able to function as well as anyone out where you're going?"

"It's the truth."

"How?"

"Unfortunately I can't go into that. A new technology is involved. That's all I can tell you."

"Why should I believe you?"

"Have I ever lied to you before?"

"Yes, many times."

Unexpectedly, Sam laughed. "Well, not this time, Sara." He moved his right hand in a gesture above his heart. "You've got my word of honor, for what that's worth. Physically, Danny will do just great."

Sara was looking at Danny, biting her lip. "I can't just tell him to leave me."

Sam's voice turned soothing again. "Then don't say anything. Let him decide." He reached out and took hold of her shoulders. "If it'd help, I can step outside for a few minutes. On my way across your lawn I happened to spot a number of specimens of your local wildlife I've developed a certain fascination for lately. If you want, I can wander out and commune with them for a while."

"Wildlife? What wildlife?" said Sara.

"Some slugs," Sam said.

She laughed, shaking her head. "Sam, you never will cease to amaze me. But I don't think it's necessary. You don't have to go out and play with the slugs. Danny's already made up his mind. You have, haven't you, Danny?"

He started to shake his head, but felt the gesture turn instead into a nod. As usual, she knew him better than he knew himself. "I guess so."

"You want to do it?" Sam said eagerly.

"I . . . yes. If it's the way you say and if—if she says it's all right."

"Sara?" Sam said. "It appears to be your choice after all."

She looked from Danny to Sam and then back again. "If it's genuinely what you want to do, Danny . . ."

"If my legs—I mean, if I can really do all the things anyone else can do . . ."

"You can," Sam said.

"Then yes, I want to," Danny said.

"And it'll be a tremendous confidence builder too," Sam said.

"When I bring Danny back, you won't recognize him, Sara."

"Maybe that's what I'm afraid of."

"But you'll give your consent?"

"You said it wasn't my decision."

"Danny says it is."

She lowered her gaze. "Then yes." She looked at Danny. "Sam's right. I hate him for being right, but that doesn't change the fact. My keeping you here—my sheltering you—has been selfish. This world—this poor, sad, ruined planet—it's just not enough for you, Danny. You need more. And you deserve more. Sam'll see that you get it."

Sam put a hand in his back pocket and removed a bulging envelope. He crossed to Danny and held it out to him. "In here you'll find everything you need to get from Seattle to Cape San Lucas and from there to Tranquility on Luna. I've booked a passage for you on the liner *Gherman S. Titov* to Mars. In Clarkegrad—"

"Mars?" Sara broke in. "I thought Danny was going to Triton. Wouldn't Ganymede or Titan be a more direct connection?"

"That may well be," Sam said, "but I've got an errand I want Danny to take care of on Mars first. There's a potential recruit there I want him to approach rather than me."

"Who, Sam?" Sara asked in a taut voice, as if she already knew.

Sam nodded somberly. "Yes, him. Your other son—George."

"Then he is still on Mars?"

"There's some question about that, since he seems to have pulled a vanishing act about half a stanyear back, but I tend to think he's still living in Clarkegrad, though presumably under an assumed identity—a different assumed identity."

"How is Danny supposed to find him, then?"

"In the envelope there's a number for a man named Matheson Lucero, a detective in Clarkegrad. Danny should contact Lucero and have him attempt to locate George. I've included a few thousand in Martian scrip in case of need. Also, Danny, you'll find a few jotted notes concerning the actual Neptune project, things you can tell George, if necessary, to help convince him to join up with us. George only, please—though I can personally vouch for Lucero's discretion if he happens to be nearby at the time. And destroy the notes as soon as you've read them. The Combine is pretty insistent that everything about the project has to be kept top secret."

Danny clutched the envelope firmly in his hands. He couldn't help thinking about his errand on Mars—about his brother George—but he wasn't going to let that spoil everything else for him. "I'll be sure to do that, sir."

Sam frowned. "And stop calling me sir. I warned you once, and this is going to be the last time. Say it again and I'll boot you in the kneecap." Sam went over to Sara and gave her a quick hug. He said, "I'm honestly sorry I had to do this, but the names came up—both names—and I had no choice."

"From your master computer again?" she asked.

"Well . . . yes."

"I don't believe you, Sam, but I'm trying not to care either. I suppose I knew this had to happen. If not you and if not now, then somebody else some other time. Danny is an exceptional person. As hard as I tried, I couldn't hide him forever. He ought to be good out there."

"If he's half as good as you—"

"No, better. Wait and see."

"No one could be better, Sara. Not even Mike, and you know how I felt about Mike. He was as tough as a bull and twice as brave, but there were times when he didn't bother to think twice."

Danny wondered what they were talking about. Mike he knew—Mike was his father—but what Sara had to do with Sam and space . . .

Sam turned and said, "I hope you're aware, Danny, that your mother was the best female spacer there ever was. In fact, for me, you can probably drop the female part."

"My . . . who?"

"I never talked about those days, Sam," Sara said.

"She was the third member of the Nemesis crew, Me, Mike, and Sara. Without her we—"

"No, that was . . . it was somebody else." Danny struggled to recall the name. "I saw her photograph with yours and Dad's in an old newspaper. It was . . . Sara Spencer."

Sam gestured at Danny's mother. "Who do you think this is?"

"I've changed since then, Sam," Sara said. "I've grown my hair back, for one thing. Remember how that was the style in those days for spacers? We all shaved our heads, God knows why."

"Not Mike."

"No, not him. And you, with that red beard, who wouldn't recognize you?"

"And the fat belly."

"I changed my name after we came here too. I use my mother's family name now—Dominca."

"I noticed that," Sam said. "Because of your poetry?"

"Partly—I don't want people mixing up who I am now with what I was then—but it was also to keep people away. From me—us."

"Who, for instance?"

"You, for instance."

"But I found you easily enough when I wanted to."

She nodded. "I suppose I knew that would happen too."

Later, after Sam had gone out the door, Danny went to the front window and watched him cross the lawn to his waiting car. Partway there Sam stopped suddenly, bent down, and picked up something in the palm of his hand. For a long moment he stood there, gazing at the thing in his hand, and then with a shake of the head crouched down and put it back where he'd found it.

Sam walked on and got in his car and started the engine and drove off without looking back.

Danny glanced at Sara, who had been watching too. "What did Sam pick up just then?" she asked him.

"A slug," he said.

"A slug? A garden slug?" She started to laugh, and then looked serious. "I never will understand that man, if I live to be a hundred and fifty years old."

FOUR

He was winning tonight, George Hawkins was, but that was nothing out of the ordinary. When it came to games of so-called chance, George Hawkins always won. His game tonight was blackjack—the rules as simple and straightforward as a knife blade. Each hand started with two cards dealt facedown on the table in front of you. After that the idea was, drawing from the deck, to build a total in your hand as near to twenty-one as possible without going over. Aces could count one or eleven—your choice —and all face cards were ten. Once you were satisfied with what you held —and assuming you hadn't broken twenty-one—then it was the dealer's turn to build on his hand. If you beat his final score, you won. If you didn't, you lost. Ties were ties and nobody won anything.

George didn't win every hand. That was neither necessary nor would it have been especially wise. He won when he wanted to win, when the odds shifted in his favor and the size of his bets abruptly increased. There were two reasons for his overall success at the game. First, George had an airtight, near-perfect memory; and second, he could calculate and then maintain mathematical ratios in his head over a period of time. Given these two talents, in the long run—which is when it mattered—nobody ought ever to lose.

It was a shade past midnight local time in the old Anglo-Soviet colony city of Clarkegrad in the Hellas region of the planet Mars. George occupied the last of five chairs, facing a three-armed, tarnished aluminum robot dealer at a corner blackjack table in the main casino room of the Glitznik district Club Monte Carlo. George had never been to the real Monte Carlo on Earth—he was born the year after the war had wiped it out, along with most everything else in Europe—but he liked to believe it must have been at least slightly less seedy than this dive.

Not that the Club Monte Carlo wasn't a pretty typical Glitznik casino. A booze bar jammed with the usual throng of sitting and standing, half-drunk and half-sober bodies, stretched the length of one wall. In addition to another half-dozen blackjack tables identical to the one at which he sat, the casino contained three roulette wheels, four baize-covered crap tables, and four long rows of whirring, jingling slot machines. Off in a side room behind velvet curtains, a few other tables had been reserved for poker. George invariably stayed clear of these other diversions. He despised the taste of liquor—and what too much of it could do to your brain—and while there were systems for beating both roulette and the dice, the odds were never as good as at blackjack. As for poker, it was different—a genuine game of skill, and too personal. You didn't win the house's money over there. The Petrov Affiliate which owned and operated the Club Monte Carlo took a flat percentage off its poker tables, so that when you won at poker, you won other players' scrip. And those players, being human, tended to remember the faces of people who pocketed what had once been theirs.

The Club Monte Carlo might have been slightly less packed tonight than usual, George thought, which meant it was possible to walk a full meter across the sandy red concrete floor without bumping into somebody else. About three quarters of the customers were sandhogs in from the surrounding airless desert—rock miners, haulers, salesmen, prospectors. There were even a few genuine homesteading colonists scattered here and there among the mob, and a handful of vacationing tourists from Ganymede and Titan also. The last you could easily spot from their clean, neat, well-pressed attire, always a good five years out of style and never what the poor saps wore in their daily miserable lives. (If Mars was a stinkhole, Ganymede and Titan were worse—George had spent time on Ganymede and knew.) The rest of the crowd was the normal collection of Glitznik flotsam, sharpies and scammers for the most part, along with a few professional gamblers off in the poker room, where they were expected to remain. Men outnumbered women approximately ten to one, and nearly all the women worked for Petrov, even if some would never admit it even after you paid their price. (If they hadn't been affiliate employees, they would never have gotten past the front door.) The air was thick and dank and saturated with the combined odors of whiskey and perfume, sweat and smoke—tobacco, untobacco, chemically herbal—the whole mess adding up to something that made George's eyes water and nostrils drip. The funny part was how in spite of the flash and glitter, the dance of dazzling neon everywhere, the casino was basically a somber place. It was because of the money, George thought. People never laughed about money unless they had more than they needed, and nobody who had more than he needed ever hung out in the Glitznik district. Since losers always outnumbered winners—the odds said that had to be so—what was there to be happy about?

Except for George. George liked to think of himself as the exception who proved the rule—a winner. Right now, with a big bet on the table in front of him, he took a quick look at the two cards the robot had dealt him —a king and a four—glanced at the dealer's one exposed card—a nine of diamonds—and then shifted his gaze to the right to observe the other players—a couple beef-faced miners, a skinny female tourist from one of the outer moons, and a spacer from the shuttle run who acted drunk and probably was—as each played out his or her hand in turn. Three of them broke and one—the drunk—didn't.

Then it was George's turn.

A survey of the various ratios he was keeping in his head of cards played to cards unplayed informed him that the dealer's hidden hole card was in all probability something low, most likely a three or a five. George knew this with the certainty he did because he'd latched onto this particular dealer the moment it first reached the floor, and had been playing against it now for almost a solid hour. The store of a hundred-fifty-two-card playing decks the dealer had originally brought with it to the floor was by now pretty much exhausted. It was when this happened that the odds shifted in George's favor, and it was when his bets grew large.

The pile of scrip on the table in front of him right now marked his biggest bet of the night so far.

George laid his fist on the table and thumped his knuckles. Interpreting the gesture, the dealer fired a card from the slot at the blunt end of its middle arm. The card landed faceup on the table in front of George. It was one of the fives he had been expecting.

That gave him a total of nineteen.

"I'm good," he said.

The robot flipped its hole card—a three of clubs—and dropped another card on top. Five of hearts. Nine plus three plus five. Seventeen.

"The casino will pay all hands totaling eighteen or above," the dealer announced.

George showed his hand and collected a pile of scrip from a slot in the dealer's chest just above its middle arm.

"Luck was with you on that one, my friend," the dealer said as George placed his winnings on top of his original bet.

"Go blow a transistor," he muttered in a voice too soft to be picked up. George hated robots, always had, always would. Especially their voices— those dead, flat, pleasant voices—it always turned his stomach to have to listen to them.

He removed another fifty in script from his wallet and added it to his bet.

"You seem certain lady luck's smile won't fade," the dealer remarked amiably.

"There is no such being as a lady luck." George said heatedly. "Only the Buddha can bestow good fortune upon a mere mortal such as I." It sounded pretty dumb even to his own ears but he was only trying to keep in character. His identity for the evening was that of a freelance Chinese prospector named Chen Punan, in from the desert for a few hours of serious gambling. He had the ID to prove it too—as well as the clothes and facial makeup.

"I am programmed never to discuss religion with customers," the robot said.

"A policy of wisdom," George agreed, nodding curtly. On the other hand, he was thinking, maybe he actually ought to love robots. After all, if it wasn't for them, he'd have had to find a new line of work long ago. Given a human being dealing the cards rather than this animated hunk of metal and circuitry, and sooner or later—probably sooner—anybody with half a brain would have figured out what he was up to, would have noticed that he was winning too often and at too regular intervals. But not a stupid robot. No, George corrected himself, that wasn't right. Robots weren't really stupid. Any of them—even a cheap piece of junk like this blackjack dealer—could put two and two together and come up with a four. The problem was—and it wasn't really stupidity—not a one had the least inkling what a four was, what it signified beyond the word itself. Night after night the robot dealers of the Glitznik district watched George cheating— what the affiliates regarded as cheating—and not a one ever realized what it was seeing. Robots weren't stupid, no, but they were dumb. And thank the Buddha for that, George thought with a grin.

The dealer swiveled on its perch, dealing new cards facedown for everyone. A couple months back, George remembered, he'd had a real scare when the Dawson Affiliate decided to get rid of its robot blackjack dealers and install a computer system instead, one utilizing random numbers. Randomness—that was another thing that turned George's stomach—just the sound of the word. Luckily for him the new system proved about as popular with the gamblers of Mars as an outbreak of the plague, and people stayed away from the Dawson casino like vegetarians from a meat market. Gamblers, George knew, were conservative by nature and always felt most secure around what they knew best. What that meant when it came to blackjack was a dealer who dealt cards from a deck, not a panel of blinking numbers. Within a few days the robot dealers were back behind their tables where they belonged, and George dropped by the Dawson casino long enough to triple the amount of script in his wallet.

Not that he ever could have done it alone. None of it. Without Vladimar Arabatov he never would have gotten a foot past the front door of any casino in the district. George owed Vladimar everything. (And vice versa, too, of course.)

George reached for his cards on the table.

FIVE

It had all begun approximately half a stanyear back, when a seemingly foolproof scam George had been running on these three Albanian brothers had unexpectedly blown up in his face. A month-long, planetwide sandstorm had driven the brothers into Clarkegrad from the north basin, where they owned and operated a small but lucrative gold mine, and George's scam had involved selling them oil leases on some nonexistent land he claimed to own. After two days intensive bargaining—a tradition among Albanians, he understood—one of the brothers had caught him totally off guard by angrily pointing out that Mars, lacking any past plant or animal life, contained no deposits of oil.

Later, while being chased through the sporadically illuminated nighttime streets of Clarkegrad by three angry men waving knives—the transparent glass dome two hundred meters above still blanketed by swirling waves of sand—George had, to his vast relief, spotted a partly open door in the sandy red concrete wall ahead. Aiming for the gap, he skidded inside and managed to slam the door shut before anybody could follow. Fumbling in the dark for a lock, he bolted the door, then whirled, took three or four running steps, and found himself bathed in an eerie blue light.

He was standing on a stage. In a small auditorium. And there was an audience out there, too, though not a very big one from what he could see. A short distance from George another man knelt, holding what appeared to be a human skull cradled in the palm of his hand. The man had shoulder-length blond hair, wore what resembled a woman's leather blouse and black elastic tights, and had a sword and scabbard belted around his waist.

The man seemed to be talking out loud to the skull in a strong, firm, insistent voice.

George heard a burst of applause punctuated by hoots and whistles, and suddenly realized it was him they were clapping for. "I, uh, I think I made a wrong turn," he said, spinning on a heel and scampering back the way he had come. He had one hand on the outer door when he heard the sound of angry voices coming through it in a language he didn't immediately recognize but which he had a sinking feeling would turn out to be Albanian.

He swiveled, searching for another way out, and saw the blond-haired man charging down on him with his sword thrust outright in front of him.

George fell back, throwing his hands in the air. "No, please don't kill me!" he cried as the man, never hesitating, rammed him square in the chest with the point of his sword.

The blade bent nearly in double.

"Rubber?" said George, reaching down to touch the sword.

"Next time I run you through," the man promised.

"But—" said George.

"Never mind. The audience calls to me."

The man hurried back to the center of the stage, bowing from the waist as he did. If the audience had been calling, you couldn't have proved it to George. Two or three people were clapping politely—and that was it. "Hey, send the other guy back," somebody shouted. "He was funnier."

The blond-haired man walked past George as he exited the stage. "Next comes Othello," he muttered, crouching in front of a large metal trunk filled with old clothes and other assorted junk. As he pawed through the trunk with one hand, he used the other to peel off his face and hair.

Underneath he was almost totally bald and a good ten years older than George would have thought.

"Anything I can do to help?" George asked, leaning over his shoulder.

"You do enough helping already tonight," the man snapped. He seemed to find what he wanted in the trunk—a wiry-haired wig—and slipped it on over his scalp. "Now the blackface," he murmured, standing. "But where is the stupid blackface?"

From behind, George heard a steady thumping noise. It took him a moment to identify the sound. Someone was pounding on the outer door with a fist.

The man in the wig noticed it too. "Now what?" he asked. He had located his blackface—a jar of creamy makeup smelling of fish oil—and was applying it to his face and neck. "More company to spoil the show?"

"No, wait," George said, getting between him and the door. "Those are maniacs out there who want to kill me. You can't let them in."

The door was shaking on its hinges now. It looked and sounded as if it were being kicked—by several heavy boots simultaneously. "I think maybe they get in anyway," the man remarked.

"Then hide me," George said.

"Hide?"

"Yes. Anywhere. In . . . wait. Yes. In here." He climbed inside the trunk, crouched on his knees, and tried to band his spine. "I think it'll work," he said. "Is there a lock? I can hide in here till you get rid of them." It was going to be an awfully tight fit—and some of the clothes definitely smelled of sweat and dirt—but there was no other obvious choice.

The man seemed to be thinking. Finally he shrugged. "Okay, I get rid of the maniacs for you."

The lid of the trunk came down with a clang, squeezing George into the shape of a flattened pretzel. He heard the click of the padlock snapping and figured ten minutes at the most. Sounds were very much muffled inside the trunk, but after a while George thought sure he heard voices. Albanian voices? They didn't last long. Then nothing. Silence. And the silence dragged on. And on. And on. Hours seemed to go by. He's locked me in here, George thought, the crazy maniac, and he's not going to let me out till I starve or suffocate or—

George considered screaming, crying out for help. But what if he were wrong? What if the Albanian brothers were still hanging around? They were as stubborn as a pack of bloodhounds, that kind. It was better not to run the risk. After all, how many lives did he have to lose? Just one that he could think of.

The light, when it finally exploded above him, was like a burst of enlightenment. George managed somehow to extract himself from the locker, rolling to the floor. He lay flat on his back, savoring the luxury of freedom.

"What took so long?" he asked, straining to sit up.

The man—he was wearing a false nose now which stuck out about a foot in front of his face—nodded toward the stage. "I am busy."

"And the Albanians?"

"The maniacs, you mean?"

"Right, them."

He shrugged. "I tell them you run out the front. They go that way, chasing you with knives."

"And that was it?"

"What else?"

"You mean you kept me in here all that time for nothing?"

"For my show. The recitation. I decide not to let you screw it up again."

George felt his rage boiling up inside him like water in a tea kettle. Everytime he moved a muscle, he discovered a new source of pain. "You—"

"Come on," the man said, walking away. He beckoned over his shoulder. "We split a bottle of booze and become fast friends."

George didn't drink alcohol and he already had all the friends he needed, but he tagged along anyway. What else could he do? The Albanian brothers knew where he lived. He'd been cocky enough—and dumb enough—to bring them to his hotel room the night before last, when he was setting them up for the scam. He'd been intending to move to plusher surroundings as soon as he had their money in his pocket, but now he didn't have any safe haven. Or anything else in the world, either, for that matter. Except for the clothes on his back.

The man sat cross-legged in the middle of the stage with a bottle of vodka on the floor in front of him. The blue spotlight shone squarely on the side of his face, giving his foot-long nose a ghostly sheen. George turned his head and looked out over the auditorium. The place was even dumpier than at first glance. Probably a converted service garage for desert crawlers. He thought he could see the sunken place where the lube pit had been. The chairs—about thirty of them—were cheap wooden stools, and the walls and floor were made of the same reddish-brown concrete as everything else in Clarkegrad—Martian sand was used in the mix instead of rocks and gravel. The stage was a concrete block too—and cold when you sat on it.

The man took a long swallow from the stem of his vodka bottle and wiped his lips with the back of his hand, bumping his nose as he did, tilting it slightly askew. Then he told George the story of his life. His name was Vladimar Arabatov. Born on Earth thirty-nine stanyears ago in the old Union of Soviet Socialist Republics. A passion for the theater gripped him from an early age, and at ten he was playing juveniles on the Moscow stage. "By the time of my twentieth birthday party, all the critics agree: Vladimar Arabatov is the finest actor in all of Europe."

"You were in movies and television?" George asked, having heard of such things.

Vladimar frowned. "Acting, I say. No stupid machines taking pictures. The stage. The theater."

"So what are you doing on Mars?"

That was the rest of Vladimar's story. According to him, he'd come to Mars on a cultural mission from his government to spread the beauty and truth of the theater to primitive lands. "Three days after I land in this crazy domed city, the Americans attack my homeland for no known reason. Russia fights back valiantly, but the weapons are all too horrible. In hours there is no place left for me to go back to anywhere."

"So you stayed here?"

"They give me this place, my sponsors, the men and women of Clarkegrad who say they appreciate culture. It will be your little theater, Vladimar. Fine, I think, and prepare to begin. I find stagehands, crew, fellow actors and actresses. Much time is spent teaching and training and rehearsing. Finally it is opening night—Chekov's immortal *Cherry Orchard* —and fourteen citizens appear to watch. By act three five are sleeping. The second night, nine people. The third night we close. There is no money to pay anyone but me, and the others all quit. Since then— fifteen of the old years—I gave recitations here alone. Great scenes from the world theater of Earth, I call them. Few come, but enough that I do not go hungry for long. Then tonight I see you and I think maybe there is hope yet."

"What do you mean?" George asked.

"I mean your friends, the Albanian brothers who want to chop you into pieces with knives. They tell me of their hotel room and say, when you see this fellow, you come see us."

"Why should you do that?"

"Exactly what I am thinking also." Vladimar beamed and took another swig from the bottle. "So you stay here with me and become my apprentice. I teach you everything I know about the theater, which is everything there is to know. You are a good-looking boy. Wonderful profile, straight teeth, smooth white skin. Together we give recitations from the world theater of Earth—two characters now, not one. Many old admirers will, I think, come back to see and applaud."

So George stayed. It wasn't so much that he was afraid of the Albanians —the sandstorm let up after a few days, and he figured they'd gone back to their gold mine—he simply liked being an actor. It was a lot of fun pretending to be somebody else for a change, and he thought he was fairly good at it, too, though Vladimar was pretty sparse with his praise. So was the audience. Sparse in every respect. Vladimar had been mistaken about that part. His old admirers—assuming there were any—never did come back to see and applaud. George and Vladimar ate—and there was always money for Vladimar's vodka bottles—but that was about all.

It was Vladimar who one night came up with solution to their financial difficulties. It was following a recitation that had drawn a grand total audience of five, and they were sitting together on the stage with the vodka bottle between them and the blue spotlight shining on their faces, George dressed in a shimmery white gown that clung to his hips and bared his shoulders, and Vladimar in his black tights, leather blouse, sword and scabbard. Hamlet and Ophelia. It wasn't George's favorite role. He much preferred Lady Macbeth, because it gave him a chance to rant and yell and that was always the most fun.

By now, a little at a time, George had been telling Vladimar the story of his own life. Tonight he was talking about when he had first arrived in Clarkegrad.

Taking a drink, Vladimar nodded, already looking sleepy-eyed. "So you were a player of cards in those days. I have seen these casinos in the Glitznik district, as it is called, but I do not go into them. Gambling is not in my blood, only the theater. I like to win money, sure, but there is too much losing in these games of cards."

"Not for everybody," George said. "Take me for instance. I never lost."

Vladimar looked mildly suspicious. "That is not possible. The odds of these games make it so."

"So I change the odds," George said. "Take blackjack. Do you know how it's played?"

"That is the one where the player tries to make twenty-one."

"Right, and if you know what you're doing, you can tilt the odds as much as sixty-forty in your favor."

"It is easy to do this?"

"Easy for me. All it takes is to be able to remember every card when it's played and then keep track of them in your head, what they are and how many of each kind."

"And you do this?"

"No problem."

"Then why are you not a rich man?"

"Because the casinos got to know me too soon. I mean, there just aren't that many kids hanging around the Glitznik district all night on their own. After a couple times in each casino, somebody'd always take me aside and suggest it would be a smart move if I made myself scarce and stayed scarce. There's only fourteen casinos, so pretty soon I'd been kicked out of every one, and that was the end of it. If it hadn't worked out that way, who knows? Maybe I would be rich by now."

There was a tiny gleam glowing in the back of Vladimar's eyes. He nodded slowly. "And this system of yours, you could teach it to me?"

"Only if you've got a memory like a camera and think you can keep track of five thousand cards at a time."

Vladimar considered. "That would not be easy."

"Then forget it. If it's not easy, it isn't going to work."

Vladimar was still thinking. All at once he smiled. "And what of young Ophelia?"

"Huh?" George said, looking down at himself. "What about her?"

"Do you think she could possibly learn this system?"

George was about to say "Huh?" again when it hit him. Oh my Lord, he thought, starting to laugh. How come he'd never thought of it before? "It would be as easy as slicing pumpkin pie," he said.

Vladimar, beaming, ran his palm over the mouth of his vodka bottle. "Here, my friend." He held out the bottle. "Now you must share a drink with me."

George drank, but jeez, the stuff tasted miserable. He had to fight to keep it down.

The following night at the Club Monte Carlo, a sallow-faced young woman in a white gown and golden braids more than tripled her stake at blackjack within a few hours time.

The next night she appeared at another casino, again winning.

And then another.

The following night it was a round-cheeked man with a black silken moustache and a reedy voice. He won too.

And so on. Night after night. The players varied—as did the casinos—but the winning never ceased.

Vladimar was a real genius when it came to costumes and makeup, and George was what he'd come to believe he must be—a heck of a fine natural actor.

After three months steady playing—and steady winning—George calculated they were already close to being rich. He asked Vladimar, "So what do you plan on doing with all the loot we're making?"

The two of them were sitting on the stage of Vladimar's theater shortly after George's return from the Churchhill Affiliate's Silver Casino, where he'd enjoyed an especially profitable night. Outside, dawn clawed at the horizon like a cat at the trunk of a tree. There was a major sandstorm brewing to the east, and the Martian sky was a ruddy shade of pink.

George was made up to resemble a Chinese prospector in dirty baggy clothes with a tight black pigtail snaking down his back. "There is a dream I have been having," Vladimar said. He drank from his vodka bottle. (The label claimed the liquor inside has been distilled in the old Soviet Union— probably a lie, but considering what it cost, George wasn't about to argue.) "Shall I tell it to you?"

"Sure," George said, yawning. He was physically exhausted but wide awake at the same time. It always took hours to wind down totally from the stress and excitement of the casino.

"My dream," Vladimar said, "is to leave this petty, ugly building that surrounds us with its stupid brown concrete and to build a new theater in a new place, a real theater with seats made of wood and acoustics that are true. Then I will hire a stage crew and teach them all my knowledge and find actors and actresses who can learn all the many roles. It will be a true repertory company as in the old days. When all is perfect, I shall announce an opening night's performance. Throngs will come to see and applaud. It will be a triumph for all concerned."

"You mean you want to build a whole new theater?" George asked, turning his head and looking around. "From scratch?"

"There is no other way," Vladimar said firmly.

"But we can't have that much put away yet."

"No." Vladimar's face sagged. "Tonight while you are gone, I count scrip. The wood alone—imported from Earth—it will cost a fortune."

"You figured in my half too?"

"Only my own. We are even partners, you and I."

"Then go ahead and throw mine in," George said with a shrug.

Vladimar looked genuinely startled—and moved. "For me you would do this?"

"Why not? The whole thing was your idea to start with, wasn't it?"

"Ah, but the card playing—that is your genius, my friend."

"What do I need with a lot of money? I mean, look around you." He waved at the concrete walls, the tattered stage curtains. "I've got everything I need right here, don't I?"

Vladimar looked solemn. "Then you shall have a key role in my new company."

"Well, I sort of expected that."

"Nevertheless there is still not enough money—not nearly."

"So? We've got all the time in the world to make more, don't we?"

And they were close now, from what Vladimar told him, very close. A few more weeks, two of Mars' sixty-day months maximum, and they'd be

over the top. Then it would be time to start work on the new theater—
Vladimar had already picked out a site near the eastern slope of the dome,
as far from the Glitznik district as you could get—and if that didn't work
out, if the audience Vladimar insisted was out there waiting failed to mate-
rialize, well then, heck, George could always go back to the blackjack
tables.

Speaking of which—

George examined the cards he had been dealt.

SIX

George had a good hand. In fact he had a great hand. Ace of diamonds. Ten of clubs. An improbable combination given present odds, though not, of course, an impossible one. Twenty-one. Natural blackjack. An automatic two-to-one winner—unless the robot dealer dealt itself the same.

Which present odds said it definitely should not.

And it didn't. The dealer drew a seven of clubs faceup. George put on a deliberately happy grin and then waited with obvious impatience while the players to his right played out their hands, George taking care to observe the identity of each new card as it was revealed.

Then the dealer's aluminum head, swiveling on its shoulders, fixed on him. "Does your Buddha continue to smile his good fortune?" it asked.

George started to turn over his winning cards, but something hard and heavy landed on his shoulder. Puzzled and irritated, he looked back.

There were two people standing directly behind him. One was a little bald-headed man, sharply dressed, and the other a pasty-faced kid about twelve. "Move away from here," George told them in his clipped Chinese voice. "All seats at this table are taken."

It was the little man whose hand had fallen on George's shoulder, but it was the kid who spoke. "Hello, George. Remember me?"

George? He couldn't have heard that right. Nobody ought to know his real name except Vladimar, and Vladimar wasn't around tonight. He'd said earlier he was going out to check over the new theater site one more time.

"You have found the wrong person," George said. "I am not your George. I am Chen Punan of the Hellas Basin." (Never, no matter what, deviate from your character, Vladimar had advised him more than once. George understood what that meant. Even if one of the affiliates caught on to him, they couldn't do much permanent harm unless they also found out who he actually was.)

George turned back and flipped over his cards. A voice close to his ear said, "Give him a hit."

It was the little man again.

"The player has achieved a natural score of twenty-one," the dealer explained. "Under the rules of the Club Monte Carlo, that is an automatic two-to-one winner, and nothing is gained by obtaining additional cards."

"He still wants one," the little man said. "You tell the tin head, Mr. Hawkins. Tell it to give you a hit."

George felt a leaden weight in the hollow of his stomach. Not just George—Hawkins too. Who were these guys? Affiliate enforcers? Then why not simply toss him out on his ear? The cops? No, that was even loonier. There weren't any police on Mars.

"Hit or stay, my friend?" the dealer inquired in its maddeningly pleasant voice.

George could feel the other players at the table watching him. Too much more of this and they'd attract a crowd. The last thing George needed was a crowd.

"All right," he said in a soft voice. "Hit me."

The dealer fired him an eight of hearts. "Nineteen," it announced.

"One more," the little man said.

"I'll bust," George cried.

"You never can tell," the little man said philosophically.

The puzzled stares of the others were getting oppressive. The best thing, George decided, was to cut his losses and clear out while he could. "Okay. Give me a hit."

The dealer dealt him a seven of diamonds. "Bust," it said, vacuuming up the pile of scrip on the tabletop through its middle arm.

George jumped to his feet, feinted right and darted left. He'd gone about two meters when a hand like a steel vise clamped around his wrist. "Hold on, George," the little man said. "We'd like a word with you."

"Leave me alone," George cried.

"Uh-uh," the little man said. He began forcing George across the casino floor. "This way. I've reserved a private room."

They edged down a narrow passageway flanked by rows of clattering slot machines. The players—some operating two and three machines at a time—danced back and forth, jerking handles as if in the throes of a fit. A shrill jingle of bells went off, followed by the rattle of tumbling coins and the flutter of falling script. A woman was shrieking joyously. Another winner, George thought bitterly, swinging his head in hopes of somehow finding someone to help him.

"Don't bother," the little man said. "Vladimar won't be around tonight. He's gone to see a doctor."

"A doctor?"

"He tried to shoot me. I shot him back."

"You killed him?"

"A doctor, I said, not a morgue. He'll live to steal again another day."

"Vladimar's not a thief."

"Maybe not—but you are."

They'd come to a blank wall between two packed roulette tables. The little man stuck out his hand and banged the wall with his knuckles. A portion of it swung back, revealing a narrow gap through which a light was shining. "Mr. Petrov's private office," the little man said. "He was kind enough to lend it to us."

"You know Petrov?" George asked nervously.

"We've done business in the past."

"You're his trigger?"

"Just a friend. Don't worry. If somebody decides to kill you, it won't be me."

They were waiting for the boy to catch up. There was something wrong with his legs. He walked with a limp. No, not a limp, George thought, more like a shuffle, as if his shoes were weighted down.

It was only then that George recognized his brother. "Danny?" he asked tentatively when the boy reached them.

He nodded. "So you know me after all, George."

"I just never expected . . . I mean, what are you doing on Mars?"

"Looking for you, as a matter of fact."

George got angry then. "What I'm doing—my life here—it's none of your—"

"George, shut up," the little man said wearily. He gave George a hard shove, propelling him through the opening in the wall. On the other side the little man hit the wall with his fist and waited for the gap to close. Then he turned around. "Now listen to me, George, and listen good. Your brother's got something he wants to say to you, and you're to keep your big mouth shut till he's finished. Understand?"

"Go to hell," George said.

"I'm glad you understand me," the little man said grimly.

SEVEN

The room they found themselves in—Petrov's private office—was cramped, windowless, sparsely furnished. Dirty green wallpaper covered two bare walls, while in the center of the third, four television monitors—the most Danny had seen at one time in one place in his life—displayed images of the casino floor. Alongside the TV monitors hung a pair of worshipful oil portraits Danny recognized as the last known Soviet leader, Olga Tomorova, and the final king of Great Britain, the teenage George IX. There was no carpeting on the floor, only more of the usual Martian concrete.

Matheson Lucero crossed to the middle of the room, slid a leather chair out from behind a mahogany desk, and sat down. Leaning far back in the chair, Lucero raised his legs and dropped his glass heels on the edge of the desk. Slipping a hand inside his plastic jacket, he removed an untobacco cigarette and let it dangle unlit from his mouth. "It's your move next, Danny," he said. "There's nothing more I can say to him."

"Thank you, Mr. Lucero." Danny looked at his brother, but the stony-faced Oriental who gazed back at him could have been a total stranger. It had only been four years since the last time they'd seen each other, but for all the recognition and affection George displayed, it might as well have been a lifetime. "You don't like me, do you?" Danny heard himself asking.

George looked surprised. "I don't know." He shrugged. "I've never really thought about it."

"Well, don't bother. Because it doesn't matter. Why I'm here—what I've got to say to you—it's got nothing to do with either one of us. It's not personal. I want you to understand that."

"Whatever you say, Danny-boy." George glanced covertly over his shoulder at the wall behind, but there was nothing in the hard, flat, concrete surface to indicate the existence of the doorway through which they had entered the room.

"You remember that?" Danny asked. Danny-boy was the nickname his mother had called him when he was a kid growing up.

"I've got a good memory," George said. "I remember all sorts of crap. Like for instance I remember how my poor lame brother used to follow me around everywhere like a puppy dog with his stupid legs dragging behind him. I guess that's something else that hasn't changed any. I mean, you even followed me here, didn't you?"

"Only because a man asked me to, George."

"There's always a reason, isn't there? Like there was a reason why I had to go away to school and you got to stay home."

"You told us you wanted to go."

"I said that so they wouldn't take you. That was the best deal Mom could make with the bluesuits, even with the help of her bigwig friend in Perth. One of us had to go. So guess who?"

"I'm sorry," Danny said. "I didn't realize—"

"Forget it." George stepped away from him, squeezing past the desk where Lucero still sat. Then he stood in front of the far wall, gazing up at the television monitors. "It was all a longtime ago anyway. The heck with it."

"Isn't there anything personal you'd like to ask me?" Danny said, speaking to George's back.

"Personal?" George didn't turn around. "Like what, for instance?"

"Haven't you wondered about Mother?"

"What's there to wonder about?" George did turn around now. He stood directly behind Lucero's chair. The fat little detective appeared to be asleep.

"Don't try it, George," Lucero murmured, without opening his eyes. "One false move and I'll put you through the wall."

"Who said I was going to try anything?" George reached up and began clawing at his face. Strips of plastic peeled away in his fingertips. He dropped the residue in a wastebasket beside the desk. "I sent Mother a gram from here, letting her know I was all right. I don't remember her ever bothering to answer."

"How could she? You didn't tell us your address."

"Well, I probably didn't have one at the time. I did a lot of freebooting when I first came to Mars."

"Then for all you know, Mother could be dead."

George paused in removing his makeup. "She's not, is she?"

"No, of course. If she was, I would've told you."

"I didn't think so. I spotted one of her books at the bazaar a while back. I didn't buy it, but I looked through it. Do you know what those poems of hers are supposed to mean? I never could make sense out of them. When I was a kid I'd ask her. They don't always make sense to me, either, she'd say. Always a helpful person, that was my mom."

"Why do you have to hate her so much? She always tried to do the best she could for both of us."

"Well, not always equally."

"I had polio. I couldn't help that."

"It seemed to have its advantages."

"Is that what you think? Then, great. I'll trade legs with you anytime."

"Now, that I'd like to see." George cupped a hand under his mouth and spat out two wadded balls of cotton. "Besides," he said, removing his eyebrows, "you've got things completely mixed up as usual. I don't hate Mom. It's just that . . . well, I've got my own life now. I'm grown-up."

"You're fourteen stanyears old. And you call this a life? Gambling? Making a living at cards? Doing all sorts of—?"

"Hey, it beats sitting around all your life watching the slugs crawl. You ought to try it sometime, Danny-boy. No, wait. Being a cripple, you couldn't do what I do. Somebody's trigger would spot you in ten seconds flat."

Behind the mahogany desk Lucero cleared his throat. "Look, boys, I know you've got plenty to talk about—family reunion and everything— but this office does belong to Mr. Petrov. I don't want to tie it up all night."

Danny knew Lucero was right. Once he and George really got going, it could last forever. "I told you at the beginning, George. None of this is personal. That's not why I'm here."

"Then if you don't mind my asking, why are you here?" George rubbed at his cheeks and forehead with a handkerchief, removing the last of the makeup. For the first time he looked approximately his own age. Which made things a little easier for Danny. At least now he could try to think of George as just another kid.

"I'm here because a man asked me to come and talk to you," Danny said.

"A man? What man? Not a bluesuit?"

Danny shook his head. "His name was Dr. Samuel Goble."

"Goble the spacer? Dad's friend?"

"That's right."

"What would Goble want with me?"

"There's something he'd like for you to do."

George looked instantly suspicious. "Such as?"

"Dr. Goble is in charge of a project to explore the planet Neptune. Right now he's trying to put together a team of explorers—spacers to undertake the mission. There's been a discovery on Neptune—a really important discovery—and Dr. Goble feels we've got to get started right away."

"So? What's any of that got to do with me—or with you?"

"This isn't the first time the Combine has tried to send a mission to Neptune."

"I know. Dad was killed there five years ago."

"Yes. And that's part of it too. Because Dr. Goble feels that one of the things that went wrong that time was that they used the wrong sort of people. He says it's better—safer—to use younger people, adolescents and even little kids, because they have more imagination than adults, a greater ability to adapt to new and different circumstances."

George was staring. "Don't tell me. You're one of these kids. Goble wants to send you to Neptune."

"He came to the house personally to ask me. It wasn't totally his own decision cither. He said they used computers to prepare a master list of kids all through the Solar System who were in the right age group and who—"

George broke in, chuckling. "Then somebody sure screwed up this time."

"What do you mean?"

"Your legs, Danny-boy. How are you supposed to explore a world at the edge of the Solar System when you can't even walk across a room without falling flat on your face? I see you get around a little better here than you used to on Earth, but the gravity on Neptune's got to be—"

"I asked Dr. Goble about that," Danny said evenly. "He told me my legs wouldn't make any difference."

"Then he must be nuts. Or senile. Jeez, the guy's got to be a hundred and fifty years old by now. He's been around forever."

"I don't think that really matters, George," Danny said as coolly as he could manage. That was always one thing George could do better than anybody—get Danny steaming. "Dr. Goble commanded the expedition that explored Nemesis. He's done things the rest of us can only dream about. He and Dad went everywhere and did great and wonderful things, and if the two of us ever—"

"Hold on," George said. "The two of us? How did I get roped into this?"

"Your name's on Dr. Goble's list, too, George. He wants you on the project team."

George shut his eyes, groaning. "And that's why you came here, hunting me down."

"Dr. Goble felt it would be better if I was the one who talked to you."

"Well, great. Lovely. Tremendous." George opened his eyes and grinned. "Okay, this'll be easy enough. You go back to your old nut friend Goble and tell him George Hawkins says thanks but no thanks."

In spite of how well he believed he knew his brother, Danny was surprised. "Do you mean that? You don't want to go?"

"Of course I mean it, Danny-boy. Exploring Neptune? Why would I want to get mixed up in something like that? I already told you I'm as happy as a peach right here on Mars."

"You may not be happy for long," Lucero said from behind the big mahogany desk. The unlit cigarette still dangled from his mouth. "The affiliates don't appreciate card sharps who steal their money. If I was to turn your print data over to, say, Petrov and fill him in on your little scam, your life wouldn't be worth sneezing at come tomorrow. I don't care how many funny disguises you put on, some trigger'll track you down."

George seemed genuinely appalled. His voice rose slightly in pitch. "Why would you want to do that?"

"Wanting's got nothing to do with it. I said it was something I could do. It's really up to Danny here. He's the one I'm working for—him and Sam Goble. If Danny says to clue the affiliates, then I clue them."

"I hardly think Danny wants to sign his own brother's death warrant," George said. "You can forget your whole crazy idea."

Lucero shrugged. "Whatever Danny wants."

Danny decided to try a different tack. "You remember how Dad died, don't you?"

"Sure. I told you I remembered. It was on Neptune. Which to me is just another reason for staying away from there."

"Well, this—our mission—it's actually part of the same thing, a continuation of what Dad was doing when he was killed. The discovery I told you about on Neptune, it was—"

"What is this famous discovery anyway?" George asked.

"I . . . I can't tell you," Danny admitted. "I don't even know myself.

Dr. Goble said the Combine wouldn't let him say a thing until we're all together out on Neptune. But I do know it's the same thing Dad was trying to find out about when he died, so we'll be following in his footsteps, finishing something he couldn't finish himself."

"And maybe getting killed too. Sorry, but I hardly knew the man. How many times when we were growing up did he even bother to come and see us? About three times is all I remember."

"No, five," Danny said. "Once when I first got sick, and before when—"

"Not very many," George said. "When you talked about how I hated Mom, you were way off base, but him . . . if I wanted, I could learn to hate him real easy. He was nothing but a selfish jerk, as far as I'm concerned."

"George, I'd like you to do this. I . . . I really would." Danny was surprised by the urgency of his own plea. "I think it would be good for you and, well . . ."

"Well, what?"

"We need all the people we can get. Dr. Goble says there's only a handful of special kids in the entire Solar System who fit the qualifications he needs, and some of the ones he's already contacted—especially on Titan and Ganymede, and even in the Belt—he couldn't always talk them into going with him."

"Smart kids. They'll live to a ripe old age."

Danny could see how thoroughly hopeless this was. He remembered how George almost never changed his mind once he thought he'd made it up, and how trying to argue with him was like trying to cut water with a sword. He looked across the room at where Lucero sat. Lucero's eyes were open and alert now, and he seemed to be following the conversation with interest. "What you were saying before, Mr. Lucero. Were you serious?"

"Sure I was, Danny. Why not?"

"Then I want you to go ahead and do it. Tell the affiliates everything. Give them George's fingerprints, voiceprints, whatever you have and whatever it takes."

Lucero nodded. "I can do that."

"Danny, for God's sake," George said.

Danny ignored him. "And I want you to do it right away, too, Mr. Lucero. Tonight if you can."

Lucero removed a watch from his jacket and studied the dial thoughtfully. Danny thought he could hear it ticking in the sudden total silence that surrounded them. Apparently the room was soundproof. Not a jingle or a jangle could be heard from the casino beyond. "Petrov's due in later this morning," Lucero said. "I'll hang around and talk to him. He'll let the other affiliates know. When it comes to stuff like this, they manage to get along."

"You're going to get me killed," George said.

"No." Danny swung back. "You may be stubborn, George, but you're not stupid. There's a freighter scheduled to leave Phobos five hours from now carrying a synthfuel shipment for the colony on Triton. I talked to the booking agent earlier and he said there was enough extra room on board for the two of us. The entire trip will take fifty-four standays, but it's the soonest we can get away from Mars."

George's eyes seemed to narrow. He cocked his chin. "And if I agree to go with you, then you'll call off your tubby friend over there?"

"No," Danny said. "Mr. Lucero is going to tell the affiliates about you no matter what."

"But if I'm on my way to Triton, what's the big deal?"

"George," Danny said, "I'm sorry, but I just don't trust you at all."

"There's still nothing to prevent me—once we get out there—nothing to stop me from turning around and catching the next ship back. Okay, maybe I'll have to steer clear of Clarkegrad for a while, but Mars is a big planet."

"Not big enough," Lucero said.

George looked at him. "What's that supposed to mean?"

"It means," Lucero said, "that I wouldn't try that if I were you. The affiliates have long, long memories when it comes to counters, especially successful counters. What they'll do is supply Phobos with your ID data—including prints. The moment you step off a ship from anyplace, a bell'll go off and you'll get tossed in a locked room. The next time the door opens, a trigger'll be standing there. He won't be smiling either."

"There are other worlds in the Solar System," George said. "Titan, Ganymede, the newer Jovian colonies. Or the Asteroid Belt. From what I hear, the Belt's even more wide open than Mars."

"You can give it a shot out there if you want, George," Lucero said, "but the Belt's a pure freebooter economy. Unless you're born or adopted into one of the clans, you'll need a hefty stake—hard mineral, no scrip— just to gain a bottom slot on a rover ship, and then you either work your butt off or else you get jettisoned. As for Titan and Ganymede, don't kid me. I know your history, remember, and you tried Ganymede before you even came to Mars. They expelled you as a lazy bum. Come on, George, let's quit kidding each other. Is hard work something you're really fond of?"

"Then I'll go back to Earth," George said.

Lucero grinned. "Right, and the Reconstruction Corps will gobble you right up as a deserter and assign you to a work crew in one of the hot zones. Did you know World President Armelino just issued a proclamation that the Corps was going to begin major clean-up operations in Russia? Think about that for a minute, George. How about Moscow? It's got to be hotter than the inside of the Sun around there."

"This whole thing," George said, "is the meanest, rottenest, dumbest, lousiest—"

"Oh, George," Danny broke in wearily, "why don't you just shut up?"

Amazingly, that's precisely what George did. A smile stole across his lips. Rocking on his heels, he began to chuckle. "Okay, little brother. I guess you win this round. Triton it is. But jeez, whoever would have guessed that George Hawkins, of all people, would turn out to be some kind of daring spacer in the end?"

PART
TWO

THE KITH

EIGHT

Seated in a big soft chair, Sam Goble arched his neck, tossed back his head, and strained to see directly overhead. There, centered in the middle of a round window, the blue-and-gold sphere of the planet Neptune could be glimpsed shining hazily. Sam sighed softly, pursing his lips. It was a spectacular sight—and a somewhat rare one, since more often than not, Triton's methane-rich atmosphere hid Neptune from view—but not quite enough to rivet his attention for now. His chin dipped and his eyes glazed over. Dreamily, half consciously, he began to hum a mournful tune.

The only other person in the room with him, a raven-haired, sharp-boned woman named Eileen Kinugasa, turned from the computer terminal where she had been punching keys and glared irritably. "All right, Sam. I'll bite. A day's salary if you'll share your thoughts with me."

Sam lowered his head and shrugged. "I'm afraid you'd be wasting your fortune."

She snorted. "You mean to tell me you sit over there staring at that gorgeous planet in the sky and you're not thinking one brilliant thought after another? I thought you were supposed to be a genius."

He laughed. "So people have told me all of my life. But people have been wrong before. To be honest, I wasn't even thinking about Neptune. That's what I ought to be doing, but it's Earth I can't seem to get out of my mind."

"What about Earth?"

"The last trip I took there—it was different than ever before. I didn't feel at home. Not once. And I even went to America, where I was born. Not there either."

"Why should you feel at home?"

"Earth is my home."

"How much time have you really spent there? Since you first went into space, I mean."

He shook his head. "That's not the point. Months and days and years have nothing to do with it. Home to me is a mental concept, a feeling you carry in your heart. Or your soul. If you believe in souls, which most of the time I do. And it's gone for me. I no longer have a home, it seems. Unless . . ." He spread his arms to encompass the room they occupied. It was spacious, high-ceilinged, white-walled, and largely empty except for Sam's chair and Eileen's computer terminal. On the wall directly above the terminal a television monitor showed a static picture. "Maybe this is all the home I've got right now."

"Is that necessarily bad?"

"I wish I knew. It's part of what I've been trying to make up my mind about."

"And the rest?"

He shook his head. "I'm afraid you'll have to bear with me awhile longer. I haven't been feeling in the cheeriest of moods lately. Tomorrow— counting standays—will be my birthday. I'm starting to feel old."

Eileen reached back to flick off the computer terminal. The viewscreen, until it went blank, displayed a cross-section model of an oblate sphere— the planet Neptune. "How old are you anyway, Sam? I don't think I've ever heard you say."

"I don't think I have either."

She frowned. "Does that mean you're not going to tell me?"

"It's in your basic data file on the project." He nodded at the computer terminal. "Why don't you look it up?"

"I have. And I don't believe it. That was from your own input, Sam. I'd like to hear you say it yourself so I can study your face and see if you're telling the truth."

Sam shrugged, raised a hand close to his face, and counted the fingers with his other hand. Then he tried to look sincere. "Fifty-nine, I calculate."

"Stanyears."

"I was born on Earth."

"Then uh-uh. You were a founder of the Combine, right?"

"Myself and seven others, all of them now dead, by the way. Practical visionaries, we called ourselves, and maybe we were. The ridiculous nation-states of Earth were going through another of their periodic economic slumps and consequent war scares, though nothing would eventually come of it, not this time anyway. So a group of us got together—spacers, philosophers, freebooters, the Martian colonial governor—and decided we didn't need Earth anymore. We formed the Combine—the name was partly whimsical, partly braggadocio—there were only eight of us after all—and fomented a rebellion to take space into our own hands. Within a short time we'd founded the new colonies on Ganymede and Titan, expelled the Russians and British from Mars—their governments, anyway—and developed concrete plans for the first manned mission to Pluto. Also we—"

"And all of this was when—fifty, sixty stanyears ago?"

"Fifty-four," he said.

"Then, Sam, how in God's name can you be only fifty-nine years old?"

His expression resembled that of a small boy caught with a handful of matches. His eyes wavered. "I may have overlooked a year or two someplace . . ."

"Sam," she said in a firm, commanding voice, "How old?"

"Eighty-nine," he said without flinching. "I'll be ninety tomorrow."

She whistled, shaking her head. "I knew you weren't young, but I never—"

"And those are stanyears too."

Eileen was still shaking her head. "I wouldn't have guessed."

"Well, at least that's reassuring. Actually, few people ever come close."

"You don't look it at all."

"That means nothing. Not in this day and age. Also, I've spent most of my adult life in low-gee or zero-gee environments, and that's helped a lot. But I don't think it's the way I look that confuses people. It's my mind—my mental processes."

"I never thought all old people had to be senile."

"I'm sure you didn't. And they're not—far from it, in most cases. The older a person gets, the greater his or her knowledge. When things go properly, the greater their wisdom too. But something else is lost along the way. Another quality—something separate and distinct from either knowledge or wisdom. Call it inspiration. I don't believe it's any accident that most of the major scientific breakthroughs of history—and many of the artistic and philosophic ones as well—have been made by people under the age of thirty. That's what I've struggled all of my life against losing. I want to hang on to that quality of inspiration as long as I possibly can, the ability to look at an old, old problem and see a new solution."

"Have you done it?"

"Better than most, I think."

"How?"

"By constant thinking. And by constant not-thinking too."

A hesitant smile played across her lips. Sam could see that she wasn't sure whether he was kidding her now or not. He wasn't.

"Not-thinking?" she asked tentatively.

"It's an Oriental philosophic concept I picked up when I was about your age, traveling through Earth's Far East. I ended up spending five years in a Buddhist monastery near Kobe, and learned more while I was there than all the years that followed, because most of what I learned I still have difficulty putting into words. All I know is that it's just as conceivable for a person to not-think as it is for him to think. Zen is when you're thinking not to think, somebody once said. He was probably trying to be silly, but he wasn't far from the truth either."

"By not-thinking, do you mean making your mind blank—empty?"

"Oh, no. More the exact opposite. It means opening and filling your mind totally—with everything there is."

"Now you're losing me again. I guess I'm not very mystic."

He feigned astonishment. "How strange. And you being Japanese too."

Eileen looked angry. "What's that supposed to mean?" Even after two stanyears together, she still flared up when he teased her. "The closest I've ever been to Japan is lunar orbit. I was born on Ganymede, and you know it."

"Yes, I know it." The mirth had gone suddenly out of his face. His voice was soft, distant. "Do you know where I was born, Eileen?"

"Why?" She gestured at the computer terminal. "Do you want me to look that up too?"

"No, I'll tell you. It was a little town known as Laramie, Wyoming, a part of the old United States of America."

"The country that started the war."

"Nobody started the war, Eileen."

"That's not what I've heard."

"No. But you could have heard it as easily the other way, too, that it was the Soviet Union that began the horror. Both rumors have had currency off and on, and both, I can tell you, are lies."

"That's not possible, is it?"

"It's true. When I was last in Perth, serving my time, we sent robot squads into both the old capitals, Washington and Moscow, in hopes of uncovering some remnants of the final data flows from both nation's command centers. The robots found much more than we had anticipated—the command centers were apparently built to survive, unlike damn near everything—and everyone—else. An examination of the recovered data revealed that both sides fired their first missiles at almost the same exact instant—a few seconds difference at most."

"How could that be?"

"Simple human psychology. Picture two men, fists raised, both convinced that the other intends to strike a killing blow which, when struck, will allow him no chance of retaliation. Two men dangling at the end of wires stretched drum tight. Eventually the wires must snap and the blows will be struck. In this case the fact that both wires snapped simultaneously is not surprising."

"Why hasn't the Combine publicized this?"

"Because it's so goddamn depressing, that's why. Three quarters of the human race exterminated, and for no reason, not even good old-fashioned revenge, no reason whatsoever."

Eileen nodded, looking depressed. "Yes."

"But we were talking about when I was born, and the situation was somewhat different then. The USA was still a democracy of sorts back then, and one of the various peace scares was in full flower. It didn't last, of course—they never did—since eventually one or both nation-states would realize that except as armed entities bent on the other's destruction, neither possessed the slightest reason for daring to exist."

"Spoken like a true anarchist," she said, managing to smile.

"Or a realist. But in any event, this last time when I was on Earth I happened to fly directly above Laramie—my first visit, I believe, since I originally left home as a teenager. It was a cloudy day—it usually is everywhere on Earth at the moment—but I asked my pilot to drop down so that I could take a look at the old homestead. It was a mistake, I'm afraid. There was nothing there; nothing, Eileen, but a flat, blank expanse of burnt ash and black filthy soot. I asked the pilot if the area was classified as a savage zone, thinking for some insane reason that I ought to have him land. He said no, it was way too hot even for savages. This is where they used to store a lot of their big missiles, he explained, and the Russians just bombed hell out of it. The only living things down there, he said, were maybe a few ants and roaches. Later I realized he was being optimistic. Even the roaches would have starved years ago."

"So that's why you've been thinking so much about not having a home."

"That's what got me started. Because it personalized the subject. But" —he managed to force a laugh—"maybe it's time I stopped thinking, and started not-thinking instead."

"It can't hurt, can it?"

"No." Sam rose to his feet, stood without moving for a moment, then shook himself like a cat rising from a nap and strode purposefully across the room. He stood in front of Eileen's chair and looked above her at the television monitor mounted on the wall. "Still no Kith about?" he asked.

Eileen glanced over her shoulder. The image on the screen showed a smooth, nearly featureless landscape of white ice broken here and there by thirty or so randomly spaced forms resembling hemispheric domes of translucent black glass. "They haven't stirred," she said. "I've programmed the central computer to monitor the transmissions as they arrive and to sound an alarm if anything changes."

Sam looked at the lower right corner of the screen, where a digital clock flashed the passing seconds. "Over thirty-seven hours now. Is that a record?"

"It's getting close. One camera probe survived intact forty-two hours. That was another period when the Kith weren't stirring much."

"I recall it."

"I'd give my left hand to know what it is they're up to when they hole up inside all alone like this."

"It's still spring on Neptune, isn't it?"

"For another forty-two stanyears."

"Then maybe they're doing some house cleaning, sprucing things up for their new visitors."

Eileen frowned. "They don't know we're coming, Sam."

"Are you sure about that?" He hadn't been entirely teasing this time.

"There's no reason to think they can predict the future—or read our minds."

Sam stepped back from the monitor and gazed down at Eileen. She was a tiny, delicate creature, he thought, who always put him in mind of a fine glass figurine. He had hired her as his personal assistant two stanyears before, at the urging of an old friend—her father, a former spacer, who felt she would be wasting a brilliant mind on a colony world like Ganymede, where sheer physical labor remained the primary requirement for life.

He said: "I recall during the first project that Pyotr Romanov, when he returned from Neptune—he was the third scrambler to go down after Nina and Mike—Pyotr told me they had been waiting for him. He was a health-food fanatic and strict vegetarian, and the Kith had prepared an enormous banquet table for his arrival, heaped end to end with the finest, sweetest, ripest, most delectable fruit imaginable, everything poor Pyotr had had to do without since coming to Neptune. He described the feast in the most intimate detail and then reached up with his fingers and tried to claw out his eyes, as if what he was remembering was so beautiful he couldn't bear to think of never seeing it again."

"He was hallucinating, Sam. There was no fruit."

"Ah, but can you prove that? About Pyotr or any of the others?"

"I know he was insane. A permanent schizoid psychotic."

"Are you sure? How can we really talk about insanity without first knowing what sanity is? And since nobody knows what's real or not real on Neptune, there's no place to begin."

"You forget, Sam. I visited Pyotr Romanov on Luna. He wasn't talking about fresh fruit then. He was lying on the floor of a padded cell, writhing like a snake and screaming at the top of his lungs. I stood there for two endless hours watching through a mesh window and waiting for him to stop. He never did. You should have been there, Sam. You wouldn't talk this way now."

"No. I shouldn't have been there. Pyotr Romanov was a friend of mine, a colleague. I want to remember him—all of them—the way they were."

The computer terminal began to emit a shrill whistling beep. Eileen swiveled in her chair and flicked a switch.

"What is it?" Sam said. He looked at the television screen. "Not the Kith?"

"No. An incoming radio gram."

"Play it on the screen."

Eileen flicked another switch. The viewscreen brightened, and an instant later the message—letter by letter—began to appear on the screen. Sam put a hand in his pocket, removed a pair of eyeglasses, then thought better of it and tucked them away again. In spite of what he'd told Eileen about his own excellent physical condition, there were still a few minor ailments connected with aging that couldn't be avoided. A low-gee environment did nothing to prevent one's eyes from growing weak. "Tell me what it says."

"It's from Danny Hawkins on the freighter."

"I was hoping we'd hear from him again before they got here. What does he have to say?"

"There's been a crisis of sorts. It seems brother George tried to blackmail the crew into turning back to Saturn orbit and letting him out."

"Blackmail? How did he pull that off?"

"Danny says most of the crew owe George at least a stanyear's wages. They've been playing poker with him since the ship left Phobos."

Goble chuckled. "And the crew wouldn't do it? That's strange. They must have higher ethical standards than the merchant crews I once served in."

Her brow wrinkled. "I never knew you were a merchant crewman, Sam."

"An engine mechanic, actually."

"Is there anything you haven't been?"

He laughed. "A few things. But give me time. Now go on with the message."

"Well, the captain caught wind of what was going on—"

"They usually do," Sam broke in, smiling.

"—and he sealed the crew in their quarters and threatened to charge them all with mutiny. Danny says the crew then agreed to turn George over instead. The captain tossed him in the brig, and he's been there ever since, on a strict water and vitamin diet."

"That won't do him any lasting harm. A few days fasting is good for almost anybody."

"Danny also wants to know if you've thought over his last message and decided to release George from the project."

Sam looked grim. "You'd better answer him straight off on that. He's not serious, but he may not know it yet. Tell him George is essential—no, make that absolutely essential—George is absolutely essential to the success of our mission. Nothing else—just that. I want to be sure it sinks in."

"It's not true, is it?" she said, wiping the incoming message off the viewscreen and beginning to type.

He shrugged. "Who knows? It's the adaptability factor again. And while we can measure intelligence, imagination, creativity, and a host of other critical factors, we can't measure adaptability—not precisely enough to matter—and that's the one category where George truly excels. I may have to take back all the nasty things I've said about computers in my life. When they came up with George's name, they gave me a winner."

"Well, somebody certainly did," she muttered.

He cocked an eyebrow. "Are you trying to tell me something?"

Done typing the message to Danny Hawkins on the freighter, Eileen turned in her chair and fixed him with a frown. "That famous list of potential recruits you used to carry around. I never did get a real close look at it, Sam."

"You're not implying I might have invented it out of whole cloth?"

"I didn't say that. But a few of the names . . . Raymond Liu, for instance. Since when has any computer system contained data for Belters? You know how they are about privacy rights."

"There are always sources," Sam said.

"Right. And I know who too. Your own private network of friends and buddies throughout the Solar System. If you ask me, that's where you came up with most of the names on your list, and no computer had anything to do with it. Like the Hawkins brothers. What a neat coincidence that their father happened to be your all-time best friend. Danny I'm not going to raise a fuss about. From what I know, he's certainly intelligent enough, even if his range of experience is pretty limited. But George . . . George is nothing but a slick little con artist."

"And what's wrong with that?" Sam demanded. "Slick means adaptable, and adaptability, remember, is one of the things I was looking for when I set out to put together a project team. Take what we found out just now about George. The crew of a merchant freighter. The toughest, meanest, hardest bunch of men and women in the Solar System. But George goes in there among them, age fourteen, and not only adapts almost immediately, he thrives—and conquers."

"But you said that adaptability couldn't be measured. So that still doesn't explain how George's name managed to show up on your mysterious computer list."

"Why shouldn't it have been there? George's IQ is one hundred sixty plus. He has a near photographic memory, a—"

"And the moral character of a shark," Eileen said. "I thought that was one of the factors you were intending to have checked out."

"I thought about it, yes, but in the end I decided no. I don't care how many psychologists say otherwise, it's my belief that you just can't measure moral character. Not by computer you can't."

"George Hawkins is a liar and a thief, Sam. What's so difficult to measure in that?"

"Nothing. But if that's all there is to it, then name me one person who isn't a liar. You can't and I can't, and the reason we can't is because the ability to lie, to twist the truth to suit our own purposes, is one of those rare traits that sets the human species apart from the so-called lesser breeds. The best of us, when we lie, we do it unconsciously—knowing exactly what it is we're doing—while the rest, the majority, they have to lie to themselves first—believing their own lies too—before they can go out and tell the same lie to everybody else, pretending it's really the truth. George, I think you'll agree, belongs in the first category. As for stealing, what's so extraordinary about that? Our entire Solar-System-wide economic system remains based on stealing, only we prefer to call it the profit motive."

She shook her head. "You're talking like an anarchist again, Sam."

"Well, I can't help that. I am one. Most of the time anyway. But we were taking about moral character, and when it comes to moral character, what's really essential, I think, is motive. Everybody makes mistakes, but if the road to hell is paved with good intentions, then it's a road I wouldn't mind traveling anytime. And intention—motive—is one thing no computer can measure. They haven't built one yet that can peer inside somebody's head and report for certain what's going on. Until that happens, my opinion is just as valid as anything else, and in this instance my opinion tells me that the motive behind George's stealing—if you can call what he's done stealing—has been a desire to exercise and challenge the resources of his own brain. I think it's a natural thing, an outgrowth of his intelligence and his adaptability. It's certainly not a character flaw. In fact, let me put it this way: If George were here in this room now, I'd feel no hesitation in placing my life savings on the seat of that chair and turning my back on him for any length of time you might suggest."

Eileen smirked. "Is that what you're planning to do when he gets here?"

Sam took her question at face value. "No. Because I've already decided about George. It's my opinion I'm going with this time—my pure gut instinct."

She looked straight at him. "But is that enough, Sam?"

It was one question he'd hoped she wouldn't ask, because it was one that haunted him too. He said, "I wish I knew. But what else is there? This is my project, Eileen. I'm the one responsible for taking a bunch of kids, placing them down on the surface of Neptune, and then getting them out of there again alive and in one piece—physically and mentally. If it doesn't work, if anything goes wrong, then I'm the one who'll bear the blame—and the guilt."

She nodded slowly, falling silent for a long moment. "Sam, there's something I'd like to ask you."

He laughed. "What do you call what you've been doing?"

"This is different. It's about the project, not just George. I want to know what chance you think we have of pulling it off."

"Well, that depends on what you mean by pulling it off."

"What you just said. Getting the kids down and getting them back again."

"That's not our real objective."

"I understand. But it's where we have to start, though."

He nodded. "Then make it, say, seventy-thirty."

She looked surprised. "That's all? Only a seventy percent chance we can do it?"

"No. A seventy percent chance we won't do it."

"My God, Sam, that's not what you've been telling everybody."

"I know. I lied. But my motives were pure. It's imperative that the human race establish a physical presence on Neptune. At the moment there's only one conceivable way of accomplishing that—by scrambling and by using these poor kids I've collected. We have no real choice, Eileen. We've got to go with it, we've got to try no matter how dangerous it may be, and if it doesn't work, if we fail again, then God help us all."

"I didn't know you believed in God, Sam."

He shook his head. "It was only a figure of speech."

Her eyes were locked on his. "But do you?"

He sighed, twisting away from her gaze. He loved Eileen as if she were his own daughter, but like his own daughter—not that he'd ever had one, alas—she could also drive him nuts on occasion.

His eyes strayed to the ceiling and focused on the blue-and-gold orb that shone through the window up there. Neptune, he thought. A planet of mystery. A mystery wrapped in an engima shrouded by a riddle.

"Wait," he told her, turning back. "When the project's over, ask me that question again. Maybe then—finally—when we've learned who the Kith are I'll have an answer for you."

NINE

As naked as a bear in the woods, Sam sat cross-legged on the cold stone floor of the windowless chamber that served as his present home. To his left a fat candle was burning, the flame rich and red in the artificial air of Triton's domed colony Tsiolkovsky. Sam's room here was nearly identical to most of the temporary homes he'd inhabited the past two stanyears since last leaving Perth, as spartan and impersonal as a medieval monk's cell. But that was how he chose to live these days. It meshed with his own concept of the proper progression of material life. Properly, he believed, you began with nothing, and then, as you aged, you acquired objects—possessions, friends, beliefs too—until, as the declining years set in, you began to pare these things away—or had them pared from you—so that when the end arrived, you found yourself full circle at the beginning, at nothingness. And that was called death.

Not that Sam had come that far yet. He certainly wasn't dead—far from it, he thought—and so, along with the burning candle, he permitted himself a few other material objects in the room: a stack of papers—his mail—and several bottles of Martian beer. Sipping the beer—the best obtainable in the Solar System these days, though still a far, sad cry from the genuine pre-war Earth varieties made from natural grains and pure fresh water—he went through the stack of mail, holding each paper up to the candle and squinting through his eyeglasses until he could decipher the text. The candle was a personal eccentricity—one of his twitches, as Eileen called them—although perhaps it was actually connected to what he had been thinking about before, about paring things away as one grew older, about simplifying. In any event, even if the candle did make reading a bit difficult at times, Sam figured what the heck, if he couldn't read it right away, then it was probably not worth reading at all.

Now here was something he had no trouble deciphering. It was a radio message from Danny Hawkins in response to Sam's earlier message emphasizing George's value to the project. Danny's reply consisted of two words: YES SIR. Sam grinned. Now what was that supposed to mean? Could it possibly be that Danny was being sarcastic? Probably not, Sam decided regretfully. The kid was just polite to a fault. Well, wait until he gets here and falls in with the rest of the kids. That ought to be enough to cure him of his yes sirs. There was nothing like a little peer pressure to turn a sweet, gentle lad into a sneering, cynical adolescent. Sam knew. He'd been a teenager once upon a time himself.

The next sheet was a considerably lengthier message, the complete text of a presidential edict forwarded from Perth for his information and apparent approval. Sam wasn't happy. He'd tried to make clear to the others when he'd left Earth that he was through with the business of ruling a world. Sam skimmed the text quickly, nodding agreement here and there, and then placed his thumb against the bottom of the page next to his name and set the approved text aside for retransmittal. He'd send a few sharp sentences along with it too, telling them to leave him alone from now on. The edict concerned the proposed Chicago cleanup and set a firm date for the initial recolonization of the lakefront suburbs. That had been one of Sam's pet projects during his term as World President Armelino—he kept telling the rest of them, you couldn't really have a civilization till you first had some real cities—and he decided that must be why Vim Mebi, the new Armelino, had felt it necessary to pass on the edict. It was a nice gesture on Vim's part, but Sam had too much on his mind out here already without adding anything else. It was World President Armelino's job to dictate the affairs of Earth, and Sam wasn't Armelino anymore. (Though he might again be someday, he knew, assuming he survived the Neptune project. The original concept of a World President Armelino had been largely Sam's. Once it became clear in the aftermath of the war on Earth that only the Combine possessed the necessary wisdom, wealth, and power to reestablish a semblance of order on the devastated planet, Sam had argued for the creation of a mythical charismatic leader-figure to serve as a front for their unified efforts. People believe in other people, he'd told the other Combine directors, not in organizations. The Earth needs a symbol—a savior—and it's up to us to provide one. And it had worked. There were even reports of Armelino cults in some of the savage zones that worshiped the nonexistent world president as a sort of neo-Christ.)

Sam picked up the next sheet of paper in the stack and held it up to the candle. This was yet another message from Matheson Lucero on Mars. Vladimar Arabatov was out of the hospital now, Lucero reported, and back in his theater, having happily accepted the wad of scrip Sam had told Lucero to slip him—claiming it came from George—and was now full of plans for his new repertory company. Sam wished him luck and regretted he likely wouldn't be able to make it to Clarkegrad for the opening curtain. Lord, he hadn't watched a real stage play in more years than he cared to remember. He had a few vague recollections of Vladimar Arabatov from Earth too. A competent classical actor, Sam recalled, if a little too florid. (But maybe Vladimar also had learned something about paring things away as he grew older.) Lucero also wanted to know about informing the affiliates concerning George. Sam had been thinking this over, and he'd now made up his mind. He'd tell Lucero to do nothing for the time being. The idea had been to force George to come to Neptune, not to destroy his future. When the project was over, Sam would take George aside and inform him he was free to go wherever he wanted. Somehow Sam doubted that life as a Martian gambler would hold much appeal for George by then, though you never could tell.

After Lucero's message, came several sheets of computer-generated technical data. Sam flipped through these quickly. The data had originated on the space station *Leverrier,* which had gone into orbit around Neptune a year and a half before the first project. Sam had asked Olga Kropotkin, the commander there, to inspect the MAGMOS hardware, and the bottom line of her reply was that everything appeared to be in working order, although there was no way of being absolutely certain until a biological run-through could be conducted. Because of a certain fondness for dramatic gestures, Sam had already told Olga to hold up on that till he and the project team reached *Leverrier.* A MAGMOS biological run-through, whether successful or not, was about as dramatic as gestures could get. Sam thought it would be a fine way to start the kids out on the right foot.

The last sheet of paper in the stack was a handwritten note in a childish scrawl. Now what's this doing here? Sam asked himself, grinning. The note was from Nina, telling him to please be sure and visit her room before he went to sleep because she wanted him to tell her another of his stories about adventures in space. Another of my lies, Sam thought, still smiling. He made a mental calculation of the precise time—he hadn't needed to consult a clock since entering the Buddhist monastery decades before— and decided he could finish another beer before Nina came pounding on his door, demanding to know what was keeping him. Sam popped the cap on the next bottle in line—the beer would be slightly warm to the taste, but Sam had developed a fondness for warmish beer as a youth while studying comparative economic systems at the old Cambridge University in England—and raised the bottle to his lips. Pausing momentarily, he cocked his wrist and spoke out loud: "To Neptune," he intoned. "To Neptune, where we must conquer."

Then he sipped.

Actually, of course, it never ought to have come to pass. Neptune, that is. Not now and probably not ever. Since its inception in the latter half of the previous century, the human conquest of space had progressed in an orderly pattern, one largely predictable in advance. The nearer Earth a particular world—and the more similar to it—the more certain it was that human footsteps would soon march across its surface. Luna was the obvious initial target, and shortly thereafter, the planet Mars beckoned. And it was on these worlds that the first human colonies had come into existence. Later—after the formation of the Combine—the larger satellites of the Solar System had been colonized each in turn, beginning with Jupiter's Ganymede and Saturn's Titan and proceeding more recently through the three remaining major Jovian moons, until at last reaching even here to distant and remote Triton. (Though the total population of its single domed settlement numbered only a few thousand.)

Nevertheless, even with eight worlds now bearing permanent colonies in one stage of development or another, the fact stood that the vast bulk of the Solar System remained off limits to the human species. Mercury and Venus were simply too hot, Pluto too cold, and the remaining uninhabited moons too small to arouse much immediate interest in their colonization. (The rapid development of the Asteroid Belt was a different matter, since there the motive spurring the people who came was the accumulation of wealth—and the pursuit of individual freedom—rather than any wish to create a permanent human abode.) As for the four great gas-giant worlds of Jupiter, Saturn, Uranus, and Neptune—which among them constituted ninety percent of the non-Solar mass of the system—human beings not only couldn't live on them, they couldn't even stand on them. (Even apart from their crushing gravity, none of the four appeared to possess a truly solid surface area.) Lovely worlds, the lot of them, Sam had believed, but —in strictly human terms—utterly useless as well. Ornaments in the sky— only that and nothing more. The next orderly step in the conquest of space lay outside the boundaries of the Solar System—in the stars. As a result, the majority of the Combine research and development budget had for years been devoted to a search for a practical means of interstellar flight.

It was as an offshoot of this search that the so-called scrambling process had come into being. How scrambling worked was simple enough to describe. Take an object—a brick, say—and break the brick down into its component molecular structure. Transform these particles into corresponding waves and beam the waves through space at light-speed velocity to a chosen point of destination, where the waves could then be converted back into molecules and joined to recreate the original brick. In theory what this constituted was an excellent means of very rapid transport throughout the Solar System. In practice, however, the energy expended in scrambling, beaming, and recreating the brick was considerably greater than the energy necessary to propel a thousand conventional space freighters—each loaded down with a million bricks—across an identical distance. In other words, although scrambling might work, it did not pay.

A number of biological experiments were conducted as well. What could be done with a brick could also be done with a mollusk, a fieldmouse, or even a human being. But again the cost in terms of energy proved prohibitive. If you wanted to send a mollusk from Luna to Mars, there were other, considerably less expensive means available than the scrambling process.

Over the succeeding years some degree of scrambling research did continue, in hopes of making the process less expensive. It was during the course of this research that a physicist working in the Combine labs on Luna had developed the MAGMOS Process. MAGMOS, an acronym standing for Manipulative Genetic Molecular Scrambling, had been inspired by an earlier failed biological experiment during which a dog, after being scrambled, had somehow been reconstituted with its tail sprouting from the center of its forehead. Contemplating this incident, the physicist —a man named Jared Duncan, an old friend of Sam's—had come up with a new idea, or more accurately, a new twist on what was by then a rather old idea. Take an object—a brick, say—and break it down into its component molecular structure. Transform these particles into corresponding waves and beam the waves through space at light-speed velocity to a chosen point of destination, where the waves could then be converted back into molecules and eventually jointed to form—what? Well, anything you wanted, was Jared Duncan's idea—anything you wanted, so long as the basic molecular structure remained that of the original brick.

And, again, what would work with a brick could also work with a mollusk, a fieldmouse, or even a human being. In theory at least. At this point Jared Duncan's request to proceed with actual biological testing was rejected by the Combine directorate. Any such genetic tampering, it was felt, would not only be expensive and dangerous—for the subjects involved, that is—but virtually pointless as well. How many uses were there, after all, for dogs with tails sprouting from the centers of their foreheads? Given the ability to create such a creature, what then?

In due time an answer came, the source for this response turning out to be—of all conceivable places in the cosmos—the bleak, forbidding world of Neptune. Suddenly and unexpectedly, a critical need arose to devise a means for placing a human being upon the surface of that planet. Sam, having thoroughly reexamined Jared Duncan's original research, brought up the possibility of using the MAGMOS Process as a way of attaining that end. As he put it to his colleagues during a meeting of the directorate convened to discuss the Neptune situation: "We're all aware that it's not physically possible to place a human on Neptune—even the altered Neptune that seems now to exist—and expect that person to survive more than a few brief instants. What is possible, however, is to place a Neptunian on Neptune instead, a being as biologically suited for life on Neptune as we in this room were once suited for life on Earth. Since no such being appears to have evolved in nature, I suggest we make an attempt to invent one for ourselves."

Because of the MAGMOS Process, as Sam went on to point out, it was indeed possible to invent such a Neptunian. A crash program was approved with Sam at its head. Two stanyears furious labor followed. A number of major technical problems had to be met and overcome before the project could proceed. The most critical among these was devising a method by which to convert a scrambled object—in this case a human being—into its chosen material form on Neptune, where it would not be possible to have any hardware waiting to receive and capture the beamed waves of energy. It was like trying to figure out a way of playing baseball without using a catcher, one engineer bluntly told Sam. But the project had the best possible minds in the Solar System laboring in its behalf. In time a tentative solution was arrived at. Sam ordered an immediate test. A frog was beamed from the project laboratory on Luna to a chosen spot on the face of the Earth—a swamp in old Louisiana. The frog remained in the swamp for a full hour and then returned to the Lunar lab. To Sam—and to the biologists working for him—it was still the same old frog, none the worse for wear. A second test followed, this time utilizing the MAGMOS Process so that when the frog reached Earth, it wasn't a normal frog anymore—it looked more like a hairless chipmunk—but when it returned to Luna, it was a full-fledged frog again. And a totally healthy one, too, as far as anyone could determine.

At this point Sam began to put together a mission team, eventually composed of five veteran spacers he knew and trusted. The entire group then set out for *Leverrier,* the new space station in orbit above Neptune, where the MAGMOS hardware had already been installed. Once there, Sam put the team through an intense pre-mission training period. The five scramblers—as they'd taken to calling themselves—each passed through the MAGMOS Process several times, being changed on each occasion into a physical form progressively more alien from their original human bodies. Each also spent considerable time huddled in hypnosimulators, undergoing the subjective psychological experience of moving about the surface of Neptune in the form of a native Neptunian. (On Luna Sam had assigned a group of biologists the task of creating the perfect Neptunian, using the identical molecular composition of a human being; he believed they had done their work well.) Following each training session, the scramblers were given thorough physical exams, but nothing medically amiss was ever discovered. Sam began to feel confident, and one day called the entire team into his office and said he needed a volunteer, without bothering to say what for. A woman named Nina LeClaire, who wore her carrot-orange hair shoulder length, contrary to the usual spacer practice, put up her hand when it became clear nobody else would. "What do you want this time, Sam? Do I have to get scrambled into a monster again?"

Sam nodded. "If you're going to Neptune, you do."

"Neptune? Me?"

"You put your hand up, didn't you?"

"Sure, Sam, but . . . well, okay. When?"

"What about right now?"

"You're kidding me."

"Are you ready?"

Nina looked suddenly grim. "Damn right I'm ready."

"So let's do it."

Nina did it, her basic molecular structure converted into corresponding energy waves and then beamed to a preselected location on the cloud-shrouded surface of Neptune and there reconverted into the form of a meter-long, methane-breathing, multilegged creature resembling an enormous slug. For approximately two hours Nina the Neptunian lumbered about the sleek icy surface of what was for all intents and purposes her native environment. Back on *Leverrier* Sam paced outside the empty scrambler chamber. He lit an untobacco cigarette he borrowed from a technician, took two puffs, realized how lousy it tasted, crushed it out underfoot, and borrowed another before he realized what he was doing.

Then a bulb flashed red above the chamber's iron door. Sam stood stock still as the door cycled open and there was Nina, stark naked on the other side. With a whoop of joy Sam rushed forward and caught her hand in his. "What was it like down there?" he asked gently. "Did you see them—see the Kith?"

Nina opened her mouth as if to reply, emitted a piercing scream Sam could still hear echoing in his ears five stanyears later, and bit her tongue cleanly in two. Blood splattered the front of Sam's white lab jacket like droplets of scarlet rain.

The chief project psychiatrist, Dr. Frederik Berman, found Sam later, sitting on the floor of his own spartan quarters, a pile of empty Martian beer bottles on the floor beside him, one of the few remaining full ones gripped in his big red hand.

Dr. Berman kicked the door shut and knelt on the floor in front of Sam. "Spare a sip of that stuff?"

"I didn't know you psychiatrists drank beer."

"Why shouldn't we?"

Sam shrugged and passed over the bottle. Berman took a swallow and made a face. "That's not beer. It tastes like salt and piss. Have you ever drank a really good German beer, Sam? Thick and brown like molasses, and the taste of hops just seems to melt into your tongue. You're not drunk, are you?"

"Not yet, no."

"Then keep drinking." Berman gave Sam back his beer. "The news I've got isn't good."

"I was there when she first came out of the chamber," Sam said. "It was like getting a glimpse of the inside of pure, raw hell. Once you looked, you could see it in her eyes."

"I know." Berman folded his legs beneath him, grabbing the knees and forcing them into a lotus position. "Nina's suffering from psychotic shock, a full-fledged schizophrenic seizure. We've injected her with enough Thorazine to make an elephant comatose, but she's still fully conscious and fitfully violent."

"She bit her tongue off."

"That can be reattached, but it'll have to wait until we can calm her. She wouldn't be able to talk rationally now, even if she could."

"Then when?" Sam drained the beer bottle and opened another with the tip of his thumb.

"I took a brainscan. There's some apparent neurological damage, but it doesn't seem to be severe. My hope is, when she comes out of this, she'll be perfectly all right."

"I asked you when, Fred."

"I know you did. I can't tell you. Not when or, frankly, if ever."

"What do you intend doing with her?"

"In time she might have to be sent back to Luna, where I can arrange care for her on a permanent basis. For now I think the best thing to do is keep her right here and hope for some sudden improvement in her overall condition. If that happens, and if we can get her to respond to questions, then you might be able to start up the project again without too great a delay."

Sam was shaking his head. "I'm not shutting the project down, Fred."

"I meant the actual missions to Neptune."

"That's what I meant too. Mike Hawkins just left here. He and I talked things out. Mike wants to go down next, and I gave him my okay."

"If what happened to Nina happens to him . . ."

"Then we've found something out," Sam said. "We've found out there's a flaw in the process, even if we can't be sure where or what it is. As things stand, what happened today may have simply been Nina's own fault."

"I don't think that's the right word to use, Sam."

"It's the one Nina would use if she could."

"People seem to think you spacers are brave. If you ask me, you're just crazy."

"Is there a difference, Fred?"

"There certainly ought to be."

"Perhaps. But the truth is what is, Fred, not what ought to be. What ought to be is a damn lie."

"Or a dream."

"Only when the dream comes true."

The next standay Michael Hawkins went to Neptune. What happened to Nina did not happen to him, or if it did, no one ever knew. Michael Hawkins vanished. When the iron door to the scrambler chamber cycled open, there was no one on the other side.

Sam ordered a shutdown of all further missions to Neptune until a thorough inspection of the scrambling systems could be conducted. A team of human and robot technicians carried out the inspection, going over every last wire and circuit in the MAGMOS Process. It was thirty-two standays after the disappearance of Michael Hawkins before their report reached Sam. There was nothing wrong with the scrambler systems, he was assured. Hardware had worked as it was intended to work. There had been no mechanical malfunctions. Michael Hawkins had definitely reached Neptune in the form he was intended to reach it. What happened then—what happened to an alien being on an alien world—there was no way of knowing. When the time had come to bring Michael Hawkins back to *Leverrier* and make him human again, he simply wasn't there.

A few hours after receiving the report, Sam gathered the remaining three scramblers in his office. He told them, "Mike Hawkins has vanished on Neptune and must be presumed dead. Nina LeClaire is on her way to Luna and must be presumed insane. If both of them were dead or both insane, we wouldn't be holding this meeting right now. As it is, I'm going to ask for a volunteer."

All three hands rose in seeming unison.

Sam nodded at the individual he'd already picked out in advance, a smooth-faced, wide-eyed, ever-grinning young man in green dungarees. "Pyotr Romanov, I believe you had your hand up first."

When the door to the scrambler chamber cycled open and Pyotr Ramanov stepped out, he was grinning from ear to ear. Rushing up to Sam, he grasped his shoulders in a hug.

"Do you know me?" Sam asked curtly.

"You are my dear friend Sam Goble."

"And who are you?"

"I am Pyotr Romanov."

"Then tell me what happened to you down there, Pyotr."

He shut his eyes. "It was wonderful, Sam, like a warm dream in winter. The Kith creatures took me into their home, where there stood a great banquet table stretching farther than the eye could see and heaped with fresh ripe fruit. I ate pineapples with the juice squirting down my face and sweet pears and red delicious apples with hard thick skin. I ate golden peaches and nectarines and strawberries plucked fresh off the vine, and I— I—"

Pyotr Romanov threw back his head and began to scream. It was a staccato sound like the cracking of a repeating rifle punctuated by sharp intakes of breath. His hands flew up to claw at his eyes, but before he could do himself any harm, two robots sprang forward and caught and held his wrists while a third injected him with a massive dose of Thorazine.

Pyotr Romanov's round head lolled on his shoulders. His eyes were open now. "It was a feast fit for a god," he muttered. "For a god."

When Dr. Berman entered Sam's quarters later that day, he found Sam seated with his back to the wall, writing in a spiral notebook.

"What are you up to, Sam?" Berman asked, sitting down across from him.

"A draft of a letter. To Pyotr's clan in the Belt. I'm telling them he was killed on an experimental mission to Neptune."

"He's a long way from dead, Sam."

"But he might as well be."

"Well, the amount of actual neurological damage remains slight, for Nina too, but—"

"You think they're not going to recover."

Berman nodded slowly, looking down. "I'm afraid so."

Sam closed the notebook. "That's what I thought you thought. Now do you mind telling me why?"

"It's what I came here to tell you."

"So I figured. But why now? Why not before, after Nina? You must have had some inkling then."

"Would you have listened to me, Sam?"

"I think I would have listened, yes."

"And shut down the project?"

"No. Not unless I was sure you were right."

"You wouldn't have been. Because I wasn't sure myself. Not then I wasn't."

"And now you are?"

"It's happened twice, Sam. Twice that we know of for certain, and probably three times. Anything can happen once, but very few things ever happen twice."

"That sounds like something I might say."

Berman smiled. "It is. I'm quoting you."

"Then tell me your theory. It's MAGMOS, isn't it? The MAGMOS Process is driving them insane?"

"To a degree that's correct, though I think it would be more fully accurate to say that it's their own minds that are doing it. The human consciousness is a limited domain, Sam, possessed of only so much capacity to withstand a vast and steady stream of new and radically different perceptions. What we've been doing here is taking human beings and changing them into something else, something alien—"

"Into Neptunians," Sam said.

"So we like to think. But it's not true. Not completely. Because there's always one part that remains unchanged—the human mind itself, the individual consciousness."

"That's necessary. There wouldn't be any point to sending people to

Neptune if they didn't retain enough sense of human identity to be able to interpret what they experience there."

"I understand that. But it's a fatal flaw. The human consciousness remains a closed system, and like any closed system when it's overloaded with input, sooner or later it's going to blow. With Nina I think it must have blown almost immediately, moments after she reached Neptune. With Pyotr it appears to have remained intact somewhat longer."

"What makes you think so?"

"The memories he's clearly retained. They may not be rational memories—the banquet table, the fresh fruit—but something did happen to him down there, and he remembers it."

Sam nodded. "Why the difference?"

"Probably because Pyotr is eleven years younger than Nina and his consciousness less fully formed. The older we are, the more we've seen and experienced, the less we're able to adapt to the new and radically different."

"We see what we expect to see," Sam said.

"Exactly. You've seen those picture puzzles where there's a crude drawing of some very ordinary scene and the idea is to find the five or six things in the picture that are wrong. Perhaps a man's hat is on sideways or a fish is swimming in a bowl without any water in it, but whatever, it always takes a while to sort things out. Why? Because, as you said yourself, Sam, our first reaction is always to see what it is we expect to see, even when it's not actually there. We automatically put the man's hat on the right way and we fill the fishbowl with water, because that's the way we've learned all our lives that it should be. Well, on Neptune nothing is the way it should be."

"And the hypnosimulators?" Sam asked. "My idea in using them was to duplicate the actual experience of being on Neptune."

"Well, clearly it didn't work. I know because I examined Nina and Pyotr after each training session and there was never the slightest indication of mental instability on the part of either. The simulations may well have been objectively realistic, but they were also a product of a human mind, filtered through human consciousness. The best most of us can do is show the expected unexpected. We create from the well of our own experience. Paint me a picture of God, Sam, and make me believe that's who it really is."

"I can't. I've never seen God."

"Exactly."

Sam frowned, spreading his hands. "Then maybe what we ought to concentrate on first is trying to improve the realism quality of the simulations. What if we scrambled our people first, changed them into Neptunians, and then put them through hypnosimulation . . ."

"And if it worked," Berman said, "what then? You'd only be driving them into psychosis even before they actually had a chance to reach Neptune."

"If we did it gradually, built up their resistance . . ."

"Psychosis isn't a disease you develop a resistance to."

"So what is the answer?"

"Maybe there isn't one, Sam."

"You know that's not what I want to hear."

"It's the only answer I've got for you right now."

"Then find me another," Sam said, rising to his feet.

Four stanyears later on Luna Sam burst into the inner sanctum of Dr. Berman's private office in Tranquility's third commercial level. A well-dressed woman seated in a soft leather chair slapped a hand over her mouth as if trying to seal her lips.

Ignoring her, Sam looked at Dr. Berman behind his big mahogany desk. "I want to talk to you, Fred."

Dr. Berman was on his feet, pointing stiffly at the open door. "I want you out of here before I—"

"Not now." Sam's voice was a hard, thick whisper. "This is important, Fred, damnably important."

"For you to come barging in here like this, it had better be as—"

"It is. You have my word."

A robot secretary, rattling on four wheels, rolled through the door. "A security patrol will be arriving momentarily, sir."

"I—No, never mind. Go tell them we don't need them." He looked at the woman in the leather chair. Her hand hadn't moved from her mouth. "Madelaine," he said softly, "can I ask you to please come back in . . . ?"

"An hour will do," Sam said.

"In one stanhour. We'll start over then. This man is a patient of mine and extremely disturbed. I'm sure you can understand."

"Of course, Dr. Berman." The woman rose to her feet. "I understand perfectly." She shot Sam a look that mixed pity and anger and strode from the room.

Sam went over and threw himself down in the chair the woman had vacated. "Do you frequently lie to your patients, Fred?"

"Only when it's in their own best interest."

Sam's head swiveled on his shoulders. "I thought you people always used a couch."

"Only when the patient feels more comfortable that way. There's one in my other office if you—"

"Thanks, but no thanks. I didn't come here because I need your professional services, Fred. What I came here for was to show you the master list I've prepared."

"Master list?"

"Of people I believe can be sent to Neptune without their going insane."

"You're starting the project up again?"

"Yes. Want to see the list?"

"Are they human?"

"Of course."

"Then I'm afraid I'm doubtful already." He held out a hand. "But let me see it."

Sam dipped a hand in a pocket and pulled out a thick wad of papers. Slowly, he separated the sheets, removed one, and handed it to Dr. Berman. "Here you go."

Dr. Berman studied the sheet of paper. He shook his head. "I thought I knew every spacer working for the Combine, but these names—"

"They're not spacers. Not yet anyway,"

"Then who . . . ?"

"Not who, Fred—what. It's what they are that's important. They're a bunch of kids, Fred."

"Kids?"

Sam nodded. "That's the answer to the question you failed to come up with four years ago on *Leverrier*. There's nothing new under the sun. You've heard that expression, I assume."

"It's from the Book of Ecclesiastes originally."

"Do you agree with it?"

Dr. Berman smiled thinly. "Some particularly dreary mornings . . ."

"Precisely. But to a newborn infant right from the womb, it would be the biggest lie there could be. To a newborn infant *everything* under the sun is new."

"You can't send newborn infants to Neptune."

"Well, I could, but you're right, there wouldn't be much point to it. So what I'm going to do is come as close to that ideal as possible. The kids on that list—the oldest are barely in their teens, some considerably younger, and every one of them exceptionally open to new concepts, new experiences. If anyone can survive Neptune, it's them."

"Well . . . I wish you luck, Sam."

"I wish you'd do a bit more than that, Fred. I need a project psychiatrist. You're still caring for both Nina and Pyotr Romanov, I believe."

"I see them occasionally. There's been no significant improvement in their condition—"

"Yes, I know."

"You've seen them too?"

"My personal assistant has. But I'm offering you a job, Fred."

"I have patients here."

"And they'll still be here when you get back."

He shook his head wearily. "Sam, you don't know one goddamn thing about psychiatry, do you?"

"As little as possible, to tell the truth. I'm a Buddhist, you know. I'm going to need your answer today, Fred. Right now, in fact."

"I . . . you're lying to me, of course, but—all right, I'll go. I don't know how, damn it, but I'll go."

"Then . . ." Sam was going through his wad of papers again. He extracted one. "Here's your travel itinerary. You'll be leaving eight standays from today—see, I'm giving you plenty of time to clear up your business here—for Ganymede, connecting there with an inspection ship bound for Triton. When you arrive, contact *Leverrier* and arrange for a shuttle. Olga Kropotkin is still in station command, so she'll know why you've come."

"Sam, can I ask you one thing?"

"Certainly. Go ahead."

"When did you figure this thing out with the children?"

"Oh, about . . ." He screwed up his face. "About ten minutes after you and I had our last talk on *Leverrier.* That's when the idea first hit me. I've had it checked and studied and examined from every conceivable angle by every conceivable means since then. And it's still alive and kicking."

"But you waited until now—almost four stanyears—to get the project rolling again."

"I wanted to be sure. As absolutely sure as anyone could be without going ahead and actually doing it. I'm not a sentimentalist, Fred, but I am a human being. These are just kids whose minds are going to be put to risk. It's not a responsibility I look forward to assuming. And there were the kids themselves. I had to wait until they were ready too."

"Then, I gather, these aren't just ordinary kids we're talking about."

"No. None of them are that, and several are quite special."

"Special in what way?"

"In various ways. And numerous ways. I'll go into more detail, I promise you, as soon as we're both on *Leverrier.*"

"When will that be?"

"As soon as—" Sam reached down and scooped the list of children off Dr. Berman's desk. "As soon as I've got my project team together."

And now that moment had very nearly arrived at last. Of the children on his master list who had been able to accept Sam's offer, all but the final two had by now reached Triton.

There was a sharp, impatient knocking rattle at the door. Sam sighed, placed his beer bottle on the floor, and called out: "I'll be right there, Nina darling."

But it wasn't Nina this time. The door opened and Eileen Kinugasa stood in the gap. Sam frowned but made no effort to cover his nakedness. "I wasn't expecting you this late, Eileen."

Her expression was dark, her complexion pale. "You'd better come, Sam."

"Why? Something's up?"

"The Kith are back and they—they—"

"They what?"

She lowered her head so that he couldn't see her eyes. "You'd better come for yourself."

TEN

Danny Hawkins on board the Combine space freighter *Yevgeny Zamiatan* was having one of those crazy dreams that never seemed to make sense till after you woke up and mulled it over. An anxiety dream, a psychiatrist would've called it, except that right then Danny couldn't have cared less what words they used to try to explain things.

He was the one having the dream—and the dream seemed real. Danny was walking on the surface of the planet Neptune. At least, he knew it was supposed to be Neptune, except that—since this was actually a crazy dream—the landscape around him was red and bleak and sandy, much like the surface of Mars as he'd observed it during his recent sojourn on that world.

Head down, breath coming hard, Danny plodded forward, struggling to hurry. He knew he was headed someplace in particular, seeking something —or someone—and that if he failed to arrive in time, truly awful conse- quences would transpire.

The trouble was, Danny didn't have the slightest memory of who or what or when or where. He was as ignorant as a lamb marching to the slaughter.

As he tried to hurry, Danny kept glancing at his wristwatch, but half the time the face of the watch was blank and the other half the dials were spinning madly out of control. To make matters worse, the sand at his feet kept moving and shifting as if being shaken by unseen hands, with the result that his legs kept sinking deeper each step he took. Also, overhead— he wasn't looking now, but he'd noticed it before—an enormous god-like face hung suspended in the sky. The face was creased and leathery and wreathed by a red beard. Danny knew it was observing him with a definite purpose. The face was judging him.

Another step, and this time Danny's leg sank almost to the knee. Pausing, he reached back, clawing at the sand till he managed to jerk his other leg free. Then, swiveling his hips, he took another lunging step. It's not my fault, he thought, glancing up at the face in the sky. How can you look at me that way? It's not as if it was my own idea to fail.

Danny's front leg was buried clear to his thigh. He again reached back to pry himself loose. But there was something there now, something alive way down under the sand. He felt it brush his leg. Something cold and wet and slippery. Like a snake or an enormous worm. Danny struggled to free his leg, but the worm caught hold of the ankle. Danny kept trying, but the leg wouldn't budge. He was trapped, held tight.

Danny told himself to remain calm. Panic was the worst thing he could let happen now. As long as he kept his wits and concentrated on the problem at hand, a solution would eventually emerge. He tried to think. But the worm—or was it another one?—now had hold of his other leg too. And it was pulling him down, dragging him down. Danny felt the sand cover his thighs. His waist was buried. And there was nothing to cling to, no way to stop it. He was being sucked down, buried alive, and he was as helpless as an infant.

The giant face still watched from the sky. Danny gazed at it imploringly, willing to concede his own ultimate failure. But the face looked away, averting its eyes. Danny looked too. There was something in the distance. He squinted. The sand edged past the level of his chest. But now he could see. A light—a brilliant orange-yellow light like a shining globe. It burned dazzlingly against the impossibly distant horizon. Danny knew it at once for what it must be. Call it salvation. Release. Why, this was the thing he had been seeking all along.

And now it was coming for him.

The face in the sky began to weep; precisely why, Danny did not know. Its tears poured down around him like a heavy violent rain. The wet sand swirled against his throat, tickled the bottom of his chin. The shining globe would never reach him in time, Danny decided. It was coming closer but not nearly fast enough. He had to find a way to save himself. But how?

Then Danny remembered. None of this was actually real. It was merely a dream. All he had to do was wake up. If he did, then everything else, everything terrible—Neptune, the worm, the face in the sky—would vanish like a raindrop hitting the ground.

Danny wanted to scream. A scream was the surest way of waking from a dream. But when he opened his mouth, the sand poured in like an onrushing tide and the scream died in his throat. He tried again. It was useless. He couldn't scream and he couldn't—

"Hey, Danny wake up."

Something was clutching his arm. He jerked free

"Hold on. Go easy. Were you having a nightmare or what?"

A face hung in the air above him. But this wasn't the face in the sky over Neptune. It was the soft, unlined, beardless face of a young boy. "George," Danny managed. "What are you doing in here?"

The face drew back. "Nothing much. I heard you screaming and thought I'd better look. It sounded like somebody was getting killed."

"No, I was just . . ." Danny tried to sit up, but discovered that he could not move. For a moment, feeling as if he were back on Neptune, buried and trapped in the shifting sand, panic returned.

George was laughing. "Here, let me give you a hand. I forget those straps sometimes too."

Reaching down, George unfastened the four straps that held Danny bound on his back to the bunk. The centrifugal force generated by the ship spinning on its axis was sufficient to produce some degree of gravity here in the freighter's outermost deck, but the effect was barely a twentieth of a gee, and precautions had to be taken while sleeping.

Using care, Danny twisted his body until he was safely sitting up, his legs dangling over the edge of the bunk. "That was the weirdest dream I can ever remember having. I thought I was on Neptune and there was this giant face in the sky and this thing like a big worm—" He broke off, shaking his head. "What time is it anyway?"

"Five-thirty or so," George said.

"What are you doing up so early?"

"I haven't been to bed. Marion Broznik and I were watching some vids in the crew lounge—they've got a great version of *Hamlet* that must be fifty years old—this guy I knew in Clarkegrad would go nuts—and then we went to her room and Clara was there and the three of us played some cards, poker, until—"

"Didn't you get in enough trouble over that before?"

George raised his hands defensively. "This was different. The Brozniks aren't part of Captain Flatface's crew. He's got no say over what they do with their money." The Brozniks, sisters in their twenties, were traveling to Triton as colonists. Marion was a biomedical technician and Clara a chemist. Besides George and Danny, they were the only paying passengers aboard the *Zamiatan*. George chuckled. "Anyway, they cleaned me out."

"What do you mean, they cleaned you out?"

George ran his hands over the silver lamé jumpsuit he was wearing, the only part of his poker winnings the captain hadn't forced him to give back. (He'd won it from a spacehand named Quigley.) "I'm broke."

"Well, don't expect me to help you out."

George frowned. "Who asked?"

"Isn't that why you're here?"

"I told you. I heard screaming."

Danny pointed at the door. "Through that? It's duralloy, twenty centimeters thick."

"The way you were screaming, little brother, I could have heard you on the other side of the galaxy." George turned, bent his knees, and vaulted across the room in a single bounding leap like a dancer in slow motion. He paused with a hand resting on the door. "Are you going back to bed or what?"

Danny shook his head. "No, I'm awake now." Sliding off the bunk, he drifted toward the floor, hit, kicked, and stood upright. Like someone wading through water, he crossed the room with his arms extended straight out from his shoulders. "Why do you want to know?"

"Clara said you can see Neptune now. She said it's about the size a big fist. I was thinking you and I could go up to the observation port and take a look at our new home."

Danny pulled a drawer out from the wall. "That sounds like fun. Let me get dressed and I'll go."

"Need any help?"

"No, I can manage." Danny removed the pale blue spacer's nylon jumpsuit he'd taken to wearing and rolled the fabric down to the waist. Then he stepped in, one leg at a time, and drew the suit up around him like a second layer of skin. He zippered the front.

"We could grab something to eat afterward too," George said. "The galley should be open by then."

"Sure, if you want."

"Better bring some money too. Remember, I'm cleaned out."

"Okay. I guess I'd better not let you starve."

"Your friend Dr. Goble wouldn't like it if that happened."

Danny maneuvered a path back to the bunk, put a hand under the mattress, and withdrew his billfold. He checked the contents, then slipped it away in a side pocket.

"That's a smart idea," George said. "Hiding your money under the bed. On a junk freighter like this there's probably fifty thieves in the crew who'd love to steal you blind."

"Especially when they're all broke—thanks to you."

"Not anymore. Good old Captain Flatface made me give it all back."

"His name is Captain Flatmeyer, George."

"You call him what you want, I'll call him what I want. You ready or what?"

"Let me get my boots." Danny's boots each would have weighed close to five pounds on Earth and were intended to provide him the necessary stability to move about easily in a low gravity environment without turning a somersault.

George watched as Danny stepped into the boots and then bent down to snap them snugly around his ankles. "It must be a kick for you out here," he said. "Being able to get around just like anybody else. You ought to think about getting a job as a spacehand or something."

"Actually," Danny admitted, "I have thought about it now and then."

"Of course, Mom might not want you to."

"I'm going to be grown-up pretty soon. She understands that."

"You *are* grown-up, Danny-boy," George corrected. "That's what I've been trying to get through your head since we left Mars."

George gave the door a push and the two of them went out. The corridor was a high but narrow tunnel with padded walls and gently curving floor and ceiling. Iron rungs evenly spaced at shoulder-high intervals ran along both walls to serve as handholds. George led the way, stretching to grasp the iron rungs and then vaulting forward, swinging neatly from rung to rung, touching the floor only with his toes and then immediately pushing off when he did. Danny had to struggle to keep pace, but once he got the hang of it, found that he could manage. It was just as well, though, that George seemed to know where they were going. Danny had gotten hopelessly lost in the confusing maze of the ship's corridors more than once already. The freighter resembled a giant beehive with a hollow core— the central storage chamber where the primary cargo of synthfuel was kept —and a half-dozen layers of encircling decks. The four fusion engines that actually propelled the ship were housed in pods attached to the main fuselage by long thin sprockets.

Danny and George had the corridor to themselves this early in the day. Those crew members not at work somewhere in the bowels of the ship would doubtlessly be in their cabins sleeping. The only sound other than the regular slap of their own boots touching the floor was the gentle hum of the ship's oxygen recycling system. The sharp, sweet, artificial air seemed to carry odors more strongly than normal. Besides an omnipresent oily scent that appeared to be part of the freighter's general nature, Danny could detect cooking odors presumably emanating from the galley two decks below. There'll be bacon for breakfast today, he thought, feeling suddenly hungry.

George turned sharply left into a branching corridor, slowing momentarily to allow Danny to catch up. "Does this mean you're changing your mind?" Danny called out as he pursued.

George glanced back over his shoulder. "Does what mean what?" His voice boomed sharply in the emptiness of the corridor.

"Your wanting to see Neptune," Danny called back. "I would've thought it'd be the last thing you'd want to look at."

George laughed, facing front now. The corridor, following the curvature of the ship's hull, arched like a bowed stick. "I guess I've gotten reconciled to my rotten fate."

"That's kind of a negative way of looking at things," Danny said.

"Then tell me another way. Your Mr. Lucero took care of the rest of my life for me back on Mars. I'm a guy with no future left."

"Is that why you tried to get the crew to head back to Saturn?"

"Oh, that was a big joke," George said. "Why would I want to go to Titan? I lived on Ganymede, remember. All they do in those places is work you to death. Work and I don't get along, if you haven't noticed."

"Then why did you do it?"

George stopped now, hitting the deck, turning to emphasize his point. Danny stopped too. "It's just something I figured I had to do. Under the circumstances, I mean. Look, I'd won everybody's money, right? But they weren't going to pay up. Why should they? So I had to make the gesture. But that's all it ever was—just a gesture. Then Captain Flatface decided to take things seriously and started talking about the brig and a vitamin-and-water diet."

"He could've had you jettisoned. Into space. For inciting a mutiny."

"But there wasn't any mutiny. That's why the whole thing was so stupid. Besides, it might have been better if he had jettisoned me. Better than the brig. Have you ever gone three days without a bite of real food? You start to forget what it's like."

"He did let you out, though."

"I know. What a sweet fellow, huh?"

George turned, swinging forward again. He led the way down yet another branching corridor and after a short distance stopped. A ladder climbed the wall to where a rectangular indentation showed in the padded ceiling. "Here we are," George said, pointing. "It's up through that trapdoor. You going to be able to make it up the ladder okay?"

"Sure," Danny said, gazing at the trapdoor a good two meters overhead. "If there's a problem, I can always take off my boots."

"Okay, great." George ascended the ladder easily, pushed the trapdoor aside, and disappeared through the gap.

The observation port was a glass turret big enough for several people to stand in at once, jutting out from the approximate middle of the ship's hull. Danny had gone up there once to look back at Mars shortly after they left Phobos. Since the ship's navigation systems were computer directed, the port was the only place on board where a passenger could actually see what lay beyond. There would be television monitors on the bridge, of course, but the bridge was strictly off limits to anyone except the crew.

Climbing the ladder proved even simpler than Danny had hoped. Once inside the glass turret, he got to his feet, raised his head slightly, and immediately lifted his hand to shield his eyes against the blazing firmament of stars that seemed to explode above him. It wasn't really that bright, of course—not even as bright as the twilight on cloud-and-dust-shrouded Earth—but it seemed that way after such a lengthy time spent living under artificial light alone. "Wow," he said very softly, shaking his head. "I never realized . . ."

"I forgot you hadn't been up here before," George said, grinning.

"Only when we first left Phobos. So I could look back and see Mars. I had one of the robots bring me. But . . ." He was still shaking his head. "After that I didn't think there was anything to see."

"You were wrong."

"I know." Danny swiveled his head. "But I don't see Neptune."

George pointed. "It ought to be down that way—by the bow. With the ship spinning, it might—"

He broke off as the planet swept suddenly into sight around the burnished curve of the freighter's bow. A slightly oblate blue-and-yellow sphere that seemed to coolly glisten against the star-studded blackness of space. Danny felt his throat grow dry and constricted, but he couldn't have said why.

"Pretty," George remarked flatly. "But—"

"Remote," Danny finished. "Alien."

George glanced at him curiously. "What makes you say that?"

"I don't know"—Danny shrugged—"but Mars, even when you're looking back at it from space, there's something nice about Mars, something familiar. It feels warm and—and friendly. But Neptune . . . it's like something out of a completely different universe. It's cold and far away from everything else, and it . . ."

He shook his head. "I don't know. That's just how it makes me feel."

"It's the place where Dad died," George said.

"I was thinking about that too," Danny said.

George nodded, and for a long moment in mutual silence the two of them observed Neptune as it appeared to resolve through the sky in a tight circle—although it was actually the freighter that was spinning. Eventually the planet again disappeared out of sight around the bow of the ship.

"We're headed toward Neptune at a slight angle," George explained, "and that's why it acts the way it does. See that star right there, almost dead straight ahead, the really bright yellow one? That must be Triton. It's where we're really headed."

Danny sat on the floor, continuing to peer at the blanket of stars overhead. Neptune would be back in a minute or two, he calculated. "George, can I ask you something?"

George was sitting now too. "Why not? I don't have to answer, do I?"

"There's something I've been wondering about. The Reconstruction Corps. Was it really that awful? That you had to desert and go clear to Mars to get away? If you'd only waited a few years, they'd have let you come back home to stay."

"But I didn't want to come back home." George dropped his eyes from the ceiling—even though Neptune was back now in full splendor. He spread his arms wide. "Don't you see, Danny-boy? That was the whole point of everything. It's why I joined the Corps in the first place. I knew it was time to get away."

"Because you were still mad about having to go to school when I—"

"No," George said sharply. "Hell, no. I wasn't even mad. I . . . okay, maybe I was a little upset, a little resentful, but school wasn't that bad anyway. It was just boring. Small and silly and boring. You look at Seattle from the island, and though it's a mess, you think it must be full of people. But there were only fifty kids total in the whole school, and most of them acted like they were brain-damaged."

"Savages, you mean."

"Oh, no. Not in Seattle. The bluesuits keep them away from there. Seattle's what they call in the Corps an Active Reconstruction Zone. That means someday—supposedly really soon—they hope a lot of people will live there again."

"But you didn't like it."

"Not the school. They were trying to teach things like art and history and poetry. Dumb things—pointless things. I was giving them a lot of trouble, and one day a bluesuit showed up and asked me if I wouldn't be happier in the Reconstruction Corps. The thing was, I felt I was already grown-up, and it was silly wasting time being bored when there was a whole Solar System out there waiting to be explored."

"George, you were only ten years old."

"Eleven before I actually went into the Corps. And even then I was way younger than anybody else I ever met. They had to get approval from way up the chain—from Perth—but I managed to talk them into it. The fact is, certain people grow up a lot faster than others. It's called a maturation rate."

"But why run away? Why go all the way to Mars and never try to contact us?"

"I sent you a gram once."

"But that was it. One time in four years. Didn't you miss us? Miss Mother?"

George appeared to consider. "I don't mean to hurt anybody's feelings, Danny-boy, but I've got to say no. Why should anybody go around missing somebody else? The way I see it, if you like a person and they're there with you, then swell, but if they're not, then you've still got to go on living. Like I said, it was just that I figured I had my own life to live."

"On Mars."

George smiled. "Mars is where I ended up, but I was on Luna for a while first and then Ganymede. Ganymede is wretched. That's how I know I wouldn't like Titan either. They're both pretty much the same. You've got to work like a slave or else, and there's always somebody telling you what to do."

"Is that what happened in the Corps? They made you work?"

"Not in the beginning. They were going to make a bluesuit out of me, believe it or not. The tests I took said I was a genius—heck, I could have told them that—so they put me in a school for engineers over near what used to be Idaho. I was going to learn how to build bridges and highways and all that wonderful stuff President Armelino is always issuing proclamations about. I was the only person in the place under twenty years old too. What a great future I had, they kept telling me. I stuck it out as long as I could—jeez, it was boring—and then I went for a walk one day. I don't think anybody had ever run away before. It took months for the

bluesuits to track me down. I was living up around Lake Chelan with a
bunch of crazy fishermen, savages supposedly."

"So what did they do when they caught you?"

"They dithered. I was a deserter from the Corps, but they didn't seem to
want to shoot me or anything, not like they were supposed to. They
dragged me back to the school and locked me in a room and they'd come
in and ask me questions and then go away and then come back and ask
more questions. What they seemed to want to know was if they let me
back in the school, would I run away again?"

"What did you say?"

"I lied and said no, but I don't think it fooled anybody. One day they
took me into the headquarters building and there was this big dark blanket
set up and somebody sitting behind it and he kept asking me questions, all
sorts of questions, about myself, my feelings, about you and Mom and
Dad."

"A psychiatrist?"

"I suppose, except"—he shook his head—"they had one of their own at
the school, and it wasn't him. I could tell by the voice, even if I couldn't
see him. Anyway, it was right after that they put me in a bus with no
windows, and when they let me out, I was in California and part of a hot-
zone squad."

"And what was that like?"

"Like spending time in the middle of hell. San Francisco—which is
where my squad was assigned—took four direct hits in the fifty-kiloton
range, and there were still spots all over the city so hot you looked at them
and damn near died. Five guys in my squad came down with rad sickness
in one month, and they made them keep working till they couldn't lift a
hand. It was enough to make anybody throw up."

"Were the others deserters too?"

"I was the only one, I think. We didn't talk much. There was something
about the situation that kept you from wanting to make friends. Mostly
savages, I suppose. Whenever the Corps reclaims a savage zone, the hardest cases—the leaders—get put in the squads. Some mutants too. Kids
born with all sorts of terrible deformities. One I worked next to had a face
like a fish, except with a regular mouth and teeth. One time I watched
when he was going through decon, and like I figured, he had scales up and
down his legs and back, and a little tail—a fishtail—growing out of his
butt. It was funny in a weird way—like a cartoon."

"How did you get away from there?"

"Well, it was a lot tougher than the engineering school, let me tell you that. Five of us made the break—me, the fish guy, and three others. None lasted more than a couple hours that I ever found out. Only me. But I'd made up my mind. The only way I was going back was if they killed me."

"So how did you do it?"

"Partly by luck, partly by brains, and partly because I was normal-looking, so people didn't look at me twice and get to wondering. I made it down into Mexico—Durango—where I felt a little bit safe. I was eleven years old, no papers, no money, but I lived day by day and I got by. What I'd decided by then I really wanted was to get off Earth completely."

"And that's what you did do, right?"

"I met a lady, a really nice lady. Dr. Miriam Delahunt. About fifty. I was selling relics on the street—junk from back before the war—me and a gang of other kids, a lot of them mutants, and she seemed to pick me out of the crowd. She took me to the place she was staying—a hotel—and made me wash and put on clean clothes she bought for me. I knew a good thing when I saw it, so I conned her, told her some lies about my past, and she let me stay with her. I found out she was a scientist with the Combine. She couldn't have kids of her own—she'd caught a nasty rad dose during the war—and since I was an orphan—it's what I'd told her I was—then why didn't I come and live with her in Perth when she'd finished her work in Durango? I thought it over—it was an idea—but it wasn't what I really wanted either. Instead, I started telling her how much I wanted to go and see another world, any world. I figured she had to have some connection with space since she was a wheel with the Combine, and one day she told me she was supposed to go to Luna for a conference and would I be okay while she was gone. I made a sad face and begged her to take me along, ended up crying, throwing a fit, and finally she said all right. As soon as we got to Tranquility I rifled her suitcases, took every scrip note she had with her, and ducked out. But Luna was kind of boring too. Living underground the way they do makes everything rigid and dull. So when I came across this Ganymede recruiter, I told him to count me in. He wanted to know what my skills were. I told him I could work hard. He said that wasn't enough. I had to give him all the money I had before he'd let me sign up as a colonist."

"But you didn't like it when you got there."

"Not Ganymede, no. They put me in hydroponics, growing ferns all day. Talk about boring. And then I'd have to suit up and go out and help with the terraforming process, the huge recycling machines, chemical ponds, and of course more ferns. Ugh. I used to play sick a lot, biding my time, till I ran into this old-time spacer who operated an indy shuttle between Ganymede and Phobos with stopovers in the Belt. He asked me if I knew how to play poker. I didn't—not then—so he went over the rules of the game, and I saw right away where it was mostly memory, a few basic calculations, and a lot of playacting. A short time later I'd cleaned the poor old guy out, including a half interest in his ship. I told him I'd forget the ship if he'd give me a free ride to Mars. As soon as I set foot in Clarkegrad I knew I'd found my true home. Eventually I ran into Vladimar and everything was starting to turn out just great."

"You've led an awfully full life," Danny said, unable to prevent an undertone of bitterness—or was it sheer envy?—from invading his voice.

"At least I did till you turned up and I ended up out here."

"Then you still want to go back?"

"I guess." George shrugged slightly. "But what really worries me is what I'm going to do when we're done with the Neptune stuff. The way you and Lucero fixed things, I can't go back to Mars, and there's no place else in the Solar System I really want to go. When this is over I'm really going to be stuck."

Danny saw that George had a definite point. His own primary concern had been just getting George to Neptune. He hadn't given any thought to what might happen afterward. "We'll have to talk to Dr. Goble. He'll figure out something to do."

George looked less than convinced. "If your guy Goble can pull that one off, then he must be a big genius. But look"—he waved at the transparent ceiling above—"what say we go grab that breakfast now? The galley ought to be open."

Danny nodded. "I guess I've seen enough of Neptune for now."

"Come back," George suggested. "It's not going away, and there's still plenty of time before we get to Triton."

He gave a bounce and hurtled through the open trapdoor, not even touching the rungs of the ladder as he dropped down. Pausing at the bottom, he waited until Danny followed at a more careful pace, reaching up to grab his waist and help him down the last few rungs.

"You didn't have to do that," Danny said. "I could've managed."

"No trouble," George said. "What are brothers for except to help each other out?"

George turned down the corridor, moving in the direction of the galley. He'd only gone a few meters, though, when he dropped to the floor with a sudden thud and turned back. "You know, Danny," he said, "I think I was wrong. I'm not as hungry as I thought I was. What I really need is a few hours sleep. Why don't you go ahead without me and I'll grab breakfast later?'

Danny made no effort to conceal his disappointment. He had definitely enjoyed these moments with George. It was like discovering a friend—a brother—he'd never known he'd had. "Are you sure?"

George yawned into his palm. "I'm afraid so."

"Well"—Danny reached for his side pocket—"then let me—"

George caught his wrist. "I don't need your money, Danny."

"But I thought you said—"

Without loosening his grip, George grinned. "I was kidding around. Do you think your big brother's stupid? I didn't let the Brozniks clean me out completely. I can still eat."

"Well, if you're—"

"And it's a matter of personal pride too."

Danny's armed relaxed. "Okay. If that's what you say."

George let go of Danny's wrist. "Why would I lie about it—"

His voice broke off, interrupted by a loud clanking noise. Both boys looked up to discover one of the older, cruder robot models, which resembled nothing so much as vacuum cleaners on stilts, moving relentlessly down the corridor in their direction. George gave a sudden good-bye wave and attempted to slip past the robot. A steel arm shot out of its side and blocked his path.

"Hey," George said, tugging at his arm. "What gives with this stupid thing?"

"It must be looking for something," Danny said, hurrying up. A camera lens protruding from the robot's torso was surveying George. Suddenly a green light flashed and there was a steady beeping noise.

"Look." Danny pointed. "Here comes a message."

The message emerged from a slot in the robot's side. Danny tore off the sheet and started to read, but George grabbed it out of his hands. "Oh, great." he said, shaking his head. "Oh, wonderful."

"Why? What is it?" Danny asked, leaning over his shoulder.

"It's your buddy Goble on Triton. For some reason, all of a sudden he wants both of us there with him right away. He can't wait for the freighter. He's sent a high velocity shuttle to pick us up."

"When will it get here?"

"In an hour. Or less." George crumpled the message into a ball and tossed it on the floor. A vacuum hose snaked out of the robot's bottom and sucked up the wad of paper. There was a burning smell.

"Here," George said, putting a hand inside his jumpsuit. He removed a leather billfold. "I won't be needing this after all."

Danny found himself staring at his own billfold, a Christmas gift from his mother three years ago. "You—You took that?"

"Picked your pocket. When you were coming down the ladder. Clean as a kazoo. You didn't even guess, did you?"

"Well, no, I—"

"Never let anybody touch you where you keep your money."

"But I said I'd buy you breakfast."

"Breakfast wasn't what I wanted it for. I told you it was personal pride. I was going to win back what those Brozniks took me for or else die trying."

"With my money, you mean," Danny said bitterly.

George was gazing gloomily at the robot. "What difference does it make? Where we're going money isn't going to mean zilch." He sighed. "Come on, Danny-boy. I'll let you buy me that breakfast after all."

ELEVEN

Encased in the bulky armor of a pressure suit and glass helmet, Danny emerged from the windowless interior of the shuttlecraft, craned his neck, and tried to take a good long look around. So this was it, he thought, struggling to swivel his head to see better. This was Triton. Neptune's major satellite.

His first emotion was one of vast, overwhelming disappointment.

His second emotion—his third, if he'd bothered—was precisely the same.

What a dreary, ugly, totally uninspiring world, he thought.

Everywhere Danny looked, a thin sheen of mustard-tinted ice blanketed the craggy, rock-strewn landscape. Even the sky itself was a yellow-brown color, the stars showing only faintly through the hazy, methane-dominated atmosphere. It wasn't as if he had been anticipating something warm and wonderful, a paradise planet, but . . . well, he *had* been expecting something more dramatic. Triton stood at the very edge of human civilization, after all, but it—there was really no other way of putting it—it seemed utterly dismal.

Then it began to snow—huge, fat, fluffy, brown flakes.

"Now I know why I didn't want to leave Mars," came George's voice as he touched his helmet to Danny's to be heard. "I thought Ganymede had to be the armpit of the Solar System, but this place . . ."

Danny knew what he meant. But there was no point in preying on it. Besides, they'd only just arrived. First impressions could be deceiving, he liked to believe.

"That must be Tsiolkovsky over there," Danny said, raising a gloved hand to point at the ice-shrouded glass dome that rose a quarter kilometer in the distance.

"Home, sweet home," George said.

"Well, only for a little while. Neptune's where we're really headed."

"Now there's something to look forward to," George said.

Tsiolkovsky, Triton's only human settlement, dated back to the era of Combine colonization fifty years before. Danny recalled there had been serious talk of launching a terraforming project here like those already under way on Ganymede and Titan, but clearly nothing had as yet been accomplished. It would surely be a massive undertaking. If nothing else, the outside temperature on Triton averaged near two hundred fifty degrees below zero. Standing here in the open, Danny thought sure he could feel the chill in the tips of his fingers and the ends of his toes, even though—dressed in the pressure suit—that should not have been possible.

At the edge of the landing strip a treaded vehicle resembling a stream-lined army tank sat idling. "Is that our welcoming party?" George asked, bumping helmets.

"It must be," Danny said, straining at first to see through the snow. Then, as suddenly as it had begun the snow stopped falling. Triton clearly was going to be a world that took getting used to.

"Maybe we ought to go over and say hello," George leaned over to suggest.

"Uh, sure," Danny said. He was looking at the sky. "I guess we better."

The two of them headed across to where the treaded vehicle sat waiting. A crawler; Danny recalled the proper term. Walking was proving as difficult for him as he had feared it might be. Even with his braces again strapped to his legs, his knees still acted as weak as water. And the extra weight of the pressure suit hardly helped. Triton was a big moon—the most massive in the Solar System after Titan—with a surface gravity a quarter that of Earth. Following the prolonged near weightlessness of the freighter, it seemed to Danny as if there were lead weights hanging from every one of his limbs.

It reassured him only slightly to see George having nearly as much trouble maneuvering a path across the icy, rocky landscape.

There was a driver in a pressure suit and helmet sitting alone in the crawler cockpit. As Danny and George edged closer, a door slid open in the side. Danny piled through the gap, collapsing in the rear seat. His own labored breathing sounded like a series of explosions in his ears. George dropped into the front seat. As soon as he had, the driver shut the door, raised a hand as if signaling, and then brought it down again about thirty seconds later.

Then she removed her helmet and smiled at them.

The woman was somewhere between twenty and thirty stanyears old, with the sharp, angular features of an overexposed photograph. Her skin was the color of Triton's sky. A thick mane of black hair fell past her shoulders. "I'm Eileen Kinugasa, Sam's assistant. You're George, and you must be Danny, right?"

"On the button," George said, removing his own helmet and letting it rest in his lap. "I knew everything about this place couldn't be dreary. You're the most beautiful girl I've seen in my life, Eileen."

"You must not have seen very many girls, George."

He grinned and winked. "A lot more than you'd think."

"Oh, I don't know about that. If you had, then you'd know I'm not one."

"You're not? Then what are you?"

She patted his arm with mock familiarity. "I'm a woman, George. Not a girl. There's a difference, you know."

Danny leaned over from his perch in the back. "Has something gone wrong, Eileen? Is that why Dr. Goble wanted us here right away?"

"Nothing's wrong, Danny." She shook her head crisply. "Sam just got impatient. He's like that sometimes, you know. He'll throw a fit waiting for a kettle of water to boil."

"He didn't seem that way to me," Danny said.

"Of course he didn't. Not Sam. Sam would seem the way he wanted to seem. The man of a thousand faces. Only with Sam every one of them is real."

"I can hardly wait to meet this guy," George put in. "I've got a couple of things to say to him anyway."

"I imagine he has a few things to say to you, too, George," Eileen said with a grin.

"A real tough old bird, huh?"

"Not a bird," she said thoughtfully, reaching out to press the ignition. An electric motor hummed to life, gently vibrating the interior of the crawler. "More of a bulldog. A bulldog who bites and then won't let go. That is"—she chuckled softly to herself—"if you can imagine a bulldog who looks like a teddy bear."

The crawler rolled forward, rocking across the jagged land, maneuvering around the occasional large boulder. Ahead, gradually, the domed settlement of Tsiolkovsky grew in apparent size.

"Kamasaki," George said musingly. "Is that what you said your last name was?"

"Close. Kinugasa."

"I like it. Kind of musical. What is it? Chinese or something?"

"Japanese, actually. Though I've never been there—Japan. Or Earth for that matter. I'm a purebred colonial. Dad took me with him to Mars once. I didn't like it. Sleazy."

"When this is over," George said expansively, "I'll take you to Japan." He said nothing about his own period of time on Ganymede.

She burst into laughter, fighting to maintain her grip on the steering wheel. "George," she said when she could, "if you tried that, the bluesuits would pick you up in about two seconds flat as a deserter from the Corps. Then where would we be?"

George looked somber. "You know about that?"

"George, dear, I know everything about you." She patted his arm again. "Probably more than you know yourself."

George fell silent for the remainder of the journey, presumably mulling over what Eileen had said. Leaning back, Danny twisted his head and tried to watch what passed for scenery on this world as it crawled by. Since there wasn't much to look at, he focused his attention straight ahead, where the ice-shrouded glass hemisphere of Tsiolkovsky loomed. Gazing at the dome, he felt a strange emotion come over him that he didn't at first comprehend. It was pride, he finally decided. The dome represented the human race (of which he was a part) clinging to a frozen ball of rock where it had no real right to be. Danny's whole life on Earth—even as relatively isolated as he had been on the island with his mother—he had been surrounded by evidence of past destruction, reminders only of humanity's failures. Tsiolkovsky, unlike anything on Earth, was an achievement. It was something to feel proud of.

At the sloping edge of the glass dome Eileen eased to a stop. Someone— or something—inside sensed their presence and a gate slid open in the face of the dome large enough to allow the crawler to enter. It was the first stage of a two-phase airlock, so they had to wait momentarily while the poisonous natural atmosphere of Triton was filtered out and replaced by a breathable oxygen-rich brew.

Then a second gate opened and they drove inside.

Tsiolkovsky—named by the Combine in honor of the pioneering intellectual forefather of all space travel—was a cluster of ramshackle fiberglass and plastiform hovels, most of which looked as if they'd blow away in a strong wind, not that any wind would ever blow here. Also, here and there stood a handful of much larger, concrete blockhouse structures, probably storage facilities. The crawler wound a circuitous path among these various buildings—there seemed to be no definite streets as such—and pretty soon Danny was hopelessly lost. There were only a few people outside at this time of day—by twenty-four-hour stantime it was presently 0230—but most of these paused and waved. Either Eileen—who always waved back —knew just about everybody on Triton, or else the colonists were an exceedingly friendly group. Perhaps it was a combination of both, Danny concluded.

George, whose thoughts had apparently paralleled Danny's own, broke his silence at last. "What's the population of this dump?" he asked.

"About three thousand," Eileen said.

"Then maybe you can answer a question for me: How come?"

She glanced at him curiously. "How come what, George?"

"How come anyone wants to live way out here? I'm sorry, but I just don't see it."

"You should. Didn't you run away from home to go into space, to see new worlds?"

"That was different."

She nodded. "Maybe it was. Because the reason these people live here is the only one that ever makes any real sense: this is their home."

"That doesn't make sense to me."

She smiled thinly. "No, it wouldn't."

"And besides," he went on, spreading his arms, encompassing the entirety of the domed settlement, "what do they do all day? How do they keep from getting bored to death?"

"They do pretty much what people everywhere do. They live, eat, sleep, bear children, study, think, work, examine, explore. Mostly what they do is survive. Life here is a long way from easy. I don't think you can even call Triton a real colony yet, not even in the sense of Ganymede or Titan, to say nothing of Mars. It's really only a settlement—an outpost—but the second generation is now well on its way to reaching adulthood, children born here who've never lived anywhere else, and to me that's when a colony truly gets its start. The rate of population increase is high, too, even with no coercion, like on some of the other satellite colonies."

"On Ganymede," George said, "they have a law—I'd guess you'd know since you lived there—"

"So did you, George, though we never met."

"Uh, yes, right. But, anyway, they have a law that either you have at least one kid every other year or else you pay a fine in personal resources. I was too young to have to worry about it when I was there—"

"Thank God for that," Eileen put in.

"But it sure was one of the reasons I got out when I did," he finished.

She nodded. "They've got something similar on Titan too. But it's not necessary here, even if it would work, which I'm not too sure about. Living space is limited as it is. They've laid out plans for two more domes, one to the south and another to the east, both close enough for regular crawler contact but far enough away to permit autonomy to develop. All they're waiting for is a Combine grant, and Sam says that ought to be coming soon."

"Seems a waste, though," George said idly, glancing at a couple of young women in shorts and tee-shirts who were walking past, arguing heatedly. The women were among the few they'd passed who failed to stop and wave.

"That might have something to do with what we were talking about," Eileen said, pointing at the two women. "Those are both council members, and there's been a lot of discussion about who gets to go to the new domes and who doesn't. In the end I imagine they'll just draw lots. It seems the fairest way. That's how the council itself is chosen, too, by the way."

"Do you mean nobody wants to go?" Danny asked.

"More the opposite. Everybody wants to go. The older people remember the early days here, and they're nostalgic, and the younger ones—well, like George said, everybody craves a little excitement in their lives." She was looking at George now as if remembering something. "What seems a waste?" she asked.

"This whole world," he said. "These people, their lives. I mean, there doesn't seem anything to it except work and more work."

"Some people find satisfaction in that, George."

"I guess. But isn't there anything else? What do they do for entertainment? What do you do?"

"Me? Mostly the same as them. I work. Not as hard, perhaps, but I run a computer, talk to Sam, monitor the—"

"And when you're not working?" he broke in. "What I'm trying to find out about is recreation."

"Like gambling dens, you mean?"

"They have some?" George asked eagerly.

She laughed. "No. But there's two public vids. One of them's full tridee, too, when it works, which is less than half the time. And there's a community center with regular concerts and dances. There's a church—two churches now. Both are nondenominational Christian. Tomorrow's Sunday. You could go if you wanted. Sam does sometimes when he's feeling in the mood, but I'm an atheist."

"The dances sound more like my style," George said. "When's the next one?"

"A few hours from now, 0600 stantime. It's for the third shift getting off work."

"Great. Let's go."

She looked genuinely taken aback. "Are you asking me for a date?"

"Sure. Why not?"

"I'm nearly twice your age, for one thing."

"How old are you?"

"Twenty-seven."

"Stanyears?"

She nodded.

George was clearly straining to look incredulous. "You sure could fool me."

Her cheeks puffed out, and Danny guessed she was stifling another burst of laughter. "And you're fourteen, George."

"Do I look it?"

Eileen twisted her head, scrutinizing George as if for the first time. "No. But you act it."

"Then give me a chance. Maybe I can improve. With your help."

This time she did laugh, shaking her head wearily. "George, you're hopeless. But forget the dance anyway. Sam has his own plans for you. And don't worry. You won't get bored."

She braked in front of a white fiberglass-walled building, a conical-shaped edifice rising to a pyramidlike point that towered a good twenty meters above every surrounding structure. Danny had noticed the building a long time before they arrived, and now he understood why Eileen didn't have to worry about getting lost. "Combine headquarters for the colony," she explained. "Sam will be waiting inside."

The building contained an elevator that swayed and rattled as it hauled them toward the upper reaches. Eileen laid a reassuring hand on Danny's arm as he winced from the jolt of acceleration. "Does that hurt?" she asked in a soft voice that barely rose above the clatter of the elevator.

"No, I'll be okay. I'm just not used to the gravity yet."

"Well, you won't have to put up with it for long."

"What do you mean?"

She shook her head curtly. "I'd better let Sam explain. He's apt to throw a fit if I spoil his little revelations."

The elevator opened into a narrow, curved hallway facing a single door. Eileen opened the door and ushered them through. There was a circular, white-walled room on the other side, plainly the building's apex. The ceiling was a round glass window through which the yellow-tinged sky of Triton could be seen.

Sam Goble, dressed in a purple kimono and matching slippers, stood at the front of the room. He broke into a grin when he saw Danny and George.

"Danny, my boy, damn good to see you again. And this must be the infamous George. Well, well. So we are whole at last. Come on up, boys, and grab a chair. You've arrived just in the nick of time."

Seated in a semicircle facing Sam were five children of varying ages. Three were boys and two girls. All five turned as if at a signal and gazed at Danny and George.

Sam was pointing at the two remaining empty chairs in front of him, one at each end of the row. "Come on, boys. Let's not keep everyone waiting. I was about to launch into a little briefing on our impending mission. Danny, you sit right here. George, we'll put you down at the other end."

Danny shuffled forward, aiming for his chair. He could feel the puzzled stares of the others as he moved awkwardly. One of them, a little redheaded boy with big eyes and a loud voice, said, "But he's a cripple."

"No more than any of the rest of us, Benny," Sam said smoothly. "Eileen." He pointed above their heads. "There's no reason for you to stay and hear this. I want you to go back out and stand guard in front of the elevator. As long as I'm in here talking, I don't want anyone—I don't care if it's World President Armelino himself—coming through that door."

"Why don't I just shut off the elevator, Sam? That would be the simple way to do it."

He frowned. "Please do as I say. And if there's any indication of trouble —any at all—I want you to yell the top of your head off."

"And you'll come and rescue me?"

"We'll all come and rescue you," Sam said.

Her cheeks puffing again, Eileen backed through the door.

When she was gone, Sam cleared his throat and looked down the line of chairs from one of them to the other, each in turn. "Gentlemen. Ladies. Little people. Whatever you want to call yourselves. Right now I'm going to fill you in on a certain few basic facts concerning your mission—our mission. All of you already know why you're here. You know you're a project team and that your task is to explore the surface of that planet right up there."

He pointed. Neptune—a blue-and-gold hazy ball—now stood poised in the round window above their heads.

"What you don't know," Sam went on, "what I couldn't tell you till now, when we're finally far away from the possibility of prying ears, is why you're going to be doing that."

"Because it is there," George murmured in a voice shaky with awe.

Sam's lips twitched in what might have been the start of a smile. "Let me simply state here and now that within a relatively brief period of time, if all goes well, at least one of you—and perhaps more—will have inscribed his or her name in the history books for all time to come as the first human being to have communicated directly with an intelligent species other than his or her own."

"You mean there's life? Life on Neptune?" Unexpectedly, the speaker was again George.

"There is indeed life on Neptune, George, and a good deal more besides. Now, if you'll only sit quietly in your chair like a good little boy and keep your damn mouth shut, you'll find out what I mean."

The silence in the round room at the top of the conical tower was total.

TWELVE

Sam went on in a more subdued tone, while Danny—and his six fellow project-team members—listened with rapt attention.

Sam said, "I suppose to be polite I ought to start by introducing myself, even though all of you know me by now except George over there, who I'm sure has gotten an earful from his brother. In any event, Sam Goble's the name and I'm a doctor of one sort or another—several different sorts, actually—though as long as we're working together, I'd prefer if you'd just call me Sam. That happens to be the way I think of myself, and it'll make life easier among us all the way around. Now, Sam's what you call me, but while you're doing so—with my blessing, remember—I also want you thinking something quite different: I want you thinking *boss*. And the reason for that is because, one way or the other, it's what I'm going to have to be for this team of ours. The boss. And not because I'm necessarily smarter than the rest of you. I'm not. Next to the lot of you kids, I'm pretty much of a dope. I am a few decades older, sure, but that's not the reason, either, because, I'm also old enough to have realized that age doesn't necessarily equate with wisdom—all it equates with is getting old. But the sad fact is, like it or not, we need a boss. Democracy is a marvelous invention, and I believe in it more deeply than I believe in anything else, but the smaller the group, the less well democracy functions—until in the end you come down to one lone individual, and then it doesn't function at all. Every one of us has to act as the absolute dictator where his or her own life is concerned. In this team of ours—eight people counting myself —I'm going to have to be the dictator, and the only reason it's me and not one of you is because I'm the one most likely to remain alive—and sane—

the whole time. The rest of you, any one of you, all of you, might die at any given instant. Here. Let me show you what I mean."

Sam turned in a rustle of silk kimono and strode to where a computer terminal stood with a large blank television monitor on the wall above it. Sam tapped several keys, and the smaller terminal viewscreen flickered. On it appeared the blue-yellow sphere of Neptune.

"I want you to look at this," he said, turning back to face them, "and look carefully. Engrave the image in your brains. This is the planet Neptune—a most lovely bauble, I'm sure we agree—but it's also something else in terms of your present lives. It's death. A number of years ago I headed another project whose mission was precisely the same as yours. By the time the project ended, one brave and veteran spacer was dead and two others were in a condition where those of us who loved them wished they, too, might have died. What happened to them can most definitely happen to you. Make no mistake about that. This planet—this bauble in space—can kill you. For you—from now on—Neptune is death."

As Sam spoke, the image of Neptune over his shoulder grew, eventually filling the entirety of the screen. Danny found it impossible to tear his eyes away. The person seated next to him—a pretty, fresh-faced girl with a crown of blond ringlets—let out her breath in a sudden whoosh, as if she'd been holding it in her lungs the whole time without being aware.

Sam stepped away from the terminal and let their eyes slowly catch up to him. "When I came to visit each of you in your own homes, I was only able for security reasons to describe our project in the broadest outline. What I intend doing today in this meeting is to proceed beyond that. I'm going to tell you everything. I'm also going to be fair about it. When I'm done, if any of you feels you've been cheated or fooled or lied to, you may, if you wish, ask to go home again. I'll see that you get there. This isn't an offer I'm supposed to make." His voice was a throaty whisper, as if to ward off possible eavesdroppers. "But it's a personal promise. If people are going to risk their lives under my command, they're going to do so voluntarily and with full knowledge of the circumstances."

Danny looked down the line of chairs to where George was seated, to see if he could catch his eye, but George was gazing straight at Sam, his chin cupped thoughtfully in a hand. Did Sam really mean what he was saying? And if he did, why had he brought them all the way to Triton first? Would anyone really be apt to change his or her mind after already coming this far?

Sam went on: "A few hours after the conclusion of this meeting, we're all going to leave Triton and take the short shuttle trip to our permanent base of operations, the space station *Leverrier,* in orbit around Neptune. Once there, you will all undergo a process of training which will last several months. When that's finished, one or several of you will then be sent to the surface of Neptune. Once there, your goal will be to contact and if possible open communication with the intelligent alien beings who presently inhabit that world."

With this last remark still hanging in the air—and still unexplained—Sam crossed back to the terminal. Turning, he faced them. "Now, many of you are no doubt bursting at the seams to point out that much of what I've just told you is scientific nonsense. Neptune has no solid surface—all the standard reference works agree—and even if it did, the gravity and atmospheric pressure would be more than sufficient to crush any human being who attempted to land there. In fact, if I remember correctly, several of you had something to say along these lines when I first approached you about our project. I evaded your questions then. I promised to explain at a later date. Well, today is that date. To begin with, the standard references are in error. Neptune does possess a solid surface area. In a few moments I'll show you photographs. As for the matter of gravity, here is your answer to that."

Again tapping the computer keyboard, Sam erased the image of Neptune and replaced it with another. Danny involuntarily jumped in his seat. This new image was a side view of some sort of horrible monster, a squat hunched creature resembling an armor-plated slug standing on a dozen short thick legs.

"Is that—" It was the boy seated in the middle of the row, a gangly Oriental with the long braided hair of a resident of the Asteroid Belt, a Belter. "Is it one of those aliens you were telling us about?"

"No, Raymond," Sam said. "I'll be getting to the Kith shortly. As a matter of fact, this is actually you."

"Me?" Raymond said, peering down at himself in confusion.

Smiling, Sam spread his arms. "Not just you personally—all of you. This is the physical form each of you will assume when you visit and explore the surface of Neptune. This is a Neptunian, and you, my friends, are going to be Neptunians."

Sam then proceeded to describe in some detail the character, history, and nature of scrambling and the MAGMOS Process, including its use during the first Neptune project. When he finished, still standing beside the image of the hideous monster, he asked if there were any questions.

Several hands rose in the air.

Sam nodded at the farthest in line. "George?"

"I'm still wondering about that offer you made, that personal promise of yours. Does it apply to me?"

"Certainly it does."

"Then when can I leave?"

"I told you—as soon as we've concluded this meeting."

"And what about the way you and certain others"—he frowned in Danny's direction—"have made it sort of difficult for me to go back home, since as soon as I set foot anywhere on Mars, I'm apt to get my head blown off?"

Sam shrugged. "It's your problem, not mine. The offer still stands."

"But it's not much good to me, is it?"

"You can take it or leave it, the same as anyone else." Sam looked at the blond girl beside Danny, who had her hand in the air. She appeared to be in her early teens, approximately Danny's own age. "Carolina?"

"I'm still confused about the MAGMOS Process, Sam, and the way it connects with that thing up there on the screen. How can you take the basic molecular components of a human being—and I have a pretty fair knowledge of what those are—and no matter how you combine them, end up with something looking like that?"

Sam turned his head, peering thoughtfully at the screen. "It can be done. I'm afraid that's the best I can tell you. But I'm in a position to know. That creature up there happens to be none other than yours truly, Sam Goble. The original photo was taken some six stanyears ago in a lab on Luna. I was the first Neptunian, a privilege I insisted upon. Others followed, though, as I've explained."

"It's still hard to believe."

"Think of it this way, Carolina," Sam said. "Suppose we have a quantity of bricks. Stack the bricks one way and we build a soaring tower stretching far into the sky. Stack them another and we build a broad plaza where a thousand people can walk. The plaza in no way resembles the tower, except that both are made from the exact same bricks. This creature in no way resembles me, except that its molecular structure and mine are nearly identical."

"Nearly?" Carolina said. "I thought it had to be exact."

"For all intents and purposes, yes. In this instance—or so I understand —a number of component molecules have been further broken down into their base elements, particularly oxygen and carbon, and then recombined to form different molecules. But I'm not a chemist or molecular biologist. The members of the team that designed the Neptunian were, however, and a summary account of their work will be made available to each of you once we reach *Leverrier.*"

The Belter kid—Raymond—spoke up. "I've been trying to remember anything I might have heard about this before. There's not much that happens in the Solar System that doesn't get around the Belt pretty quickly. But the only thing I can recall is a spacer getting killed on Neptune three or four stanyears ago, and he was supposed to have been crushed during a surveying expedition aboard a bathyspheric glider."

"That's the story the Combine chose to put out," Sam said, "since it jibed with both the common scientific knowledge concerning Neptune and the standard exploratory techniques used previously on the other gas-giant worlds."

"Do you mind telling us how the man actually did die?" Raymond said, nodding at the computer screen. "Did it have anything to do with the MAGMOS Process, the transformation from man into—into thing?"

"No, it didn't. The spacer—Michael Hawkins was his name—simply vanished. We know Mike reached the surface of Neptune, and we actually traced his movements for a period of time. Then all at once he was gone. My personal theory is that a local quake too small to be recorded—and quakes were extremely common on Neptune at the time—claimed him. But there's no evidence. I'm not trying to minimize the dangers of the MAGMOS Process. There have been accidents, some of them fatal. It's an extremely complex process, and mistakes can certainly occur."

"Such as?"

"Do I really need to go into detail?" Sam said, frowning. "The point is —and I'm not trying to keep this from you—the mission you seven will be undertaking is going to be extremely dangerous in a great many different ways."

"None of which," George broke in, "you bothered saying a word about till we'd come traipsing across the Solar System to do your bidding. Do you mind if I ask how come all the tight-lipped secrecy?"

"No, that's a fair question. As for scrambling—and the MAGMOS Process—it's Combine policy to keep a firm lid on its existence. At the present time scrambling is not a practical means of interplanetary transport. It's too expensive. But if there's ever a change—a breakthrough in technology —the Combine would very much like to be the ones to make it. We—they —are a non-profit corporation. But to be a successful non-profit corporation entails having to make a great deal of money. Scrambling, to put it mildly, could well be an absolute bonanza at some future time."

"Okay," George said. "That's money, and I understand money, though I can't figure out who you think your competitors might be."

"Oh, you'd be surprised," Sam said. "There are more than a few wealthy individuals in the Asteroid Belt, for example, with sufficient free capital to undertake large-scale research and development projects. One of them happens to be sitting in this room, as a matter of fact."

George glanced at the boy with the braided hair and looked puzzled. Then he shrugged. "Okay, but what about this other thing, these aliens you keep mentioning on Neptune and then not saying anything else about —does the Combine expect to make a bundle off them too?"

Sam shook his head, smiling wanly. "No, George. With the Kith— which is what we've chosen to call the aliens—hopefully—with the Kith our motives are much purer. We're trying to protect the human race, not just our own selfish financial interests. With the Kith, if word of their existence ever leaked out—their existence and their powers—it would scare the living daylights out of every human alive."

"Why?" George said. "I know. I'm not scared." He peered down the line of chairs. "I don't think any of us are."

"I'm definitely not," piped up the little redheaded boy who had called Danny a cripple. He was seated directly next to George. To his right sat a somewhat older boy—perhaps eight or nine—a Negro with a bald skull and no nose or ears. A mutant. Not that Danny was a mutant hater, like some people on Earth. He supposed, when you came down to it, they had a right to live like anybody else.

"I'm sorry to say, Benny," Sam told the redheaded boy, "that both you and George are victims of your own ignorance. I said the Kith's existence —and their powers. It's what the Kith can do—what they already have done—that's truly frightening."

"So how about telling us?" George said. "So we won't be so ignorant anymore."

Nodding curtly, Sam turned to the computer terminal. He tapped the keyboard with the fingers of one hand. "This is what you ought to see first," he said.

THIRTEEN

The image that flickered into existence on the computer screen appeared to be a static photograph. At first the image meant nothing to Danny, but as he looked harder he began to make sense of it. The photograph seemed to depict a series of randomly spaced translucent glass bubbles—about thirty of them—rising from an otherwise bare, smooth, icy plain. Tall, sometimes jagged ridges of ice gleamed in the background, while beyond these the hazy horizon appeared an exceptionally long distance off. Overhead the sky formed a mottled green-brown pattern of swirling splotches. Whatever this scene was—and wherever—it was like no place Danny had ever seen before.

"This is a photograph depicting a certain small portion of the surface of Neptune," Sam said. "Those glasslike structures you see in the foreground are the primary Kith settlement at the present time."

"Gosh, and I'm still not scared," George said, turning to the others with a crooked smile. But no one was smiling back. Danny didn't feel especially frightened—not yet anyway—but there was definitely something about this scene, the longer you looked at it, something ominous and . . . well, disturbing.

"The fact that we human beings were no longer alone in the Solar System," Sam went on, "first came to our attention seven stanyears ago when an event utterly without precedent—or immediate explanation— took place on Neptune. During a period of approximately thirty-two hours, Neptune appeared to explode within itself. My terminology isn't very exact, I'm afraid, to describe what actually occurred—in fact, we still don't know precisely what took place—we know the results but not the process. But at the very least, observations made at the time of the event indicated that temperatures in the upper planetary atmosphere of Neptune —all that could be readily measured—reached levels approaching one thousand degrees. This controlled explosion—this contained burst of energy, this thermonuclear event—ended quite as suddenly as it had begun."

Carolina, sitting beside Danny, said, "Thermonuclear? Then it was a bomb?"

"Only if you choose to think of the Sun as a bomb."

Raymond, the Belter boy, was nodding to himself. "I remember hearing about this when it happened, though I was only a kid. But the way I heard it, the Combine was experimenting on Neptune with an atmospherical terraforming system they were thinking of using in an attempt at colonizing Venus, and something went wrong and the whole thing blew up."

Sam's smile was tight-lipped. "That was the story that was rather hastily given out to the public, since there wasn't any way of concealing the fact that something extraordinary had occurred on Neptune."

"But if it wasn't anything like what they said—and it wasn't a bomb—then what was it?" Raymond said.

"It was the Kith," Sam said. "Though it would be sometime later before anyone found that out. What was plain from the beginning, however, was that Neptune was no longer the same world it had been before. The chemical composition of the atmosphere had been altered. There was somewhat less methane and more free oxygen. The period of rotation had slowed by nearly a full stanhour and there was a significant dwindling of mass. And, most amazingly of all, Neptune now had a solid surface area it most definitely had not possessed before."

"And all this stuff," George said, "you say it was these Kith who did it?"

"The Kith and their technology."

"What technology?" George pointed toward the viewscreen. "All I see are a bunch of glass domes that look like igloos sitting in the middle of an icy wilderness. I don't see any machines, that's for sure."

"Nor has anyone else," Sam agreed. "We are merely assuming that they exist. It's one of the things we'd like you to discuss with the Kith when you meet them—how they've done what they've done."

"But when this explosion—or whatever you want to call it"—this was Raymond again—"when these changes happened, nobody knew anything about the Kith then, right?"

"No. Not then nor for sometime afterward. Two dozen of our brightest scientists—the Combine was reluctant to send a larger party, for security reasons, since we wanted to find out for ourselves what had happened on

Neptune before going public with any part of it—these people converged on Triton to study what was for all practical purposes a new planet in the Solar System. Work began on the construction of *Leverrier* at the time and was completed within a few months, thus allowing for closer observation."

"And that's when you found out about the Kith?" Carolina said.

"Yes. One of the first things we did once we'd established a base on *Leverrier*—I say we, though I wasn't yet personally on the scene—we launched a series of probes in an attempt to obtain a photographic survey map of the new planetary surface. It was during the course of this survey that a Kith settlement was first discovered. A mobile robot was immediately softlanded in the vicinity for a closer look. Here's one of the initial photographs that robot transmitted back at the time."

Sam punched some keys. The new image on the screen showed a two-legged creature standing in front of one of the glass domes. A Kith, Danny realized with a start, gaping at the sight. Despite knowing it had to be coming, he couldn't help feeling more than slightly awestruck. Unlike the hideous monster Sam had shown them before, this was the real thing: a genuine alien. There was no connection with the human race whatsoever—or with Earth.

At least there wasn't supposed to be. Nevertheless, looking at the Kith, Danny kept thinking how much it resembled a turtle—a squat, flat-headed turtle, but with six limbs instead of four and a short bushy tail jutting from the back of its shell. Sam showed them a series of photographs depicting the Kith—or perhaps several Kith—from a variety of angles.

"So that's a Kith," broke in the very young girl sitting between Raymond and Carolina. "Sam, it's cute."

"This is indeed one of the Kith, Nina," Sam confirmed, "though as far as being cute, I ought to mention that shortly after obtaining these first photographs, our robot was set upon by this Kith and a number of others and systematically destroyed."

"The Kith don't like robots?" George said. "Hey, good for them."

"That's assuming the Kith have any idea what a robot is," Sam said, "which there's no reason for believing they do."

George looked unconvinced. "But if they're smart enough to change an entire planet, aren't they smart enough to know what robots are?"

"Not necessarily," Sam said. "What does intelligence have to do with anything? The philosopher Plato was as intelligent as any man in history, but he knew nothing of robots."

"That's beside the point," George said.

"Of course it is," Sam agreed. "Because Plato, smart or dumb, was a man—a human being. And the Kith are not. The Kith—this is something I want all of you to remember—not just George, all of you—the Kith are not human. They are alien beings. They're not just different from you or me or Plato, or strange, or peculiar, or odd. They're *alien*. And what that means is that no matter how much we may find out about them, we'll never really be certain about anything."

There was a moment of silence as Sam let the meaning of his words sink in.

"I still think it looks like a turtle," Danny heard himself mutter.

"What was that?" Sam tilted forward. "Did someone say something?"

"I . . ." Danny twisted uncomfortably as the eyes of the others focused on him. He cleared his throat. "I just said it sort of looks like a turtle to me, sir."

Sam turned and peered at the screen. "I . . . yes, I suppose there is a faint similarity."

Danny thought the similarity was a lot more than faint, but he was reluctant to get into an argument about it. Unlike George—and some of the others, too, it seemed—Danny found it difficult to be the focus of attention. He just wasn't used to it. How could he be, having lived alone with his mother for so many years?

"What's a turtle?" It was the little girl, gazing down the line at him.

Danny was surprised. "Don't you know?"

"It's an Earth animal, right? But I've never seen one. A lot of us haven't. Raymond, Carolina, me. We've never been to Earth."

The little boy sitting next to George spoke up. "A turtle," he told the girl in a bored voice that sounded years older than he clearly was, "is a usually amphibious reptile with toothless jaws and a soft body enclosed in a bony shell. Turtles—or tortoises, as the land varieties are called—can still be found in most regions of Earth. In my opinion, Danny's observation concerning the physical similarities between the Kith and turtles is accurate in at least seven respects. Firstly, there's the characteristic of the bony shell, and then there's the matter of the absence of any—"

"Good point, Benny," Sam cut in smoothly, "but all of this, I want to remind you—the initial discovery of the Kith, the first robot landing—all of this occurred seven stanyears ago. In the days and weeks that followed, every effort was made to establish communication with these aliens that had so unexpectedly appeared in our midst. None of these efforts succeeded. When we sent down additional robot probes, the Kith destroyed them also. When we beamed radio signals from *Leverrier,* they ignored them. When we tried to set up a two-way television system by landing equipment close to their settlement, they ignored our efforts at first and eventually destroyed the equipment. It finally became obvious that only direct human-to-Kith contact had any hope of bringing about their recognition that we even existed. There was only one known practical way of bringing that about: the MAGMOS Process. As a result, the first project was launched."

"The one that killed my father," George said flatly.

Sam nodded. "Yes, George. It's how your dad died."

"His father?" Carolina broke in.

"George's father was Michael Hawkins," Sam said. "He was Danny's father, too, of course."

Carolina turned her head and gazed at Danny with a rapt, almost awestruck expression. Danny felt himself twisting uncomfortably under her gaze. It was his first real experience of what it meant to have a famous father.

"Like father, like sons, let's hope," said the Belter boy, Raymond. He was looking at George with an expression that seemed more curious than awestruck.

Sam then went on to describe the first project, its initial success—human beings reached the surface of Neptune—and its ultimate failure.

"So there we stood—with one individual missing and presumed dead, two others in permanent psychotic states, and the chief project psychiatrist, a man you'll be meeting soon, assuring me that the situation couldn't be altered, that the fault lay not so much with the MAGMOS Process as with the limitations of human consciousness. So the project was suspended indefinitely. The final decision to do so was mine. From *Leverrier* efforts continued at establishing some form of contact with the Kith. There were more robots, more radio signals, more probes. Nothing worked any better than before. We were stymied. Eventually it was decided to maintain as close a watch on the Kith as they'd allow, but to proceed no further for the time being. Even in this, however, it only seemed that the more we learned, the less we really knew."

"That's because they're *aliens*, Sam," the little girl Nina said brightly.

He nodded, smiling. "Yes, exactly. But to give you an example, the location of the Kith settlements has often changed. New settlements have appeared, and the old ones simultaneously disappeared. Does this mean that the Kith are physically moving from place to place? But if so, why? And how? The settlements are often thousands of kilometers apart. Do the Kith possess a form of instantaneous transport, a practical scrambling technology or something even more advanced? Sonic probes set up to examine the internal transformation of the planet discovered the presence of a network of tunnels beneath the Neptunian surface. How many Kith are living down there totally hidden from us? Is that where their machines are located, assuming they have machines, an assumption there is as yet no evidence to support, as I mentioned. And so on. I'm only giving you a sampling of the unanswered questions we have concerning the Kith. Where do they come from and what do—"

"How do you know they weren't just born on Neptune?" Danny was startled to hear the sound of his own voice. When nobody laughed or looked at him weirdly, he decided it hadn't been such a dumb question after all.

"Have you found the wreck of a starship or something like that?" Carolina asked, turning her head and smiling encouragingly at Danny as she did.

"No, no starship," Sam said, "though we'd dearly love to uncover any such artifact. No, the general belief that the Kith are not native to Neptune is based entirely on negative factors. Where life ought not to exist— where in fact everything we know says it cannot exist—then we have to conclude that it doesn't. And when, contrariwise, suddenly there it is, then either everything we know is wrong or else that life has come from someplace else."

"But if the Kith came from someplace else," Carolina said, "from another planet or star, then what do they want here?"

"That," Sam said, "is perhaps the biggest unanswered question of all."

George made a snorting sound. "I don't buy that. I mean, how can you even be sure the Kith want anything from us at all? Maybe their ship just crashed on Neptune—it's probably buried somewhere under all that ice— and now they're just trying to figure a way to get the hell out of there. That's what all this other stuff is about, too, changing the planet and everything. All they want from us is to back off and leave them alone."

"But if that's true," Carolina said, "why won't they tell us so?"

"When a bug's crawling on the floor next to your foot," George said, "you don't bend down and ask it to go away. You step on it."

"I wouldn't know about that," she said. "We don't have bugs on Titan."

"But you know what I mean."

"And besides," she said, "the Kith haven't done anything like stepping on somebody. Right, Sam? The Kith have never actually harmed a human being, have they?"

"To the best of our knowledge, no."

"You mean my father," George put in at once.

Sam nodded. "I meant that since we have no clear idea what happened to Mike down there, we really can't say."

"But there's no reason to think the Kith might be capable of harming anyone, is there?" Carolina said.

"I . . ." Sam paused. "That's something I'd rather go into a bit later. Before I do, though, let me first explain why the seven of you are here and why I believe you can achieve the primary goal of our mission where the members of the first project could not."

Danny listened intently as Sam expounded his theory as to why certain exceptional children—exceedingly bright and imaginative children—possessed an innate adaptability that would permit them to survive the psychic shock of living in an alien body on an equally alien world.

"Of course, my theory could be wrong," he said, "but if it is, I hope to find that out before any one of you actually sets foot on the surface of Neptune. When we arrive on *Leverrier* you will undergo an extensive training period. As with the first project, much of this will consist of hypnosimulator sessions during which time each of your minds—at least the conscious portions of it—will have you believing that you are actually a Neptunian wandering about Neptune. Since this wasn't by itself sufficient before to prevent madness, the technicians have come up with a new concept that should prove helpful. They call it an environmental chamber, and what it consists of is a big room, a chamber, in which as near as possible the actual conditions of the surface of Neptune are duplicated—including the immense gravity. Each of you will be scrambled into your Neptunian form and beamed into the chamber. After each training session —whether hypnosimulation or in the environmental chamber—you can expect to be put through an immediate and extensive psychological evaluation. At the first sign of significant mental instability in any one of you, that person will be dropped from the project team. If it happens to more than two of you, the project will be canceled. If there's any way I can avoid it, I'm not sending another person to the madhouse for life."

"So what about the Kith maybe harming people?" George said when there was a pause. "You said you'd tell us about that."

Sam nodded. "Actually, it's something I want to show you. After I have, I'm going to decree this meeting to be at an end. I imagine every one of you still has a hundred questions you'd like to toss my way, but I'm going to ask you to sit on them for the time being. When we reach *Leverrier* you'll each receive a briefing book thicker than either of my arms, and somewhere in those pages, I'm willing to wager, your questions will be answered. A supply shuttle is scheduled to depart for *Leverrier* at 0730 stantime, and I've managed to squeeze the lot of us on board. That gives you"—he shut his eyes—"three hours and few spare minutes in which to wander about Tsiolkovsky to see what mischief you can stir up and still get back here in time to leave as a group for the shuttle pad. All I ask is that you say nothing to anyone of what you've learned during the course of this meeting, that you steer clear of alcohol and other intoxicants, and that you avoid contracting a contagious disease. No gambling either. It's a waste of mental energy."

"Oh, Sam," Nina said, giggling, "we're just kids. We're not going to do any of that."

"Some kids," Sam said, "are a lot more grown-up than others."

Danny didn't think it was purely his imagination that Sam was looking at George as he spoke.

Sam leaned over the computer terminal and tapped the keyboard. "What I'm going to show you now is the latest tape of Kith activity, recorded less than a half-dozen hours ago by our most recent camera probe shortly before its own destruction. The primary reason I'm showing you this is to again emphasize the alien nature of the Kith."

At first the screen showed only the same scene of the Kith settlement Sam had shown them before: the bubbles of translucent glass spread across the icy plain. For a long moment, as the scene remained static, Danny felt his attention drifting away, until a sharp gasp of breath—from Carolina, beside him—jerked his eyes back to the screen.

The Kith had emerged. Seven of them, Danny counted, spread out in a line, approaching where the camera presumably stood. Their squat thick legs, he now noticed, ended in broad flat flippered feet, and they moved painstakingly but gracefully across the ice, sliding almost, as if they were skating.

The Kith in the middle of the line was carrying something in its upper set of arms, a long narrow object wrapped in a cloth fabric. (At least it looked like a cloth fabric.) As the seven Kith continued to approach, they gradually separated, three eventually disappearing off the edges of the screen. What they seemed to be doing, Danny thought, was forming a circle with the camera at its center.

The remaining Kith halted. All except for one that had some sort of bony outcropping on its skull, like a big twisted horn. After a moment's pause it continued forward until it nearly ran into the camera. Then it stopped, turned its green-speckled shell to the lens, and twitched its bushy tail rapidly up and down.

He acts like he's nervous, Danny thought, watching the tail. Then he quickly corrected himself. No, Sam was right. The worst mistake was trying to impose human characteristics on an alien being. The twitching tail might mean almost anything. It might also mean nothing at all.

The Kith carrying the covered object now slid forward too. As it drew closer to the camera, it removed the cloth, revealing what lay underneath. It was a long, thin metallic object, resembling a sword without a hilt or definite handle. Slowly, still edging forward, the Kith raised the sword over its head. As it did, it extended its middle pair of arms straight out, perpendicular to its torso, presumably for added balance on the ice.

The Kith halted about a meter in front of the other Kith, the sword still poised overhead.

It's some sort of ceremony, Danny decided. Like what used to occur on Earth during the so-called Age of Chivalry. The king would lay the flat of his sword on a brave knight's shoulders and proclaim him a knight of the realm.

Watching, Danny waited for the Kith to lower the sword and complete the ceremony. But when the sword finally came down, it seemed all wrong. Because of the gravity or something, the sword was falling way too fast. Before Danny realized what was happening, the sword reached its goal and lopped the green-shelled Kith's head from its body. The head toppled to the ice and lay there, face up, eyes seeming to stare at the camera. An instant later a spout of blood erupted from the neck, splattering the lens.

Then the body collapsed lifelessly beside the severed head.

Somebody in the room let out a scream. Somebody else was yelling and shouting. Danny, in his chair, felt numb and out of breath. The image on the computer viewscreen was all a crazy jumble now, swinging spastically from side to side. Then it went blank. Out of the corner of an eye Danny spied George on his feet. He was holding the little redheaded kid by the shirt front and shaking him for all he was worth. "Look what you did, you moron. You puked on my shoes."

Danny's eyes met those of Carolina. She gave him a wan, exhausted smile and wagged her head from side to side. Danny didn't know why she was smiling, but he couldn't help smiling back too.

It seemed the only human thing to do at the time.

FOURTEEN

Among the Kith, whose name for their own kind means People, lives one Gornami (the dunce), who suffers most dreadfully from a disruption of personal warmth-fabric in the wake of the brutal demise of one Nykol (the believer), who twice in other realm-times has born Gornami sister-brothers through his own blood.

To ease his grief-anxiety, this Gornami soon undertakes a long-burrow to the interior sea, slurping the methane-water ice into his material form and absorbing simultaneously those misty fragrances that bring a welcome if transitory forgetfulness. For Gornami, alas, there can exist no permanent relief from the anguish that pierces his soul as if cut by the same sheath-blade used by Zorm (the uncaring) to effect the murder of poor Nykol, who has harmed none during nine counted lifespans.

And so finally (short of the interior sea) Gornami reverses his descent and up, up from the ice mantle he rises to storm the lodge-home of the many-elder Potrum (the dispenser), who has lain dream-sleeping.

"I seek soul communion," demands Gornami, voicing in blatant first-tongue the one plea that can never be denied.

Roused from his trance, the many-elder of seven acknowledged spans responds grudgingly. *You are too stupid,* he replies, refusing to expend precious life-breath by using the first-tongue. *You are too young.*

But even stupid and young, Gornami is aware of what can never be denied. "I know that my mother-wife-father-husband Nykol has suffered a full disruption of his life-force because of your will."

Among those of many, yes.

"Then who were the others? I, Gornami (the dunce), demand to know."

Then lay supine, my idiot. Your demand of soul communion is one that cannot be denied.

And so it comes to pass that these two Kith lie prone upon the mottled floor of the many-elder's lodge-home with their skulls touching while between them intimate forces flow.

Gornami (now able to speak voicelessly from the soul as an elder): *My warmth-fabric endures a terrible pain, my Potrum, for never until now did I conceive that the life-force of one such as Nykol could be dispersed to the void.*

Potrum (patiently): *If you believed such, my infant, then you have neglected to observe the cosmic flux.* With this, Potrum displays for Gornami a brief series of tableaux testifying to the creation and destruction of the universe.

Gornami (impatiently): *I know of the flux, many-elder, but these are suns and planets, balls of gas and rock, while Nykol had born my sister-brothers twice in other realm-times.*

Potrum then envisions a sun exploding from within and raining death upon a hundred billion living beings on four planets.

Gornami (repelled): *Stop, please. Why do you envision for me this . . . this senseless slaughter?*

In response Potrum reveals the spectacle of a primeval nebula spewing forth a fiery sun and thirteen companion planets, upon one of which life eventually emerges. This is Xob, the ancient home world of the Kith, a realm-time Gornami has witnessed before through soul communion.

Gornami (pondering): *Then what you are teaching, my Potrum, is that for every one thing which dies, another soon is born?*

Potrum (with a searing blast of anger): *No, fool! You have lived much of your first alloted span and yet have failed to understand even this much. There is no such obscenity as a balancing scale in the universe.*

Gornami (appalled): *Then there is no sense to the universe, no meaning or purpose.*

Potrum (with joy): *Exactly, my brilliant pupil. You are wise beyond your span, as therein truly lies the rub, for while death is without sense, life is nothing but the purest of sense, and thus when the two refuse to balance, what emerges is the cosmic flux.*

Gornami (confused): *But what does this have to do with the murder of Nykol by the sheath-blade of Zorm?*

Potrum: *The murder and the flux are the same.*

Gornami: *Then you admit that the murder was carried out through the will of the many-elders in order to impress the peeping glass eye of these human beings.*

Potrum: *Eye?* He depicts mocking laughter. *It is called a television camera, ignorant one.*

Gornami (heatedly): *A primitive mechanical contraption to spy on us.*

Potrum: *Or a window through which many eyes can peer.*

Gornami: *Many-elder, I grow weary of such riddles. Don't you understand that Nykol was not only my mother-wife-father-husband but also my friend? His death diminishes my past-present-future.* Here Gornami struggles to concoct a vision to express his anguish but fails to produce more than a splatter of colors. *Once upon this Neptune-world Nykol and I burrowed to the interior sea and there cleansed ourselves of all we had brought from before, laughing as the delirium of freedom tickled our warmth-fabrics and made us seem as one.*

Potrum (nostalgically): *Nykol was indeed a rare spirit who encompassed fourteen separate visions of truth and beauty.*

Gornami (with passion): *Then why did you kill him? Wasa it merely to teach those . . . those human beings a lesson?*

Potrum: *What lesson mlight we Kith possibly teach such a race?*

Gornami (bitterly): *The cosmic flux, of course. Isn't that what many-elders always teach?*

Potrum: *The human beings already know the flux.* Here he provides for Gornami a visionary sequence of horrible warfare, giant armies clashing, cities burning, millions dying.

Gornami (disgusted): *These human beings are unworthy of us—of the flux.*

Potrum (amused) *Then they are not alone.* And here he shifts the perspective of his vision slightly so that when one of the warning soldiers turns, he is shown to be a Kith.

Gornami: *No! You cannot show me lies, many-elder.*

Potrum: *Peer closer, young dunce, and see the truth of the truth.*

Unwillingly, Gornami looks, and discovers that the Kith is his dead friend Nykol. *No, no, this cannot possibly be.*

Potrum (with firmness): *Such it was upon the home world of Xob many eons ago.*

Gornami: *Kith killing others. I will not believe—*

Potrum: *Yet you dared to accuse me of willing the death of Nykol.*

Gornami: *That was one. This is millions, madness.*

Potrum: *It is what?*

Gornami: *It is madness.*

Potrum (triumphantly): *)At last! Finally! Then you do understand, my son.*

And with this Potrum ruptures the soul communion, springing upright and kicking at the still supine Gornami. *Come, get along with you. I have described the lessons you demanded to learn. Nothing remains to be revealed.*

Gornami, on the floor, rocks back and forth on his shell. "You taught me nothing!"

On the contrary. If you failed to learn, dunce, that is not my responsibility. Potrum gives Gornami a solid kick. *Now go. There is much essential dream-sleep in my future.*

Clutching his underbelly where he has been kicked, Gornami staggers out. It is late in the day on Neptune, the sun a faint streak in the low sky. Smeary clouds converge like birds of prey. Driven by a furious rage, Gornami trudges across the ice-coated land until, at the edge of the Kith settlement, he spies an object that makes him pause. It is another of the peering glass eyes of the human beings—television cameras, Potrum called them.

His anger now overwhelming, Gornami attacks the camera, smashing it to pieces with his hands and flippers.

As he is finishing, from behind he hears cheerful laughter.

Turning, he discovers a Kith he has never seen before. "Who are you?" he demands. "What do you want of me, the dunce?"

The strange Kith continues to laugh.

Leaving the battered remnants of the camera, Gornami lumbers toward the Kith. "I demand your name and your reason for being here. Speak or I will kick you until you cry out in the first-tongue."

"But do you not recognize me, my friend?" the newcomer asks gently. "I am Nykol, who has twice born you sister-brothers."

"No!" Gornami cries, halting in his tracks. But although the shell is speckled blue and the face is without the sagging gravity lines of age, the scent of the warmth-fabric is identical.

This is indeed Nykol (the believer).

Gornami advances into the four waiting arms of his friend. The two Kith embrace, turn, rub shells, link tails.

"Nykol," cries Gornami, "how can this be? You were dead, for with my own eyes I witnessed your slaughter. Zorm (the uncaring) severed your head from your body with his sheath-blade."

Nykol touches his skull with all four hands. "It appears to be intact, friend Gornami."

"I shared communion with the many-elder Potrum, who showed me nothing but lies."

"How peculiar. In ten spans I have never known an elder to deceive."

"Potrum told me you were dead!"

"So I was." Nykol vanishes.

"Nykol! Gornami wails.

"Here—behind you."

Gornami turns to find Nykol again standing before him.

"Then we cannot truly die, we Kith," Gornami muses. "That is the secret the many-elder Potrum refused to reveal to me."

"All entities bearing the gift of the life-force must in due time die," Nykol softly explains.

"And the-one-who-is-nothing?" Gornami asks tremulously, as the Neptune-world seems to stir beneath him.

"The-one-who-is-nothing does not live and so can never die. That, too, is part of the cosmic flux. But the life-force of a mortal, when it so chooses, can emerge within a newly formed body and thus stop short of the void."

"And that's what you did."

"Reluctantly, my friend, and only because of them"—he gestures at the sky, a maelstrom of bleached yellow-gold—"the humans. Now, with you, I must await the stirring of the-one-who-is-nothing and voyage to yet another realm-time."

"But the humans are unworthy, fools and murderers and even worse."

Nykol raises an upper arm to silence Gornami. "The human beings will soon walk among us one more time, and that is why I have returned short of the void. When the humans come, I will stand to welcome them, you at my side."

"Me?"

"The elders have so chosen."

"But I am a dunce."

"A former dunce, my friend."

"But then I—" Before Gornami can complete his astonished outburst, a flash of lightning ignites the sky. Gornami tilts his head, staring. *Then I have become Gornami-yev (the former dunce).*

You have .

But— (He is speaking the soul speech of the elders.)

As the lightning fades, there is a thunder on Neptune.

PART
THREE

LEVERRIER

FIFTEEN

In the sanctum of his office in the outer rim of the spoked wheel of *Leverrier,* Sam stood with his back to the door, his eyes focused on the far wall. Beyond the wall (actually a vast window) Sam could observe a portion of the blue-and-gold oblate disk of Neptune as it appeared to float majestically through the surrounding void of space. As usual, an old quotation came into his head, one having originally nothing to do with planets or space but seemingly appropriate nevertheless. *A mystery wrapped in an enigma shrouded by a riddle.* (That was close anyway.) The mystery? That would be Neptune. The enigma? The Kith, of course. And the riddle? Maybe that's us, Sam thought. Humanity.

And maybe it's everything else, too, he decided wearily. Maybe it's the whole damn universe as well.

With a sigh Sam averted his gaze from the big window. None of this was doing any good, he realized. Contrary to his usual practice, he had returned to his office this evening (according to stantime it was evening, though of course that had no practical meaning aboard an orbiting station) in hopes of being able to come to a certain decision here with all the data he might require at his fingertips. So far, however, his mind had refused to cooperate, drifting instead like a ship tossed in a rough sea. Well, maybe that's the best way to do it, he thought. Let the old subconscious be the guide.

The trouble was, as far as this decision was concerned, the subconscious didn't seem to be doing much guiding either.

I hate having to do this, Sam thought. I hate having to pick and choose. Any other time, no problem, but now—with life and death at stake—I just hate it.

Tomorrow was going to be the day. That much had already been decided some hours earlier, when Sam had met with Fred Berman, the project psychiatrist, Bob Mobuku, the chief MAGMOS technician, and Olga Kropotkin, the station commander. He had asked each the same question in turn: "Is there any overwhelming reason, in your opinion, why we should not launch our first scrambling mission to Neptune at the earliest available moment?"

The three of them, taken aback, had hemmed and hesitated at first but finally provided Sam with their honest responses: after six months testing and training, examinations and evaluations, simulations and dry-runs, no such overwhelming reason existed.

As far as they were concerned the first mission could proceed whenever Sam—and the kids—felt ready.

Sam tried to look pleased. "If they're not ready now, they never will be. I think we ought to get right to it. How does tomorrow sound? Tomorrow at noon stantime?"

As Sam had anticipated, all three raised immediate objections then, Bob Mobuku demanding one last biological dry-run—scrambling a lab animal through MAGMOS, beaming it to Neptune, and bringing it back—before granting his approval.

"How many biological dry runs have you already conducted?" Sam asked. "Quite a few, if I recall."

"Thirty-seven," Mobuku said. He was a lean, full-bearded black man who always bore himself with immense dignity, claiming to be the direct descendant of a Central African emperor despite having been born on Mars. (The claim was true, Sam happened to know.) "Twenty involved insects and spiders, five reptiles including a young turtle, and the other mammals, lab mice and gerbils."

"But you still want another."

"Nine of the thirty-seven were failures, Sam," Olga pointed out. She was one of Sam's oldest friends, a dyed-in-the-wool spacer, half Russian, half American Indian, and still damn beautiful, in spite of being nearly as old as he. Sam and Olga had had a lot of interesting times together back in the early days of the Combine—and even before. He could remember one night with Olga in Clarkegrad when the dome sprung a leak and everyone had to huddle in their emergency airlocks till morning . . . There was nothing like twelve hours alone with somebody in a two-meter cube to learn the meaning of real intimacy.

"But those were early on," Sam said, "and due to malfunctions in the MAGMOS hardware, the fact that everything had been sitting around here on *Leverrier* the last five years. I thought you told me you had all the glitches ironed out, Bob."

"We believe we do, yes, but—"

"But you're not sure?" Sam arched an eyebrow.

"In the proper sense that one can seldom be certain of anything, yes."

"Okay, then. I'll let you have your dry run. But I want it done right away, before tomorrow morning. And I get to pick the animal you send. Agreed?"

"Within reason, yes. Our laboratories do not contain a full complement of animal species, by any means."

"I'm aware of that. So what do you say we go outside the lab this time? What I want is a representative of the only species other than we humans that's ever ventured into space of its own free will and thrived there."

"What species is that?" Fred Berman broke in, looking puzzled. "I know some ship crews keep cats, especially the rovers in the Belt, but—"

Same was smiling. "Not cats, Fred. I said of their own free will. Rats."

"But we have utilized rats on a number of occasions—" Mobuku began.

Sam shook his head. "I don't mean those scrawny little white things you've got in your lab, Bob. I'm talking about the real thing—a wharf rat."

"You've got one in your pocket?" Olga said, smiling with him.

"No. But one shouldn't be too hard to find. Right?"

Olga nodded. "They're all over the station. You don't see them very often, but they're there."

"I figured they would be. Think you can trap one for Bob?"

"Sure. I'll program a robot."

"Why a rat in particular, Sam?" Berman asked. The three of them stood side by side in front of Sam's desk, Mobutu looming over the other two.

"Because," Sam said, "as long as Bob wants one last shot, I think we ought to try to get something out of it. What was the primary evaluative factor in picking the kids for the team? Intelligence, imagination, and creative potential were important, but the really crucial factor was adaptability."

"That's what you told me anyway," Berman said.

"It's true. And what can be more adaptable than a rat living in an artificial space station a billion-odd kilometers from its natural habitat? Let's send one of these highly adaptable rats to Neptune and see what we've got when it gets back. Now, Fred." Sam gazed straight up. "I get the impression you're not fully satisfied with my decision either. What's the problem? Do you want more tests too?"

Berman shook his head. "I would if I felt it would do any good, but I don't. Bob's got the easier responsibility here, because his machines either work or they don't, and which is which it's fairly easy to tell. Me, I've got to deal with human beings, and the difficulty with people is that they often keep right on functioning even when they're broken."

"Some do, Fred. But not all. Or even most."

"I'm sure that's true, Sam—as a generality—and if you'd given me seven relatively normal, more or less ordinary kids and said, 'Keep an eye on them, Fred, and let me know at the least hint of psychological instability,' I would have been able to pull it off with no major problem. But these kids aren't ordinary, Sam."

"If they were, they wouldn't be here. They're *extraordinary.*"

"You're telling me." He shook his head, smiling grimly. "Look, Sam, what it really comes down to is that after six months—after hours and hours of testing, countless one-on-one interviews, more psychological profiling than you could ever read—all I can tell you definitively is that none of the kids is completely crazy."

"But isn't that what we're concerned with?" Olga put in.

"On Neptune, yes, but there . . . Training is training and only that, no matter how realistically it may duplicate the actual experience. And how close is that duplication? Internally, subconsciously, how close? I don't know. Nobody does. And psychosis is a continuum. The dividing line between sanity and insanity is a blurred gray area. And sometimes it's damn hard to locate."

"The line between genius and madness," Sam said, "is a thin one."

"Or an invisible one," Olga said.

"No," Sam said. "No, I don't agree."

"Neither did I," Berman said. "Till now. After living in these kids' back pockets the last six months, I'm not so sure of anything."

Sam folded his hands on top of his desk. "What'll make you sure?"

Berman thought for a moment, then shrugged. "Short of an actual mission, probably nothing."

"Then you're telling me to go ahead?"

He didn't look especially pleased. "I guess I am."

"Then in that case—"

"Who's going?" It was Eileen Kinugasa. She had slipped into the office partway through the meeting and sat in front of a computer terminal on the opposite side of the room.

"My dear?" Sam said, lifting his head.

"I asked who's going. To me that's the big question. I gather you've

made up your mind tomorrow's D-day. Okay, swell. Now who's the big
D?"

"Two D's," Sam said, showing his fingers.

"Two?" Berman said, surprised.

"Bob and I have discussed this. More than anything, I want to avoid
another Mike Hawkins situation—where I lose a scrambler and have no
idea why. Frankly, I'd send an even bigger group, but Bob says there
would be technical complications."

"It's a question of fusion energy expenditure, limited reserves, and consequent replenishment in the MAGMOS Process," Mobutu said.

"We might be able to send four or five of the kids down," Sam explained, "but we couldn't bring them back for at least a standay. And
that's not a good idea—not in the beginning. For the kids' sake and also
the Kith. I don't want to overwhelm or frighten them."

"Hah!" said Eileen.

"Eileen doesn't believe it's possible to frighten the Kith," Sam said with
a smile. "She may or may not be correct, but two still seems our optimum
mission size at present."

"So which two is it?" Eileen asked. "That's what I asked in the first
place."

"To tell the truth," Sam said, looking across at her now, "I haven't
decided yet."

"Want some recommendations?" she said.

"No. This is something I'm going to have to do on my own. The responsibility is mine if there's a failure, so the authority to choose has to be mine
also."

"But you will let us know, though?" Olga said.

"Of course. As soon as I've made up my mind, you'll all hear."

But he hadn't said a word. To any of them. Not yet. Which was fair
enough.

He hadn't made up his mind either.

It was this unusual—for him—state of indecision, combined with the
growing lateness of the hour, which had driven Sam here to the office
largely in hopes of finding something concrete upon which to base a final
decision.

Standing with his back to the wall-length window, Sam glanced quickly
over his shoulder, saw to his relief that Neptune had temporarily vanished
from view, and took advantage of the moment to cross the room. Because
of the law gravity on *Leverrier* —the only reason there was any gravity was
due to the station's rotation in space—he moved in a series of short, easy,

lilting bounces, like a slow-motion jackrabbit. Reaching the computer terminal where Eileen had been working earlier, he dropped into the chair, activated the system with a fingertip, and pecked briefly at the keyboard. The viewscreen at eye level lighted up. Sam slipped on his eyeglasses and read:

PSYCHOLOGICAL DATA SUMMARIES

NEPTUNE PROJECT TEAM

SERIES 19B

His fingers went back to the keyboard. This time he typed: HAWKINS, DANNY.

On the viewscreen a succession of graphs, charts, notes, and memos began to appear, one fading rapidly into the next. Sam dropped a hand to slow the pattern, then thought better of it and instead shut down the entire system.

"This stupid waste of time," he muttered to himself, removing the glasses.

What was it he expected to find here anyway? It wasn't as if the computer and its data summaries were apt to contain any hidden secrets previously unknown to him. The problem for Sam wasn't that he didn't know the kids well enough. The problem was the opposite: He knew them too well. And because of that knowledge, the choices—the possibilities—seemed almost endless. It was from among the myriad of them that he had to decide.

Foregoing the stream of computer data, Sam decided instead to rely on his own personal knowledge. If that wasn't enough by now, then God help them in the days to come.

He began where he had intended to begin before with the Hawkins brothers. Dear sweet Danny, the least likely candidate of the seven. But Danny had surprised everyone—surprised even Sam himself—with his rapid progress. Bright and eager, smart and quick, Danny had emerged from the six months of training a long way from the bottom of his class, having coped well with every situation, real and simulated, and having shown in the end no psychological signs of being any the worse for wear. And none of the others had grown as much—or made a real effort to. Nevertheless, Danny's limitations remained clear. If adaptability still loomed as the primary criterion in putting together an initial mission, then Danny had perforce to be left behind. It wasn't his own fault, of course, but as Fred Berman had once pointed out: "I'm sorry to say I just don't get it, Sam. Danny's a sweet kid, but he's spent his whole life more or less tied to his mother's apron strings. What's he doing here?" Sam had tried to parry by arguing that the past was not necessarily a guide to future behavior and that Danny's overall lack of experience granted him the freedom to respond openly to new phenomena. But Berman had been basically right, even though (Sam had noticed) his objections to Danny had pretty much stopped lately. Apparently Berman had also recognized Danny's rapid growth during the training period.

Then came brother George. In support of his innate adaptability, George could always point to the undulations of his entire life up until now and the undeniable fact that he had not only survived, but prospered, under circumstances that might have killed people years older. But was that really enough? George's life was his life, but was there any real proof that what he had accomplished lay beyond the capabilities of the others—even Danny, for that matter—if they'd found themselves in similar circumstances? But George hadn't just found himself. He had to a degree created his own circumstances. And that, too, had to be taken as evidence of innate adaptability. But adaptability wasn't everything either. A multitude of other factors had to be considered. George was the one member of the project team who wasn't here on *Leverrier* of his own free choosing. Which led directly into the matter of George's loyalty, his trustworthiness as part of a group. There would be someone with him—a second scrambler —and the two would necessarily have to cooperate for the mission to succeed. Would George be willing to do his part? Could he? And what about the flipside of the matter? Carolina McClellan seemed oddly fascinated by George, and little Benny Sims had come nearly to idolize him but did any of them—Danny, too, for that matter—really like George? Raymond Liu, for one, made no secret of the fact that he couldn't stand the sight of George. No, thought Sam with a sigh. What it came down to was that if George had a great deal going for him, he had almost as much going against him.

As for Carolina of the blond ringlets and Raymond of the braided ponytail, Sam tended to think of the two of them together. Both came from the outer reaches of the Solar System, both were achievers at ages when in Sam's own more limited youth he had been fortunate to have escaped elementary school in one piece, and both were mature, intelligent, knowledgeable, thoughtful. At twelve stanyears, Carolina served on Titan's ruling council—and also happened to have three husbands—while Raymond at eleven was among the most successful freebooting miners in

the Asteroid Belt, an extremely wealthy man. The major distinctions between the two derived from the drastically opposed environments in which
each had grown up: Raymond in the Belt, with its scattered population of
clans and rovers; Carolina on Titan, where every individual action was
rigidly controlled because independence could too quickly lead to death.
They ought to make a good team, Sam thought. The problem was convinc-
ing them of the fact. Each regarded the other with considerable suspicion,
an attitude largely an outgrowth of their contrasting societies.

Then there were the two little ones, the babies. ("The brats," George
called them.) Benny Sims, age five; Nina Kropotkin, age four. Had it been
possible, Sam wouldn't have hesitated to pick the entire project team from
kids that young, but Benny and Nina were actually exceptions. While the
openness of early childhood was a desirable characteristic, so too was the
fully formed personality—the sense of self—that usually developed much
later in life. Benny and Nina knew who they were, however. Nina, who
had spent all of her life in space—mostly on *Leverrier*—had from birth
been given the freedom necessary to develop as an individual. (Even Fred
Berman remarked that Olga had done a marvelous job of mothering. "But
I'm not her mother," Olga pointed out. "Biologically, no," Berman said,
"but that's not what matters in mothering.")

As for Benny, it was hard to think of any person of any age who was
more of a true individual. His parents were old friends of Sam, the mother
a member of the Combine directorate in Tranquility, the father a brilliant
exobiologist who had once headed the terraforming on Ganymede. Sam
had had to argue long and hard—even longer and harder than with Sara
Dominca on Earth—to talk Mr. and Mrs. Sims into letting him borrow
their son, though in the end, he suspected, they were more than a little
relieved too. Benny Sims had to be the Solar System's most obnoxious five-
year-old. It wasn't so much that Benny was a genius with an IQ in a range
that could not be accurately measured, or that he knew more facts in more
fields than most grown, educated men and women. It was that Benny
could never stop letting you know just how smart he was. His solitary
saving grace was his ability to play superb classical piano for hours on end.
After less than a single standay on *Leverrier* with Benny Sims—Triton had
been bad enough, but at least there you could sneak away—Sam had
ordered the robot engineers to build a piano and install it in the recreation
zone, solely as a means of keeping Benny's fingers busy—and his mouth
shut—for a time. The bottom line for Sam was clear, though. Despite
Benny's youth—Nina's, too, for that matter—Sam could not allow himself

the slightest hesitation when the time came to send him to Neptune. The only remaining question was when that time ought to be. Now? Or later? The seventh and last member of the project team, eight-year-old Duncan Broadhead, was the hardest to evaluate. Duncan—not un-coincidentally—was also the only team member to have been selected by means of an actual computer scan of a population group, though the group from which his name had emerged was a somewhat select one: the several thousand mutant children born since the war who were presently under the care of the Preservation Corps in a number of camps on Earth. Not all mutants belonged to this group—the large majority did not—only those who did not appear capable of arranging their own care. Outwardly Duncan's mutations were relatively minimal: his hands and feet were webbed; he had no ears, nose, or body hair. Nor had he ever spoken a word in his life, though apparently this wasn't physical in nature. But inwardly—which was what interested Sam—the central Combine computer network seemed to think Duncan possessed the proper characteristics. He was special—and extraordinary.

So there you had it. The group. The team. Seven kids. Danny and George. Raymond and Carolina. Benny and Nina. Duncan Broadhead. From the seven, pick two.

Leaning back in his chair, Sam shut his eyes and did just that.

He picked two:

George and Carolina.

Raymond and Duncan.

Benny and Danny.

George and Nina.

Carolina and Danny.

And so on.

Every choice made sense. Every choice had its limitations, its drawbacks. And every choice might mean death—or madness—for those chosen.

I must be getting old, Sam found himself honestly thinking for the first time in his long life. In the past he'd never had any trouble making up his mind and had had little or no patience with those who did.

But the past had always revolved around adults, and these were kids. There was something buried inside every civilized human that made the harming of a child among the worst conceivable sins. So I'm human, Sam thought bleakly. What can I do about it?

Seek volunteers? He considered the option only briefly before discarding it. If he asked for volunteers, he'd more than likely get six (George the exception) and end up right back where he was now. Which was no place.

Twisting his head, Sam saw that Neptune had floated within range of the window again. (Actually it was *Leverrier* that was floating—or, rather, spinning.) Gazing at the vast looming object, Sam thought back to what he'd told the kids on Triton: *this is death.* Melodramatic? Yes—of course. But not inaccurate either. Death. Or worse.

Sometime later, his decision still unresolved, Sam bounced wearily down the station corridors on his way back to his own room, where, if he recalled correctly, two bottles of Martian beer were waiting. Passing a door, he was brought up short by a burst of laughter like the braying of a mule.

That laugh he'd know anywhere: Benny Sims. But where it was coming from intrigued him.

It was George Hawkins's room.

Curious, Sam rapped on the door. He heard furtive noises, then a whisper. "Carolina?"

"Yes, George," Sam murmured in a soft, shrill voice.

The door swung open and there stood George. "Jeez, Carolina, you've gotten fat," he said.

"And grown a beard too," Sam said, peering around George. Inside, Benny Sims sat cross-legged on the floor. Beside his knee were several stacks of Lunarian scrip, the solidest currency in the Solar System. A little beyond the money lay a deck of playing cards.

"What's going on here?" Sam demanded in his most authoritarian tone.

"We're playing poker," Benny called out. "George taught me how."

"He did, did he? Who's winning?"

"Me," Benny said. "I'm way, way ahead so far."

George was trying to shut the door, but Sam jammed his foot in the gap. "I didn't know you had any money, Benny."

"Economic speculation was an interest of mine, Sam. I'm actually extremely rich."

"And your parents let you bring all that money out here with you?"

"It wasn't any of their business. It's my money, not theirs. They're not rich."

Sam supposed they weren't. For that matter, neither was he. "I think—" he began, then stopped, looking at George. It was the oldest hustle in the book. Let the sucker win for as long as it took him to catch the fever and lose his head, and then clean him out before he could think twice. It was a game of chance with every move coolly planned in advance.

And that was when it happened: serendipity.

All at once Sam had the answer he had been seeking all night.
He broke into a sudden smile and put a hand to his mouth to stifle the
urge to laugh out loud. "I—make sure both of you get to bed before too
late. I'm calling a meeting in the morning, and I want everyone bright and
awake."

"What's the meeting about?" George said, staring at Sam

"Oh . . . oh, nothing." Still grinning broadly, Sam shook his head.
"You'll find out."

"Does that mean we're finally going—"

"In the morning, I said." Sam drew his foot out of the doorway and
turned quickly away. By the time he reached his own room a short distance down the corridor, he was whistling brightly. Good old George, he
thought. Count on him to come up with the solution to everyone's problem.

Sam realized now that he had very nearly stumbled upon this same
solution himself earlier. Volunteers. But it wasn't the volunteers who mattered, it was the one person who would never volunteer, whose sole alle-
giance was to the gods of chance and their ultimate wisdom. Wisdom was,
after all, a quantity often to be found lurking in the darkest, least illuminated corners of existence. And if it wasn't truly wisdom, it was still good
enough. It was an answer.

Sam had made up his mind at last.

And he was starting to feel young again too.

SIXTEEN

Danny couldn't believe what was happening to him. Here he was, sitting in a stiff-backed chair in the project office along with not only the other six team members, but also Dr. Berman, the psychiatrist, and Bob Mobutu, the chief MAGMOS technician, and Olga Kropotkin, the tiny granite-faced woman who commanded *Leverrier*—a gathering that just had to mean something important was up—and what was he doing?

He was falling asleep.

True, he'd stayed up sort of late yesterday in the recreation zone with Raymond Liu and off and on with Nina Kropotkin—like most little kids, Nina was restless, darting constantly in and out—drinking coffee and listening to Raymond's fascinating stories about life as a freebooting miner in the Asteroid Belt. But it hadn't been that late—hardly much past 2300 stantime—and, besides, after six months abroad *Leverrier*, Danny was getting used to getting by without a lot of sleep. He should've been wide awake right now. Not only that, but given the circumstances—this meeting—he should've been tense with excitement, taut with anticipation. Instead here he sat with his eyelids drooping, his chin sagging.

It was Sam's fault. He was the one who'd called the meeting, summoning them by intercom as they slept, and here he stood at the front of the room, his arms stationary at his sides, his expression blank, as he recited in a dull, flat monotone the most basic sorts of facts that might have been cribbed wholesale from an elementary encyclopedia. Right now he was telling them about Neptune. Neptune as it used to be—before the Kith. It was the one planet in the Solar System that generated a magnetic field outside its rocky core. Its mean distance from the Sun was four billion kilometers. Its day lasted eighteen hours, twelve minutes. It . . . and on on and on, the sort of material all of them had picked up from their briefing books within days of reaching *Leverrier.* (Later, orally, Sam had given them the currently revised, post-Kith figures.) What was the point? Did Sam think they'd all turned suddenly dumb on him, that he had to start over again at the beginning? Did he—

Jerk. Danny's chin snapped upright. This was getting silly. There he went, nearly snoozing again. Glancing to his left, he noticed Carolina McClellan with her eyes definitely shut. He heard snoring too—but it wasn't Carolina. From behind. He turned to look. George?

Bam!

That did it. Ten chins snapped upright, Twenty eyelids flew open.

At the front of the room Sam stood grinning. His knees were locked, his back curved, his hands hanging nearly to his ankles. He'd just finished hurling a huge thick book—an elementary enlcyclopedia, Danny had a feeling—through space to the floor.

"Well, my friends," Sam said, standing straight, "I thought that might shake things up. My apologies for being as boring as a teaching robot till now, but I thought it might be wise to lower the adrenaline level in the room before getting down to brass tacks. Eileen!" He was bellowing. "Eileen, bring in the specimen."

The door opened and Eileen Kinugasa strode through. A wire cage hung from a handle in her right hand. She passed the cage to Sam and then took a chair at the rear of the group. Sam held up the cage and peered through the wire mesh.

Danny looked forward, trying to see also.

Squeak-squeak.

Danny realized what he was seeing. There was a rat in the cage. A scrawny, black-furred, beady-eyed rat about thirty centimeters in length.

"Yuck," Nina said. "Sam, that thing's creepy."

"Oh, no." Sam placed the cage on top of a chair so they all could watch. "This rat is no creep, Nina. In fact, he's a hero, because unlike any of us, this rat has been to Neptune and back. He's here now to share his experiences with you."

"It's not a he, Sam," Eileen broke in. "Her name is Gloria. Right, Bob?"

The tall African nodded solemnly. He sat in a chair beside Dr. Berman and Olga Kropotkin, off to one side of the room. "I believe that's the designation my robots have chosen to use."

Bob Mobutu and his robot engineers had been beaming scrambled animal specimens to Neptune ever since the project team first arrived on *Leverrier.* Sam had allowed them to be present at the first demonstration—

it was only their second full day on *Leverrier*—but none since. Danny studied the rat as it darted around its cage, attempting to scale the mesh walls, falling, hanging helplessly, relentlessly seeking a way out.

"How is she going to share her experiences with us, Sam?" Nina asked from over Danny's shoulder. "I thought only people and robots knew how to talk."

"Gloria is talking," Sam said, "if you know how to listen. What she's saying is, kids, look at me. I am alive, I am healthy, and I am not crazy."

It was George who snickered. "Are you sure about that last part?"

"A human being is classified insane," Sam said, "when he ceases to act like a human being. This rat is acting exactly the way a rat should act—a rat trapped in a cage."

"Is that what we're going to turn out to be?" George said. "More rats in cages?"

Sam looked somber. "You've gotten a step ahead of me, George, but to answer your question—I'm assuming you meant it metaphorically—yes. Gloria here is our last animal experiment. The next step is you seven. We're going ahead with an actual mission."

"When?" George said.

"Today."

Despite the fact that all of them had figured it might be coming, Sam's announcement was greeted by stunned silence. It was so quiet in the room, you could have heard someone breathing—if anyone had been breathing.

"What time?" Carolina said, breaking the silence at last.

Sam looked across to Bob Mobutu, who nodded curtly. "Twelve noon stantime," Sam said.

"How many of us are going?" she asked.

"Bob, Fred, Olga, and I discussed that particular question all last night. We decided together on the mission team of two. That's the optimum number, technically and otherwise."

"Are you taking volunteers?"

Sam shook his head, smiling thinly. "If I did, I'm afraid I'd be overwhelmed. Instead . . ." He put a hand in the side pocket of the pale blue cotton robe he was wearing and withdrew an object he kept concealed behind his back for the time being. He took a few steps closer to the group, paused, held up his hand, and opened the fist. "I hold here in my palm a deck of ordinary playing cards," he said.

It was no lie. That was exactly what he was holding. Sam turned his wrist, fanned open the cards, and showed them both sides. "We're going to let chance decide. Since all of you are equally prepared and presumably equally eager—"

There was a snort—from George.

With a sharp nod, Sam darted forward, moving with his usual unexpected grace. He stopped in front of George and thrust out his hand. "Does that mean you'd like to pick first, George?"

"Pick what?" George said, his own hands folded in his lap.

"Top two high cards go," Sam said.

George was looking at the deck. "No cut?"

"If you want to cut, cut," Sam said.

"I want," George said. He took the cards from Sam, patted them shut in his lap, cut, shuffled, cut again, shuffled again, cut. He handed the deck back to Sam. "Okay—ready."

Sam fanned the cards open. "Pick," he said.

"Not with you looking."

Sam twisted his head ostentatiously aside and shut his eyes. "Good enough for you?"

"Great." George picked. He looked at the card right away and broke into a broad smile. "Aces high?" he asked.

"Aces low," Sam said. He closed the deck in his fist.

George glared. "You didn't say that before."

"Why? Is that what you've got? An ace?"

"None of your business. Not yet. Let's let everybody pick, then we'll show what we've got. It's more fun that way."

Sam didn't argue. He headed back toward the front of the room and paused next to Danny's chair. But he turned the other way. "Carolina? How about you?"

"I'm ready."

"Do you want to cut too?"

"That's okay." She was wearing a snug-fitting nylon jumpsuit and heavy steel-soled boots that made walking easier under the low-gee conditions of *Leverrier*. Danny thought she looked absolutely gorgeous, but he'd always thought that, even if he'd certainly never told her so. Carolina kept largely to herself. Raymond—who was easily Danny's best friend among the team, and who didn't seem to care much for Carolina—said it was because she was a big wheel on Titan and thought she was better than the rest of them. "I think she's very pretty," Danny confided once. "Maybe," Raymond said, shrugging, "but she's married, too, I hear." "Married?" said Danny, who could hardly believe it. "She's got three husbands back on Titan." About the only person Carolina ever really palled around with was, of all of them, George. Raymond said that was only because they had something in common: nobody else liked either one of them. But Danny didn't dislike Carolina. He just didn't know her.

As she picked from the deck, Carolina noticed Danny staring at her and winked in his direction.

His face flushed, Danny averted his eyes.

By the time he looked back, Carolina held her card in her hand. She looked down at it. He saw her swallow hard.

Before Danny could decide what that might mean, Sam spun on a heel. "Okay, Danny, you're next."

"Uh, sure, Sam." Danny's stomach was suddenly as tight as a drum, his mouth dry as a desert. Well, at least I'm not falling asleep anymore, he thought bleakly. Reaching out quickly, he grabbed a card and held it against his chest. For a long time he didn't look. Which was it? High or low? Was it Neptune now or better luck next time? The strange part was that Danny didn't know which he wanted it to be. As Sam had said, after six months training, after countless hours in the hypnosimulators—where the mind, if not the body, actually seemed to be on Neptune—after a dozen MAGMOS voyages into the environmental chamber, where the opposite seemed to be true, Danny was as ready as he ever would be. But he was nervous. No, not nervous. Danny tried to be honest with himself. He was scared.

Danny looked at this card. He peeked at the corner. But it was enough. The ace. The ace of hearts.

Danny felt an instantaneous wave of relief wash over him, and realized the truth about himself. His fear had overwhelmed every other emotion. He was a coward.

Sam continued to roam the room. Benny Sims, like George, demanded a cut, and also like George, he cut, shuffled, cut. The two of them—George and Benny—had been spending an increasing amount of time together lately. Maybe because—like Raymond said about Carolina—nobody else really wanted to be around either of them. George was teaching him how to play cards, Benny said. Once, after a long day of hypnosimulator training, when they were all—even Carolina—eating dinner together in the station's tiny mess hall, Raymond had accused George of stealing money from a baby but George had just laughed, waved his fork at Benny, and said it was actually the other way around. "Don't sell the kid short. He's probably smarter than the rest of us put together."

Benny had beamed in utter delight at the compliment.

Now, poker-faced, Benny picked a card and examined it without changing expression.

Raymond was next. He picked his card without saying a word. Then came Duncan Broadhead. Duncan was silent too. But Duncan was always silent. According to Raymond, Duncan had probably been born without vocal cords, a fairly common condition among Earth mutations. Danny liked Duncan. Both of them were cripples of a kind, when you thought about it. Actually, everyone liked Duncan. Even George was always nice to him. It would have seemed cruel—given Duncan's other problems—not to be. Raymond said on Earth in the years right after the war, a number of mutants—just babies at the time—had been killed by mobs. That's why World President Armelino had decided to keep many of the worst separate from the rest of the population.

Raymond seemed to know a lot about Earth. He said it was because in the Belt as a freebooter with his own rover ship—he'd been born into a clan but had legally split as soon as he could at age nine—he'd spent so much time alone drifting in space from one rock to another that he'd had to find some hobby to fill the time. "So I listened to every radio or TV transmission I could pick up—a lot of them beamed from Earth and Luna. I knew someday I was going to take a few stanyears off and travel around the whole Solar System, seeing everything—I was already rich enough to afford it—and I wanted to know as much about the rest of the universe as I could before I got there."

It was little Nina's turn next—Olga Kropotkin's daughter, everyone had assumed, since their last names were the same and Nina had apparently grown up on *Leverrier* till Sam picked her for the project. But once Benny had gotten into a fight with her—Benny was always getting into fights—and said, "If you don't like it, why don't you tell your mother on me?"

"My who?" Nina had said.

"Your mother, Commander Olga, that's who."

"She's not my mother."

"Then who is?"

"I don't know."

"Then who's your father?"

She looked suddenly confused, as if it were a question she'd never considered before. "I don't know that either."

Benny smirked. "You sure are ignorant, aren't you?"

"No! I . . . I just never thought about it before."

It would have sounded utterly absurd coming from anyone else. But

Nina—Nina was such an otherworldly person, always lost in a universe of her own, that it was more than believable.

Benny seemed to have struck a chord, however, and later at dinner in the mess room, Danny happened to overhear Nina asking Olga and Sam at the far end of the table about her mother and father. Sam's reply was too soft for Danny to hear, though Sam was shaking his head when he said it.

Now, as Nina chose her card from Sam's deck, she suddenly let out a whoop of joy upon seeing it.

The trouble with that was, Danny thought, a whoop of joy might mean either of two things under the circumstances.

So, done, seven cards gone from the original fifty-two, Sam faced the entire group with a suddenly very serious expression on his face. "All right, my children. Shall we see what each of us has got? George"—he pointed a thick finger—"you picked first, you show first."

George needed no further prodding. He turned his card in his hand so that all of them could see. The two of hearts. A deuce. "Fooled you with that talk about aces, didn't I?"

Benny grunted in surprise. "But George, I thought you—"

Sam's finger was already pointing deftly. "Carolina, your turn."

She raised her hand and waggled the card overhead. Danny stretched his neck to see. A six. The six of clubs.

"In the middle," Sam said. "So far you're it, my dear, but we've a ways to go. Danny, how about you?"

Danny showed his ace of clubs, feeling reluctant somehow, as if exposing the low card also exposed his own fears. There was a gasp from somebody, but Sam smoothly said, "Aces low, we all agreed, so that puts you out of the running, Danny."

"I guess it does," he said, shrugging casually.

George snickered. "Beaten out by my own flesh and blood."

"Benny?" said Sam.

Benny turned, glaring at George, and held up his card. "Read it and weep, everybody." He was still looking at George. "Almost everybody, I mean."

The card was the king of spades.

Sam's expression was as solemn as a priest at a funeral. "It appears you're going to be it, son. They don't come much higher than that."

"They don't come *any* higher," Benny corrected in that ostentatiously adult tone of his.

"Raymond," Sam said, "would you—"

Nina was bouncing up and down in her chair, no mean feat under low-gee conditions. "Sam, I want to go next. Can I?"

Sam turned to her with a patient smile. "I don't see why not."

She showed him her card. It was a queen. The queen of hearts. "See, I'm going too. A king is the best, and then comes the queen. It's me and that loudmouth over there."

Sam, betraying no emotion, turned cooly. "Raymond, you can go ahead now."

Raymond turned up his card. It was another king—diamonds this time. "Sorry, Nina," he said, "but there are four kings in the deck."

"Oh, foop," she said, which made everybody smile, some brighter than others, though.

Sam said, "Duncan." Unlike some of the rest of them, Sam never fell into the trap of shouting at Duncan, who might not be able to speak, but whose hearing seemed as keen as anyone else's, even if he didn't have any actual ears.

Duncan held up his card. It was another queen. Hearts.

"Close," Sam said, "but not close enough."

He then went around the room, collecting the cards from everyone.

Back at the front, he said, "Raymond, Benny, you'll stay after I've dismissed the others. I know Bob will want to go over everything with you one last time, and I suspect Fred has some final words of advice also. After that I'm turning you both over to the physicians and medtechs for yet another total examination. The least indication of anything amiss and you're off the mission. For substitutes we'll start at the other end of the deck and work back up. That means, Danny, you're next in line, then George."

"Hey, we didn't—" George said.

"Shut up," Sam said crisply.

Surprisingly, George did just that. As for Danny, he wasn't going to protest, but he was definitely nervous again. Not scared, though, just nervous, and that was an improvement.

Sam said, "I've only one more thing to share with you, and it's a story I've carried around in my head more years than I can remember. It's a good story, though, one that may help all of you."

He cleared his throat and then went on. "Once upon a time there lived in the East—this is Earth, of course—a sage and his three young disciples on a mountaintop overlooking a thriving village. One day the sage called his disciples to him and told them that he was soon to die. 'I have ninety-nine days remaining to my earthly existence,' he announced, 'and then one of you must inherit my duties. Which of you shall it be?'

"The disciples, who were well-trained in matters of modesty, each declined the honor, suggesting that either or both of their fellows was more deserving.

"The sage grew angry, and reaching into a basket of dung he always kept beside him, removed three large handfuls and hurled them one after the other into the faces of his disciples.

" 'Fools!' he cried. 'If you were as unworthy as you state, then I, as your teacher, must be even less worthy. Go, I say. Go forth into the world for ninety-eight days, and at the end of that time return here bearing the wisdom of the universe that you have learned. Then I shall decide which of you shall assume my place.'

"The three dung-faced disciples went forth as ordered, and for ninety-eight days remained absent. At the end of that time the sage sat upon his mountaintop and awaited their return.

"The first disciple appeared soon after dawn's first light and bent to kiss the hem of his master's saffron robes.

" 'Ah,' said the sage, 'and what is it that you have brought me?'

" 'I have brought only what you asked: the wisdom of the universe.'

" 'And where is it?'

" 'In the valley below. Laden upon the backs of two hundred elephants. A great library of writings, the knowledge of the ancient scribes and scholars.'

" 'A welcome gift,' said the sage, 'for when winter comes, the people in the village shall have much fuel with which to feed their fires.' The sage reached into his dung basket, removed two handfuls, and hurled them into the face of his disciple. 'If knowledge and wisdom were one and the same, there would be little use for one such as I. But ignorance can sometimes be wisdom also, and it is only fools who have failed to learn this lesson from life. Now go, for I have no desire to entertain such stupidity on this my last day on Earth.'

"The sun stood high in the sky when the second disciple appeared and knelt before his master.

" 'Ah,' said the sage, 'and what is it that you have brought me?'

" 'I have brought only what you asked: the wisdom of the universe.'

" 'And where is it?'

" 'Here in my hands,' said the disciple. And he showed the sage a blue sapphire of perfect shape and tremendous size. Peering into the depths of the jewel, the sage saw much that he had himself long since forgotten. He bowed his head and wept silent tears. 'You have done well,' the sage proclaimed, 'in bringing to this humble place an object of true beauty.' He put a hand inside his dung basket, removed one small handful, and flung it into the face of his disciple. 'Beauty is only one particle of wisdom. If it were all, then we would have no need for men such as I, since our senses alone would suffice to show us all that is truly wise. Now go. The hour is getting late.'

"It was dusk when the third disciple appeared at last. He was the youngest of the three, not yet old enough to shave the hairs upon his chin. He stood before his master, holding his hands clenched in front of him.

" 'Ah,' said the sage, 'and what is it that you have brought me?'

" 'I have brought only what you asked: the wisdom of the universe.'

" 'And where is it?'

" 'It is here,' said the disciple, opening his hands and showing the empty palms.

" 'You have brought me nothing,' the sage said.

" 'I have brought myself, master, for it is certain that no other wisdom shall I know or ever need seek to know.'

"The sage rose to his feet. 'Sit,' he said, pointing to his place beside the dung basket. 'From this moment you are the sage.'

"And with that the old sage went down from his mountaintop and was found the following day in the valley below, dead in the shade of a banyan tree."

Sam again cleared his throat. "Benny, Raymond," he said in a soft voice, "you know to stay. The rest of you, when there's news, will be informed. Until then, keep busy."

SEVENTEEN

Danny eyed the distant circle of the iron hoop on the other side of the room, a good twenty meters from where he was standing. It was an impossible shot to be sure, but the way the game was going, that was the only way he was ever going to win: by making impossible shots.

Ready at last, he locked his hands over his head, bent his knees, tensed, and then sprang, hurling his body into the air as high as it would go, letting the ball sail off his fingertips, using sheer physical momentum as a propellant. As he fluttered back to the floor, Danny never lost sight of the ball as it arced rainbowlike through the air, struck the rim of the hoop, bounced high, dropped, hit the rim a second time, bounced, and then fell cleanly, piercing the net with a sound as pretty as music. Stunned by his own success, Danny let out a yelp, tossed both arms in the air and cried, "I did it! You'll never top that shot! Never in a hundred billion years!"

Placidly, Duncan Broadhead chased the ball down and retrieved it. He dribbled slowly over to the spot on the floor Danny had occupied while shooting, and stopped there. Danny, now sitting on the floor, watched in fascination as Duncan eyed the basket, cocked his wrists, and then with an apparently effortless leap, let the ball slide off the tips of his fingers. The moment it left Duncan's hands Danny knew there was no way it was going to miss. With a groan he shut his eyes and kept them shut till he heard the distant *whish* that signified Duncan's shot had been as straight and true as it had appeared from the beginning, hitting nothing but net.

"All right," Danny said. "That does it. I quit. Don't you ever miss, Duncan? I pull off an impossible shot and then you go and do the same thing, like you've been doing it all your life. It isn't fair, I'm telling you."

As stone-faced as always, Duncan crossed to where Danny was sitting

and offered his hand. With a helpless shrug Danny took it and stood upright. He was wearing his electric leg braces, although he'd set them at the lowest power. Maybe if he turned them up a notch higher, got slightly more spring into his leap . . . But, no, that would be like cheating. And winning when you cheated just wasn't as much fun.

It was more fun than losing, though, right?

Still, Danny made no move to adjust the braces.

He and Duncan were here, just beyond *Leverrier*'s central hub, trying to do what Sam had told them: keeping busy. Danny assumed this place was supposed to be the station gymnasium. He had stumbled upon it by accident a few nights ago after a particularly arduous hypnosimulator session. Apart from the basketball hoop, there was also a set of barbells in one corner and a long rope dangling from the ceiling for climbing. Nothing in here looked as if it had been disturbed in ages. Didn't scientists and engineers ever exercise? he wondered. Even the basketball had been as flat as a waffle. He and Duncan had had to hunt around for a pump to blow it up again. Still, it was something to do. And it didn't cause him to think about what might be happening on Neptune right now.

According to the rules of the game, it was Danny's turn now to duplicate the shot Duncan had just made, which had in turn been a duplication of Danny's original shot. If Danny made his shot, then it would be Duncan's turn again. And so on. Whoever missed first, it would count one point for the other person. So far they'd been playing about an hour, and the score stood at Duncan ninety-eight, Danny two.

Taking his position, Danny bounced the ball a couple times and heaved a sigh. The hoop appeared farther away than ever. He pumped his knees, rocked on the balls of his feet, cocked his wrists, and sprang. His heart wasn't in it, though. The impossible sometimes happened once, never twice. His leap lifted him barely a meter off the floor. For a moment he hung there, the ball cupped in his hands as heavy as lead. He knew he wasn't going to make this shot. Or even come close.

Then, just as he let go of the ball, something amazing happened. As the ball slid off his fingertips, it was as if an invisible hand swept down from nowhere, caught hold of the ball, and carried it through space toward the hoop. Back on the floor Danny watched incredulously as the ball plummeted through the net as clean as a vacuum tube.

He just stood there, mouth agape, unable to move. How in the universe . . . ? He pointed at Duncan. "You did that, didn't you?"

Duncan stared back at him, slack-jawed and stone-faced.

That got Danny mad. It was enough to lose all the time. It was worse having somebody cheat so that you could finally win.

He raced across the floor, shaking his finger. "I want to know how you did that. If you—"

He stopped, realizing how ridiculous he must sound. Duncan hadn't been anywhere close to the ball. How could he possibly have directed its flight? It must be my imagination, Danny thought. Okay, so I made two impossible shots in a row. It was a miracle—but maybe it could happen after all.

"Okay, your turn," he mumbled.

Duncan chased eagerly after the ball, grabbed it off the floor, took up his place, dawdled an instant, then leaped and fired. The ball didn't come anywhere close to the hoop, ricocheting harmlessly off the wall.

So that made it Duncan ninety-eight, Danny three.

Thoughts of a comeback stirring in his head—miracles could indeed happen, right?—Danny went after the ball. For his next shot he stood considerably closer to the basket, turned his back toward it, and arched his neck, letting his head hang nearly upside down so that he could just glimpse the rim of the hoop. As he stood there, mentally mapping a trajectory, a voice broke through his concentration. "Okay if I come in?"

Danny let go of the ball, lowered his head, spun, and saw Carolina standing in the doorway. She was wearing denim shorts, a blue long-sleeved jersey, and knee-high cotton socks. "What is this weird place anyway?" she asked, stepping inside. "It's huge."

Much of the interior of *Leverrier*'s spoked wheel, exclusive of the docking facilities in the hub and the various offices and laboratories in the outer rim, was honeycombed with a myriad of separate cubicles, many of them small and most of them empty. The station had clearly been designed in anticipation of a much larger permanent population than now existed. But that wasn't especially surprising. The Combine was well known for always trying to plan several decades in advance.

"I think it's supposed to be the gym," Danny said. "Nobody's used it in a long time, though."

"That's no big surprise. Dr. Mobutu looks great, but most of these people, the scientists and stuff, ugh. If they lived on Titan, we'd make them exercise till they dropped. It's a law there that you have to keep in shape."

"A law?" Danny asked.

"Well, not officially. I proposed it once just after I came on the council, but the others said it wasn't necessary. They said on Titan, with so few people and most of them living under the one primary dome, you didn't

need a lot of laws to force people to do things for their own good. I don't know. I just hate fat people. They're so lazy and self-centered. Don't they make you kind of sick too?"

"Well, Sam's fat," he said before he could stop himself. He didn't really want to get into an argument with her.

But she seemed more taken aback than put out. "You know, I never thought of that. You couldn't call him skinny, that's for sure. But Sam's so old. It seems different."

"Aren't there any old people on Titan?"

"Not really. They almost always leave once people start pointing out that they're not carrying their full load anymore. If they don't, the council steps in. We have a common fund set up to take care of them on Mars or Luna or wherever they want to go."

"That must be tough. Having to leave your home after so many years."

"That's where most people make their mistake. Thinking of Titan as a home. It's not. A home is what we hope to turn it into someday. Right now it's just a place where a few thousand people try to cling to life and survive."

"And you like it?" he said.

"I love it."

Danny shrugged. People were so different. And, besides, how could he be sure? Maybe if he went to Titan, he'd love it too. Not that they'd ever let him in. Not with his legs. That would be worse than being fat.

Carolina was looking across the room to where Duncan stood bouncing the basketball up and down. "Were you two playing a game?"

"Well, in a way. Why?"

"I didn't mean to break anything up. I was just curious when I heard noises in here."

"No, that's okay. We were almost finished anyway."

"Is it a game three can play?" she asked.

"Not really, no, but—look, why don't you and I just play?"

"If he doesn't mind."

"Who? Duncan? No, he doesn't mind."

"Then show me how the game works."

Danny took up his previous position with his back to the hoop. He waved at Duncan to pass him the ball. Duncan did. Hard. The ball seemed to explode when it hit Danny in the gut.

He frowned, started to say something, then thought better of it. He turned and stood with his head hanging nearly upside down. "The idea is,

I try to make a really difficult shot like this one." He tossed the ball in the general direction of the hoop. "Then if it goes in, you have—"

Whish.

Danny stopped, unable to believe his ears. He'd just given the ball a toss, not even aiming.

He turned and looked at Carolina, who was staring at the hoop. "Did that go in?" he asked.

"It sure did. Wow, what a shot. You're good."

"No, just lucky." He glared at Duncan, who was sitting on the floor, holding his knees in his hands and looking innocent. Danny didn't care how absurd it might seem, he was positive now. Duncan could definitely control the flight of the ball.

"Now, what do I have to do?" Carolina asked.

"You, uh, if I make the shot, you have to make it too."

"And if I don't?"

"Then it's a point for me."

"Maybe we ought to skip the game and just let you give me lessons."

"I'm not really that good," he said, speaking the truth.

"You couldn't prove it by me."

Carolina ran after the ball. Danny looked across at Duncan and moved his lips silently. *Knock it off. She's not hurting anything.*

Carolina put her back to the hoop, blond curls spilling off her head, aimed, and launched the ball. It didn't miss the net by more than an arm's length. All in all, an excellent shot.

"It's going to take me time to adjust for the difference in gravity," she said. "I'm still used to Titan."

"That was a great shot," he said.

"It was also a point for you."

Danny took the ball and went in for a lay-up. It wasn't as easy a shot for him as for most people, because of the importance of timing the leap. He didn't get it exactly right this time, but it was close enough. The ball banked off the backboard, hit the rim, spun a circle, and dropped through the net.

"Hey, don't be easy on me," she said, making the same shot without difficulty.

"I'm not." It was his turn now. He had to make the same lay-up. This time something went wrong. When it came time to leap, his legs refused to respond. He barely cleared the floor. The ball bounced futilely off the bottom of the backboard.

"You slipped," she said.

"No, it was my legs. The muscles get tired all of a sudden, and I have to adjust the braces to compensate."

"We can quit."

"Oh, no," he said quickly. "I don't want to quit."

But Carolina just stood, holding the ball. "Can I ask you something, Danny?"

"Sure. What?"

"This morning. You knew what was going on, didn't you? With George. That he fixed the deck."

Danny wasn't surprised. Knowing George, he'd certainly had his suspicions. "Sam would have stopped him if he'd tried that."

"If Sam knew."

"Sam's not dumb."

"I know," she said, "and that's what bothers me." She dipped her knees and threw up a gentle set shot. The ball cleared the net with a soft whish. "If Sam knew, why did he let George get away with it?"

"Well . . ." Danny had been wondering about that himself.

"All George could really have done was fix his own card. So I guess Sam felt, if he doesn't want to go, then why force him?"

She nodded. "The trouble is, that isn't all George did. He fixed the next card too—mine."

"How?"

"Creased the edge. When he was shuffling, I suppose. Only a little, but when Sam held out the deck, it was the first thing that caught my eye."

"You didn't pick it, though?"

"I picked it."

"But why?"

"Curiosity. After all, George couldn't have known it was going to be my card. You were the one sitting closest to him. The obvious thing would have been for Sam to go to you next."

"You think the card was supposed to be mine, then?"

She shrugged. "At first I did."

"George should have known I wouldn't have gone along with anything like that."

"Maybe, maybe not. But what if you had? That to me was the strange part. It wasn't an ace or a deuce. It was a six. Why a six? I mean, with seven of us picking, the odds against your going—or my going, since it ended up being my card—were pretty slim. But not impossible either."

Danny thought he understood. That would have been George's way of being scrupulously fair, of avoiding absolutes. And he would have thought it was funny. George must have had a ball watching Carolina's face when she pulled his six out of the deck.

Danny started to explain his reasoning to her.

Carolina cut him off with a nod. "I know. That's pretty much what George said too."

"You asked him?"

"Sure. Why not? Just before I wandered down here I went by his room. He was in there, taking a nap. Can you believe that? Taking a nap, with everything else that's going on."

"George is a cool one, that's for sure."

She nodded. "Anyway, he said the card wasn't just meant strictly for you. He said he figured it was probably going to be either you or me, but whoever it was, he wanted to give them a better than even shot. He said it was no big deal. Benny did it, too, he claimed. Stacked his own card. I don't know about that."

It wasn't something Danny had considered before either. But Benny had certainly been spending a lot of time with George lately. Usually playing poker too. "I wonder if Sam knew about that," he said.

She shrugged. "Who can tell? With Sam, I'm beginning to understand almost anything's possible. What did you think of that weird story he told us there at the end? Did it make any sense to you at all?"

"Well, a little," Danny admitted.

"Not me. But I'm different from the rest of you. I'm the only real colonial in the bunch, you know."

"Is that why you've—you know—sort of kept to yourself?"

"Have I?"

"Except for George you—"

"Oh, George." She smiled. "Don't think I like George. I don't. But when I said you were all different—well, George is the most different of all. When I first saw him in action back on Triton, I thought he was a complete jerk, but, you know, he's a kind of a fascinating jerk too. George was an actor on Mars, he told me. He appeared in stage plays and everything. We don't allow anything like that on Titan. It's frivolity, we call it. George is like an entirely different universe for me."

"George lived on Ganymede for a while," Danny blurted out.

"He didn't tell me that."

"They kicked him out of the colony—for not working."

She laughed. "Isn't that just what I said? George could have done it, but he didn't want to. By the way, whose turn is it anyway?"

"Yours,'" he said sullenly. It was actually his turn—she'd thrown up that set shot while they were talking—but he was tired of giving her all the breaks. "You get to pick your own shot this time."

"Oh, lovely." She went after the ball, stood for a moment seemingly lost in thought, then dribbled the full length of the floor clear to the opposite wall. Turning, she faced the hoop and gave it a long careful stare. Then she shut her eyes, making a broad face. "Watch me," she called out. "I can't see a thing, right?"

"Sure," he said.

Carolina appeared to curl herself up into a tight knot of hard muscle. Danny hadn't noticed before how physically powerful she was. When the knot of muscle unraveled like an explosion of energy, the ball came spurting cleanly from the middle of it, rocketing into the air. The shot was certainly long enough. Too long, he thought. The ball hit the backboard and banged high. Then it took a weird bounce, plummeting straight down. *Swish* went the net as the ball plunged through. Incredibly, Carolina had made her blind shot.

She was gaping in wide-eyed astonishment. Then she burst out laughing. "I can't believe it. I—honestly, I never thought . . . not in fifty hundred million years . . . not that shot. I was trying to give you a break."

"I don't need any breaks," Danny said, running down the ball.

Now it was his turn again. When he got to the far end of the room and looked back at the hoop, it was like peering through the wrong end of a telescope. This is nuts, he thought.

"Don't forget to close your eyes," she called over to him. "No peeking either."

From this distance peeking wasn't apt to do him much good. With a sigh Danny shut his eyes. Let's get this over with, he thought. Hunching down low, he strained to make his muscles hard and tight, the way she had. Then he uncorked. His feet came off the floor and the ball floated free from his hands.

When he opened his eyes it was just in time to see the ball flutter through the net.

He stood there, open-mouthed and staring.

Carolina wasn't laughing anymore. She was staring too.

"My God," she said softly.

"What happened?" Danny asked.

"You didn't see?"

"I forgot to open my eyes."

"It—Your shot—it wasn't even coming close. Then all of a sudden the ball was in the middle of the air—you could see it happen—it changed direction. The ball did. And it went through."

"But that's—"

"I saw it. Do you think I'd make up something like that? How did you do it? Is it the way you grip the ball or what?"

Danny glanced at Duncan, who was sitting impassively on the floor with a blank, distant expression on his face. Danny went across to Carolina. "I think it's him," he said in a soft voice, a whisper. "He was doing it before you came too. I think he can control things, objects, control them with his mind."

"And what else?" she asked anxiously.

"Huh? What do you mean?"

"You say he's got psych powers, right? So what's the limit? Can he read minds too?"

"I don't know. He doesn't talk. How could you tell?"

"Well, at least it makes sense now."

"What makes sense?"

"He does. Duncan. I knew he was a mutant, of course, but it still didn't explain what he was doing here with the rest of us. We're supposed to be a special group, the best there is in the whole Solar System. So why Duncan?"

"Because Sam must have found out what he could do."

She nodded. "You bet. So now there's only one of us I can't figure out."

"Me," Danny said automatically.

She touched his arm reassuringly. "Not you. I admit I had my doubts in the beginning, but the way you breezed through training, I saw I was wrong. And then George told me some things about your life. You're shy and kind of insecure, but none of that really matters. You're also smart and quick and everything else you need to be. No, it's Nina I can't figure out. The little girl."

Danny had to admit Carolina had a definite point. Nina was such a sweet, likable kid, he'd never really thought about it. She was intelligent, certainly, but exceptionally so? Special? It was hard to see.

Carolina was looking at Duncan. "Do you know what we do on Titan if a mutant happens to be conceived? It hardly ever happens, because we do a genetic screen on everyone who comes from Earth, but every once in a while. We require the mother to abort the fetus. If for some reason there is a birth, the baby is killed."

"That's horrible. Not all mutants—"

"Oh, sure, and on Earth you just pen them up in camps."

"For their own protection."

"Not from some of the things I've heard. I've heard if they're considered dangerous, like Duncan over there, then they're killed."

"Duncan's not dangerous."

"Then what's he up to? Why did he do that with the ball?"

"He likes me. He was trying to help me win the game."

"Well, he did a swell job." She looked at the hoop. "I'll yield you the point." She fumbled with her wristwatch, one of the big spacer models that could tell the exact time anywhere in the Solar System at the press of a few buttons. "Look, it's been almost two hours since they were supposed to be scrambled. Maybe we ought to head out to the rim and see if there's any news."

"Don't you want to finish the game first? We could play up to ten."

"With him around?"

"I'll tell him to knock it off."

"Never mind. Besides, Sam might not know where to find us."

Danny turned to glare at Duncan, angry at him for spoiling everything. But he stopped short, staring.

Carolina was looking too. "Is something the matter with him?"

Something was definitely the matter with Duncan. His noseless face was covered with a sheen of sweat, the veins in his forehead as tight as wires.

"I don't know," he said, walking across. "I've never seen him like—"

Duncan's scream smothered Danny's words. It was like a howling, shrieking crescendo, rising and falling. Duncan sprang to his feet, his whole body shaking as if each muscle were being jerked on separate strings.

Danny grabbed Duncan's shoulders and held him. "Duncan, what's wrong?"

Carolina came hurrying up from behind. She swung her hand, slapping Duncan hard across the face.

The scream died out. The blank look left his eyes. His muscles relaxed. He was crying silently, tears running down his face. "Benny," he said suddenly. "Benny is . . . hurt . . . real awful."

They were the first words any of them had ever heard Duncan speak.

EIGHTEEN

Gornami-yev (the former dunce) feels the atmosphere of the Neptune-world tingling around him as if the air itself is a living thing, churning with anticipation of events yet to come. A mighty storm rages as the heavens clash, thunder roaring, lightning crackling. Gornami-yev squats in the open beyond the translucent lodge-homes of his fellow Kith, hunkered down on six splayed limbs while the brutal rain beats a rhythm against his upturned shell. His loving friend Nykol (the believer), returned from the dead, huddles at his side. Both Kith observe the approach of the two former human beings.

"So you were correct!" Gornami-yev cries, speaking duncelike from habit in the first-tongue. "Again they venture to poke about in matters which do not concern them."

It is the normal pattern among these human creatures, Nykol says, utilizing the clarity of the soul speech. *It is a thing called curiosity, an unquenchable thirst for pure knowledge.*

"Of which there is no such thing among the many-elders of the Kith."

Alas, no. When it is understood that everything will eventually be learned, then curiosity ceases to exist. Only patience is required. (There is warm laughter.) *For you, the once born, however, all is quite different.*

"I am no human being!" Gornami-yev flares.

But there are similarities. Youth itself, this thing of curiosity, and the death that is final and absolute.

"I will die?" Gornami-yev asks, trembling suddenly. "Die forever?"

The possibility lessens with each passing moment. You have grown much, my friend. But these humans . . .

"When first they came among us—"

Enough! Use the speech of your elders. My ears ache from your duncelike shouting.

My apologies, many-elder.

That is better. Now proceed.

When first these human creatures came among us—Gornami-yev is surprised and pleased at the eloquence of his voice—*it was said that they lacked the life-force, that death for them must be absolute and final.*

In the ignorance of youth you misunderstood. All living entities possess the life-force, but the humans have not yet detected its presence within themselves.

Will they?

Look for yourself. The future lies open to the internal eye.

But I see nothing.

Look again, my young friend.

Gornami-yev looks, but the riddle of the future does not reveal itself. What he glimpses is a misty cloud, indefinite and shifting.

Do you see? Nykol inquires.

No. Nothing. It is vague—shapeless like a gas.

But only because you have not yet learned to see totally. It is the same with humans and the life-force that lies within them.

But I know of the life-force.

You have been told. That is a different thing.

But—

Hush. The humans draw near. It is our task to observe them.

Gornami-yev observes as the humans in their transformed shapes slither and slide clumsily upon the icy slick surface of the Neptune-world. One slips and tumbles dangerously before being brought up short against an outcropping of ice. The other human rushes to his side, the scent of fear filling the fabric of the air like a rude stink.

"They stumble like fools," Gornami-yev says, reverting to the smugness of the first tongue.

Or children, Nykol says wistfully.

Children? (The concept is a puzzle.) *What do you mean?*

Nykol forms the image of a tiny shell-less Kith. *This is a child.*

"I have never seen—" Gornami-yev blurts out.

Not that you remember, but the truth is that you yourself were a child not long ago, and even I, Nykol (the believer), nine times reborn, was one, though very long ago. A child is the initial particle riven from the cosmic flux into which the life-force is injected.

A brother-sister, two of which you have born me in other realm-times?

No. A brother-sister is an act of simple division. A child is pure creation.

But why have I never seen one?

They are most rare, my friend. Among us Kith, one is created for each winking of the cosmic flux. Among the human beings, many billions appear within the same span.

An amazing feat.

They are an amazing race—young, while we Kith are truly ancient.

The two wait alone. Their fellow Kith remain ensconced within their lodge-homes, or else, having long-burrowed, engage upon other, unseen labors.

"Nykol, look over there," Gornami-yev says with sudden excitement. "There is another human being—a third."

Ah, yes. (The severity of the storm having lessened considerably, the two now venture to peer farther beyond the limits of their own shells. Abruptly, as if to caution against complacency, a blast of thunder rattles the air.) *That is the one often called Dav.*

The wanderer?

And the seeker, yes.

I did not realize that Dav—of whom many tales are told—was a former human being.

Once, yes, but now . . . it is uncertain. His life-force melds separate strands, some human, some Kith. He seeks to know the-one-who-is-nothing.

But that is death.

And life. Dav is one who must be respected.

And feared? Gornami-yev asks, staring at the watchful figure in the distance.

Not feared. Pitied perhaps. His spiritual essence lies torn.

But what does he want here now?

The same as you and I: to observe the coming of these new human beings.

Gornami-yev is struck by a sudden thought. *Will he seek to return with them to his own kind?*

I cannot answer. His personal warmth-fabric remains too human. His future cannot be glimpsed even by one of ten lifespans.

I think that's why he's come here, Gornami-yev rushes on. *I think Dav is* —he pauses to search for the concept—*homesick.*

We shall see. Come. It is time for us to greet these new human beings.

The two Kith edge forward. Above, masses of clouds form radiant whirlpool patterns. A steady, gentle wind sweeps the icy land.

The thunder stands mute—as if in wait.

NINETEEN

"**A**ll right, son," Sam said in a voice as gentle as a falling feather. He edged his chair closer to the cot and then bent forward to peer down at the boy lying there. "Just take your time. None of us is in that much of a hurry. Collect your thoughts, arrange them in sequence, and then tell us exactly what happened down there and when it happened."

"But that's just it, Sam," Raymond cried. "It's what I've been trying to get you to understand." He sat up slowly, spreading his arms, looking beyond Sam to where Fred Berman and Bob Mobutu stood, each slightly behind and to one side of Sam's chair. The room was a tiny, cramped cubicle next door to the station dispensary and packed tightly with an assortment of medical gadgetry, the specific purposes of which were not immediately discernable. "There isn't any sequence. It's all mixed up, a crazy jumble. It's like everything happened at once."

"It didn't," Bob Mobutu said. "You and Benny were down there exactly forty-seven minutes, fifteen seconds. We monitored your separate positions the entire time. If you want, I can let you review the readouts."

"And what would that prove?" Raymond said. "I don't care what your computer says must have happened. I'm telling you what really did happen. I was the one who was down there, damn it."

"Of course you were," Sam said soothingly, twisting his head and grimacing at Mobutu, cautioning him to pick his words more carefully. "Forget what I said before, Raymond. That was thoughtless of me. Tell your story whichever way you remember it, the best you can. If it doesn't seem to make sense right away, maybe it will later, when we know more. And maybe it's not even supposed to. Remember, what you've gone through has driven every other person who's tried it insane. You're not insane, Raymond. That's an achievement."

"If it's true," Raymond said, with a sound that was half laugh, half sob.

"Oh, it's true," Fred Berman said. "I ought to know. I'm the psychiatrist here, don't forget."

"Sorry, Doc," Raymond said, smiling thinly. "I didn't mean anything."

"Then stop questioning my judgment. If you're insane, then I'm the reincarnation of Napoleon Bonaparte, and that fellow over there"—he nodded at Mobutu—"is the last emperor of Ethiopia."

"Okay, you win." Still smiling, Raymond lay back on the cot and shut his eyes. It was as if the reassurance Berman had just provided was what he'd been waiting for all along. "God, I'm tired. Forty-seven minutes, huh? The way my body feels, I could have been down there forever."

"That's only to be expected," Mobutu said. "The MAGMOS Process itself is physically draining. You should have been prepared after the various run-throughs we put you through in the environmental chamber."

"That was a big joke," Raymond said. His eyes were open again.

"It was? In what sense?"

"In every sense. It wasn't real. This was. And that's what made it a joke."

"Forget about that for now," Sam broke in. He didn't want this to degenerate into an argument over training procedure. "We can go into specific mission details later on. Right now what we need to know, Raymond, is what happened to you on Neptune. And what happened to poor Benny."

"All right." Raymond took a breath and swallowed hard. "I'll try to remember, Sam. Just give me a couple more seconds, okay?" Reaching up with his hands, he rubbed his temples as if to jar the memories loose. "I told you there were two of them, right? Two Kith. That's the first really clear memory I can dredge up. Before that . . . only it's not really before. It's before, but it's also during and afterward too. You never had any definite sense of time down there. It was—" He laughed suddenly. "Maybe I should have worn my watch. Anyway, it was like I said before—it was a jumble, like being trapped inside one of those toy kaleidoscopes kids play with and a big hand kept jerking it back and forth. Colors everywhere, colors that kept changing, and jagged shapes like rocks, and you'd take a step forward, try to take a step—remember, we had twelve legs, and it wasn't easy—and there might be nothing there to stand on, and you'd think you were going to fall through the heart of the world. Part of the time I thought I was going to die, and the other part I was sure I was dead already. It was like clinging by your fingers to the edge of a cliff, and when you finally pulled yourself up, there'd be another cliff there and you'd be clinging to that one the same as before. I've never been as scared in my life. Except—and this is probably what got me through—fear is a feeling, and I didn't have any feelings. Feelings are human, and I wasn't human anymore."

"That's something I tried to inculcate during the final hypnosimulator sessions," Berman said. "An attitude of apartness, separation from self. When you come down to it, that may be what keeps the mass of us from going collectively insane. If we felt all of our real emotions—felt them truly all of the time—we'd probably go mad, too."

"Well, I didn't," Raymond said. "It was like there were two of me. One part was the Neppie part—"

"Neppie?" Mobutu asked.

"That's what we kids call ourselves when we're the slugs," Raymond said.

"The MAGMOS forms," Sam said. "But go on, Raymond. You're doing fine."

"So everything was jumbled, and then suddenly there were these two Kith standing right in front of me, with a sheet of ice underfoot and the domes, their city, whatever you want to call it, a little ahead. Things made sense, and you don't know what a relief that was. It wasn't cold, though. Even the ice. It should have been cold, shouldn't it?"

"Presumably it was," Mobutu said. "The MAGMOS form was designed deliberately to contain severely limited nerve endings in the extremities. There seemed no point in providing an acute sensitivity to pain."

"Was Benny with you then?" Sam broke in. "When you first saw the Kith, were the two of you still together?"

"Oh, sure," Raymond said. "Benny was always there. Even when nothing else was making sense, I always knew Benny was close. Sometimes he was right next to me and sometimes he was inside me. That was scary, though."

"But unreal," Berman said.

"The hell if it was. If you think it was unreal, why don't you go down there and look for yourself. It was as real as you are, Doc."

"Now we're getting into metaphysics," Berman said lightly. "That's more Sam's field of interest than mine."

"And how was Benny doing?" Sam said. "Could you tell?"

"Well, in a way. He was doing better than me. I'm pretty sure of that."

"Why?"

"Two things that I can remember. Once I looked over and he was doing something really crazy with his feet. Sliding them back and forth on the ice and shaking his whole body at the same time. It was the funniest thing you'd ever want to see. I think he was trying to do a dance. And another time I remember slipping and falling and Benny came rushing over to help. I couldn't have helped anyone then, not even myself, so Benny must have been doing better than me."

"And you were together when you saw the two Kith?"

"Right. Nykol and Gornami-yev. Benny and I were together."

"You know their names?"

"The Kith? Sure."

"How?"

"I . . . don't know. I . . . they couldn't have told me. They made noises sometimes, and maybe it was supposed to be speech, but of course it wasn't any language . . . wait. Now I remember. They could speak inside your head—mostly images, but sometimes sounds too."

"Telepathy?" Sam said.

"Yes, though like I said, it wasn't so much words as images and moods and feelings and . . . but you could usually figure it out. That's how I learned their names. I don't know if they'd say it the same—Nykol and Gornami-yev—but that's as close as I can come."

The door opened then and Eileen stepped inside, accompanied by Olga Kropotkin. The already cramped room was getting very crowded now. "Raymond was just describing his first encounter with the Kith," Sam explained. "I'm having a tape made, of course, but it may be helpful if both of you stay and listen."

Raymond lifted his head and looked at the two women. "How's Benny doing?" he asked.

Eileen glanced at Sam, who nodded. She said, "His condition's no different. He's been sedated—enough so that he ought to be out like a light—but the medtechs say he's still fully conscious. If there's any change, they'll let us know. Nina's sitting with him right now."

"He's still in that trance, then?"

"Catatonia. But it may not be that bad a sign. During the first project—"

"Our best hope," Berman said smoothly, "is that Benny's present catatonia represents an internal psychological struggle to reconcile his experiences on Neptune with his own ordered sanity. If he succeeds, then he may be able to return to us in a relatively normal state of mind."

"But you don't know that for sure," Raymond said.

"We don't even know what happened to him down there."

"I know. That's what I'm supposed to be trying to remember. It's in there somewhere, but it's so—"

"Just continue the way you have," Sam broke in reassuringly. "It seems to be working. After you and Benny first saw the Kith, what happened next?"

"They took us inside one of their domes. That's the next thing I seem to remember, anyway, and it couldn't have happened before we met them. It was one big room, very bright, with pinkish-white walls that moved in and out like they were breathing. Benny and I both rested on our stomachs. I don't care how many muscles we're supposed to have in our legs, trying to move around in all that gravity—especially on ice—still wears you out. One of the Kith went away—it was Gornami-yev—and when he came back, he had this big bowl filled with this sticky-looking goo. He put in a hand, pulled out a gob, and stuffed it in his mouth. Then he passed the bowl to Benny and he ate some too. It was like a ceremony of some sort. Then it was my turn. Benny pushed the bowl over toward me with his front legs and I—"

"You were both taking an awful risk," Eileen said. "What if you'd poisoned yourselves?"

"Not likely," Mobutu said. "Since the MAGMOS form was never designed for extended life, it lacks any sort of digestive system. Basically, if something's eaten, it will be excreted almost immediately in its original state."

"The Kith must have appreciated finding that on their floor," Eileen said.

Raymond looked acutely embarrassed, which Sam chose to interpret as yet another favorable sign. Sam was beginning to shed much of his initial anxiety that at any moment Raymond might slide into the schizophrenia of his predecessors and be lost to them forever. Yes, certainly, his memories were garbled. Yes, certainly, he'd had a tough time of it. But he'd come through. He'd survived, he was sane, and it appeared likely he was going to stay that way.

"Well, I ate some of it anyway," Raymond went on. "If you're careful about what you're doing, you can stand upright on just ten legs and use the front two as sort of handless arms."

"That was intended in the original design," Mobutu said.

"Anyway, it worked and I managed to get my head close enough to the bowl to grab a mouthful. The first bite tasted like pineapples. The second was more like fresh bananas. It was delicious too."

"Pyotr Romanov's banquet of fresh fruit," Eileen murmured softly.

"I know," Raymond said. "As soon as I swallowed the first bite, I remembered reading about him in our briefing book. It was funny, in a way. Sometimes I could remember everything, who and what I really was, and other times I was nothing more than this twelve-legged slug on a frozen ball of a world, standing around with a couple of giant turtles, eating goo out of a bowl."

"In actuality," Sam said, "you were both. So what happened next, son?"

"Well, when the bowl was empty—we kept shoving it back and forth between the three of us—the other Kith, the one called Nykol, didn't eat any—Benny went straight into action. That's another reason why I think he was handling things better than me. He got right down on the floor and started drawing circles. He drew one big one in the center and nine smaller ones on the outside, the Sun and the major planets. Then he pointed at the eighth circle and to the Kith, and then at the third circle and to him and me. He was trying to get across who we were and where we'd come from. Then Nykol went over and picked up Benny's foreleg and moved it away from the circles and put it back down on the floor. Then he pointed to himself. I think he was trying to explain that the Kith weren't originally from Neptune, that they'd come from somewhere else."

"Another star system," Mobutu said.

Sam flashed him a warning look. It wasn't that he disputed his conclusion. It was simply too soon yet to be sure about anything.

Sam looked down at Raymond. "You told us earlier, son, that the Kith are telepathic. What I fail to understand is why it is necessary for Benny to go through this rigmarole with the circles when he could have communicated his thoughts directly."

"He . . . he did," Raymond said, sounding surprised by his own memory. "Everything I just told you about, the only way it actually happened was in our heads. Benny couldn't have drawn circles on the floor anyway. It was hard and smooth as plate glass. And that's also when I found out their names—Nykol and Gornami-yev."

"But did you find out anything else concerning the origin of the Kith?" Mobutu put in impatiently. Sam had long since given up any thought of attempting to control the gathering. And besides, it seemed to help Raymond to participate in the give-and-take. "Did you bother to ask how they'd reached Neptune if their origin was outside the system?"

"Well, I meant to," Raymond said. "It was the next thing on my mind. But then I looked around and Benny wasn't there."

"He'd left?" Sam said. "How?"

"I had no way of knowing. I hadn't seen a thing, though that wasn't too surprising, not with all that other stuff going on inside my head. It was like listening to loud music on earphones and trying to hear a conversation in the room at the same time. You can do it, but it's not easy. The Kith were still there, and I figured they had to know something, but either my thoughts weren't getting through or else they were ignoring them. So I decided to show them how upset I was and took a run at the wall—ran as hard as I could run—and rammed my head against it. That wasn't too smart a move. The wall was actually kind of soft—almost squishy—but I still nearly knocked myself cold."

"The MAGMOS form lacks much bony protection in the skull area," Mobutu said. "Because of the need to place additional mass in the legs and underbelly."

"So I remembered," Raymond said. "After I'd hit my head. Anyway, it seemed to work, because I was standing there, reeling, when a hole oozed open in the wall just where I'd rammed it. That's the only way I can describe it—it oozed—like seeing a wound open up in your flesh. I took a last look back to see what Nykol and Gornami-yev were up to, and they were both lying on the floor on the backs of their shells with the tops of their heads touching. I had no idea what that was supposed to mean—if anything—so I went on out, looking for Benny. And it was awful."

"What was?" Eileen asked anxiously. "Benny?"

"I didn't see him. Not right away. No, it was a storm. An awful storm. Now that I think about it, that might have been part of the reason things were so mixed up in the beginning. There was another storm raging then. But this one was even worse. The wind was blowing so hard I could barely stand up. I tried to walk, but with the wind in my face and nothing but ice under my feet, I was afraid of falling and not being able to get back up again. A bolt of lightning hit the ground about ten meters from where I was standing and burned a huge hole in the ice. Then—whammo—in an instant the whole thing froze solid again. It was like being trapped in the middle of a nightmare with no way out."

"And no Benny either?" Sam asked softly.

"Not right away, no. But this is where things get even stranger. The storm kept getting worse. I could hardly see ten centimeters in front of me, with the wind and everything. Then it let up. All of a sudden. Maybe it was like the eye of a storm. And there he was. Benny. He was up on this low ridge of ice between two of the Kith domes, and he—he wasn't alone. There were two of him, two Bennys, both standing on their hind legs— which I didn't think you could do—and they were hanging onto each other with their other legs. It was like they were hugging or—or like they were dancing, turning in a little circle, dancing in the middle of that awful storm. I know it sounds totally crazy, Sam"—Raymond was sitting up again now—but that's the way it happened, I swear to you. I wouldn't make up something like that. I—"

Mobutu started to interrupt but Sam, sensing his intention, turned and waved a quick hand, cutting him off. This was something Sam felt he ought to handle for himself. Gently he pushed Raymond back on the cot. "You say there were two Bennys there, son. By that do you mean two of the MAGMOS forms?"

"Yes, right. Two Neppies—slugs."

"And you weren't seeing a double image? With the atmospheric pressure at Neptune's surface, a phenomenon like that is not impossible. On Venus, according to some of the spacers who have gone there, a person can look straight forward and glimpse the back of his own head."

"No, this was different. I mean, they were dancing together, Sam, not standing side by side."

"And they were identical, you say."

"Well . . . a Neppie's a Neppie, right? One of them did look bigger than the other, but everything was so weird, who can say?"

Sam nodded thoughtfully. "Then what happened, son?"

"Well, nothing really. That was pretty much the end. The scrambler must have beamed us back right about then."

"It did. That was entirely my decision, by the way. We'd been tracking both you and Benny when we could—the signal wouldn't penetrate the Kith dome—and when the storm showed no signs of letting up, I decided it was best to bring you back before things got worse. We knew your positions but not your actual situation, and since you'd already established contact with the Kith—"

"No, I'm glad you did it, even if it meant I didn't have time to find out more about Benny. That's definitely the last thing I can remember too—from Neptune. After that it was just the transformation—you're actually conscious for a split second, and the pain is horrible—"

"We knew about that from the preliminary run-throughs," Mobutu managed to break in at last. "Unfortunately, there doesn't appear to be any means for getting around the momentary discomfort of the process."

Raymond smiled. "It's a little more than momentary discomfort, Doc. It's like having your whole body ripped apart bit by bit while you sit inside feeling it happen. Anyway, the next thing, I was back in the lab, in the scrambler chamber, and you two were helping me out. I was pretty dazed, and then Benny arrived and he was . . . well, you know. Catatonic."

"Although the last time you'd seen him on Neptune he wasn't."

"No. I . . ." Raymond was silent for a moment, thinking. "Do you think that's a good sign, Sam? Maybe we're wrong. Maybe it was the transformation that tipped Benny over the edge and Neptune had nothing to do with it."

Sam didn't think that was very likely. Benny had gone through the MAGMOS transformation in training as often as any of them and ought to have been psychologically prepared for its consequences—the "momentary discomfort," as Mobutu called it. "I certainly don't think it's a bad sign," he said truthfully, patting the boy's shoulder. To Sam this seemed to be the end of it. They had Raymond's story now—from the beginning to apparent end. There was nothing to be gained from pursuing it further at this time, especially considering the boy's present delicate state. Sam turned and glanced questioningly at Fred Berman, who nodded firmly.

Sam stood up. "I want to tell you, son, how grateful I am to you for doing a superb job under very difficult circumstances. Being the first at anything is always the toughest challenge, and you've a right to be proud of yourself. Right now we're going to let you rest. I'll have a medtech sent over with something to help you sleep if you feel you need it."

"No, I think I can sleep all right."

"Fine. Then later we'll go through your story again and see if you can add any details."

"Sam, one more thing," he said urgently.

"Of course, son. What is it?"

"This won't be the end, right? I mean, even if Benny doesn't come around, you won't give up?"

"We're not quitting, no."

"Then I'd like to be on the next mission team too. I think with my experience that would make sense."

"I'll keep it in mind," Sam said, "in making my choice."

"You're not going to have them pick cards again?" Eileen put in.

"No," Sam said gravely. "No more cards."

The door burst suddenly open behind them. Turning, Sam saw Carolina standing in the doorway with Danny a short distance behind her. Sam had given strict instructions to all the kids to stay clear of this room until he told them it was all right to visit Raymond.

Frowning grimly, he took a step across the room. "What do you two think—"

Carolina caught him partway, grabbing his arms. "Sam, come quick. Hurry." She tugged at his sleeves. "It's Benny. He's awake."

TWENTY

If there was one thing George regarded as absolutely pointless and mindless, it had to be solitaire. And the version he was playing now—sitting cross-legged on the floor of his room—had to be the most mindless of all. The way it worked, you turned over the cards off the top of the deck one after another, laying them out one by one in a long row. If the card you turned over happened to match either of the previous two cards—by denomination or suit—then you placed it on top of that card, creating a stack. The objective was—by matching up cards as you went along—to end up with a single stack of fifty-two cards at the finish, the same as you'd started. The game was presumably winnable—George had never bothered to calculate the precise odds—but only just barely. And he never had. Which was presently fine with him. Winning would have ruined the whole point of the game for him—its utter pointlessness—a pointlessness that just happened to match his mood perfectly.

And my life, too, George thought, turning over a card and letting it drift slowly to the floor.

Take this Neptune thing, for example. Winnable too—somehow, he supposed—but even if you did, what would it mean? To him that was the one big problem with this entire project, and why he still just couldn't see it. So what if the Kith were powerful enough to alter the molecular composition and mass of an entire huge planet? So what if nobody knew what they were or where they came from or what they wanted here? (Assuming they wanted anything at all, something of which George was far from convinced.) The way he saw it, as long as the Kith left the human race alone, why go through all the effort risking people's lives—and their sanity—especially a poor dumb little kid like Benny Sims, who'd never even really lived yet—trying to solve a mystery that might not even have a solution? Leave the Kith alone and maybe they'd leave us alone too. It was worth trying, wasn't it? If it didn't work, then worry about it.

But when he'd tried this line of reasoning on old fat Sam, all he'd gotten for an answer was a dark look—eyebrows scrunched together to form a V —and a lecture to the effect that human beings were innately curious creatures who demanded to know the answers to all the big questions of the universe.

Big questions, big deal, George thought. It was the little questions he cared about, the stuff that actually mattered in one's own life. Like this stupid pointless card game. Like whether Benney Sims was ever going to be sane again. Like whether he himself was ever going to be able to go back to Mars without getting his head blown off.

So if that's how you feel, what the hell are you doing here? It was a question he must have asked himself a hundred million times already, and so far he still didn't have a satisfactory answer. He knew what Sam would say if he asked him, how brilliant and singularly adaptable he was. George wouldn't deny that. But he still found it tough to believe Sam couldn't find one other person almost as brilliant and almost as singularly adaptable somewhere in the Solar System who would furthermore actually *want* to be turned into a twelve-legged slug and dropped on an alien planet to lumber around trying to talk to giant turtles. There were millions of kids around. Why didn't Sam go out and recruit one of them?

So far, though, he had to admit it hadn't really been that bad. Even the actual training part had proven bearable. Reading books and studying papers and committing facts to memory had never been a problem for George, and the hypnosimulators—glass tanks filled with warm salty water in which you lay immersed, sweetly floating, naked except for a breathing tube and earphones, till you drifted off to sleep, and when you woke up, feeling totally rested, all you had to show for the experience was a fuzzy memory of a dream that invariably involved lumbering around Neptune dressed up (that's how it felt, since your mind remained your own mind) as a Neppie, meeting emergencies like quakes and storms and trying to talk to some six-legged turtles—the hypnosimulators were basically a breeze for him too. Oh, now and then the dreams would turn sour—two of his, he recalled, had ended abruptly with his own death—and some of the other kids, poor Benny in particular, had had it much worse—but since a dream was still only a dream, any lasting effects had been meager. What they'd gotten into later in training, the actual run-throughs involving the MAGMOS hardware, Dr. Mobutu's pet baby, had been a good deal more traumatic simply because of the genuine pain involved in transformation. (George was no fancier of pain, especially his own.) What happened was that you climbed inside the so-called scrambler chamber, had an iron door slammed shut in your face, got transformed into a Neppie while you screamed screams nobody could hear, including yourself, and then woke up in your brand-new body, beamed inside a specially constructed, rapidly spinning, circular compartment located in the center of *Leverrier*'s hub in which all the conditions normally prevalent at the surface of Neptune were supposedly duplicated. For the most part, what George had done once he found himself inside the environmental chamber was just stand rooted in one spot while Mobutu or some robot engineer bellowed in his ear to move, till they finally gave up and brought him back. "The spinning makes me dizzy," he lied when Sam confronted him. "And anyway, if you don't think I'm cooperating, why don't you send me back home?"

"But if I did that, George my boy"—Sam laid a fatherly hand on his shoulder—"you'd get your stubborn little head blown off."

Which, it seemed, was what it always kept coming back to. It was certainly the one thing George couldn't get out of his mind and the one thing that made the whole question of what he was doing here on *Leverrier* not only answerless, but unanswerable.

He'd given a lot of thought to surveying the possible alternatives. Heck, even if he played this thing through to its end—whatever that might turn out to be—someday he'd have to leave. And where would he go? Mars was definitely out of the question, and Earth as well. Ganymede was a big boring hellhole, as he knew from personal experience, and Titan, from what he'd picked up listening to Carolina, was pretty much the same. As for the newer Jovian colonies, logic said they, too, had to be more of the same, only under more primitive conditions. So what was left? The Asteroid Belt? That had been his first thought, but the more he saw of Raymond Liu, the less appealing it seemed. Life in the Belt was the life of the pure freebooter. Nothing wrong in that—George didn't like people telling him what to do any more than the next person. (A lot less than the next person, actually.) But was it the sort of life where he could succeed? Oh, he was ambitious enough, no question about that, but his ambition didn't run toward a lot of hard work, it ran more toward finding the right corners to cut to get to the top of the heap as quickly as possible. In the Belt, Raymond would gladly tell you, there were no corners to cut, and trying to find them could get you killed. Well, Raymond could talk. He'd done his hard work and now he was eleven years old and rich as hell. (He hadn't done it entirely alone, George eventually found out; there were several partners involved when he'd made his first big strike. Apparently the free-booter ideal only went so far in practice.) But George had a feeling he could spend thirty stanyears in the Belt and still come out as poor as when he'd started. (Or maybe dead from trying to find those corners to cut.)

And all of this, of course, was assuming none of the Martian affiliates managed to track him down wherever he was and kill him. A pretty optimistic assumption, he knew.

Brother Danny, of all people, had come up with another possibility when the two of them happened to hit the mess hall at the same time. "There's something you said to me a long time ago, George," Danny said, "back when we were first on our way out from Mars, about how it would be better for me if I didn't live on Earth. Because of my legs, I mean."

"Well, isn't it better?" George wasn't blind. A couple of days ago he'd spotted Danny actually running down a corridor—a stiff-legged, bouncy kind of run to be sure, but a run—rather than dragging his legs behind him like so much dead meat.

"So I was thinking," Danny went on, "when this is over, maybe the two of us could sign up with the Combine for freighter duty."

"Mom wouldn't like that."

"But she'd understand. I didn't used to think so, but now I think she would. And I talked to Sam and he said he thinks he could get us both midshipman commissions, and after that—"

"Freighters have to put in at Phobos now and then," George pointed out. "I show my face around there and I lose it."

Danny shook his head. "Sam says the affiliates wouldn't dare touch you if you're working in the Combine."

George replied noncommittally, wanting time to digest this last bit of information. As a matter of fact he still was digesting it. A midshipman on a Combine freighter. And that was only a start, too, as brother Danny loved to point out. What came after? Well, there was lieutenant, then captain, then admiral of the fleet, and then . . . no, the whole idea was so absurd it was laughable. But maybe there was a germ of a notion lurking in there someplace anyway. If George could only figure out a way to hang on to the Combine part of it while somehow avoiding having to spend the rest of his life stuck in a boring space freighter, then maybe . . .

It was awfully vague though. Worse than that, he conceded, it was desperate. Almost as desperate as this stupid solitaire game.

But wait. Somehow, while continuing to play more or less by rote as his thoughts whirred elsewhere, he'd reduced the stacks in front of him to a mere four. And—he slid his thumb along the edge of the deck—there were only six more cards left to play. Six cards—four stacks. It was a chance—a desperate chance, sure, but a chance.

George played more carefully then, concentrating, turning over five more cards. In the process he reduced the stacks in front of him to two. How about that? he thought. Two stacks—and one card left to play. The first of the stacks was topped by the ace of diamonds, the other by the jack of hearts.

George peeked at the card in his hand. There it was, all right. The jack of diamonds, leering right back at him. Unbelieving, George laid the jack gently down on top of the second stack, picked it up, and dropped the whole thing on top of the first stack.

Then he just sat there, elbows on his knees, shaking his head, staring and grinning.

Fifty-two cards in one neat pile, the same as when he'd started.

That could mean only one thing: victory, for the love of God.

There was a knock on the door. "George? Are you in there, George? It's me, Danny."

For a moment, savoring his triumph—how many years had he been playing this stupid game, always losing?—he was tempted to ignore the knocking. But maybe the cards had been given as a sign. Maybe his old protectoress, the goddess of chance, was clueing him in to the fact that his luck had turned at last. Anyway, he needed to ask Danny a couple more questions about this freighter deal.

"Sure, come in."

Danny wasn't alone, unfortunately. Not only was Carolina with him—since when had those two started hanging out?—George couldn't remember them exchanging a dozen words—but the ugly black mutant Duncan as well.

Carolina peered down her long nose at him on the floor. "I thought you were taking a nap, George. It looks more like you're praying."

"Sort of." George winked at the deck of cards in front of him. "Actually, I was playing solitaire."

"Is life that boring for you?" she asked.

"Almost always." He stood up. "What do you guys want?"

"We were going to see Benny in the dispensary," Danny said, "and I thought you might want to come along. Eileen says it's okay."

"You sure there'll be room in there for me too?" he said, looking past the two of them at Duncan.

"It's a big place, George," Carolina said.

"Well . . . I'm kind of busy right now too."

George turned his head, searching the room for something to be busy with.

"I know—playing solitaire. Look," she said, "don't you think you owe it to Benny to at least look in on him? Considering all the money you stole from him at poker, I'd think—"

"I didn't steal a thing." She'd almost gotten him mad—almost, but not quite. "What I won I won fair and square." (In truth, a bit later on, when Benny had picked up the game better, George had lost it back the same way. The little guy had been a pretty quick study. No, George corrected himself, he *is* a quick study.)

"The same fair and square way you cut the deck this morning?"

George glanced at Danny to see if he also knew. "I didn't hear you letting out a peep at the time," he told Carolina. "Especially when you drew that six."

"If I'd wanted a favor from you," she said, "I would have asked."

"Don't worry. It wasn't you I was trying to help. It was Danny-boy over there, my flesh and blood. Old fat Sam crossed me up, though."

"That's not what you told me before."

"I was trying to sweet talk you then, acting like I cared."

"Besides, Danny doesn't need any favors from you either."

"Look." George took a deep breath, playing at being calm and reasonable. "Why don't the three of you go down and say hi to Benny, and maybe I'll drop by later? I thought he was supposed to be in a coma anyway."

"He's catatonic," she corrected. "A coma's physical—this is psychological. There's a major difference, George."

"But either way, he's not going to know who visited him and who didn't, correct?"

She put her hands on her hips. "Haven't you done one thing in your life just because it was the right thing to do?"

"Let me see." He pretended to think. "There was one time—I must have been about three—and I—"

"And have you bothered to realize that some day soon any one of us might be in the same position as Benny and want—?"

"Uh-uh. Not me. I'm not that dumb."

"Oh, drop dead." She spun on a heel, neglecting to compensate for the low gravity and nearly losing her balance. Recovering, she managed to storm toward the door. Reaching it, she stopped and turned back with a glare. "Well, are you coming with me or not?" she said to Danny.

"Uh, sure, Carolina."

George gave Danny time to reach her side before calling, "Hey, hold on. Not so fast."

Danny glanced back. Carolina didn't.

George rose to his feet and shrugged. "What the heck. It beats solitaire. I'll tag along."

Which is exactly what he ended up doing, tagging along, bringing up the rear. Except for the central hub, *Leverrier*'s corridors were only wide enough for two people to walk side by side. George ended up walking alongside Duncan, with Carolina and Danny's bouncy glide of a walk ahead of him. Watching Danny got George thinking again about the freighter berth idea. Chances were good, after poor Benny, Sam would now come to his senses and shut down the project. But if he did, George realized, that wouldn't give a lot of time to figure out an angle to use on the Combine. Something like a medical disability might do it. He'd take his midshipman commission and then suddenly come down with a bad back. He could then retire—while retaining his Combine status—and live happily ever after.

The four of them passed through one spoke of *Leverrier*'s revolving wheel, cut quickly through the hub, and entered another spoke before reaching the station dispensary.

The door was shut. Instead of just walking right in, though, they stood around in the corridor, each reluctant to be the first to see Benny. From the next door down came a murmur of voices punctuated by a sudden shout.

"That was Raymond," Danny said.

Carolina nodded. "They brought him over there, away from Benny, to get his story, Sam and the rest."

"But not us," George said.

"Sam's supposed to brief us later. Eileen said he'll tell us anything important."

"How's Raymond doing anyway?" George asked. "When I was grabbing a snack earlier in the recreation zone, a couple human medtechs were in there watching a vid, and one of them said Raymond was raving out of his mind."

"They didn't know what they were talking about. Eileen said he's in excellent physical shape. Mentally, he's confused, but we all knew from training it was going to be confusing down there."

Another shout from the room next door.

George cocked his head. "He sounds just great to me."

Carolina hurled open the door to the dispensary and charged through. It was a big room—for *Leverrier*, enormous—with white walls and a dozen beds in two long rows. Only one of the beds was presently occupied. Little Nina, seated in a chair beside the bed, glanced up at their entrance and smiled wanly. Two robot medtechs lurked nearby.

In the bed Benny lay flat on his back, covered by a single thin white sheet drawn up to his chin. Underneath the sheet his chest rose and fell with rhythmic regularity. His eyes were open—but as blank as a blind man's.

George felt himself driven to approach the bed. He waved a hand in front of Benny's face.

"He won't even blink," Nina said, watching him. "He won't do anything."

"Christ," George said, "this is ugly."

"From what Eileen told me," Carolina put in, "it's a moment by moment situation. Benny could snap out of it while we're standing here."

"Five years old," George said. "Can you believe it? When I was five, I was a baby. That jerk Sam is worse than a murderer."

"George, it's got to be done," she said. "The Kith—"

"Oh, screw the Kith." He turned his back on the bed and stepped away. He'd been right to begin with. Coming here had been a really dumb move.

Somebody was standing next to him. Glancing up, George saw Danny. Danny said, "I think you're right, George. I think . . . I didn't tell you before, but I—I appreciate what you tried to do this morning. With the cards. I was scared. I—"

"Being scared has nothing to do with it," George said. "It's just crazy, is all."

"Because Dad did it, because he died, I thought I—you and me—I thought we had to—"

"But we're not him," George said softly.

"Then we'll tell Sam. All of us. He's got to give up and send us home. We can—"

"Hello, everybody."

The familiar boom of that hoarse bass voice burst through the room like the crack of a gun. George spun and gaped at the bed. Nina looked back at him helplessly, her arms spread.

"He didn't—didn't—" she said.

Carolina was pointing past George and Danny to the door. Turning, George saw Duncan with his back against the wall. His hands were clenched into fists at his side, his head thrown back, his face a frozen mask of strain and exertion. Sweat beaded his forehead. His lips moved.

"I don't want anyone to worry about me," said the voice of Benny Sims. The words poured from Duncan's lips in a rush of sound. "I'm doing perfectly okay. It's just that I have to adjust myself to everything I found out on Neptune. There was so much. I can't wait to tell you."

"Benny, I—" George took a halting step toward Duncan. "Are you really going to be all right?"

"I am all right, George. I told you that. How about some cards tonight? Poker? Jacks or better?"

"Sure, Benny. That sounds great. You'll have to stake me, though. I'm cleaned out, you know."

"You're a good player, George." He actually laughed. Or Duncan did. (Though it sounded like Benny.) "Almost as good as me. But I'm tired, George. I might want to sleep instead."

"No, that's fine, Benny. Do what you have to do. We can always play poker later."

"Is Nina there?"

"I'm here, Benny." She was standing rigidly at the foot of the bed, her head swinging back and forth between Duncan and Benny.

"I thought it was nice of you to come and sit with me. I always thought you hated me."

"Oh, no." Having apparently made up her mind, her eyes were fixed on Duncan now. "Not me."

"Is Danny there?"

"He's here," George said. "And Carolina. We're all here except Raymond."

"Poor Raymond. He kept missing so much. They tried to help him, but he didn't know how to listen."

"Who tried?" Carolina said. "The Kith?"

"And George," Benny/Duncan said, "I almost forgot." The voice was growing softer now, as if coming from a farther distance. "I have a message for you. It's from your father."

George wasn't sure he'd heard correctly. The voice was very soft now. "My father?"

"Yes. From Michael. I met him down there. We talked and communed and danced. He knows everything. He wants to see you. That was the message. He wants to see you. Danny and Nina too. And quickly, he said. The-one-who-is-nothing is stirring strongly now, and soon the cosmic flux will appear. Time is growing short."

"You're saying my father—that he's alive? Down there? On Neptune?"

"Oh, definitely. When I informed him you were all here, he said, 'Damn that Sam Goble.' " The voice was a hoarse whisper now. "He said, 'I should have known Sam wouldn't leave me in peace.' "

"But it's been five years," George cried. "He can't be alive. Not down there. He can't—"

But Benny was gone. It was obvious to see. Duncan's chin lolled on his chest and shoulders sagged. Then his knees buckled and he fell in a heap.

The four of them rushed to his side. Danny cradled his head in his lap. "Duncan, are you okay?"

The eyes snapped open. The noseless face broke into a smile. The head bobbed up and down. Once. Twice.

From behind they again heard Benny's voice: "Boy, am I ever hungry."

When they turned to look, there he was, sitting up in bed, looking exactly as if he'd just awakened from a nap. He was rubbing his stomach and grimacing painfully. "I bet I could eat a whole horse," he said.

TWENTY-ONE

Neither Danny nor George had ever been here before—in Sam's private room next door to the project office. It certainly wasn't anything like what Danny would have expected. It wasn't just the room's spartan austerity that surprised him, it was the complete lack of personality. Sam was such a strong individual, one naturally expected him to dominate any environment he became a part of, but this room could have belonged to anyone. To Danny. Or George. To Duncan, for that matter. There was just a single narrow cot with a pillow and blanket, and a tiny, square, wooden table. There was no rug, no lamp—the only light came from a fluorescent bulb in the ceiling—and hardly anything personal, no books or vids or taped music, nothing except, casually tacked to the wall above the bed, a single blown-up photograph. The photo, dog-eared and yellow and torn at the edges, showed a view of the full round Earth taken from space. This was the old Earth from before the war, blue as a sapphire and wreathed by delicately streaming white clouds.

Sam noticed the direction of his gaze. "Know what this is, Danny? It's a copy of one of the first photographs ever taken from space of the full Earth. It's from one of the earliest Apollo missions."

"I know. The one that first circled the Moon prior to the actual landing."

"Apollo Eight."

"It's a great picture."

"I only wish . . ." Sam sat down heavily on the edge of the cot and waved at them to sit too. Danny knelt on the floor—there was no other place—while George remained on his feet. "What would make that picture truly great," Sam went on, "was if anybody had ever learned anything from it. But the fools went ahead and blew up the planet anyway, when all they had to do was open their eyes, look at that picture, and see for themselves what it all came down to: one round, lonely ball floating in a sea of emptiness. If they'd learned that lesson, they would have done something to keep that sea of emptiness on the outside, where it belonged, instead of inviting it in and thereby destroying their world in the process."

"Look, I thought we came here to talk about the Kith," George broke in. "Not a lot of history."

"I am talking about the Kith," Sam said softly. "If the war on Earth had never happened—and it never should have—not only would millions of human beings be alive today, but we wouldn't have the Kith to deal with either."

"Sam," Danny said, "are you saying the Kith and the war are connected?"

"I'd stake my life on it, boys. Or my soul. Whichever you think is more valuable. In my opinion the Kith are here in the Solar System only because of the war. I just can't accept the idea that a species can get away with destroying an entire world without somebody, someplace, somehow noticing. The Kith noticed. I've studied the astronomical records of the time. I've found evidence of an unexplained surge of energy emanating from Neptune at almost the same exact instant as the war. Nobody paid any attention to it at the time. Naturally enough. But it happened. And I think it was the Kith. Their arrival among us."

"It still could just be a coincidence," George said.

"Perhaps. Coincidences do exist. But they're rare, George, damn rare. Rarer than a truly new idea or a genuine work of art. My personal policy has always been to dismiss the possibility of coincidence from my thinking unless and until I receive overwhelming evidence to the contrary. With the Kith I've seen no such evidence. Not a scrap."

"But if the war itself was an accident . . ." Danny said.

"It wasn't. The war was a tragedy. An accident is blind chance, like a piece of mortar falling on your head as you stroll casually past a building. Tragedies, on the other hand, are the inevitable consequences of purposeful acts. The war was a tragedy because it was inevitable. Knowing that, it was why I founded the Combine years before the war actually took place."

"You founded the Combine?" George said.

"By myself, no. There were eight of us to begin with, equal partners, and several others who joined later, when it became clear what we were up to. Throughout history, I'm convinced, there has always existed a tiny handful of truly exceptional people, those few knowing how to accomplish the most difficult act for any being to accomplish: to think. Socrates, Confucius, and the Gautama Buddha all lived at more or less the same time. Suppose they'd been able to meet, to pool their thoughts. They could not. We in the Combine could. Thanks to the existence of system-wide computer networks, it wasn't terribly difficult for us to locate each other once we started looking. And we were looking. We'd glimpsed the same future, realized it was inevitable, and knew what had to be done to ensure that the race as a whole, the human species, did not perish in the ruin of its own planet. The examples I cited earlier—Socrates and the Buddha—I don't mean for those to confuse you. We were not famous people. Because we were thoughtful, we were wise enough to remain largely invisible, to live at the peripheries of human society, where the mind is always its freest. Of the eight of us, six were nevertheless wealthy, although that wealth was primarily a means—a way of guaranteeing invisibility, for instance—and never an end in itself. Without hesitation we pooled our wealth. It increased. Making money when you have money to begin with is one of the easiest tasks ever invented, kids, believe me. We used our wealth to proceed with our goals. The first of these—and the most crucial—was space, the faltering colonies hesitantly established by various Earth governments on Luna and Mars. We bought the Moon. You won't find that written down in any ledger book or tax record, but that's what we did. From there we moved on to foment rebellion on Mars, and eventually founded our own colonies in the outer satellites. If Earth was destined for destruction, other environments had to be created where people could live—and live freely. Most of the other details you know. They're part of the public record. And when the war finally did occur—three of our original eight directors died in the course of the initial exchanges—we were thoughtful people but not, alas, prophets—we were poised to step in and try to salvage what remained."

"But what about the new Earth government in Perth?" Danny asked. "And World President Armelino?"

"The Combine and the Earth government are for all purposes identical. As for Armelino, you're looking at him, son. One of them."

"You're Armelino?" George said, sounding slightly less skeptical this time.

"I've held the position from time to time. How do you think you got out of your school assignment so easily, Danny? As for you, George, remember the various strokes of good fortune that allowed you to escape a hot-zone squad and somehow reach Luna—and then Mars."

"What did you have to do with that?"

"I had everything to do with it."

"Uh-uh," George said. "It was a lady named Dr. Miriam Delahunt who helped me get to Luna. She worked for the Combine, sure, but I conned the hell out of her."

"The lady worked for me," Sam said. "You might say both she and I conned the hell out of you, George."

"I don't believe it."

Sam smiled. "Maybe that's for the best."

Danny felt overwhelmed by this onslaught of revelation, finding much of it hard to believe and yet also impossible to disbelieve. After all, why would Sam lie?

But George—George just looked angry.

"You smug—" He broke off, taking a breath. "Look, are you trying to tell me everything—my whole damn life—has been manipulated by you?"

"No, George. Not your whole life. Only since your father's disappearance, and only to the degree necessary to ensure your survival and prod your education."

"But what gave you the right?"

Sam thrust a thumb toward the ceiling. "They did—the Kith. I needed both of you ready when the time came."

"Then this crap about how our names just happened to pop out of some big computer network, that was another lie?"

Sam nodded. "In your instances, yes. I knew I wanted both of you on my team from the time I conceived it, before I learned the first thing about you."

"But why us, damn it?"

"Because of your father. Who else could bring him back?"

"Then," Danny broke in, "Dad really is alive down there?"

"I've always believed so," Sam said.

"Benny wasn't hallucinating?"

"Raymond saw him, too, though he wasn't aware of what he was seeing at the time. No, boys, Mike's down there. We can be certain of that."

"But, Sam . . . how?" Danny asked.

"You'd have to know your dad the way I knew him, a chance he never gave you, I know. Michael Hawkins was more than simply a strong man, a powerful personality. Hell, I'm all of that, and I'm not Mike, I guarantee you. Charismatic? Yes, but even that only tells part of it. Mike was the brightest flame of his time, the true child of the gods, the shining star that seemed as if it could never burn out. Take our famous expedition to Nemesis." Sam smiled as if in fond remembrance. "That was pure Mike Hawkins from beginning to end. You think you can con people, George. You should have seen your dad in action—a true master of the art. Not only was I his victim—and your mother—but the whole damn Combine directorate fell under his sway. Nemesis was, frankly, a pie in the sky. The sun's dark companion star, something the majority of astronomers considered a myth. But not Mike. Mike thought otherwise, and he wanted to go see for himself. In the end it turned out he was right—he nearly always was, by the way—but I don't think that was really the point with him either. Mike didn't care about Nemesis, whether it was out there or wasn't. He cared about himself—about Michael Hawkins. In Mike's private cosmos there was only one star that burned brightly, and that was himself." Sam stopped long enough to shake his head. "And the funds it cost the Combine, the diversion of resources. Do you know what Mike's crucial argument was, the one that—believe it or not—swayed us over? Dreams, he said. People need dreams, and it's up to us—those who can—to create and share those dreams. He spoke of the Earth on the verge of war and about the grueling daily existence on the colony worlds. And he won us over. We were the thoughtful ones, remember, but Mike was something more. Give them dreams, he said, drama, give them heroes. Mike was ready to be that hero. Hell, to be truthful, he was mine too."

"But that doesn't explain why you're so sure he's not dead," George said.

Sam smiled. "Always the practical one, aren't you, George? Well, if it doesn't explain things for you, then it's because faith is always a difficult thing to communicate. I believe Mike's alive because there's no way I could ever believe otherwise. Me, I might die down there—I probably would—but not him, not Mike. Heroes don't just die, George. They burn out—like the brightest stars—they explode in a blast of heat and fire. The one thing they never do is fade away."

"But how could he survive all those years?"

"Without help he couldn't," Sam said, practical now as well. "We have to look to the Kith again to answer that."

There was a knock on the door then. "Yes, come in," Sam called.

It was Nina, looking tired and drained. She tottered up to Sam, dropped down on the cot beside him and lowered her head to his shoulder. "I'm sleepy," she said.

"You've had a long day." He patted the top of her head. "Sitting up with Benny like that."

"I know. I was so scared for him and now he's awake and he won't shut up and let me say one word. What a jerk. Eileen said you wanted to see me."

"Yes. Do you know these boys?"

"Sure." She looked at them, sleepy-eyed. "That's Danny, and that's George the jerk."

"They're your brothers, Nina."

Her face scrunched up as she squinted. "Really?"

"Yes, really."

"Good. I always wanted to have brothers." She looked at him pleadingly. "Will you come to my room and tell me a story, Sam? Before I fall asleep? Another space story, okay?"

Danny was on his feet, too stunned to speak or move. George looked enraged. "What are you talking about?" he growled, advancing on Sam.

Glancing at him, Sam spread his arms wide. "It's the truth, son. Nina here is your and Danny's sister. Your father—"

"Liar!" George swung his fist. Sam reached out in a blur of motion and caught the fist in midair. He held it frozen there. George shifted his weight and swung the other fist. Sam caught that too.

"Don't kick, George. I've run out of hands."

"I ought to kill you."

"I agree."

"Then let go of me."

"Only if you promise we won't have to go through this again."

George was straining to break loose. "I'm not promising anything."

"Then just listen to me."

"I—All right." He relaxed. "I'll listen. Now let me go."

Sam let him go, remaining tense. After a brief moment's hesitation, George stepped back and folded his arms on his chest. "All right. I'm listening. If you've got something to say, say it."

"I'm sorry. That's got to be the first thing I tell you. I just finished boasting about what a brilliant man I am, and then I go and act like the biggest fool in the universe. I have an addiction to dramatic gestures. I like to create them for my own pleasure. Sometimes I'm too blind to see that others may not enjoy them quite so much. This was one of those times. I was stupid—and I was insensitive. I apologize to you, George—to all three of you, in fact."

"What did you do bad?" Nina asked, looking up at him wide-eyed.

"You're still saying it's true," George said.

Sam met his gaze. "It is true. Let me begin at the beginning." He draped an arm over Nina's shoulders, drawing her close. "I don't think your father ever loved anyone in his life until he met your mother—Sara—until I brought her to him and said here's the person we need as the third member of our crew. It was a lonely journey to Nemesis—and a long one. Two stanyears out and another two back. By the time it was done, the three of us were all in love in one sense or another. And that was most fortunate. It could as easily have been hate. The love between Mike and Sara was both potent and pure. It began, I think, when Mike discovered to his considerable astonishment that Sara alone among the women he'd known did not worship him. Given that—and given who and what Sara was—their love may well have been fated from the start, if you want to believe in fate, which sometimes I do."

It suddenly struck Danny—why hadn't he realized it before?—that Sam was in love with Sara himself.

"But, as you know, eventually they separated. The war came, a world was destroyed, everything changed, and Sara was changed by it. But not Mike. Mike was the same brightly burning flame he always had been. Outside events never influenced him; he influenced them. But Sara no longer cared to spend her life as a nomad, a spacer, chasing his flame as it flared here, flared there, from place to place and world to world. She sought a measure of security, peace, tranquility, concepts alien to Mike. Above all, I think, she wanted a home, and Mike carried his home with him—he was it, it was he. She chose Earth—partly from the guilt and nostalgia we all shared, and partly because the Earth, unlike the colony worlds, offered a place where she would be let alone. Mike went with her. For a time I think he honestly tried. You were born, George, and then you, Danny. He stayed that long. Sara wanted children, and he gave them to her. Then he left. He showed up at my office one day in Tranquility and asked for a job. I gave him one."

"He did visit us," Danny said. "Every once in a while when George and I were growing up, Dad would suddenly pop up one day."

"Of course, Danny. I never said he stopped loving her—or loving you. As for Nina here"—he gave the girl another squeeze—"her mother, as you may have guessed, was poor Nina LeClaire from the first project. Nina was another of my protégées—bright, young, energetic—much like Sara, in fact, though lacking her intricacy or depth. Nina was a doer, not a poet. Did Mike love her? That's not for me to say. She clearly loved him. She definitely worshiped him."

"According to you," George said, "they had a baby together. That ought to count for something."

Sam shrugged. "Possibly. I'm certain it was never Mike's intention to make her pregnant. The circumstances under which they met—the first project—Mike would have known better. He was self-centered but never selfish. As for Nina, I could only venture a guess. Nothing was known of the child's conception until after Mike's disappearance on Neptune. Nina, psychotic, was on her way to Tranquility when the discovery occurred during a routine physical examination. The embryo appeared healthy. I ordered it born. When the child—when Nina was born, I had her brought out here for Olga to raise."

Nina, amazingly, was sound asleep, curled in Sam's big arm.

George was gazing at her. "Okay," he grunted. "I believe you. Now what?"

"I want you to go to Neptune. The three of you."

"When?" Danny asked.

"Immediately."

"Can we, so soon after the last mission?"

"I've discussed that with Bob Mobutu, and he says we have the resources available to scramble the three of you, beam you down to Neptune, and keep you there for as long as two hours each. And he can get you back too. After that, it may be several standays before we can mount another mission."

"And you want us to look for Dad?" Danny asked.

"Yes. I don't want you to ignore the Kith, especially if they try to establish contact, but I want Mike found. From what Benny said, he wants to see you. The three of you."

"I thought you just got through telling us he didn't know anything about Nina," George said.

"Apparently he does," Sam said. "How? I don't know. You might ask him."

"Will we be able to?" Danny said.

"Benny managed. I hope you can too."

"Do you think he wants to come back?" Danny said. "Do you think that's what this is all about?"

Sam pursed his lips thoughtfully. "If that turns out to be what he wants, tell him we'll give it a try. I don't know how, but we'll find a way. We might be able to shuttle him up here in his present form and rescramble him in the lab. Tell him not to worry. One way or the other, we'll pull it off. But frankly, it's not what I expect."

"Why?" Danny asked.

"Because I've never known Mike to change his mind once he's made it up. Five stanyears ago he decided he wanted to stay on Neptune. He must have had a reason—an overwhelming one—and I don't imagine that's changed."

"Maybe he just wanted to get away from all these kids he kept having," George said.

"I don't think that's funny," Danny said.

"Who's laughing?" George asked.

Danny was looking at Nina, watching as she slept. It was still difficult thinking of her as his own little sister. After all, she was still the same person she'd always been, wasn't she? The fact that she shared certain genes with him—and with George—how significant was that?

"How come nobody wants to ask me anything?" George broke in suddenly.

"Is there something we ought to be asking you?" Sam said.

"Sure. Whether I'm even going on this nutty mission of yours."

"But you've got to," Danny said. "Dad asked for you—for all of us."

"Great. And I suppose, all my life, if I'd asked for him, he would've showed. Fat chance. No, look"—his gaze met Sam's—"I'll make you a deal. If I'm going, I want something in return."

"Such as?" Sam said.

"A commission with the Combine. You say you run the whole thing, then swell. A commission with no duty assignment. I want the status but not the job."

"For God's sake, why?"

"So that I can go back to Mars—and anywhere else I please—and not get my brains blown out."

Sam looked surprised. "You mean that's what's been eating you."

"Why shouldn't it be eating me? It's my life—the only one I've got."

"And it still is, George. Nobody has ever said a word to the affiliates about your past gambling activities. That was largely a threat designed to get you out here. I may be a lot of things, but I'm not an assassin—even an indirect one. You can go back to Mars whenever you want. You're perfectly safe."

"You could have told me that before," George said.

"Well, you never asked." Sam grinned.

Danny didn't think it was so funny. Not that he cared that much about George's feelings—not right now he didn't anyway—but he realized that their leverage over George had disappeared.

He looked straight at George. "Does this mean you're out?"

"Out?" said George, who was still glaring at Sam.

"Are you going with us or aren't you?"

"Oh, I'm going with you, all right. I never said I wasn't."

"But I thought . . ."

"That's your trouble, Danny-boy," George said, walking over and punching Danny lightly on the arm. "You think too much." He was smiling himself now.

The door swung open and Bob Mobutu looked in. "Sam, may I speak with you alone for a moment?"

"I don't think we ought to keep anything from these boys. What is it? The fusion reserves?"

"No. Neptune. It appears to be changing again."

TWENTY-TWO

The alien thinks: *My true name is Michael Hawkins. A human being. Born on the world of Earth, I was once a voyager of space.*

These words that are not truly words reach the alien indistinctly, as if originating less from the fabric of his own mind and more from without, from the soul speech of the other beings, the ones he calls Kith.

But the alien is alone. His thoughts are his own, frail memories stirring. After so long, why? He pauses in his wandering, twelve legs rooted on ice, and seeks the buried wisdom of his personal warmth-fabric. *Who am I? What am I? Why am I?*

Ancient, forlorn questions, long dismissed. The answer again rises from deep within: *Michael Hawkins. Human being. Wanderer of space.* The blue, shimmering orb of the world of his birth.

He stands momentarily frozen in thought, then plods on.

All past, all gone, thinks Dav (the wanderer). This is his world now. Ridges of ice, ravaged and torn as if by a constricting hand while overhead clouds clash furiously like armies at war. Neptune, his home. There is no other.

But again he must halt. Far below the-one-who-is-nothing (and therefore everything) (and nameless) stirs. The land rumbles like the beat of a drum. Shards of ice sprout, tumble, rise, collapse. Hugging the ground as if it were life itself, the alien holds on. *My name is Michael Hawkins. I am a man of Earth. I have seen born children of my own—two of them, my sons. And a third—a girl—glimpsed through soul communion.*

The faces of all three children appear before him as if made corporeal by the force of the quake.

Nykol? he thinks. *Nykol, is it you?*

194 ■ GORDON EKLUND

Silence. The thoughts are his own. The thoughts of a human. A father. He must go on. Ridges of ice now loom before him, remnants of the latest quake, the stirring from below. Passage will be difficult. He has grown weak. For too long a time he has neglected to enter the lodge-homes of the many-elders to sip the potion that brings renewal, life. Once before he delayed too long. He died. His life-force, set free of the smothering embrace of its body, sped gladly forth toward the welcoming mystery of the void. But, no. The many-elder Potrum (the dispenser) pursued, drawing him back, forcing the potion into his dead carcass. He lived again, Dav (the wanderer).

Potrum spoke (the soul speech of the elders): *You must never die, ignorant human. The void is not for one such as you. Wait. Learn. Behold the cosmic flux when the-one-who-is-nothing stirs.*

There is no flux, said Dav (the wanderer). He recalled the sweetness of the beckoning void, so close.

Fool! Remember why you stayed when others of your kind ran, fleeing into madness. "I want to see it happen." Potrum's voice became that of a human, mocking itself. "I want to stay here with you. Until then. Come on, help me. There's got to be a way."

That was long ago, said Dav.

Less than one heartbeat of the cosmic flux.

I have seen no flux.

It comes. When the-one-who-is-nothing rises, all will see the truth of the flux.

When?

Sooner than you will wish.

Then show me.

It is not yours to see.

Show me. Another did once. Nykol (the believer), who enticed me to stay on this Neptune-world with visions of the cosmic flux. Show me again.

Grudgingly, Potrum showed him, concocting a vision to reveal the fullness of the future. Seeing, remembering, understanding, Dav (the wanderer) burned with a sense of awe as the totality of the cosmic flux swirled before him.

Yes. His thoughts came only with difficulty, as if from afar. *That is why I stayed.*

Then go. Potrum sent him off to wander anew. *Your time will come.*

When? he called back, seeking a last answer.

You will know, Michael Hawkins.

He knows. That time is now.

A ridge of ice, newly risen in the spasm of the latest quake, stands before him. Grimly, stubbornly, hugging the ice with the sponge of his underbelly, Dav hauls himself upward to its summit. From there he is able to peer down at the lodge-homes of the Kith. Only two Kith are presently visible, lying flat upon the shells of their backs, staring up at the yellow streak of the sun in the mottled sky above.

The sun has never been this clearly seen before, Dav knows. It is yet another sign of the coming of the cosmic flux.

A memory reaches him. Dimly at first he sees two children at play. Human children—his own, he realizes. George and Danny. They run through a field of yellow grass while the sky above them is a muddy brown, the sun invisible. It is the ruined Earth, their home.

My home, Michael Hawkins thinks.

The memory runs strong, then fades, and he stands on Neptune again, a twelve-legged slug blinded by a light unseen for years.

One of the Kith is coming toward him, rising steadfastly from the domes below. This is not one of the two he saw watching the sun—they have not budged—but another. Perched upon the ridge of ice, Dav waits, thinking, They are the true aliens, not I. I am an alien only on this one world. The Kith are aliens everywhere.

Human being, calls the Kith as he draws near. *You are the one called Dav?*

And you are Nykol (the believer)? Potrum (the dispenser)? These are the Kith with whom he has shared communion before.

I am the one now known as Gornami-yev (the former dunce). I have come to speak with you.

At whose bidding, once-born?

My own. The Kith stands below him, head tilted to peer up. (His voice, apparently inadept at the soul speech, rises and falls, sometimes blaring, sometimes nearly inaudible.) *All Kith are angered by your conduct.*

With me, dunce? Why?

You spoke to the other human beings, the young ones. Now others will come. The cosmic flux is near. It is not a good time for those who have never died.

Such as yourself?

It is true that I am a former dunce, but these humans are dunces-that-will-always-be-dunces.

A lie. I am a human being.

And you are a dunce, as are those to whom you spoke, offending the many-elders.

I spoke to one. He could not listen, his mind ravaged by a madness.
The madness is gone. He listened—and heard. Now others follow his lead
to consult with Dav (the wanderer).
Which others?
Yes—your children.
I remember my children—my sons.
Now the many-elders wish you to go far away so that these children shall
not find you here. It is better now that you again become Dav (the
wanderer).
No. I am Michael Hawkins. I shall stand to greet my children.
But the flux—
They are my children! Michael Hawkins cries.

Above in the sky lightning bursts. A crackling flashes in the north, another to the east, then south—and west. The air itself seems set ablaze.

The icy ground shakes and rumbles as if driven by mighty machines concealed below.

It is the-one-who-is-nothing! cries Gornami-yev (the former dunce).

No, says Michael Hawkins, understanding now. *It is the cosmic flux.*

PART
FOUR

COSMIC FLUX

TWENTY-THREE

"**D**anny," Sam said, indicating with a glance the elongated metal box on the scrambler chamber into which Nina and George had previously vanished. "I believe it's your turn now."

Swallowing hard, Danny managed a nod. It had been a long wait—waiting for Neptune to be ready to receive them—but now it was almost over. Rising to his feet, Danny shed the linen robe he was wearing. Cocking his chin a few extra centimeters higher in the air in an effort to appear casual about his own nakedness, he stepped forward.

Sam hurried across in front of him and jerked the handle that opened the iron door. Inside Danny could glimpse nothing but blackness. With stoic indifference he aimed his steps in that direction.

They were in the MAGMOS lab. Danny didn't like it here. He never had. The lab was a big wide vault of a room in *Leverrier*'s outer rim with unpainted, dull-gray metal walls—seams and rivets plainly showing—naked light bulbs dangling from the ceiling, glowing white, and thick black wires piled everywhere, sometimes three and four deep across the floor. Danny had a sneaking hunch the lab had been consciously designed by somebody—Dr. Berman, most likely—in an effort to ease stress and forestall anxiety through an air of studied clutter. Well, Danny thought, it didn't work. At least for him it didn't. And the fact that the string of portholes along the outer wall had been painted black to prevent any possible glimpse of what lay beyond—well, that didn't help either. As long as he'd been waiting here—nearly two stanhours now—Danny had been able to think of little except what lay beyond the lab. What lay beyond was Neptune. And his father.

Much of the time, Sam had seemed to be experiencing a similar inability to be calmed. As well as he could manage with the sprawl of wires lacing the floor, he had paced restlessly back and forth from one end of the lab to the other, his hands clasped first in front of him, then behind, his big head bobbing on his shoulders as the gentle gravity caught and eased him down with each gliding step.

Just about everybody else was also present. Dr. Mobutu, of course, hunkered in a corner in front of a computer terminal, his back to the room as he monitored the winking digits that indicated the current readiness state of the MAGMOS systems. Mobutu had also been the one in contact with Olga Kropotkin during the time she was away from the lab overseeing the collection of data describing the altered conditions on Neptune. It has been primarily Olga they had been waiting on the whole time. Before going ahead with the actual mission, Sam insisted they first receive word from Olga that it was physically safe to proceed, that Neptune had at least for the time being stopped changing.

Eileen was also here in the lab, occupying the soft armchair directly to the left of Danny's own armchair—the cozy furnishings, he assumed, were another failed effort at forcing people to relax. Until fifteen minutes ago Nina had lain curled in Eileen's lap, her eyes shut, apparently fast asleep. Danny couldn't help envying his sister's ability not just to forestall anxiety, but to go blissfully on as if no such thing even existed. Sometimes I wish I was four years old again, he had thought wishfully.

And George. George, oddly silent and somber, had occupied the third armchair. The whole time they'd been waiting, George had barely muttered three full sentences. What was he thinking? Danny wondered. Was it possible George was just as scared as he was? Or, knowing George, maybe he was simply bored with having to wait. There was no clear way of deciding, and Danny knew it wouldn't do any good to ask.

Sam had also invited the other project team members to be present this time. By necessity Raymond and Benny remained in the dispensary, both still recovering from their earlier mission. But Carolina and Duncan had both shown up a short time after Sam called them. Carolina, with nothing practical to do, stayed in the background, standing unobtrusively by one wall with Dr. Berman—uncharacteristically subdued himself—beside her. She was wearing a burnt-orange pseudo-leather jumpsuit that hugged the contours of her body like a glove. Danny thought she looked a lot older than she really was, and George, snickering as she entered, muttered something about flowers budding in the spring. Danny wondered if George knew about her three husbands back on Titan. Probably, he guessed. George always seemed to know that sort of thing. Now and then as Danny surveyed the room, Carolina would catch his eye and flash him an encouraging smile. That did help—it made him feel better—but it was about the only thing that did.

And then there was Duncan. As soon as he'd entered the lab, Duncan had walked straight over and sat down in the middle of everything—on the floor right next to the scrambler chamber itself. With his eyes squeezed shut, Duncan began breathing deeply and noisily—in heavy gasps—and seemed to fall into a trancelike state. Danny had seen it happen before—in the gym, when Duncan had first told them of Benny's condition, and then later in the dispensary, when Benny had actually spoken through him. Was this going to be the same thing again?

Then Duncan spoke. The words came haltingly at first, then in a sudden violent stream. It was clear from the beginning what was happening: Duncan was describing the current conditions on Neptune. He spoke of raging atmospheric storms, thunderous rain in a kaleidoscope of colors, monumental quakes, vast upheavals of ice and rock. It was a vision of hell as seen from the inside out.

How was he doing it? Or was he? Were the eyes observing these visions actually Duncan's? As Danny listened to the words pouring from Duncan's lips, he experienced an icy sensation as if he were hearing a voice from his own deep past. *Father,* he almost said out loud. *Is it you?* He glanced at George. But George's gaze was fixed in his lap. George alone among them did not even seem to be listening.

Duncan's steady flow of words continued for several long minutes and then he broke off suddenly in the middle of what appeared to be a description of a huge quake. They all waited expectantly for him to go on, but although he remained seated as before, with his eyes shut and body tense, he didn't utter another word.

Danny couldn't help feeling shaken. If Duncan's description of the cataclysms now taking place on Neptune was accurate—and Danny had no doubt that it was—how would they ever be able to proceed safely with the mission? And how did that make him feel? Disappointed? Or relieved? No, not this time, Danny thought. This time I'm definitely ready to go.

Sam seemed to be having many of the same thoughts. He went over to Dr. Mobutu and said, "Call Olga, Bob. I want to know what she's found out for us so far."

Mobutu nodded, reached down, fiddled with the keyboard, and then spoke softly into the headset he wore. He glanced back at Sam. "Olga was just about to call again. It appears to be finally over, she says."

"Over?"

"Neptune. The changes—the upheavals—have apparently ceased."

Sam looked meaningfully at Duncan. Was that why he'd stopped talking so suddenly? "And . . ?"

"She's having a complete data summary prepared, every fact that can be determined from here on *Leverrier*. As soon as it's complete she'll bring a copy down here. Until then . . ."

"Until then," Sam finished, looking cross at the scrambler chamber, "we wait."

"She did mention one significant finding, however."

"What?"

"A heat source. An internal heat source."

"On Neptune?"

"In the planetary core. A giant furnace in the middle of the world. Preliminary estimates are that the radiation level is sufficient to melt the entire surface ice mantle in less than a standard year."

"Is it a fusion process?"

"Apparently not. In fact, according to Olga, the energy source seems to be nothing known to us."

"My God," Sam said softly.

"Well, someone's at least," Mobutu said with a thin smile.

"No." Sam's voice was sharp. "Let's be precise. There are no gods involved in any of this. It's the Kith, Bob, and presumably the Kith alone."

"And the mission?" Mobutu waved at Danny, George, and Nina in their armchairs. "Do we cancel or . . . ?"

Sam pursed his lips. "We wait for the data summary. If it's at all possible, I want to proceed. This may well be our last chance."

"What do you mean?"

Sam shook his head. "I mean that all of this—everything that's happened with the Kith so far—may well be pointing to some definite conclusion. I have a feeling that conclusion may well be about to fall upon us."

"But what is it?"

Sam shook his head vaguely. "Let's wait and see what Olga has."

It was more than half an hour later that Olga finally entered the lab accompanied by a robot bearing in its trio of extended arms a stack of papers a good fifty centimeters thick. Sam took one look at the robot and burst out laughing. "Olga, you'd better be pulling my leg."

"Sorry, Sam. Not this time."

"You call that a summary? It's thicker than the Hindu *Mahabharta,* and probably considerably less enlightening."

"And only the start, Sam. All we have so far is what we've been able to observe from here, from *Leverrier*, and we've got to assume that's only a portion of the full story. I've already ordered the launch of a series of atmospheric skimmers to give us more of the whole picture. I'm also having an instrument package put together for a soft-landing at the Kith settlement site. I'm going to send along a mobile robot unit with full video capability too. The Kith may destroy it the way they have before, but I think it's worth a try under the circumstances. Give me another two or three standays, Sam, and I ought to really be able to tell you something."

Sam was still staring in bemusement at the robot and its paper burden. Finally he said, "I'm not going to be able to wait that long, Olga."

"You want to go now?"

He nodded. "Yes."

Olga didn't seem especially surprised. She said, "Are you sure that's wise?"

"No," he admitted. "But wisdom isn't really the point. But neither is data, pure information, which is all you're actually promising me. I'm as fascinated as anyone else by what's taken place on Neptune, but what matters more, I believe, is why it's happening. That's a question only the Kith can answer. I don't want to wait any longer than necessary before asking them."

"Will they answer?"

"In their way I think they may already have. But we need to be sure." He nodded at the robot. "All I require from you, Olga, is whether there's anything hidden in that mountain of facts to preclude our going ahead with another MAGMOS mission at this time."

"If anything, the opposite. Here—see for yourself." Olga dipped a hand into a pocket and produced what looked to be fewer than a dozen stapled sheets of paper.

"The data summary?" Sam asked.

She grinned. "Yes. That"—she glanced at the robot—"that was just to give you an idea."

"Thank you, Olga. I see you agree with me that teaching through demonstration is the best way."

"You taught me that, Sam."

"So I must have." Sam was reading the summary, rifling the pages swiftly. Once or twice he grunted, and another time gasped in apparent astonishment. "This is amazing," he said when he finished, "but not unexpected. Neptune, once as inhospitable a ball of gas and ice as existed in the Solar System, is becoming compatible with life as we know it."

Olga nodded. "The Kith appear to be terraforming the planet for us," she said.

"For somebody," Sam murmured.

She gave him a long, hard, curious look. "I don't get you, Sam. What are you talking about?"

"I'm just a little skeptical that any of this"—he waved the summary in his hand and nodded at the robot—"is being undertaken for the benefit of the human race."

"Who else, then?"

"That's another question only the Kith can answer, and again I think it's one that ought to be asked right away."

"And that's why you don't want to wait?"

He nodded.

"Then go ahead. It's really up to you and them, the kids. I won't try to stop you. Even with Nina." She glanced across at the still-sleeping child. "I may not be entirely happy, but I won't stop you."

"Thank you, Olga," he said. He twisted his head slightly to look at Dr. Mobutu. "And you, Bob? What do you think? Do you want to read over the summary report for yourself?"

"No. I'll accept your word—and Olga's—for what it contains, as incredible as that may appear. All I can assure you of is that the MAGMOS systems remain in a state of readiness whenever your final decision is made."

"And Fred?" Sam turned to Dr. Berman. "I know you've been listening. Have you anything you want to tell me—from the psychiatric standpoint?"

Dr. Berman stood leaning against the wall beside Carolina. "I've heard nothing so far that seems to breach the boundaries of my territory. As far as I'm concerned, you're in charge, Sam. Do what you think's best—and good luck."

Sam nodded curtly, handed the summary report back to Olga, and started off across the room. Danny, lowering his gaze and listening to the approaching footsteps as loud as drumbeats in the stillness of the big room, knew where he had to be headed.

Sam knelt down in front of Eileen and gave the still sleeping Nina a gentle shake.

Her eyes popped open and she groaned. "Darn you, Sam. Why did you have to wake me up? I was having a dream."

"A good dream?" he asked.

"Are there bad ones?"

"For most of us, yes."

"Not me." Nina slid off Eileen's lap and stood, stretching. "Isn't it time to go yet?"

"That's why I woke you up."

"Good. I'm getting darn sick and tired of all this stupid waiting around. It's boring, Sam."

"I couldn't agree more, dear. Just be patient for another few moments, please." Sam got back to his feet. "Danny? George? How about it? Any questions? Any second thoughts?"

Afraid to trust his own voice, Danny shook his head. No, no second thoughts. His thoughts were still his original first thoughts. He wasn't any more scared than before. Or any less either. But he was ready. And he knew that was all Sam wanted to know.

"George?" Sam said again.

Danny glanced at his brother, whose face was broken by a crooked grin. Danny wondered if this was going to be the moment when George finally backed out. Maybe that was what his silence until now had been leading up to. After all, now that he knew it was safe for him to return to Mars, why shouldn't he?

"I've got a question," George said.

"Fire away," Sam said.

"The three of us are going, right? So who goes first?"

It wasn't the question Danny had expected.

"Either you or Danny," Sam said. "I want someone there when Nina arrives. Otherwise, it doesn't matter."

"Then me," George said. "I'm used to taking care of little brother. Let me go first."

"Unless Danny objects."

"No, that's okay," Danny said quickly, pleased—and surprised—that George hadn't backed out. And besides, Danny thought, ready or not, did he really want to be the one to go first?

"Then George first. Nina second. And Danny. Is that agreeable with all of you?"

They nodded.

George's crooked grin hadn't faded. "You ready for me, then?"

"If the scrambler is . . ."

"All systems remain in a readiness state," Mobutu reported from his computer terminal. "All that's lacking is a subject present in the chamber."

"Gee, I guess he means me," George said, coming to his feet in a single motion and shedding the linen robe he wore. Underneath, like Danny and Nina, he was naked.

George crossed the lab, showing neither hesitation nor embarrassment. To reach the scrambler chamber he had to detour around the still motionless and silent Duncan. Then he looked back at Sam and waved an arm. "I thought you were the one who wanted to hurry."

Danny had never thought of the scrambler chamber as anything more than a big metal box approximately three meters high propped on one end. But now that he looked at it again—and recalled how it was to be used—he realized what it actually reminded him of. A coffin. An upright coffin like those the ancient Egyptians buried their mummies in. Except that this coffin wasn't painted or hand-carved or anything else ornate. It was as smooth and featureless as a slab of granite—and as cold as the grave.

Sam hurried past George and grabbed a handle jutting out from the chamber. He gave it a swift jerk and the door in front snapped open with a clang. Inside it was pitch dark. George, without a backward glance, stepped in, immediately vanishing from view. "Better hurry," came his slightly muffled voice from within. "I forgot to tell you. I'm scared of the dark."

"As soon as you're ready, George."

"Hey, I told you I was ready." His voice was higher pitched now. "Go ahead and do it."

Sam reached out and pulled the handle again. This time the door clanged shut. "Proceed, Bob," he said in a hoarse voice. "Let's get this over."

Mobutu hovered over his terminal. Danny, preferring to focus on him instead of the scrambler box, watched as his fingers nimbly danced. There was never anything else. No dramatic burst of light, no sudden loud thunderclap, no whir or whine or anything else out of the ordinary.

Turning in his chair to face them, Mobutu folded his hands in his lap. "The subject has been transported," he announced.

"Let me know when you get a bead on him." Sam remained standing beside the vacant scrambler chamber.

"I have one." Mobutu leaned forward to peer at the viewscreen in front of him. "The signal indicates a subject presence in the vicinity of the last known Kith settlement site."

"Is he moving?"

"No. The signal is stationary."

"Has he moved?"

Mobutu started to answer, then tapped the keyboard. "No," he said.

"Goddamn it." Sam looked not only tense—they were all tense—he looked weary, exhausted. And old. "George should know enough . . ."

Danny understood. The fact that the microscopic tracking device scrambled into George's Neppie form was telling them he had arrived on Neptune, actually meant little or nothing. George could be down there—but hurt or dead. It wasn't until he moved that they would know he was all right.

There was a long silence. No one spoke or even seemed to move. Finally Mobutu murmured, "Still no movement, Sam."

"That . . . brat. What's he think he's doing down there? Is he counting the stars in the sky?"

"Because of the remaining cloud layer—" Olga began.

"Yes. I know. I was speaking rhetorically. Besides, it's the middle of the morning down there right now."

"Maybe I ought to wait in the astronomical lab, in the observatory," Olga said. "If there's a storm—or further upheavals—you'll need to know."

"You've got people on duty to inform us of that, Olga."

"Just robots, Sam. I think I'd be better if—"

"No." Sam's voice turned sharp. "Nobody leaves. Nobody. Not until we know for certain that boy down there is—"

"He's moving," Mobutu broke in. His tone was as unemotional as a robot, but Danny felt overwhelmed nevertheless. It was all he could do not to spring from his chair and let out a cheer. As it was, he contented himself with grinning a grin that threatened to break his face in two.

"Give me the particulars," Sam said, thoroughly in command again. "How is he moving?"

"He seems to be . . . yes. He's moving in a wide circle. And now—yes —he's turned back and he's retracing his steps, going the opposite way. This is excellent, Sam." Mobutu no longer sounded anything like a robot. The drama of the moment had infected even him. "A wonderful boy. Exceedingly bright. He's letting us know in the most direct possible way that he's fully in control of his own movements."

"Yes, he is," Sam said. "God, yes." With an enormous grin of his own, Sam slammed the side of the chamber with the flat of his hand. "God damn, yes." Still grinning, he swung his head and looked at all of them. "Anybody happen to have a real tobacco cigarette? I definitely feel like celebrating."

Oddly enough, no one else was. Not even Danny anymore. As if at a signal, everyone was suddenly staring at Nina. Withering under their combined gaze, she seemed to draw back into herself.

Sam, realizing what was occurring, hastened to her side. Nina grabbed his hand and pulled him down close to her. She whispered in his ear.

When he straightened up, Sam looked solemn. "If anyone in this room so much as cracks an eyelid, I'll gouge out both his eyes with my own fingers."

Nina pulled him down again.

He nodded firmly. "All right. I'll tell them." He turned. "Ladies and gentlemen, all of you. Nina has requested that you please cover your eyes. She's about to disrobe and she's a woman of modesty."

Nina pulled him down once more. This time when Sam straightened up he seemed to be choking back a smile. "She says it's all right for Eileen, Olga, and Carolina to watch since they're her fellow females, and Danny also, since he's her brother. But the rest of you—not one peek."

Still, when the time came, Danny covered his eyes too. He felt it was the least he could do for Nina, and besides, not being able to see definitely made things easier to endure. In his self-sustained darkness Danny heard shuffling footsteps followed by a clang and then the hushed murmur of voices. There was another clang and then—for a long time—nothing.

Danny's eyes popped open.

Dr. Mobutu said: "She's transported, Sam." And then, almost immediately afterward: "I'm receiving two signals now. She's made it, Sam."

Sam said, "I only hope she has enough sense to let us—"

Mobutu broke in. "And movement. I'm getting movement. From both of them. They're moving around each other and—" Suddenly, astonishingly, Mobutu giggled. "It looks as if they're dancing. Like two circling fireflies. You ought to see this, Sam. It's . . . it's lovely."

A loud cheer went up from them—from all of them—and Danny heard his own voice joining in.

And then it ended as spontaneously as it had begun.

And all eyes—Sam, Mobutu, Carolina, Olga, Eileen, Dr. Berman—all eyes except for those of Duncan and Danny's own—were focused on Danny.

TWENTY-FOUR

When Danny at last reached the open door to the scrambler chamber, Sam stepped in front of him. "Ready, son?" he asked in a soft voice.

Danny nodded firmly, perhaps too firmly. "I'm ready, sir."

Sam frowned. "I thought we'd been through this before. No more *sirs*, please."

"I'm sorry. I forgot."

"And no apologies either. Agreed?"

"I—Agreed, Sam."

"Good boy." He punched his arm fondly. "Shall we go for a little trip, then?"

Danny looked straight inside the chamber door. He didn't care how dark it was in there. It was a machine, only that, nothing more. He didn't care whether it resembled a coffin or not. Thinking that was stupid—and childish. Hadn't two other people just now gone inside and emerged intact in another place, another world? The chamber was no different from a robot, a wristwatch, a shovel. It was a tool, built by humans for the use of humans.

Sam leaned close, speaking quickly into his ear. "One point I didn't mention to the others, Danny. Duncan. While you're on Neptune, keep a watch out for him."

"Are you going to try to scramble him, too, Sam?" Danny asked.

"Physically, we can't, no, but . . . you've seen some of what he can do. He was seeing through Mike's eyes earlier, as incredible as that seems. Just be on the lookout. For his presence. His psychic presence. If he's there, perhaps he can help you."

"How?"

"You'll have to wait and see."

Sam backed off slightly, then extended his hand, a gesture he'd made with neither George nor Nina. Danny noted with surprise that the hand was shaking as he gripped it and shook.

"Give your dad my love when you see him," Sam said softly.

"Then you think we'll see him?"

"I'm certain of it. But why ask me? One way or the other, you'll know soon enough, won't you?"

Danny nodded, withdrawing his hand. Sam, as usual, was right. The time for theoretical questions had passed. The door to the scrambler chamber remained open before him. Sam's expression wavered slightly. He dipped his head.

Danny stepped forward. Eyes open, mind clear, he entered the chamber. It was just a big, empty, metal box. Narrow—barely shoulder-width—and not deep. Reaching the back wall, Danny managed to turn. Through the frame of the open door he could see into the room beyond. It was strange looking at people and knowing they couldn't see him. It made it easier to look directly at them, to watch and observe. Carolina, for instance. His gaze eventually came to rest on her. She seemed relaxed, leaning against the wall with Dr. Berman, her arms folded on her chest. But her expression was tense, a concentrated frown, the skin drawn tight over the jaw. Was she worried, frightened for him, or was she only thinking about her own turn in the scrambler chamber still possibly to come? Danny raised an arm, the elbow rubbing against the wall of the chamber, and waggled his fingers. Carolina couldn't see him of course. But her expression did seem to lighten. He waved again. This time a real smile played at the corners of her mouth. How did she know? Maybe she was another one—a psychic—like Duncan. Or maybe he was. Or maybe it was all of them—every human being everywhere, each in his or her own way—all part of one vast psychic whole that none of them individually could comprehend.

In that instant it seemed to Danny a truly transcendental insight, the first of his life.

Then the door shut. There was no warning. Blackness swallowed him like a hand turning into a fist. *I won't be afraid,* he thought. I won't be because I can't be, because there isn't the luxury.

And he wasn't afraid. There inside the scrambler chamber with nothing but blackness and silence around him—with nothing but nothing—Danny felt nothing. No fear. Nothing.

It's like the utter empty peace of the grave, he thought.

No! It's not like that at all. It's not death—it's life. Like the dark, silent, poised instant just prior to birth—like the beginning of the beginning. And it was cold. A draft seemed to tickle his bare legs. That was silly, of course. The chamber was sealed as tight as a drum. But he still felt it. He wanted to shiver.

Then the pain hit him like a hammer blow.

He'd been expecting it, from past experience, from the other times he'd gone through scrambling, but it was much worse this time, perhaps because it went on longer. Only seconds to be sure—the time it took to transport, the shattered molecules of his body from *Leverrier* to Neptune —but during those few horrible moments it was as though an invisible hand clutching a knife were working its way methodically through the innards of his body, slashing relentlessly at everything vital it could reach. Danny threw back his head—though he had no head and no body to be slashed—and screamed a voiceless scream.

Then it was over. The pain vanished as suddenly as a hand clap, and sweet, clean air flooded his lungs. Danny forced open his eyes and he saw . . .

. . . Neptune.

There it was, spread all around him, stretching from horizon to impossibly far horizon, the frozen icy plain, and above, a sky mottled with quivering brilliant clouds. For a moment it all seemed too vast for his meager senses to encompass, and he understood why others before him had gone mad.

Then, like a mixed-up jigsaw puzzle suddenly coalescing to form a whole, it all made sense. And he saw George. Nina too. Two Neppies, one perhaps three times the size of the other, standing side by side on the ice a few meters ahead of him. Other than their size, the two were identical grayish-brown slugs, torsos propped upright on a dozen short squat legs that looked as thick as an elephant's. They were both looking straight back at him, too, from eyes centered high in their foreheads and circled by crests of hard, bony, protective tissue.

Looking back at them, Danny was suddenly transformed again when he least expected it.

He became self-aware.

I'm one, too, he thought. I'm a Neppie as surely as these two. He didn't need to look at himself. He knew. The same way that he knew his heart was beating. It was part of the fabric of his self.

But if he were a Neppie, then he most surely was not—could not—he wasn't Danny Hawkins anymore.

And it was this realization that shoved him over a brink he had failed to recognize lurked so near.

With that, Danny began to laugh, and laughing, understood that it wasn't Neptune, the planet, that had driven the others insane so much as their own new selves and the incapacity of their limited minds—their limited human minds—to comprehend the totality of a changed identity, a new state of being, an essence altered beyond any point of past recognition.

The earlier experimental run-throughs in the environmental chamber had failed to prepare Danny for what he now underwent. On *Leverrier,* in the lab, the experience had never been entirely real. A portion of the mind had always remained apart, a separate witness ready to testify that nothing that was happening was valid, that Danny Hawkins was still Danny Hawkins, that this alien body surrounding him with its twelve elephant legs and its sluglike torso was no more real than a costume that could be slipped into and then slipped out of again.

But he wasn't in the lab now. He was on Neptune. He was an alien being on an alien world. With no company but other alien beings. There was nothing human here to cling to, nothing with which to stand apart.

And thus the laughter that consumed him like a flame. It was silent laughter. Danny couldn't have made a sound even if he'd wanted. In order to breathe sufficient quantities of oxygen to survive on Neptune, Neppies had been designed with mouths, throats, and lungs several times human scale, too large, it transpired, simultaneously to produce a recognizable voice. As a result, the biological engineers had chosen not to include either tongues or larynxes in their final design. So Neppies couldn't talk. Nor could they laugh.

Yet Danny was laughing.

He heard himself distinctly. It was laughter that seemed to go on and on indefinitely, like a mighty river flowing into its self, as if it never would stop, never could stop.

Why was he laughing? At himself? Why, yes, most definitely at himself. But at George too—and Nina. At Neppie George and Neppie Nina, at human George and human Nina. And more. He was laughing at this crazy absurd planet. At Neptune. And beyond. Danny was laughing at Mars and Saturn, at the Earth and the Moon and all the other planets and satellites of the Solar System. He was laughing at *Leverrier* and its scrambler chamber, at the MAGMOS Process and the lab, at Sam Goble and Carolina and Benny and Duncan, at Dr. Mobutu and Dr. Berman. He was laughing at the Kith. At cold drafts tickling his legs. At transcendental flashes of insight and winks and grins and frowns and smiles. He was laughing at words, at thoughts, at feelings. He was laughing at laughter. Most of all, though, Danny was laughing at life itself—at existence—at the whole huge crackpot universe, at the very concept that—

Ouch! His head suddenly exploded. The pain cut through the fiery furnace of his silent laughter like a knife made of ice. The laughter died out within him. How could he laugh when his head hurt so awfully bad?

It was George. Danny saw him now. Neppie George standing head to head with him on the ice, a scant half meter away. Then George charged. His head rammed forward. Head butted head. The pain reached Danny only gradually, as if from a distance, but when it did arrive, it was just like before. *Ouch!* He winced.

Danny stood reeling as George backed slowly off. What the hell was George trying to do? Had he gone out of his mind? Was he trying to kill him?

No, Danny thought. He had it wrong. He had it backward. George wasn't the one out of his mind. George was the sane one. And George wasn't trying to kill him. George was trying to save him.

For how long a time, Danny wondered, had he remained rooted in the same spot where he'd beamed down on this planet, totally consumed by his own soundless—and mindless—laughter?

For too long a time. George had realized something was wrong. And acted to save him. Though not his life. No matter what, Danny would have lived on. Others had before. What George was trying to save with the only immediate tool at his disposal—his own skull—was something more precious than life. It was Danny's sense of personal identity—his sense of his own true self.

He'd come that close to losing it too.

I'm Danny Hawkins, he thought, enunciating each word separately in his mind. I always will be Danny Hawkins. Nothing—not even this grotesque slug body—can alter the fact of who I am.

George watched closely as Danny continued to stand motionless, thinking. The two big eyes in the front of George's head were brown, Danny saw, the same as his human eyes. That helped too. It was a reassuring sight, like stumbling across an old friend in a foreign city. Danny was feeling much better. The mad, hysterical laughter—and what had brought it on—seemed far away now. He was going to be all right, Danny decided.

How could he let George know? He definitely didn't feel like being on the receiving end of another head butt. He thought about trying to smile, but with a Neppie face—if you could really call it a face—largely devoid of muscles, the best he could manage was opening his mouth and blinking his eyes at the same time.

That probably wasn't enough. So Danny decided to try a few steps. Even one would be more than he'd accomplished so far, and ought to reassure George that he'd gained control over himself.

Danny took a moment to review the necessary actions involved in walking. But George, still watching, was beginning to look anxious. So, fearing another head butt, Danny took a deep breath, raised his six left legs into the air, tilted his body at a precarious angle, and then lunged forward, bringing the legs back down again.

Amazingly, it worked. He'd taken a step. A real step. His first ever on Neptune.

Pausing, Danny shifted his weight to the left, then raised his right legs, lunged, and brought them down also. Another step. Two. It was a peculiar locomotion technique, he knew—more like a series of staggering near falls than a genuine walk—but the most effective means yet devised for getting around under high gravity conditions on a dozen short squat legs with no knee joints. When witnessed, the walk more closely resembled a half-dozen drunken soldiers struggling to march in single file than the graceful undulations of other multilimbed creatures like caterpillars and centipedes. But caterpillars and centipedes did not have to get around successfully under the gee forces of Neptune. Neppies did.

Watching, George now seemed to relax, apparently understanding the message Danny was trying to convey—that everything was okay with him. Emboldened by George's attitude, Danny took a third step, and a fourth. Oddly, the process of walking was turning out to be both more difficult than he'd expected and easier too. Difficult because it was different than when he'd practiced in the environmental chamber, and easier because the difference lay in the fact that the actual effort involved in lifting his legs and lunging forward was less now than it had been. Plainly, Neptune had indeed undergone yet another significant loss of mass and consequent lessening of gravity. As a result, though Danny wouldn't have said he felt light on his feet or that walking here was any kind of snap, it certainly was less strenuous than, say, trying to go for a stroll even on Mars in his human body without the mechanical assistance of his electric leg braces.

Danny took a fifth step and a sixth, growing more confident as he proceeded. He made up his mind to try to complete a big broad circle the way George and Nina had. He was recalling Sam now—Sam and Carolina and the others in the lab on *Leverrier*—who had been given no clue that Danny was anything other than dead.

When he finished the circle—each step more natural than the one before
—he paused long enough to turn his body completely around—a complex
maneuver, but one he managed with only two near slips—and then started
to retrace his steps.

He hadn't gone far when a peculiar feeling began to steal over him. Déjà
vu, he knew it was called. The feeling one sometimes experienced in a
strange place that one had somehow been there before. It wasn't a totally
new sensation in Danny's life—for some reason it had happened to him
quite a bit while exploring the woods close to home—but this time it
seemed ridiculous to the point of complete absurdity. Déjà vu had its place
—and its logical explanations, he was sure—but here? On Neptune?

For a moment Danny was afraid he was on the verge of losing his mind
again.

When he finally understood the significance of the feeling, it stopped
him cold in his tracks. Why, of course, he thought. No wonder he felt as if
he'd been here before. In a sense he had been.

Dr. Mobutu had set the scrambler to beam the three of them down two
hundred meters northeast of the Kith settlement site. But something had
gone awry. The scrambler had missed its target. But not by very much.

They weren't two hundred meters northeast of the Kith settlement. No.
They were smack in the middle of it.

Danny had studied enough photographs and videotapes of the settlement over the past months to be certain. Yes, one ice-encrusted chunk of
land looked much like any other ice-encrusted chunk of land. Even on
Neptune. But this chunk looked *exactly* like it.

Except for one item. And that was the problem. The settlement itself.
The thirty hemispheric domes of black glass. They weren't where they
ought to have been. They weren't here.

The Kith settlement had vanished.

And with it—presumably—so had the Kith.

Danny, George, and Nina were right where they wanted to be.

And they were alone.

TWENTY-FIVE

It was Nina who found the Kith. While Danny remained motionless in the same place he'd stumbled to a halt, stricken by the realization that their mission was a failure, too stunned—and heartsick—to want to budge another centimeter; and while George, a short distance away, was also visibly moping—he, too, plainly aware of exactly where they'd landed—Nina's ignorance of the truth freed her from the bonds of despair.

Not only did she not seem inconvenienced by her new Neppie body, she seemed to find it a major source of delight. For a moment, observing her, Danny worried that they might have lost Nina, that her mind had cracked the way his own nearly had, but then he understood that Nina was just having fun.

At one point she even managed to break into something resembling a loping trot, chasing circles around first George and then Danny, clearly urging them to join in.

Danny wished he could. It would have been fun just watching her, for that matter, if everything else hadn't been so bleak and serious.

He wondered how long they'd been down here now, how much longer they'd have to stay before the scrambler jerked them back. Time was impossible to really tell. A minute might be an hour, an hour a minute. Time was all so internal, he realized, so dependent on the body. Stuck in this Neppie torso, he was totally adrift. And, of course, there was no sun in the sky to help him either.

The weather, in fact, was turning gradually worse, if something as bizarre and tumultuous as the changing climatic conditions on Neptune could be termed mere weather. The clouds overhead, primarily bleached yellow and dingy brown when they'd arrived, were now being superseded by a lower stratum of darker, puffier, grayish clouds. If he'd been home on Earth, Danny would have guessed it was getting set to storm. And maybe it was, for now and then a real snowflake would come tumbling down from above, twisting here and there in the wind. To the south a bolt of lightning snaked against the horizon, and then to the north Danny saw another. At intervals distant thunder rattled like a big drum.

Oblivious to this as well as everything else, Nina continued her romp.

It would have looked funny when her two front legs shot suddenly out from under her and she tumbled forward on her chin—what passed for a chin on a Neppie—and slid four meters before coming to rest in a clump of disjointed legs and torso. It would have been funny, if the risk of injury hadn't been so serious. Wakened from his lethargy, Danny went hurrying to her side.

Sam had cautioned them many times about the danger of falling, though assuring them, too, that their MAGMOS forms were designed to be as physically safe as possible under Neptune's high-gee conditions. He even told them a story about how the biological engineers had gone to Earth, acquired a real slug—"a native from your neck of the woods, Danny"— transported it to the Eiffel Tower, and dropped the slug from the top. It had suffered no ill effects, Sam told them.

"But it didn't ask to do it again either," he added, "which is something I want you to keep in mind, because everytime you take a tumble on Neptune, even if it's just a matter of flopping on your faces, the practical effect is precisely the same as the slug falling from the top of the Eiffel Tower."

(Benny later insisted that Sam's calculations were exaggerated, but he didn't say by how much.)

(Danny was skeptical also. The Eiffel Tower, he was pretty sure, was in Paris, and nothing of Paris had survived the war.)

Danny blamed himself for not exercising more control over Nina. She was his kid sister, and he should have made her stop before it was too late.

Just as Danny reached Nina's side, another bolt of lightning ripped through the northern sky. Closer this time, too, he thought, pausing to stare. The icy ground underfoot quivered slightly. A quake?

Danny looked down at Nina lying on one side, her legs dangling in the air. She looked back at him—her eyes a luminous, human blue—and managed a wink.

He felt a wave of pure relief. *You're not hurt?* he wished he could ask. *You're all right?*

Nina bobbed her head up and down as if hearing his unspoken words and then swung it sharply to one side, gesturing beyond him.

Danny shuffled his feet cautiously, turned, and glanced back.

George stood there, his head bent down, peering at something lying on the ice. It was an ovalshaped object, primarily yellow, with splotches of blue here and there. From where it lay, Danny guessed the object was what had caused Nina to trip and fall.

More than anything else, he thought, it looked like a turtle's shell.

George lowered his head and bumped the object.

It sat up. As it did, a head appeared. Then two legs popped out. And arms. Four arms.

The Kith stood slowly erect, gazing at each of them in turn. *Former humans, go away,* came the voice in Danny's mind. *You disturb the sad and sullen dream-sleep of one Gornami (the dunce).*

Danny had given up any lingering hope that this might happen—that they'd find a Kith after all. He fought to get a grip on his emotions and tried to speak with his mind, projecting his silent voice. *Who are you? What happened to the rest? Where have—*

Please! The voice was an agonized shout. The Kith clutched its skull in two hands. *One at a time. I cannot listen to three fools screaming at once.*

Danny glanced at George, who stepped back. Danny interpreted this as a signal for him to proceed. Neither George nor Nina would be able to hear him, he gathered—he hadn't heard them screaming just now—but they should be able to hear the Kith.

You are the one called Gornami-yev? You spoke with the humans Benny and Raymond when they came to Neptune?

No. Gornami-yev (the former dunce) no longer exists. He has become what he once was before—Gornami (the dunce).

Are you by yourself here, Gornami?

I am Gornami-til (the lonely dunce).

Where did the other Kith go?

There. Gornami turned, facing north, and bowed his head. As he did, there was more lightning. Farther off this time. A white flash—not a bolt of yellow. *At the place of the dawning.* Thunder now rolled. *Where the Neptune world spins upon itself.*

The pole? The north pole?

Yes.

Why there?

The-one-who-is-nothing summoned them. The moment has come for those who wish to know the cosmic flux.

What is the cosmic flux?

Sad laughter. *If I knew the meaning of the flux, I would not be here now,*

Danny Hawkins. I am the dunce, he who stays while all others go. Even Dav (the wanderer) proved wiser than me.

Danny was getting pretty weary of Gornami's self-pity. It reminded him of the way he used to act sometimes, thinking about his crippled legs. And now look at him. He didn't have those legs anymore. He had twelve other brand-new ones—even if it was only for a while. *How do you know my name?* he asked.

I know, Danny Hawkins. And George. And Nina.

But how?

I have glimpsed your warmth-fabric as shared with me by others. Your shape is different now, it is true, but the warmth-fabric is the same.

Benny, you mean? And Raymond?

And the former human Dav (the wanderer). He and I knew soul communion before the-one-who-is-nothing called.

So little of this seemed to make sense. Was Gornami deliberately trying to confuse him? Or was he just being what he was—an alien? Sam would have said they were lucky to understand anything.

Who is Dav (the wanderer) and how does he know me?

He is your father, Danny, the one at times known as the Michael Hawkins creature.

Is he here? Danny swung his head, attempting to see. There was a blast of wind and the ground was shaking. Definitely a quake this time.

He felt a wave of anxiety, and realized it wasn't his own.

Gornami?

Is something happening? he asked the Kith. *Is there a reason you're afraid?*

The ground stopped shaking.

No more questions, Danny Hawkins. I must seek dream-sleep. The cosmic flux flows near, and I am not prepared for the void.

But you've got to tell me about my father.

Gornami lay down on the ice, his head and limbs withdrawing inside his shell.

It was George who came over, lowered his head, and bumped the Kith with his skull. Hard. Gornami rolled over on his back. His head popped out of the shell.

George was glaring at him, Danny would have sworn.

He has gone, Gornami said.

There was a pause.

To the place of the dawning. With the many-elders.

Another pause.

Dav was wiser than I knew. Once before he died and drew close to the void. In that time he came to know much of the flux.

Gornami was clearly responding to George's questions. For Danny it was like listening to one end of a telephone conversation. He decided to try to interject a question of his own.

Did our father say anything about us before he went away? He asked us to come here. He told Benny he wanted to see us. Did he forget?

No, he did not forget you.

Did he leave a message? With you?

Yes, with me—the dunce. There was a distinct undertone of bitterness in Gornami's words, though Danny couldn't have said how he could tell. *As the many-elders left for the place of the dawning, one following the other, Dav sought me out and demanded communion. He showed me each of you and said,* These are my children, Gornami, born of my own blood. If they come to you, send them to me. *Dav knew. He knew then that I was still the dunce, that the void was my fate.*

He said for us to go to him?

At the place of the dawning, yes.

But how? We can't very well walk.

Gornami's laughter was smug. *Perhaps Dav failed to realize that his children were mere Gornamis too. Now let me find dream-sleep. There is nothing else I can tell you.*

Gornami lay back down on the ice, withdrawing his head and limbs. This time George made no effort to interfere. Instead he strained to lift his head as high as it would go—not far, since his Neppie body lacked any real neck—and seemed to stare at the cloud-encrusted sky.

Danny looked too. *Sam,* he wished he could somehow say. *Sam, you've got to hear me. Bring us back. Bring us now. There's nothing we can do here. You've got to bring us back so we can beam right down again. To the north pole. That's where the Kith are. Dad too. He wants us to join him. He told Gornami. Sam—please. Can't you hear me?*

Sam could not, of course. And even if he could—if he had—it wouldn't have worked. In scrambling all three of them, the MAGMOS energy reserves had been drained. Even if Sam brought them back right now, it might be days before a new mission could be launched, and by then whatever was going on at Neptune's pole—at the place of the dawning, Gornami called it—might be over.

The ground was trembling again, a milder quake than some of the earlier ones. But it did seem to go on for a long time.

There was thunder too.

Danny? George? Nina? Can you hear me?

It was a voice in Danny's mind. He glanced expectantly at Gornami, but the Kith seemed oblivious, lost in private reverie. And, besides, the voice was different this time. Vaguely familiar, too, as crazy as that seemed.

Dad? Danny tried hopefully.

No, Danny. Sorry. But I've been listening in. I think there's a way I can help.

Then Danny knew whose voice it was. Of course, he thought. Sam predicted this might happen.

Duncan!

Hi, Danny.

Duncan, where are you?

Oh, just about everywhere. There was laughter, a gentle tickling sensation inside Danny's mind that made him feel warm all over. *My body's still on Leverrier, but when I want, I can go almost anywhere.*

If you're in the lab, can you talk to Sam? Can you tell him to bring us back right away?

I could try, Danny, but it wouldn't work. I've been monitoring Dr. Mobutu's thoughts. There won't be another mission for at least three standays, and then they'll only be able to beam one person down. It'll be too late anyway.

Then we're stuck here.

Not if I can help.

Help? How can you help, Duncan?

I told you I can see almost everywhere. Well, I've been to the pole—to the place of the dawning. I've communed with the Kith, the many-elders, and I've learned some of their secrets.

What secrets?

How they move from one place to another, how they teleport. It's not even really that hard—not for me—not once you know how to see beyond your own body.

But I can't do that. None of us can.

I know, but it might not matter. If I can get inside your mind, Danny—if you'll let me—then maybe I can do it for you.

How?

I can't teach you. You don't know enough yet. I'll have to do it for you.

Are you sure you can?

No. But it's worth trying, I think.

And there's no risk?

There's always a risk, Danny. It's your mind. And George's and Nina's. You guys have to decide.

Is there enough time?

It only takes an instant.

And Sam won't bring us back too soon?

Danny, you've only been on Neptune a few minutes.

Minutes? That didn't seem possible. So much had already happened. But when Danny tried to remember what, his memory failed him. There was Nina's fall. And Gornami. But what else?

So what do you think, Danny? Duncan prodded.

Danny wasn't sure what to think. It scared him, he admitted, the idea of letting someone else enter his mind and take control. But, clearly, there was no other way. *Duncan, you say you've been to the pole. What's going on there? If I knew, it would help me decide. What is this place of the dawning?*

A wonderful place, Danny. It's what everything here on Neptune has been about the whole time, what it's been leading up to, what we came here to find out.

But what is it, Duncan?

See for yourself, Danny. That's the best way. Believe me.

Can't you at least give me a hint of—

Look, damn it, broke in a different voice, though Danny couldn't have said exactly how he knew it was different. It just was, that was all. *Why don't we all shut up and get this thing over with? If we're going to do it, do it.*

George, Danny said, *George. I heard you.*

I'm hearing you, too, Danny-boy.

And me, came another new voice. *I'm hearing everybody. My leg hurts, Danny. I think I twisted it when I fell over that stupid Kith.*

Nina?

Hi, Danny. Isn't this fun?

This is my doing, Duncan broke in. *I'm trying to see if I can act as a channel among the three of you. But don't overdo it, okay? It's mostly for my own benefit. Trying to carry on three separate conversations at the same time was giving me an awful headache. George and Nina have said they're ready to go ahead and try it. So I guess it's up to you now, Danny. What's your decision?*

It came as no surprise to Danny to discover that he'd already made up his mind. *All right, Duncan. I'm with you. What do I have to do?*

Nothing really. Just stand still. And try to empty your mind, make it a complete blank. I know that's not easy, but try to concentrate on a color. What's your favorite color?

Mine's pink, Nina said.

That's a good choice. Think of pink. All three of you. Keep your eyes open and try to paint everything around you pink. A warm, soothing pink. Concentrate on that and I'll sneak inside while you do.

Danny tried. Pink. He hated pink. Blue was his favorite color, he supposed. Pink sky, pink ice. Pink Nina, pink George, pink Gornami. Pink Neptune. A pink planet in a pink universe. Duncan was right. It was soothing somehow. He felt almost like he was falling asleep, as if dreams lay very near.

Click.

It happened just like that, as if a single frame had been removed from a reel of film. A jump cut. One instant he was one place. The next he was somewhere else. There—and then here.

And here was the place of the dawning.

Duncan was mistaken, though. Danny realized that right away. Duncan said this was a wonderful place.

It wasn't.

It was an awful place.

Awful—and awesome too.

TWENTY-SIX

For Danny it was like finding himself thrust into the middle of a waking nightmare. He stood perched precariously at the sheer edge of a circular pit, an abyss some twenty meters wide, with nothing visible below except utter and total blackness.

Was the abyss real or only what his mind insisted it must be: a horrible dream?

Danny realized he had no choice but to accept what his senses told him to the contrary: the abyss—and everything else here at the place of the dawning—was as real as real could get.

Holding his breath, Danny edged gingerly back, moving each of his legs separately, aware that any one might slip at any moment and send him plunging into the unknown depths of the pit.

He made it. The abyss loomed a safe three meters away. Relaxing, Danny lowered himself carefully onto his belly and lay there, gasping for air. The process of walking had proved easier than he'd come to expect, the footing solid and firm. There was no ice here. The ground was a hard, nubby, rocky substance like a bed of lava.

But how could that be? he wondered. Neptune's north pole, free of ice?

And it had to be the pole, the place of the dawning. For the Kith were here. As many as fifty stood arrayed in a circle around the edge of the abyss, most dangerously close to the brink, their heads turned downward, their eyes fixed on the blackness beneath. Distantly, Danny could hear a noise. It seemed to be coming from down within the abyss itself. He strained to hear. It was a steady humming noise like a hive of bees—or like machinery at work.

Then one of the Kith closest to him took a step forward. One more step and then it was past the edge. The Kith fell like a shot, vanishing from the sight in an instant. There was no sound—no cry or scream—not even in Danny's mind. The Kith had apparently jumped of its own accord. And now it was gone.

A few moments later, from up out of the pit, gushed a thick stream of greenish-brown particles, like a geyser. The stream of particles rose high into the air and then, caught by churning winds, went swirling off in a dozen different directions at once.

Danny?

The voice in his mind was clear but not immediately recognizable. Danny lowered his gaze from the sky and peered across the abyss. There on the opposite side—among the Kith—stood a lone Neppie.

George? he said with his mind.

George isn't here yet, Danny. Your friend Duncan is still trying to bring him.

Nina? he said, although he knew it couldn't be her.

She'll be here soon, too, but I'm—

Dad, he broke in, wanting to be the one to say it.

I . . . I'm happy you decided to come, Danny.

It was Duncan who brought me.

Yes, I know about that. Duncan was here and we communed. I showed him the way to bring the three of you to me.

He didn't tell us about you.

I asked him not to. If you came, I wanted it to be because you wanted to see me, not just because I'd asked for you.

We wanted to see you, Danny said. It wasn't the entire truth—they were here because of the Kith too—because it was their mission. But his father would know that, Danny decided.

Danny, there's something I'd like you to tell me.

Yes, Dad.

How long—how long in human terms—have I been on this planet?

Nearly five stanyears.

That's all?

Why? Did you think you—

Danny broke off as another of the Kith marched forward. Again it was the same. Two steps—and it was gone.

Dad, he managed. *Dad, why are the Kith killing themselves like—like lemmings?*

They're not, Danny. I know it must seem that way, but . . . there's so much to tell you and so damn little time. That's the story of my life, I think.

There's never enough time. Not for everything. Not even for the things that ought to be important—the things that are important.

Danny thought this might be his father's way of trying to apologize for his years of neglect. Whether or not it was, Danny intended to accept it as such. *Duncan says we've only been down here on Neptune a little while. It'll be at least an hour before Sam brings us back.*

I wasn't talking about that. I . . . only five years, you said? I suppose I should have realized when I found out Sam Goble was involved. Nobody lives forever, not even that old goat, but . . . well, it seemed like so much more time had gone by. Ten years, twenty, even fifty years wouldn't have surprised me. I've lived so many lifetimes here. I was sure the three of you would be grown up now, adults. Maybe it's better this way, though. At least I feel I still know you a little.

Was that another apology of sorts? Danny guessed it might have been meant that way.

Abruptly there was a loud noise like two enormous hands clapping together, and a twelve-legged slug materialized at the edge of the abyss. The Neppie took one look at the gaping black pit in front of it and immediately pitched backward, all dozen feet shooting off in random directions. It was a miracle the Neppie managed to avoid toppling into the abyss. Instead it landed on its belly, seemed to hug the ground, and emitted a loud mental, *Ouch!*

George! Danny said. *You made it!*

I guess I did. George eased back to his feet and sidled away from the abyss's edge. *Do you mind telling me what that big hole in the ground over there is supposed to be?*

It's the place of the dawning, son.

Who's that? George raised his head and peered across the abyss. *Well, well. Surprise, surprise. I figured you'd be long gone again by now.*

George, I—

Another Kith jumped—from the other side of the abyss, close to Mike Hawkins. Again, after a brief interval, a stream of the greenish-brown particles geysered into the air.

George stared. *Did I just see what I thought I saw? Or am I losing my marbles down here after all?*

You saw it, George, Mike said, *and that's part of what I have to explain to you—to both of you.*

Before he could, there was another loud bang and another Neppie materialized at the edge of the pit. Nina, Danny assumed. She took one look at what lay in front of her, pedaled her legs in precise unison, and marched away from the brink.

Wow! came her voice. *That was close.*

Nina. The voice seemed gentle somehow, like a distant whisper.

Hi, Dad, she responded instantly. *I thought you might be here. And you know me too.*

We've never actually met, I know.

And now we have, except—she laughed—*I really don't look like a big ugly slug. I'm really gorgeously beautiful. These guys can tell you. Tell him how beautiful I am, boys.*

I don't need anyone to tell me that, Nina. It's something I figured out for myself. Your poor mother was one of two truly beautiful women I loved in my human life. The other . . . Danny and George know who the other was.

Somebody you decided to walk out on, George said.

It was a mutual decision. My life was out here, and hers—Sara's—she just didn't feel it could be that way anymore.

So you walked out and left her—and us—high and dry. Which is just what I said.

The depth of George's bitterness startled Danny. He'd never realized George felt this strongly about what Mike had done to them. Maybe it helped explain some things about George. Maybe a lot of things.

Mike said, *Didn't you do the same thing yourself, George? Later on, didn't you walk out too?*

That was different.

How?

I was a kid and you weren't.

Looking back now, I'm not so sure of that. Mike laughed gently.

George wasn't about to be mollified, though. *Besides, what do you know about it?* he burst out. *About anything, really? My life or Danny's or—or—*

What I know, Mike broke in evenly, *is certainly a good deal more than what little you know about me, George.*

Well . . . good. Fine. That's perfectly all right with me. Because I don't want to know about you. You're not even human. You're an alien, a slug, a Neppie.

I don't dispute that.

And how did you get that way? By running out again, by running out on everything and everyone, your own species. We all thought you were dead, and the whole time, you were down here with the Kith, alive as anything, and you—

Some of the time I was alive, yes.

George bristled. *What's that supposed to mean?*

It means, son, that the existence I've maintained here on Neptune the past five of your years hasn't been a normal one by any human standard.

So why did you do it?

To glimpse beyond, to peer beyond, to go beyond. To become a thing I never could imagine otherwise. A non-human thing. I admit that. It's true, God knows.

Then why did you have to bother us? Danny and me and Nina too. Why didn't you just hide behind a block of ice when Benny and Raymond showed up? None of us wanted to see you. As far as we were concerned, you were dead and it was better that way.

I wanted to see you, Nina broke in.

Danny said nothing. George was right. He just wasn't sure.

I can see by your feelings that that's not completely the truth, George.

What do you know about my feelings?

I told you earlier that I know a great deal about you.

Is that supposed to mean that you can read my mind or something?

Not your mind, no. I'm not like your friend Duncan. But I can read your . . . your essence. Call it a soul if you want.

I don't want to call it anything. I just want you to leave me alone. Can you understand? What I am and who I am is none of your business.

Then why did you come here, George?

I . . .

Danny was about to interrupt. He could understand George's anger—and even sympathize with his pain—but was this really the time to reopen every old wound to bleed?

Before he could break in, however, another Kith strode forward and vanished into the abyss. A few seconds later, yet another followed.

As greenish-brown particles geysered, Denny heard a boom of thunder. He glanced at the sky overhead where thick black clouds now roiled in mass.

Mike said, *That was Potrum and Nykol, two of the wisest of the many-elders. I'd hoped Nykol would stay long enough to help explain to you about the Kith and why they're here. Of them all, he seemed the one who came nearest to understanding the human essence.*

Dad, Danny said, *maybe you'd better start, then. We don't know how much longer we'll be able to stay. It's hard for us to tell time with everything so different.*

You've got thirty-nine minutes, Danny, came a new voice. *I'm looking at Dr. Mobutu's terminal as I speak.*

Duncan? Danny said.

Here. And there, too, of course. He laughed. *Heck, Danny, I guess I'm almost everywhere.*

Duncan, will you keep watch for us and let us know when it's getting close to time? We've still got to talk to Dad about getting him out of here.

I don't think . . . Mike began, but his voice faded. *Let me tell you abouth the Kith,* he said.

Dad, why are they killing themselves? It was Nina. Another Kith had jumped. And now another followed. Danny counted fewer than twenty left. *I don't want them to die. Can't we stop them?*

They're not dying, Nina, Mike said. *Their goal here on Neptune has been accomplished, and now they're going to journey to another realm-time to continue with their work. That doesn't mean they're dying. It means they're going to become one with the cosmic flux for a time.*

Then it's like what we did when we came here—like in the scrambler?

To a degree, yes. And you didn't die, did you?

But where are they going? Home?

The Kith have no home. The world where they originated—it was called Xob—vanished from the universe long ago. The Kith are a very ancient race. I think—though I'm not positive—the Kith may have been the first intelligent species to evolve in our current universe. A material species, I mean.

Danny's mind was awash with questions already. Everything Mike said seemed to demand explanation. What exactly was the cosmic flux? What kind of species could there be except material species? But there wasn't time for everything.

As if in confirmation, he heard Duncan's voice in his mind: *Thirty-six minutes, Danny.*

Dad, Danny said, *you told us the Kith have finished their work here on Neptune and that's why they're leaving. But what was their goal?*

You can see the results right in front of your eyes, Danny.

Danny peered into the blackness of the abyss. *I don't see anything.*

You do, though you don't know it. You're seeing a miracle, son, though that's the wrong word to use, because in the universe as it is there are no miracles, only natural phenomena, and those are the most wondrous miracles of all. The Kith are the seeders, Danny, the seeders of the universe.

Seeders of—of what?

Of life.

What life?

The life you've been seeing rising up from out of that pit ever since you arrived here. Those innocuous-seeming greenish-brown particles are raw pro-

toplasm, Danny, the basic stuff of life. Some millions of stanyears from now that stuff will have evolved into a race of true Neptunians—assuming the absence of anything cataclysmic to prevent it—a fifty-fifty shot, I understand.

You mean Neppies like us? Nina said.

I wouldn't think so. Evolution is always superior to the laboratory. And besides, as you must be aware, the Kith have modified the physical character of this world in order to accommodate whatever forms may evolve over time.

Another Kith stepped forward into the abyss. Watching as the protoplasmic particles came spewing forth, Danny felt a shiver of awe pass over him. If his father was correct, then this was indeed a miracle he was seeing. And Danny had never witnessed a miracle before.

It was George who asked the next question: *There's something I want to know you haven't explained yet. I want to know why. I want to know how come.*

Why what, George? Mike said.

Why Neptune? And why now?

Before I answer, there's one other thing you ought to know first: the Kith have visited the Solar System before.

To Earth, George said, understanding at once.

To Earth, Mike confirmed. *Some two billion stanyears ago, give or take a few hundred million here or there. On that occasion the Kith concocted the original primeval stuff of life from which everything since—including you and me—evolved.*

So we're sort of related, Nina put in. *Like the Kith are our great-great-great-grandparents or something.*

Or our gods, Danny added, before he could stop himself.

No, Mike corrected gently. *No Danny, this time I think Nina is closer to the truth than you are, closer than she probably realizes herself. Because, you see, whenever the Kith discard their physical bodies, as you see them doing now to merge again with the cosmic flux, the component elements making up those bodies are then incorporated into the protoplasmic brew. So in a a sense the Kith are part of every one of us here, every living thing on the Earth or from the Earth.*

You still haven't really answered my questions, George said.

I know I haven't, son. Why Neptune? you wanted to know. Because Neptune is the planet in the Solar System farthest from Earth and still possessing the necessary materials and environment to allow life to evolve. Pluto is too far from the Sun, too cold, and it's really nothing more than a big frozen rock.

But that still doesn't explain why the Kith came now, Danny said.

They came because they were summoned. And they were summoned under the assumption that the human race was extinct.

Extinct? Nina said. *Why, Dad?*

Because, by all logical and proper reasoning, we ought to be.

The war? Danny said.

The war on Earth, Mike confirmed.

How could the Kith know about that? George asked.

The Kith knew because the cosmic flux knew, and the Kith are close to the flux. The war wasn't, I gather, anything especially extraordinary. Well over half the intelligent species who develop a technology end up annihilating themselves while still in the primitive phase of evolution. The Kith very nearly did so themselves, but were spared by their knowledge of the flux. The one greatest surprise for the Kith when they arrived on Neptune was that we weren't all dead. We should have been. But we had entered space—and colonized portions of it—much earlier than normal. That was our salvation.

Then why didn't the Kith just go away? Nina said. *If we were still here, then we didn't need them.*

The Kith stayed because the flux required them to. And because the odds are very much against you—against the human race. You didn't kill yourselves this time, but there's all eternity left to complete the job. And I think you're misunderstanding one point. The Kith aren't here for the benefit of the human race. They're here to create your replacements.

Then shouldn't we tell them? she said.

Tell them what?

That we're not going to die.

There was warm laughter. *I'm glad you believe that, dear. I only wish—I wish I still believed it too.*

Why don't you? Danny asked.

Because I've seen the flux, son, and I've learned one important thing: it doesn't care. Nowhere in this universe, outside of isolated pockets like the human race, does anything exist that cares. The Kith speak of the-one-who-is-nothing, and by that they mean everything.

I don't understand, Nina said.

That may be for the best, he said.

And what about you? George broke in.

Me?

Yes, you. The longer this goes on, the farther away you seem to get from us. At the start it was always we *humans and* us *humans, and now it's become* you *humans. What happened? Aren't you one of us anymore? Aren't you human too?*

I—I wish I knew, Mike said. *If only I—*

But before he could go on, there was a noise like a clash of cymbals and a Kith materialized so close to Danny he could have touched him.

I did it! yelped the Kith in Danny's mind. *I made it to the dawning!*

Gornami, Danny said, recognizing the Kith.

Greetings, former humans, the Kith said. *But you are mistaken. It is not Gornami (the dunce) who stands before you. It is Gornami-yev-koko (the former and never-to-be-again dunce) who has ridden the great cosmic flux to come here to the place of the dawning to confront the-one-who-is-nothing. Isn't this marvelous? Isn't this wonderful?*

And with that Gornami-yev-koko broke into a lumbering little dance of apparent joy, his head bobbing above his speckled shell, his four arms waving frantically.

I express delight for your achievement, Gornami-yev-koko, Mike said. *For one who has never known the void, it is indeed an achievement of wonder.*

Gornami-yev-koko broke off his dance. *I thank you for your blessing, Dav (the wanderer), who was once a human being.*

I wander no farther, Mike pointed out.

That is true—and proper. Leaning forward, Gornami-yev-koko peered around the circle of the abyss. No more than ten Kith now remained, and even as Gornami-yev-koko watched, two more marched forward, disappearing into the depths below.

Leaning back, Gornami-yev-koko shook his head slowly, an oddly human gesture. *I do not discover the many-elder Potrum (the dispenser), with whom in soul communion I learned of the world of my ancestors, Xob.*

Potrum has gone to join the-one-who-is-nothing, Mike explained.

And the flux?

In good time, yes.

And my friend Nykol (the believer), ten times reborn? Did he not linger to greet his former dunce, the faithful Gornami-yev-koko, who alone mourned when he appeared to suffer a full disruption of life-force?

Alas, the flux called to Nykol.

And yet you remain Dav-yev (the former wanderer)?

Only so that I may speak the soul speech of the elders with these three of my own past blood.

Your . . . your children? Gornami-yev-koko said.

So they are called among their own kind.

Gornami-yev-koko stepped tentatively forward now. At the edge of the abyss he stopped, turning his head and glancing back. His voice already sounded as if it were coming from a distance: *Good-bye, Dav. Good-bye, other former humans. I, Gornami-yev-koko (the former and never-to-be-again dunce), go now to find soul communion with the-one-who-is-nothing and to discover the full meaning of the cosmic flux. Bid farewell to one who will never again be as you glimpse him now.*

Gornami, someone began (it might have been George), but it was too late. Gornami-yev-koko took a last step and launched himself over the edge of the abyss. For a moment—almost comically—he seemed to Danny to hang suspended in space, before hurtling into the darkness below.

And again, after a pause of several long seconds, the protoplasmic particles spewed forth.

Dad, said a voice that for a moment Danny had trouble identifying.

What, George?

Dad, what's down there? It was George, yes, but a different George somehow, as if something about him had changed. Or else, thought Danny, it was another aspect of George that was speaking now, the real George at long last, all disguises and facades and subterfuges stripped away to reveal what had always lain hidden underneath.

Their machines are down there, Mike explained. *The machines of the Kith. Machines that can create life and alter the shape and composition of a planet. Wondrous machines, George, a technology as far beyond ours as ours over the first tool-bearing apes.*

That's not all, Dad.

No, son, that isn't all.

There's something alive down there.

I—What makes you think so?

What you've said. And Gornami. You've both talked about the-one-who-is-nothing. At first I thought it was just something abstract, like the cosmic flux—

The cosmic flux is more than a mere abstraction, George.

But it's not alive. It's not something you can touch and feel and see. And the-one-who-is-nothing is. It's real and it's down there in that hole right now, isn't it?

That's what the Kith believe. It came to Neptune when they did, it brought them, and now it's going to take them away to another world. He moved his big, sluglike head as he spoke, peering around the abyss. There were four Kith left now. Only four. It's almost over, Danny thought.

But what do you believe? George asked. *Are the Kith right? You've been here five stanyears. Don't you know?*

Know what? Know everything? Of course I don't.

But you know what that thing down there in the pit is, don't you?

I—Yes. At least I think I do. I could be wrong but—I think I do.

What is it?

Mike was moving. Edging forward. Drawing closer to the abyss. Danny didn't know how he'd failed to notice until now.

Mike peered over the brink. *It's God, George,* he said.

Dad, don't! It was Nina, understanding now, as Danny also understood. Mike was going to join the Kith. He was going to jump.

I have to find out, he said. *And if I'm right, then I'm going on a marvelous journey.*

You'll kill yourself, she said.

No. His head raised up then and he looked away from the pit. *I won't be dying. I'll be going with the Kith. To other worlds. Other galaxies. Realms we haven't even dreamed about. And I'll be making life there, creating.*

Five minutes, Danny, came a soft voice in his brain. Duncan's voice.

Sam thinks we can bring you back, Nina said.

Sam always was stubborn, Mike said.

He says we can bring you to Leverrier *and change you back into a person again, a human. Just like us. And then we could all be together. Like a family.*

Nina, child, I'm sorry. I know you mean well—even Sam means well—but it just wouldn't work. It's too late for something like that. I can't be turned into a human being again. It's impossible. I'm not human anymore. I haven't been for a very long time.

But we could try, she said.

No, it—I'm sorry, Nina, but it's not what I want. This is what I want—the cosmic flux.

No! You're not going to do it! I'm not going to let you! You're not going to leave us again!

At first Danny thought it was still Nina whose voice he heard. But it wasn't. It was his own voice, screaming: *You can't just run out on us!*

It's what I want to do, Danny, Mike said.

That isn't good enough!

I'm afraid it's going to have to be.

No! Listen to me, you bastard, you selfish bastard, if you don't care about anybody else, if George and Nina and I don't mean anything more to you than just—

Danny, I said I was sorry. And I am. I truly am. But—

And Danny's mind suddenly filled with an image, one that blinded his eyes. The image was that of his father's face, his father's human face, looming over him, leaning over him, slightly blurred, as if Danny were viewing it from the vantage point of a child. And the face was stricken with wonder, with awe, with delight and joy. Tears flooded the eyes and flowed down the cheeks. His father was weeping.

What did it mean? Was it only another apology? Or was it something more, something deeper? A farewell—and an explanation. *I loved you then, my son, and I love you now.*

When Danny's vision cleared at last, the ground at the edge of the abyss was empty. Mike had gone.

No! Danny wailed, lunging forward. He somehow managed to keep all twelve legs underneath him as he lumbered frantically toward the abyss. *No, I won't let you do it!*

Without warning a heavy weight crashed into his side. He felt himself falling and hit the ground with a force that rattled every thick, reinforced bone in his sluglike mass of body. He lay there at the brink of the abyss, unable to move, the top of his head protruding over the edge. Below, all he could see was blackness.

Then the protoplasmic particles came pouring up, clouding his vision momentarily.

Something heavy lay on top of him, refusing to let him budge.

George, please don't hurt him, came Nina's anxious voice.

I'm not going to hurt him, George said, *but he's not going anywhere either.*

One minute, came Duncan's disembodied voice. *Hold on, guys, it's almost over.*

George, let me up, Danny managed.

Uh-uh, Danny-boy. I'm not going to let you do it.

Do what? Danny said.

Do what you were about to do before I saved your life. Jump into that pit.

But I wasn't—Danny stopped. Was it true? Was that really what he'd intended? If his father wouldn't stay, then he'd go after him, go with him? Danny didn't know. He honestly didn't. So much of what had happened here was a mad hopeless jumble. All he could clearly remember was the image of a face, of his father's weeping face. And that was something he'd never forget.

Overhead, as if pushed aside by giant hands, the clouds split apart to reveal the bright beacon of the sun in all its solitary splendor, a brilliant white pinprick in the now suddenly blue-black sky of Neptune.

And then the ground began to tremble and shake.

Thunder rattled the air like the beating of drums.

Lightning surged and crackled like tongues of flame.

And then slowly, majestically, like the passing of eternity, something rose up out of the abyss, something that was everything and nothing, something seen and unseen, something that was the Kith and the human race and a million, billion other species, something that was Michael Hawkins.

For a brief instant Danny glimpsed buried in the formless shape—in the-one-who-is-nothing, in the cosmic flux itself—the face of his father.

And Mike was weeping—with joy, with wonder, with an unknowable beauty.

In that instant Danny forgave his father—forgave him everything—forgave because he truly understood him at last.

Five seconds, said Duncan.

And then there was only oblivion and pain and more pain and then a distant tiny speck of light, a speck that grew and spread and then was blotted out by a shape, a human shape.

A face leaned close to Danny's own. "You made it," Sam Goble said. "You made it back."

TWENTY-SEVEN

Beneath the dome of Tsiolkovsky on Triton in a small windowless tavern, Carolina cradled a mug of ersatz coffee between her palms. She nodded her chin at the doorway. "Why don't we go outside and sit? I noticed a table on the way in."

Danny glanced quickly around the tavern—empty except for themselves and a robot bartender—and shook his head. "No, that's okay."

"For you maybe, but not for me. Come on." She stepped away from the bar, gripping her coffee. "It's still only a little past midnight, and Neptune's full."

"You can't see it very well from here anyway."

"Actually, now and then you can. There'll be a total break in the atmosphere. Two standays ago we were in Raymond's room—Benny and Nina were there too—and you could see Neptune perfectly for about twenty minutes. It was stunning."

"I must have missed it," Danny said.

"Anyway, this is my last chance. So let's go."

"But I don't—" he began, but she was already headed out the door. With a sigh Danny went after her, his legs dragging awkwardly. He was still trying to get around as much as possible without using his leg braces, even though after the months he'd spent in the near weightlessness of *Leverrier,* Triton's gravity seemed harsher to him than it really was. Triton would be nothing compared to Earth, however. That was going to be the real ordeal, braces or no braces. But they wouldn't be staying long, Sam said. A few days in Perth, a few more with Sara, that was all. And then back to Luna—Combine headquarters in Tranquility—where Danny would be staying. At least that's what Sam planned for him to do. Sam said there was no better way of getting an education than being around people who knew the most. And the Combine physicists on Luna were the smartest there were, as Danny knew. But he still couldn't help thinking about the possibility of a freighter berth. Sam always said that experience was important too—experience in the real-universe-out-there, as he called it. Danny would have to talk to him about it later.

Carolina was already seated at the table. Danny dropped heavily into the plastiform chair across from her and took a quick glance at the sky just to be sure. There was nothing visible but a glowing haziness. The glow would be Neptune on the other side of the clouds. But at least you couldn't see it.

"I guess you were right," Carolina said, peering up also. "It does look dense tonight."

Danny watched as two people, a man and a woman, moved past in the narrow street. Neither appeared very old—both less than thirty stanyears, he guessed—but they walked with hesitant stoop-shouldered gaits, as if bearing heavy loads. On Triton, he'd noticed, it often seemed as if everyone were bearing a heavy load.

Watching them, too, Carolina shivered. "Until we got back here, I'd nearly forgotten what a colony world is like."

"Is it the same on Titan?" he asked.

"In some ways better—conditions are less primitive and the terraforming more advanced—but there's also more work to be done."

"Is that what made you decide not to go back?"

"Partly, I suppose, but mostly it was Sam who talked me into it. He said he expected me to join the Combine in a few years, and the more experience I had before then, the better. I asked if freebooting in the Belt counted as experience, and he said that was exactly what he had in mind. I don't know. Maybe Raymond had already talked to him."

"What about your husbands back on Titan?"

She looked surprised. "What about them?"

"Won't you miss them?"

"Not especially. We lived different shifts, all four of us, so I hardly saw them. That's the usual procedure for marriages on Titan, unless you specifically request otherwise. They're my ex-husbands now, anyway. Sam said he'd take care of the divorce for me."

"Sam seems to have all our lives mapped out for us."

She shrugged. "He can't force us to do what we don't want to do."

"I suppose not."

"Look at George. I'd bet anything Sam didn't want him going back to Mars."

"What makes you think so?"

"George is going to be an actor in a theater of some kind. What kind of experience is that?"

"I think George has had enough experience in his life already. I don't think that's his problem."

"Then you think Sam wanted him to do it?"

"Sure. Why not? Sam's got at least one agent in Clarkegrad that I know of."

"You mean, that way Sam can keep an eye on George?"

"Right."

"If he doesn't change his mind and take off someplace else."

"He won't."

"Well, you know him better than me, of course."

"George saved my life on Neptune." He didn't know what had caused him to blurt that out. He regretted it as soon as he did.

"I know. I heard." Carolina put her mug down on the tabletop and looked at her wristwatch. Frowning, she fiddled with some of the levers jutting out from the dial. Then she nodded. "Less than fifty minutes till the shuttle is supposed to pick us up." She glanced at the sky and sighed. "I sure wish Neptune would come out."

"Where's Raymond, anyway?" Danny asked quickly.

"Off with Benny. Purchasing supplies and equipment. Raymond says everything's cheaper here than the Belt, since nobody's trying to gouge you for a profit."

"Are you really going to take Benny along?"

"Sure. Why not? Sam says his parents will raise a horrible fuss, but they're a billion kilometers away, so who cares?"

"Do you think you can stand him?"

"Well, one thing about Benny—if you tell him to shut up, eventually he will. I think you're the one who's really running the risk."

"With Duncan, you mean?" Danny said. "Sam says he can stay in Tranquility while the rest of us go to Earth. Nobody on Luna cares about mutants."

"I don't mean Duncan. I mean Nina. Are you sure your mother will want to take her in?"

"Sam thinks she will."

"And Sam knows her better than you?"

"I think she will too."

"She must be quite a person."

"She is."

"I read one of her books once."

"I didn't know that."

"I liked it."

"I—Good." There was a moment of silence then, and this time it was Danny's eyes that strayed to the softly glowing sky before he could jerk them back.

"Anyway," Carolina went on, "Benny isn't nearly as obnoxious as he used to be. Neptune changed him."

"Neptune changed everybody," Danny said.

"I wouldn't know. I was the only one of us who never got there, remember. Unless you count Duncan, and from what I understand, you can't."

"No, you can't," he said. "But you were lucky."

"Are you sure?"

"I—No," he admitted. "I'm not sure about any of it, and that's what really—" He broke off suddenly and shrugged his shoulders.

She reached across the table and took a light hold of his wrist. "Want to talk about it?"

"Talk about what?"

"What's bothering you."

"Nothing's bothering me."

"Danny, the whole time we've been back here on Triton you've hardly come out of your room. Everybody's been worried. Even George—and at least he's seen you now and then since you share the same room."

"He hasn't acted worried."

"You just haven't noticed. He got into a crap game with some of the natives and cleaned the poor sad suckers out, every last scrip note. When Sam found out, he told George he really ought to give the money back. And George did. Without a peep. That proves something is bothering him."

Danny laughed in spite of himself. "Maybe Neptune changed George too."

"Maybe it did," she said.

"I . . ." He slipped his wrist free from her hand and pointed at the sky. "That's why I haven't gone out. Neptune. I've been afraid I'd catch a glimpse of it up there."

"And?"

"I wouldn't know how to react."

"It's beautiful to look at. Even more than before. Remember how Sam told us that Neptune was death? When I see Neptune now, I don't think of death. I think of life."

"It took my father away from me."

"But he's not dead."

"That makes it worse. Knowing he's alive somehow, somewhere, and he's—I don't even know what he is."

"It's what he wanted, isn't it?"

"I tried to jump too," he went on, barely hearing her. "That was the crazy part. It would have killed me. I knew that. But I tried anyway. It— The cosmic flux . . . there at the end, I saw it. I saw the flux." He was looking straight into her eyes as he spoke.

"George and Nona Nina said they didn't actually see anything. George said he could feel something but couldn't see it. Duncan said that was how it was for him too."

"I saw it."

"What did you see, Danny?"

"Him. My father. I saw him in there with the rest—with all the rest— with everything, the whole universe like a giant flowing river going on and on and on, endlessly. And he was looking back at me. He could see me. He was crying. And then he smiled."

"Then he was happy?"

"I guess."

"You just didn't want to lose him, Danny."

"No."

"And maybe you didn't."

"Because he's part of the cosmic flux?"

"And the cosmic flux is everywhere," she said.

"That's what the Kith believe."

"Do you doubt them?"

"Did Sam tell you to talk to me like this?"

"No." She smiled and grabbed his hand again. "I thought it up myself."

From up the street came the sound of voices, and a moment later a group of five people swept around the corner. Danny saw Sam, George, Nina, Duncan, and Eileen.

Sam was the first to reach the table. "So there you are," he said to Carolina. "We've been hunting all over Tsiolkovsky for you."

"Why? What's up?"

"You and Raymond and Benny are supposed to be leaving for the Asteroid Belt in half a stanhour."

"I know. I'll be there. Danny and I were saying good-bye."

"The boy hermit himself," Sam said, plopping down in the one remaining chair. "So how goes it, son?"

"Better, Sam," he said. It was true, though he wasn't sure why. "A little better now, I think."

"Good. I thought it would be."

Danny glanced at Carolina and started to say something, but George broke in: "If you're feeling all that good, Danny-boy, how about a little card game tonight?"

Danny laughed. "I said I felt good, George. Not dumb."

A sudden burst of orange light bathed the tabletop, and before he could stop himself, Danny automatically turned his head and looked at the sky.

It was there. Out from behind the clouds now. Neptune.

It was glowing. A brilliant fiery-orange sphere floating suspended in a dark sky.

"I just got through talking to Olga," Sam said in a soft voice. "She sent out a third probe. The results were the same. The barrier extends totally around the planet, radiates next to no heat beyond a few hundred kilometers, and burns at a steady, constant temperature of twenty-one-thousand degrees. Nothing can enter it, and certainly nothing can penetrate it."

"And on the other side?" someone said. It was George.

"The other side, it appears, is not for us to know."

Danny gazed at the burning sphere in the sky, unable now to avert his eyes. And not wanting to either. "I wonder how long it'll be like that." he said.

"Till it's time," Sam said.

"Time for what?"

"Time for our new neighbors—the Neptunians—time for them to emerge."

"When do you think that'll be?" Carolina said.

"Not for millions of years, I imagine, tens of millions of years, but with the Kith—" he shrugged—"who can say? The barrier—it does make you wonder. Perhaps somehow they've managed to speed up the evolutionary process so that . . . well, it may be sooner—much sooner—than any of us thinks. I only hope when the time comes, we're still here—all of us. And ready. The whole sad, blessed human species."

Danny nodded as a mass of clouds stole up, slowly hiding the glowing orange planet. In his ears, as he watched, a sound rumbled, a sound he was sure only he could hear. It was thunder. In Danny's ears—one last time—there was a thunder on Neptune.